Blood Red

Anne Louise Bannon

Healcroft House, Publishers
Altadena, California

Dedication

To Michael – Of course, my darling. Who else?

Acknowledgements

I must confess, I almost completely used previous research to make Blood Red happen. But no book happens in a vacuum, and there are plenty of people out there who deserve a shout out for their support and kindness.

The wonderful volunteers of the Pasadena/Altadena Repair Café, including but not limited to Greg Marquez, Ginko Ching Lee, Michiko Lynch, Scoops Adamczyk, Evan Hilgeman, and about fifty other people whose names aren't showing up in the list of emails that go out. Your commitment to less waste by fixing things that would otherwise go into landfills is beyond wonderful. That you have become my tribe makes me forever grateful.

Then there is my sewing crew, holy buttonholes, ladies, you are amazing, taking on all sorts of bizarre tasks in service of returning clothes to wearability rather than waste.

And then Jennifer Michaud, my right-hand woman and the crazy person who talked me into starting a sewing bee in my own home. You, Paul, Kirsten, Jane, Michelle, and Hillary revive and invigorate me. Special thanks to Michael O'Brien (Jennifer's main squeeze who also brings really good lunch).

Then there are the ladies (and one guy) that are my fellow board members of the Los Angeles chapter of Sisters in Crime. We may not always agree on everything. But you are unflagging in your desire to see our chapter prosper. Better yet, you've shared yourselves with me and my life is all the richer for it.

Carol Louise Wilde, my line editor and dear, dear friend, found the nerve to tell me this one needed some more work, and better yet, told me how to fix it. Damn, you were right! Jackie Middleton and Nancy Scott both provided honest feedback and another set of eyes which were sorely needed.

Finally, there is my beloved daughter, Cornelia Ann Klarner, who calls me (and not to ask for money) every week. And is probably one of my better sounding boards when it comes to plot points, even if she freaks about the sexy bits. And, my Beloved Spouse, Michael Holland. Darling, thank you for your unflagging support.

Little Family Tree

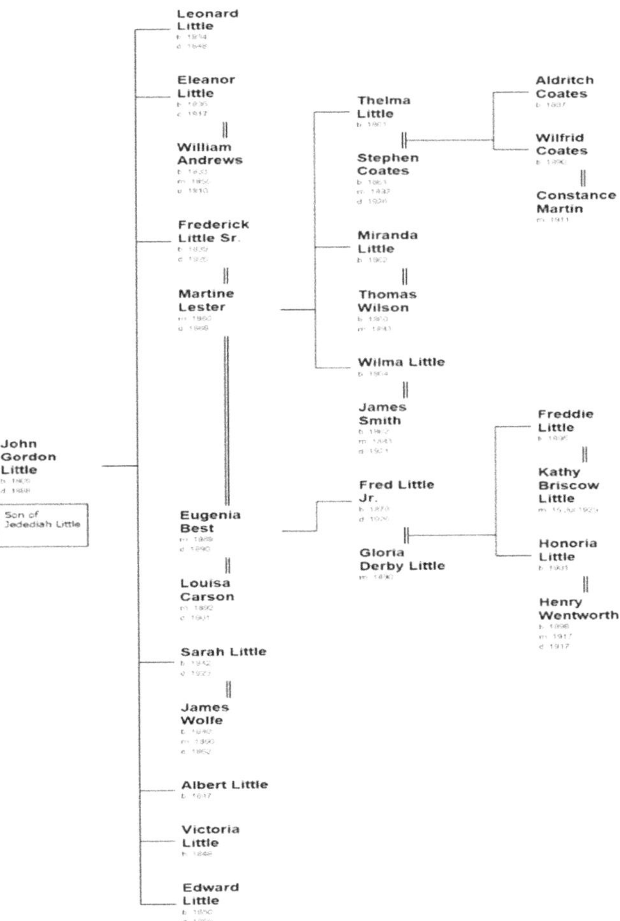

CHAPTER ONE

The gem lay in a black box lined with white velvet, the better to display the deep, rich red and the brilliant sparks of light flashing off the facets. It had been cut into a circular disc, almost two inches in diameter, and was set into a gold pendant, threaded on a string of pearls. How long the string was, Kathy couldn't say, as the rest of the necklace had been tucked under the velvet.

"Good heavens, Freddie," Kathy gasped. "You want me to wear that?"

"Yes," her husband said as he gently pulled the necklace from the box. "Well, it's what Grandfather wanted when he gave it to me."

"But, but, it's so huge." Kathy tried to gather her shocked wits together. "I mean, it's beautiful, but... I'm sorry, Freddie. I'd be terrified the string would break or that I'd lose it somehow. My God, it must be worth a king's ransom!"

"Not quite," said Freddie, still grinning. He had obviously anticipated his wife's reaction.

Kathy gazed at him as a rush of fondness filled her for her tall, lean, and incredibly wealthy husband. She seldom thought about him as being incredibly wealthy. However, every now and then, moments would come up and she would be startled by just what it meant to not only have more money than the U.S. Mint but to be included in Freddie's resulting social status.

This was one such moment. Kathy had been bathed, primped and puffed and was adorned in a beaded light green silk gown that complimented her brown eyes. Her neatly bobbed brown hair sported a jeweled and feathered band. Real diamond earrings dropped from her ears.

Freddie removed the necklace from its box and gently slid the length of pearls over Kathy's head, then picked up the ruby pendant from where it dangled just above her full bosom.

"Blood red," he whispered. "Deep and rich, like the blood coursing through our veins, like our love for each other."

Kathy looked into Freddie's green eyes and felt herself melting. "Oh, Freddie."

He gently laid the ruby pendant against Kathy's chest. Virginia, the lady's maid, approached with a mirror, but Kathy waved her off.

"No, thank you," she said. "I don't want to look. I simply want to think about what you just said, Freddie. If I think about that, I'll be fine."

"Then come, my love, our chariot awaits."

Freddie, decked out in white tie and tails, his strawberry blond hair neatly parted in the middle and slicked down, offered his arm and Kathy took it.

Her eleven-year-old brother Gamaliel was in the foyer all but dancing with anticipation as the two emerged from the back of the apartment.

"Kathy! Don't you look swell!" he yelped with a grin.

His stocky frame was clothed in knickers, shirt, and coat, like a proper little gentleman. But having only lived with Freddie and Kathy for two short months, his behavior generally reflected his life as the Kansas farm boy he was. Freddie roughed up the brown hair, so like his sister's.

"Gam, please, no slang," sighed Kathy.

She looked up to see that Freddie's sister Honoria was waiting in the foyer with Honoria's roommate and friend, Ivy St. James. Honoria had her brother's tall, slender frame and greenish brown eyes, although her hair was brown and bobbed. Ivy was somewhat shorter and rounder than Honoria, with bright red hair. Honoria wore a yellow gown with beads and gathers around the lowered waist, and a diamond hair band and earrings. Ivy was dressed in a lavender day dress with no jewelry whatsoever.

"I wish I was going," Gam sighed.

"I very much doubt that," Ivy said, in her deep, throaty voice. "They'll have to be terribly correct, whilst you and I are going to have ever so much fun."

"Mrs. Davies said he was to complete diagramming his sentences first," Freddie said, holding his hand out.

Letting out a sigh as deep and profound as a wishing well, Gam handed Freddie the copy of The Wall Street Journal he'd been trying to hide. Sliding the newspaper under his arm, Freddie snapped his fingers. Gam sighed again, pulled the pocket knife from his knickers and handed it to Freddie.

"If I catch you with it again, that's another two days without it," Freddie told him.

Ivy kissed Kathy's cheek, then Honoria's. "Do try to have fun, you three. It will make your mother so happy that she's finally able to present Kathy to her set."

The senior Mrs. Little had been trying to arrange a formal reception for her new daughter-in-law ever since she'd found out that Kathy was married to Freddie. That had happened late the previous October, but November proved to be too soon, and December became awkward because of the holidays and the fact that Freddie had brought Kathy's parents and siblings to New York City so that Kathy's mother could visit her brothers and sisters, who all lived in the city.

So, the reception had originally been scheduled for late January, but Freddie's grandfather had taken a bad fall early in the month, his health had failed and he'd passed away two days before the reception was to have happened. The reception had therefore been put off again to early March and since there had been no further complications, it looked as though Gloria Derby Little was finally going to get her wish. Kathy was nervous enough about the party without the addition of a pre-party meeting with her father-in-law, but Freddie's father had asked to see him immediately before the event and Freddie was apprehensive enough about the conference to ask Kathy and Honoria to be there, as well.

"I'm sure everything will be all right," Freddie said, aiming a quick glance at his wife and sister. "Now, ladies, it is high time we left. Thank you, Ivy, for staying with Gam."

"My pleasure, darlings," Ivy said with a wink at Gam.

Kathy was quite sure it would be a pleasure for Ivy. Both she and Gam had a most disturbing love for mischief. Not the serious kind, but Kathy doubted that Gam's sentences would be diagrammed by the end of the evening.

The ride over to the mansion near 59th and Madison was quiet. Honoria asked Freddie and Kathy how their new publishing company was doing. Kathy wished she hadn't asked but said that it was going well and chose not to elaborate. Freddie didn't say much, either. Kathy asked Honoria about how well her new magazine was doing, but Honoria said only that it was doing well enough and did not say more. What no one in the car mentioned was the coming conference to which Freddie had been summoned.

The chauffeur let the three out on the circular drive behind the mansion. It was adjacent to the formal entrance that led into the mansion's ballroom. Briggeman, the slightly stooped butler, had a footman take the outerwear from the three, then showed them down the hall to the game room.

The room's walls were cluttered with stuffed heads of lions and bears and a huge rhinoceros. Glass-fronted cases displayed a collection of all manner of guns. A large billiards table filled most of one half of the room, and several leather chairs and end tables were scattered about the other half, near a wall with a dart board hanging on it. Frederick Gordon Little, now Senior, was standing next to the billiards table polishing a small rifle when Freddie, Honoria, and Kathy entered.

"Father, we're here, as you asked," Freddie said.

The elder Little looked up from his gun, then frowned at the two women. He was tall and fair-haired, although Kathy suspected that in his younger days, his hair had been redder. He looked quite dapper in his white tie and tails, but the angry glare on his face marred his appearance.

"What are they doing here?" he asked Freddie, nodding at Kathy and Honoria.

"I asked them," Freddie said, tightly. "Now, what do you wish to discuss?"

Mr. Little, Senior, put the gun down on the edge of the billiards table, dropped the cloth next to it, then picked up a crystal tumbler presumably filled with whiskey. The liquid was amber and Kathy seriously doubted it was tea.

"We need to call a shareholders meeting," Mr. Little said.

"We could, but it wouldn't do any good," Freddie said. "Until Grandfather's will has finished probate, no one has enough shares for a quorum to make a vote valid."

Kathy watched as Freddie's father pursed his lips in anger. Even though Mr. Little held the chairmanship of the family textile business that fueled their wealth, Freddie had not only been made executor of his grandfather's will, he was to receive all of his grandfather's shares of the business. The few remaining shares were spread out among several of Freddie's great-uncles, uncles, and cousins. Mr. Little's normally bombastic temperament had not been sweetened by the terms of his father's will and the fact that his son would soon hold the controlling interest in the business.

Mr. Little moved around a chair and set his drink down on a nearby occasional table with a thud. Kathy started to walk toward Freddie, thought better of it, and ended up next to the billiards table and the gun. Idly, she looked down and saw that the long, dark muzzle was filigreed with gold.

"We're going to contest the will," Mr. Little said, looking out over the room.

"I agree it was not fair for Grandfather to leave me everything, but you still have the chairmanship of the company," Freddie said, clearly trying to hang onto his patience. "You have no grounds."

"There is undue influence," Mr. Little said, stiffly, still not looking at the others in the room.

"That's ridiculous," snapped Honoria. "The will was dated August 1925. Freddie spent hardly any time at all with him that year."

Kathy tried to swallow a sudden rush of guilt. She and Freddie had met in early December 1924. Since then, Freddie had spent a good deal of time with her, especially after they had married in July of 1925. They'd managed to keep the marriage a secret until the following October. Having their relationship made public had fortunately meant Freddie had more time to spend with his grandfather, especially after the old man's fall.

Mr. Little looked at his daughter as if he was surprised she existed, then glared at her. "I'll thank you to stay out of this."

Honoria began to protest, but Freddie held up his hand.

"You said we," Freddie said to his father. "Who else is involved?"

"Your Uncle Stephen, Uncle Thomas, and Great-Uncle Albert," Mr. Little said.

"Aunt Thelma's husband, Aunt Miranda's husband and Grandfather's younger brother," Honoria whispered to Kathy, who knew hardly any of Freddie's extended family.

"I see," said Freddie. "Well. Is there anything else you have to say, sir?"

"That is all." Mr. Little held himself up straight, then glanced over at Kathy. His face began to turn red and he pointed at her necklace. "Where did you get that ruby?"

Kathy stepped back in shock.

"I gave it to her," Freddie said. "She's my wife and entitled to it."

"How did you get it out of probate?" Mr. Little sputtered.

"Grandfather gave it to me before he died," Freddie said quietly. "It was not part of the estate." Freddie turned and offered his arms to Kathy and Honoria. "Ladies? We'll speak again later, Father."

Honoria was trembling with fury as they stepped into the empty ballroom.

"The utter nerve of him," she snapped. "So, the four horsemen are riding again. How dare they?"

"They are trying to act in the family's best interests," Freddie said calmly, although Kathy could see that he didn't believe it.

"It wasn't bad enough they forced Grandfather to retire from the chairmanship in favor of Father," said Honoria

"They didn't force him," Freddie said. "There was no way they could have. Grandfather had controlling interest and was not about to give it up."

"I don't understand," said Kathy.

"In April of Twenty-Four," explained Freddie. "Uncle Stephen, Uncle Thomas, Great-Uncle Albert, and Father all got together and suggested that since Grandfather was almost eighty-five, it was time to let Father take his turn at running the business."

"They ganged up on him, is what they did," Honoria said. "From the way Aunt Thelma tells it, the four of them all but laid hands on Grandfather to get what they wanted. And you know what a hulking brute Uncle Thomas is."

"Still, it was Grandfather's choice to retire," Freddie said. "Even if all the family had voted to have him retire, Grandfather still owned over seventy percent of the shares. They couldn't outvote him."

"But they could hurt him," Honoria sniffed. "And I'm sure they threatened to. I'd watch your back around all of them, Freddie."

"Darlings!" Gloria appeared at the other end of the empty ballroom, smiling broadly. Though not as tall as her children and considerably stouter, she was an imposing figure, nonetheless, and generally utterly confident in her bearing as a woman of society. Decked out in a steel blue ballgown and diamonds and sapphires, she looked even more regal than usual. "You came early."

"Yes," said Freddie. But Kathy could see that while he was genuinely glad to see his mother, he was not happy about the timing of their arrival.

Gloria frowned. "Oh, dear. You spoke to your father, didn't you?"

"Did you know what he had planned?" Honoria asked as she kissed her mother's cheek.

Gloria kissed Freddie then Kathy. "It was about him and your uncles contesting the will, wasn't it? I'm sorry he's being so unpleasant, darlings."

"What did he tell you about it?" Freddie asked.

"Absolutely nothing," Gloria said with a ladylike snort. "I had to find out from your Aunt Thelma. She's got some nastiness up her sleeve, the old witch. I wouldn't have invited her and Stephen or the rest of them if I couldn't have avoided it. I do so want this to be a warm welcome for our dear little Kathy."

Gloria suddenly stepped back, looking at Kathy's chest in wonder.

"The ruby," she said, then stopped.

"Yes," said Freddie. "Grandfather gave it to me before he passed. He said it was her turn to wear it."

"Of course, it is," Gloria said, slowly recovering herself. "Actually, it's perfect. You should be wearing it, my dear. It deserves to be shown off. And you deserve to show it." She paused and took Kathy's hands in her.

"I mean that."

Gloria's warmth for her daughter-in-law had surprised everyone, including Gloria. But Kathy had found herself genuinely liking the society matron and the two were becoming fast friends, perhaps even closer than Gloria was to her own children. So, once more, Kathy smiled and promised herself that she would not let herself be intimidated by New York's famed Four Hundred.

It was not an easy task. As the guests filed past in the receiving line, the men in white tie and tails, the women in a rainbow of colors covered with glittering beads and real gems, Kathy felt overwhelmed once again. Later, after the guests had arrived and she had been released from the line, she noticed many of the women furtively glancing at her waistline. Kathy did not doubt that they were speculating about when the first Little grandchild would arrive. At least, she told herself, she would have the last laugh. Not only was there no grandchild on the way, but there wouldn't likely be one if her luck held. Not that Freddie was much help that way. She smiled as she remembered the night before.

"Well, you look happy," said a man's voice next to her.

Kathy turned. The man was of medium height, but round as a ball, balding with fat lips.

"I'm sorry?" Kathy said.

"Your smile," he said. "You look happy."

There was something vaguely smarmy about the way he said it. Between that and what Kathy had been smiling about, she felt herself growing hot and flustered.

"It's, um, nothing," Kathy stammered. "Mr.... um... I'm so terribly sorry. There have been so many people."

"Everyone knows me. Miles Johnson." The man held out his pudgy hands. "Owner of First National Bank of New York. King of banking and finance."

Which Kathy suddenly realized meant that he was not a member of the Social Register. People of that caste seldom, if ever, referred to their wealth or how they got it. Mr. Johnson, it appeared, was what Mrs. Little would refer to disdainfully as a "nouveau," or someone who had only recently acquired his wealth, and by recently, that meant within the past two generations. It also occurred to Kathy that she had seen photographs of Mr. Johnson in some of the trashier newspapers she'd seen on the subway. He'd married Lovey, a girl young enough to be his granddaughter, and their stormy marriage provided all manner of steamy speculation for the tabloids. Kathy had seen several other nouveau but somewhat less notorious businessmen and their wives sprinkled through the crowd and suspected that her father-in-law was behind the invitations. Mr. Little often boasted of how democratic he was and loved showing off how many businessmen he counted as his friends.

"It's a pleasure to meet you, Mr. Johnson," Kathy said.

"Good to meet you, Mrs. Little." He grinned and pointed at the gem on her necklace. "That there is some rock you're wearing." He leaned forward. "You know, I was supposed to buy that from old Fred over there." He jerked his thumb in the direction of Freddie's father. "I could still offer you something for it."

"This is a family heirloom, Mr. Johnson," Kathy replied. "It is not for sale."

"That's what Fred said." Mr. Johnson sniggered. "I'll find a way. I always get what I want."

"I'm sure you do," Kathy said. "Now, if you'll excuse me."

Kathy pushed away through the people. It was surprisingly warm and crowded in the ballroom now that it was filled. A band was playing jazz softly at one end, while couples stiffly danced. Waiters circulated with champagne and hors-d'oeuvres, and a dinner buffet had been set up in the opposite part of the room.

"Hello, darling," said an older woman. She was tall and slender, with reddish-white hair piled on top of her head and pinned there with diamonds and emeralds to match the rest of her parure and flowing light green dress.

"Hello, Aunt Miranda," Kathy said after a second's fumbling for the name of Freddie's aunt.

"I see you're wearing the family ruby." Aunt Miranda's smile was as warm as a snake's. "It's so good seeing it again."

Kathy covered the gem with her hand and flushed. "I'm glad you think so."

Aunt Miranda smiled and moved on. Kathy began to realize that several of the women in the crowd were also gazing at her necklace. One woman, in particular, a Mrs. Everett Lewton, had smiled when she and her husband had been presented in the receiving line. As Kathy turned to take a glass of champagne from a passing waiter, she noticed Mrs. Lewton scowling at her chest once again.

Kathy sipped her champagne and wondered if she should try to strike up a conversation with somebody. The women seemed disinclined to chat with her, although they were polite. The men ignored her, beyond the occasional request for a dance, which she refused.

Her high heels were making her feet ache, so she left her glass on the first available side table and headed through the hallway to the drawing room in the hopes of finding someplace to sit. The doors to the room were wide open and before Kathy could enter, she heard the strident voice of Aunt Thelma Coates coming from inside.

"You don't know the half of it," she was saying.

Kathy slipped to the hallway side of the door and continued to listen.

"Fred is quite worried about all three of them," Aunt Thelma said. "Stephen finally did the right thing and hired a private detective to find out about her antecedents. I mean, she's obviously quite unsuitable, and that ridiculous story about her father being a landowner in Kansas. He's a farmer!"

There was a fluttering of shocked female voices and Kathy sighed. Aunt Thelma was talking about her father, who was a farmer in Hays, Kansas.

"And that's not even the worst of it," Aunt Thelma continued. "Freddie was convicted of murder last summer. How he escaped, I have no idea."

"He was let go because he was completely innocent and fully exonerated as such," Kathy said, wheeling into the room.

Four women had gathered around Aunt Thelma, a tall willowy woman with a sour face and wrinkled neck poking up out of her diamond collar necklace. She was dressed in a deep burgundy gown which made her flushed face even redder.

"You!" snapped Aunt Thelma. "You were spying on us."

"No," said Kathy. "I was walking this way and overheard you. And you know nothing about what happened last summer. So what if my father is a farmer? He's a decent and kind man, which is more than I can say for you."

"See?" Aunt Thelma addressed her companions. "Completely unstable. What more proof do you need?"

"Oh, is that going to be your strategy for taking over?" Kathy folded her arms across her chest. "Trying to prove that Freddie is unstable? I wish you luck."

She turned and left the room. Heading back to the ballroom, she looked for Honoria or Freddie. She saw Freddie near the buffet. Someone stopped her to chat with her and Kathy nodded pleasantly, still looking for her sister-in-law. Honoria, however, was absent, as was Gloria. Kathy made another circuit of the ballroom, trying to avoid conversations and mostly succeeding. The door leading out to the circular drive was open and the air was nice and cool rather than frigid. Kathy got a glass of champagne and headed outside.

The drive was mostly empty. The guests had all

arrived and were inside, and their cars were parked elsewhere. Lamps lined the wall of the mansion, and other lamps on poles lit up the driveway. At the top of the drive, one wing of the mansion, the conservatory, stood perpendicular to the main building. It was only one story and the roof was a terrace with a cement balustrade ringing it. Gloria's room opened onto the terrace, as did her husband's room.

Kathy had been standing there long enough to finish her wine when she heard raised voices coming from the conservatory. Below the balustrade, Mr. Little strode out of the conservatory through one of several windowed doors.

"You're not getting what you want this time," Mr. Little said over his shoulder to someone inside the conservatory. His voice echoed in the empty driveway. "As for that tart—" He stopped and turned back and looked up at the terrace. "What are you doing up there?"

Kathy thought she saw some movement on the terrace, but then suddenly, there was a shot and then another and Freddie's father jerked and crumpled onto his back, the bright red blood on his shirt front glistening in the outside lights.

CHAPTER TWO

There was a brief silence as Kathy gaped in horror. She could barely see him, but Mr. Little's eyes were wide-open and it was clear that he was dead.

Kathy saw another flash of movement on the terrace above them. She didn't wait and ran back through the ballroom as a couple more shots pinged next to her. She pushed through the crowd and into the main hallway to the front of the house and started up the sweeping front staircase. Gloria was coming down and stopped her.

"Kathy, my goodness!" Gloria said. "I thought I heard a car backfiring. What's happened, darling?"

Kathy choked on a sob and looked up at the landing. She sank down onto the stair as screams began erupting from the ballroom.

"It's Father Little," Kathy gasped as Gloria sank down next to her. "Someone shot Father Little."

"Oh, no," said Gloria softly. "Is he..?"

Kathy nodded, staring down the stairs at nothing in particular. "I saw someone on the terrace. Did you see anyone coming from there?"

"No. I was—" Gloria swallowed. "Oh, dear God. Fred is gone?"

"Yes," said Kathy in a tiny voice. She slowly put her arm around Gloria's shoulders.

"Gloria! Gloria!"

The woman who came running up was of average height, with a full chest. Her beads and jewels clattered as she scurried up the stairs. Kathy recognized her as one of Gloria's friends but did not remember her name.

"Gloria!" the woman gasped. "It's too terrible!"

"I know," said Gloria softly, staring straight ahead

in her shock. "Kathy told me." Gloria looked at her friend. "About Fred, right?"

"Yes, Gloria. He's dead. Shot right outside the formal entrance. Oh, Gloria, how terrible!"

"Mother! Kathy!" Honoria came running from the ballroom and hurried up the stairs, edging out Gloria's friend.

"Kathy?" Freddie called from the hallway. "Mother?" He saw them on the stairs and hurried up also. "You've heard, then."

"I saw it happen," Kathy said, her voice dull and flat.

"Oh, my God!" Freddie gasped.

Honoria was on Gloria's other side from Kathy, which forced Freddie to kneel on the stairs below them. Gloria continued to stare forward as if she was trying to comprehend what had just happened.

"How too terrible!" gasped Gloria's friend.

Freddie glanced at the woman. "Yes, Mrs. Hudson. It's too terrible." He stammered, trying to decide what needed to be done next. "The police are on their way."

"If they can get here," grumbled Honoria. She shuddered, blinked her eyes and sniffed. "As soon as the news went around, half the guests went running for their cars. We'll have a devil of a time sorting out all the wraps and hats left behind."

"Oh, no," said Kathy. "The police. They'll want everybody to stay here."

"It's too late now," said Freddie. He looked at his mother, who didn't respond, and then upstairs. "Here. Why don't we get Mother up to her room and comfortable? Mrs. Hudson, would you be so good as to bring us some brandy, please?"

The rest of the night passed in a blur for Kathy. Freddie brought her brandy and eventually, a doctor said that she needed a sedative.

"No, I don't!" Kathy remembered snapping, but nothing after that.

She awoke in a strange room. Dark oak crown

moldings lined the walls at the ceiling, and there was dark striped wallpaper underneath. Paintings and photos decorated the walls, and under them was a low bookcase filled with books. The bed Kathy was lying on was rich enough, with smooth silk sheets. Heavy dark curtains covered the window, but from the bright light leaking in, Kathy could tell that it was morning. Kathy struggled to sit up and blinked her eyes.

There was a small bell on the nightstand next to the bed. Kathy debated ringing it. She was wearing one of her nightgowns and someone had thoughtfully left her wristwatch on the nightstand, also. She picked it up. It was almost a quarter after nine in the morning.

Kathy knew she'd seen the room before but couldn't remember where or how. She set her watch on the nightstand and the night before came rushing back at her. Mr. Little's eyes wide and staring. The blood on his shirt. Gloria too shocked to do more than stare.

The sobs slowly rose up out of her chest and racked her body and she couldn't stop them. Freddie was there next to her a moment later, folding her into his arms and holding her close as she cried. It was some time before Kathy could get control of herself.

"I'm so sorry," she gasped finally.

"No, no," said Freddie. "It's perfectly understandable, my darling."

Kathy finally noticed that Freddie was in his dressing gown and pajamas and that the pillow next to her had been slept on as well.

"Where are we?" she asked.

"At the mansion. This is my old room," Freddie said. "I've been with you all night and just now stepped out to use the bathroom. It figures that's when you'd awake."

"I'm sorry."

"I'm more sorry that I wasn't here." Freddie lifted her chin so that she could look him in the eyes. "Do you forgive me?"

Kathy smiled in spite of herself. "What's to forgive?

But, yes, I do." She took a deep breath. "How are you? You just lost your father."

Freddie shrugged. "I'm managing. Someone has to keep his head straight through this."

"And your mother?"

"We had to give her a sedative, too. Honoria is watching her."

"I wasn't hysterical last night," Kathy grumbled.

"No, but you were in severe shock," Freddie said. "And no wonder, if you saw it happen."

"Well, I'm not in shock anymore," Kathy said as she moved around to get out of bed. "The police will need to talk to me. I saw someone on the terrace."

"That's what you kept saying last night. What did you see?"

Kathy closed her eyes. The image of Mr. Little collapsing, the red blood on his shirt, flashed in her mind once again. She took a deep breath and tried again.

"There was definitely someone up on the terrace," she said slowly. "I think I saw a flash of something light-colored or maybe a face but can't say more than that. Just that it was a person of some sort. Your father recognized him."

"Hm," said Freddie.

Kathy frowned. "What are you not telling me?"

"Nothing you don't already know." Freddie looked at the door to the room. "My mother's bedroom looks out on that terrace."

"As does your father's bedroom."

"Yes. But my father was obviously not in it, whereas my mother was in hers when she heard the shots. The police seemed quite interested in that bit of information."

"They don't think your mother..?" Kathy gasped. "Why would she kill your father? That makes no sense."

"Nothing makes sense at this point, darling." Freddie slumped as he sat. "As Mrs. Hudson kept saying, it's simply too terrible."

"Who's investigating it?" Kathy asked.

"There are coppers all over the house, but the person in charge seems to be a Detective John Crowley. Your Uncle Dan says he's a very good man."

Kathy's Uncle Daniel Callaghan was a detective sergeant on the New York City police force.

"That's something, at least," Kathy said. "I suppose Uncle Dan can't investigate because of me."

"Not officially, no," said Freddie.

"So he will be keeping a hand in."

Freddie nodded. "Somehow, I think he will. In the meantime, we will be heading back home. And I hope you don't mind, but I've invited Mother to stay with us until the police are done, possibly longer."

"That's perfectly all right." Kathy drew a deep breath. "At least, it should be."

"Thank you. I appreciate that. Now, shall I ring for breakfast?"

It wasn't long before Kathy had eaten, bathed, and dressed. Waiting for Gloria to do the same, she wandered the ground floor of the mansion. In the vast dining room, a policeman was laying out hats, overcoats, and ladies' wraps and furs over the surface of the dining room table while Honoria watched. She, like Kathy, was dressed in a somber black day dress. Honoria's eyes flickered up as she noticed Kathy in the doorway to the dining room.

"Good morning," Kathy said. "How are you?"

Honoria sighed and shrugged. "I'm managing. As Freddie keeps saying, someone has to stay level-headed."

"Are those the wraps that were left behind?" Kathy asked.

"Yes," said Honoria. She pointed to a red fox stole on the table. "See that? That's Aunt Miranda's. I'm sure Uncle Thomas' things are somewhere among the rest. She called this morning, in high dudgeon, demanding her stole back as if we were keeping it here on purpose. She tried to make it sound as though she'd been so upset and shocked when she left that she and Uncle Thomas forgot their things. Funny thing is, as the screaming started, I saw Uncle Thomas pulling her out of the ballroom and didn't see her again."

"Things were very confused," said Kathy.

"You and mother were lucky and missed the best part," Honoria said bitterly. "Aunt Thelma couldn't quite fake an attack of the vapors, but spent the rest of the night sobbing loudly and making herself out to be the chief mourner. She didn't quite say Freddie had killed Father, but she did let the police know about that ugliness back in Hays, Kansas, last summer."

"But if the shot came from the terrace, then Freddie couldn't have done it," Kathy said. "I saw him in the ballroom just before I went outside."

"And that just makes it look like Mother did it, which is ridiculous," Honoria said.

Kathy fidgeted with a corner of the fox stole. "I'm sure the police will get to the bottom of this."

"I wouldn't go outside." Honoria rolled her eyes. "Reporters are everywhere. Briggeman has had to bring on extra footmen to keep the pests outside. They even climbed up onto the terrace. Detective Crowley was furious."

"Where is the detective?"

"In the conservatory, I think. Apparently, there were some pots knocked over, so he thinks someone may have been hiding in there until it was safe to escape. The problem is, there were so many people here, with the party going on, that almost anybody could have killed Father and run."

Kathy frowned as she tried to remember what she saw. "Your father was talking to someone in the conservatory when it happened. Perhaps that person saw something."

"Perhaps," Honoria sighed deeply and blinked her eyes.

Kathy gently took her arm and pulled Honoria across the hall into the drawing room.

"I'm fine," Honoria said as Kathy pushed her onto the sofa.

"No, you're not," Kathy said. "Your father has just died and violently so. Of course, you're upset."

Kathy sat down next to her as Honoria began to weep quietly.

"I suppose I am upset," Honoria said, pulling a handkerchief from her pocket. It was white with a black ribbon trim around it. "It's just that I don't really know how I feel. He's my father, but he was practically a stranger to me. I hardly knew him. Right now, I feel as if there must be something wrong with me because I'm more worried about you and Freddie and Mother than I am sad about Father dying."

"Perhaps you're just saving your grief for another time," Kathy said. "As you said, someone has to stay level-headed. And you did just say that your father was practically a stranger. You're much closer to Freddie and your mother. So, it's no wonder that you're thinking of them."

"And you." Honoria wiped her nose and eyes. "Don't forget. You're part of this family, too."

Kathy took Honoria's hands. "Thank you." She took a deep breath. "Now. Freddie said he's taking your mother to our apartment for the time being. Do you wish to join us?"

Honoria shook her head. "I can't just yet. I have to help the police sort out all the coats and wraps that were left behind."

Kathy's smile took on a slightly wicked cast. "Really? Well, that's convenient. Do you think you could make a list for us, as well? Just in case the police can't find the killer? It might be useful to know who wanted to leave before the police got here."

Honoria perked up. "What an excellent idea. Yes, I will." She took Kathy's hands. "You are a lifesaver. And, now, are you all right? What a horrible thing to witness."

Kathy blinked back the vision of her father-in-law

crumpling onto the sidewalk. "It was. But I'll manage."

Honoria went back to the dining room and Kathy took yet another deep breath. Freddie found her a moment later.

"Mother's coming down," he said.

Kathy got up and hurried out to the hallway. Gloria, dressed in a black day dress, slowly walked down the stairs.

"How are you, Mother Little?" Kathy asked.

"Well enough, considering," the older woman said slowly. "And how are you, darling?"

"Much better this morning, but quite sad, of course."

Gloria got down the last couple stairs and took Kathy's hand.

"Of course," the older woman said in a flat voice, as Freddie came down the stairs behind her. "We are all quite sad."

"Ah, Mrs. Little," said a man's voice.

Both Kathy and Gloria looked up.

The man in the doorway to the game room was of medium size and fairly young, but with a long face deeply etched with long lines, and a double chin. His dark brown hair was parted on one side and bits of it stood on end as if he'd been pulling at it on top.

"That's both of you. Right." He walked fast, his eyes darting everywhere. "Gotta remember that. I'm Detective John Crowley. I'm in charge of this case." He suddenly stopped, looked over both Kathy and Gloria, then smiled gently. "How are you ladies holding up?"

"As well as might be expected," said Gloria. "And you, sir?"

"All in a day's work, I'm afraid." Crowley pulled at his hair. "I'm very sorry for your loss. It's a hard thing, I know. But I do have to ask you some questions. The sooner we can get this killer, the sooner you'll sleep better, I'm sure."

"Yes. I understand," said Gloria. "Shall we go into the drawing room?"

"Sure. Thanks."

Gloria led the way into the room, Kathy and Freddie close on her heels and Detective Crowley after them. Gloria perched herself on a chair near the fireplace then gestured to Crowley to seat himself on the couch next to her. Freddie sat down next to Crowley and Kathy took a chair next to Gloria's. Gloria rang, a footman appeared, and she ordered tea. That being settled, she turned to Detective Crowley.

"Now, how may I help you?" she asked.

"Well, let's start with what you ladies saw," Crowley said.

"I didn't see anything," Gloria said. "I had gone upstairs for a moment and heard the shots. Then as I came downstairs…" She frowned. "Kathy was coming up, quite quickly. That's when I knew something was wrong." She shook her head. "After that, I don't seem to remember much. Freddie and Honoria got me up to bed, and Kathy, I think. And then the doctor came."

"And you, Mrs. Little, the younger one?"

"Mrs. Kathy," Gloria offered.

"Um, Mrs. Kathy?" Crowley smiled clumsily, but Kathy could see the good nature behind it.

"Yes, I…" Kathy frowned, trying to remember, but again only seeing her father-in-law's body crumple. "He was coming out of the conservatory. Father Little, I mean. He was talking to somebody inside. Father Little said he wouldn't get what he wanted and then something not very nice. Then Father Little saw someone on the terrace. He yelled at him. Wanted to know why he was there and that's when he was shot."

"Did you see someone on the terrace?"

"I—," Kathy said, then closed her eyes and shook her head. "I'm sorry. All I can see is Father Little—" She choked for a second.

"That's okay. Happens a lot that way." Crowley said. "Just take your time."

Kathy took a deep breath. "There was someone up there. A person, but I couldn't see much more than a flash of movement. I'm pretty sure it was a person, though."

"I see." Crowley sat up and pulled at his hair again. "What we have here, I believe, is a crime of opportunity. I was in your billiards room, you call it?"

"Or game room," said Gloria, her voice steady but still flat.

"Seems to me, you've got a lot of guns in there," Crowley said.

"Yes, my father has, I mean, had quite a collection," Freddie said. "He enjoyed hunting."

"He went out almost every week," Gloria said. "He only lived here in the city because he had to see to the family business."

Kathy frowned. She couldn't remember her father-in-law ever talking about hunting. But then, she didn't remember him speaking about much at all since she was usually so bored by him that she simply chose not to listen.

"I see," said the detective. "Well, you'll have to tell me if there are any guns missing from the game room. But first, can you tell me who his enemies were?"

Gloria's eyebrows raised in shock. "Goodness, no. What an unpleasant thought."

"I'm afraid we really don't know," said Freddie. "Father kept to himself for the most part. He particularly made a point of shutting me out of the family business after he took over the chairmanship. The only knowledge I have of what was going on is what I've had to pry out of him to get the probate from my grandfather's will settled. I am the executor and…" Freddie sighed deeply. "The primary heir. My father was quite upset. If anything, he considered me his worst enemy. But I certainly had no reason to kill him."

"Your aunt said your father was going to contest the will," Crowley said.

"Yes. He told me that just before the party," Freddie said. He shrugged. "It wouldn't have done any good, beyond dragging things out. Grandfather's will was quite airtight, according to our attorneys. Father's death only makes things more complicated for me."

"And yet, you were convicted of murdering somebody last summer?" Crowley asked.

"Oh, that ridiculous nonsense!" Kathy snapped. "Freddie was innocent and exonerated the minute we proved it. The only reason Freddie was convicted was that they needed to get him out of the way. And Aunt Thelma must know that. After all, she and her husband were the ones who hired the detective to find all this out. He can't be much of a detective if he didn't find out that Freddie was exonerated. And if you want to look for an enemy, you might just try Uncle Stephen. He was part of the group contesting the will."

Freddie frowned at Kathy but held his tongue. Kathy suddenly realized her mistake.

"I apologize, Detective," she said. "No. It can't be Uncle Stephen, or if it was, it wasn't related to the will. Uncle Stephen doesn't benefit from Father Little's death. I should have seen that."

"It's all right, Kathy," Freddie said, his eyes filled with worry nonetheless. "It's probably the shock. It's affected all of us, I'm afraid."

"That's the way it usually works," Crowley said, as he got up. "Now, why don't we go to the game room and see if anything's missing."

Gloria looked a little frightened for a moment, then graciously rose and led the way to the room with the other following her. Once inside, she took a deep breath as she looked around at the filled gun cases. There were no empty slots.

"I don't see anything missing," Gloria said, after a moment.

"I don't see anything, either," Freddie said. "Now, if you have no further need of us, Detective, I'd like to get my mother back to my apartment so that she can recover and we can begin to make arrangements."

"Certainly, Mr. Little," Crowley said. "And I know where I can find you if anything else turns up."

Kathy took one last look around the room. There was something missing, something that had been there the night before. But she couldn't say what it was. The worst of it, she couldn't help but wonder if Freddie and Gloria both knew and were not telling the truth. But why would they lie? The only reason Kathy could think of did not make sense at all or rather, it did but in a terrible, terrible way.

CHAPTER THREE

Freddie walked into the study of his apartment very much wanting a good solid drink, never mind that it was far too early in the day to start drinking. And if he started drinking at that hour, it would upset Kathy and she was upset enough as it was.

He had settled Kathy and his mother in the living room of the apartment with his father's valet, a sour-faced man named Taylor, to run and fetch as needed. At last alone, Freddie took a deep breath and looked around the newly crowded retreat. Lined with bookshelves and filled with two desks, a large over-stuffed sofa and two comfortable chairs with a what-not table between them, it was a comfortable room. A fireplace on the side wall kept it cozy. It had been spacious enough when Freddie had been living in the apartment by himself. The desk he had installed for Kathy across the room from his had made things cozier. With Gamaliel as likely as not to be doing his schoolwork in there, the room had become a bit crowded, but pleasantly so.

Although, at that moment, Freddie would have preferred it if no one else besides him ever entered the room again. He sat down on the chair and silently took a few deep breaths. They weren't quite sobs, but the sadness and the pressure of new responsibility suddenly overwhelmed him and he trembled and gasped for several minutes.

Finally, recovering himself, he turned to the reason he'd gone into the study in the first place. Feeling along the side of the bookshelf on the left side of the fireplace, he found the small lever and pulled gently up. The bookshelf swung open to reveal a safe in the wall behind it. Freddie dialed the combination, opened it and set the box with the ruby necklace in it inside. He quickly shut the safe, twirled the dial on the combination lock and gently moved the shelf back into position.

There was a knock on the door.

"Freddie?" called a friendly male voice on the other side. "May I come in?"

Freddie made sure that the shelf was completely in place, then took yet another deep breath.

"Lowell. Of course," he said. "Come in."

Lowell Winters entered and shut the door behind him. Everything about Lowell was large, from the girth of his belly to the luxuriant dark mustache he wore, to his ego and his appetites. Freddie was one of the few people actually taller than him. The two had been friends since their college years at Harvard.

"Feel free to kick me out if you'd rather be alone," Lowell said, easing himself into Freddie's favorite chair.

Freddie gazed at the fireplace then slid down onto the sofa.

"I have no idea what I'd rather," he said after a long pause.

"Ah, yes." Lowell nodded sagely. "I remember feeling that way when my father died. According to those psychiatrist fellows, it was lingering guilt over loving my mother too much."

"Really?"

Lowell shrugged. "I thought it was because my father was a miserable, mean son of a bitch and that I was glad he was dead."

Freddie broke into a mild chuckle in spite of himself. "I concede there's been little love lost between my father and me of late." He sighed deeply. "But I am not glad he's dead. I was thinking about that last night when things finally settled down. I did love my father. I just barely knew him, is all. He tried taking me hunting a few times when I was young, but I didn't really care for it. It was cold, wet and boring." Freddie shivered at the memory. "When Grandfather was so ill that last month, Father asked me if I wanted to go hunting, and I said yes. I knew he enjoyed it but had no idea how much and thought the least I could do was spend some time getting to know him. Then Grandfather died and the will became a mess and all of a sudden my father started treating me as though I were the enemy. As if it were my fault that Grandfather left almost everything to me." Freddie shook his head. "And the worst of it is, with Father dead, everything is now that much more complicated. At least, with Father alive, he could see to the running of the family business and I could keep working on our little publishing venture. Now, I have both to worry about."

"And speaking of, is your father's death going to set back the release of Mr. Mennerly's new book?"

"I haven't had a chance to even consider that." Freddie sank even deeper into himself. "Besides, that should be as much Kathy's decision to make as ours, and right now, she is in no shape to think about anything." Freddie looked up at Lowell. "She saw it happen. It quite affected her."

"Yes, I heard. But maybe a little bit of business might help to get her mind off of it. A welcome distraction and all that."

Freddie rolled his eyes and was about to complain that Lowell's interest in distracting Kathy had more to do with his interest in the publishing company when there was another knock on the door.

"Freddie, may we come in?" came Kathy's voice.

Freddie scrambled up. "Yes, darling."

He hurried over to the door and opened it. Kathy and his mother were waiting on the other side.

"Is there something you need?" he asked, fighting to keep his voice soothing and calm.

"No, darling," Gloria said, gliding into the room. "We came to see if you needed anything. Truth be told, it was getting a bit boring and morose simply sitting in the living room and staring at each other."

Freddie looked over at Kathy, who smiled weakly. Lowell remained seated and Gloria, who had been headed for Freddie's chair, glared at Lowell briefly, then went and sat in the other chair.

"I'm getting over the shock," Gloria said. "And since there isn't much to be done about notifying people or arranging the funeral, I'm at a bit of a loss for something to do."

"See? I told you," Lowell said.

Freddie noticed that Lowell was still seated and glared. "Mother, I apologize for this cur's behavior. However, there is no cure for Mr. Winters' rudeness."

"What?" Lowell demanded.

"A gentleman stands when a lady enters the room," said Freddie.

"That's ridiculous," Lowell snorted.

Gloria sniffed. "I suppose I should be miffed, but I will forgive."

Lowell shook his head as Kathy found her favorite corner of the sofa and pulled out her knitting. Freddie sat down next to her.

"Lowell, you were saying to Freddie that you told him so?" Kathy asked.

"We were discussing the release of Mr. Mennerly's book," Lowell said. "And whether it should be put back or not on account of the senior Mr. Little's passing."

"I don't understand," Gloria said. "What would my husband's death have to do with releasing Mr. Mennerly's book?"

"It's our company, Mother," Freddie said gently. "Our publishing company, Signature Books."

"Oh. I remember now," Gloria said with a little smile. "You and those other authors got together to form your own company so Kathy would have a job."

Kathy chuckled. "Not quite, Mother Little. They merely wanted me as their editor, and since my old house wasn't going to keep me on, they thought they might do better on their own. Anyway, Mr. Mennerly's new book, The Covenant, will be the first from our company, and it's due to be released in a couple weeks. Lowell is being uncommonly polite in asking if it would be appropriate to release the book while some of the principals of the company are in mourning."

Kathy paused to glare at her knitting needles. Something in a yellow and green argyle pattern was forming or would have been if she hadn't sighed and started removing stitches from her needles.

"Although," Kathy continued. "I don't see how it would be a problem. Most people aren't going to care and at the most, it would only mean that Freddie and I are not at the release party. At the very least, the funeral will have been held by then. I hope."

"Of course, it should," said Freddie.

Gloria sniffed again. "That will depend on the police. I was just speaking with the undertaker and he said that the police wanted to have the body autopsied."

"An autopsy?" Freddie tried not to gape.

"As Kathy quite sensibly pointed out, your father was murdered," Gloria said with a shrug. "The undertaker assured me that it wouldn't delay things by that much. All to the better, I thought."

"I suppose," said Freddie, feeling rather unsettled. "It does seem rather drastic."

"Apparently, it's quite common in these sorts of cases," Gloria said, then sighed. "It does mean that we can't schedule anything, which is decidedly a nuisance."

"I seriously doubt the funeral will cause that much of a conflict with the release, which is the important part," Kathy said. "Since it's his book, we should probably ask Mr. Mennerly how he feels about it. However, I do think that with being a new venture, it would not help to hold up our first release, especially since it has gotten a lot of interest from the press and there are quite a few people who would be happy to see us fall flat on our faces."

"There is that." Freddie both winced at the thought and inwardly rejoiced that Kathy seemed to be getting over her shock.

“Are you two going to investigate the murder?” Lowell asked.

“Why?” asked Freddie. “The police appear to have everything well in hand.”

“Good heavens, Lowell, we only do that when we have no other alternative,” Kathy said.

“Investigate?” Gloria asked.

“These two are a regular Sherlock Holmes and Watson,” Lowell said as both Freddie and Kathy rolled their eyes.

“It’s true, Mother, that we’ve been caught in a few awkward situations involving some crimes,” Freddie said. “But, as Kathy said, we only resort to finding things out when we have no other alternative. And the police do seem to have things well in hand this time.” He sighed deeply. “Even if they didn’t, I hardly have the time to investigate anything, between getting our new company up and running and executing Grandfather’s will and raising Gam. I barely have time to work on my novel. If Uncle Stephen and the others want to run the company, they can, as far as I’m concerned. As it is, I’m very close to letting them have my shares.”

Gloria sat up in shock. “Freddie, you can’t! Those are family shares. Stephen and Thomas are only family by marriage and Uncle Albert is far too old. And just because you don’t have a son now, doesn’t mean you won’t.”

Freddie felt Kathy stiffen next to him. They’d only talked about it once or twice, but Kathy had made it very clear she was not interested in having children and was actively trying to avoid it. His mother’s hints that it was time for a grandchild were not appreciated.

“I know, Mother,” Freddie got up and got a cigarette from the case in his jacket pocket. He offered the case to his mother, who waved it off, then Lowell, who accepted the cigarette. “Which is why I am continuing to do what is necessary. But I see no reason why Uncle Stephen or Uncle Thomas can’t take over as chairman.”

Freddie quickly fitted his cigarette into its holder while Lowell simply lit his up, then removed a bit of tobacco from his lower lip. Puffs of smoke wafted up as Freddie took the first, deeply satisfying, drag on his cigarette.

"Hm," said Gloria. "I'd be very careful of those two. Thomas is completely ruled by Miranda, of course, and while Stephen has Thelma more or less under control, you can't say that she doesn't have her influence over him. I can assure you, Thelma and Miranda have only their own interests at heart." Gloria shuddered. "If Stephen and Thomas are showing any interest at all in our company, it's so that they can plunder it like they plundered their respective family interests."

Freddie looked over at his mother. "I had no idea they'd done that. And the Coates business has been doing very well, from what I've seen."

"That's because Stephen's older brothers are managing it," Gloria said. "Stephen has a few interests of his own and, of course, manages Thelma's inheritances. It's the same with the Wilson family, although, I've heard they aren't doing quite as well and, certainly, Eliza Wilson's debut last year was not as big as one might have expected, and the Champagne was inferior. Mrs. Wilson blamed it on Prohibition, of course, but one does wonder."

"Who's Eliza Wilson?" Lowell asked. "And I know you've explained, Freddie, but what's a debut?"

"Eliza is the eldest Wilson daughter," Gloria said. "Freddie's Uncle Thomas's niece by his older brother. And a debut is a grand party where she is presented to polite society, having come of age to get married. Naturally, you want as good a party as you can arrange so that your daughter can attract the best possible husband. Kathy, you have the oddest look on your face."

Kathy's eyes had that wicked glint Freddie loved and dreaded. "Oh, nothing terribly kind, Mother Little."

"Oh?" Gloria asked, one eyebrow lifted, her eyes also gaining a wicked glint. "Say on."

"I was just thinking how I dodged a bullet by marrying Freddie first," Kathy said, turning her focus back to her knitting.

"What do you think last night was about?" Gloria said. "I was presenting you to polite society."

"I was afraid of that," Kathy said. "At least, I only had to do it once. A debut and a wedding?"

"And an engagement party," said Gloria.

"Ugh." Kathy looked up from her needles. "I can do without the fancy parties."

"Well, it depends on the fancy party," Lowell said. "I was married to one of you society types once, and while the wedding and all the parties were quite trying, the booze was very good. And this was after the Volstead Act took hold."

Gloria was looking at Lowell and frowning.

"Mother?' Freddie asked, then sat back down next to Kathy.

Gloria smiled. "Oh, nothing. Just trying to remember something."

Freddie glanced over at Lowell. "If you're trying to remember whether you invited Lowell to last night's party, then, yes, you did at my request. I believe he even made an appearance."

"For a brief hour or so," Lowell said. "Lovely party, Mrs. Little. I would have liked to have stayed, but a director absolutely needed to speak to me last night."

Kathy smirked. "You left because you were bored silly." She looked over at Gloria and sighed. "I'm so sorry, Mother Little. It was a lovely party. It was just a bit... big for me."

Gloria chuckled. "Actually, Mr. Winters, I agree with you. That crowd is utterly boring. But they are Society and one must give them their due."

"Nor was I the only one to escape early," Lowell said. "Freddie's cousins, Wilfrid and Aldrich, and their wife left early."

"You mean Constance," Freddie said. "And she's Wilfrid's wife."

"They're Uncle Stephen's sons, aren't they?" Kathy asked.

"Yes," said Lowell. "Oh, and that ridiculous banker with the wife that could be his granddaughter. Miles and Lovey Johnson."

"I believe I met him last night," Kathy said. "He seemed surprised that I didn't know him."

"He's one of your father's business friends, as I recall," said Gloria. "One does not like to comment on what a poor choice he made in a wife."

"They're the toast of the tabloids," Lowell said, laughing heartily. "Good heavens, the grist they provide for the gossip mill. I saw them at a speak off of Broadway last night. I was just about to leave when they came in. They were having a brawl that would have shocked Mr. Winchell."

"Who is Mr. Winchell?" Gloria asked.

"The gossip columnist, Mother," said Freddie.

"Oh, I never read that nonsense," Gloria said, then gasped. "Good heavens, they weren't talking about our party, were they?"

Lowell took a thoughtful drag on his cigarette. "Now, that I think about it, they may have been. She kept screaming that something he'd done could have waited and that it was an insult to their hostess. He screamed back that he didn't give a damn about their hostess and he didn't get to where he was by waiting when he had an opportunity in front of him. Then she went into her usual tirade that he doesn't listen to her. And, of course, he stopped listening."

Kathy shot a bemused look at Lowell. "Good lord, Lowell. You were eavesdropping on them."

"Of course," said Lowell. "They're actually rather entertaining, in a queer sort of way."

There was a knock on the door bland Honoria slid into the room, with Ivy and Gam close behind. Freddie jumped to his feet and Lowell, grudgingly, hefted himself to his.

"We heard you were all hiding in here," Honoria

said as Freddie settled her on the couch.

Gam went over and stood next to Kathy.

Ivy sat down next to Honoria. "I hope we're not making it too crowded."

"Of course not!" gushed Lowell, who had already sunk back into his chair.

Freddie tried not to sigh, remembering that he'd originally gone to his study to be alone and had been thinking just how crowded the room was becoming. Still, as he gazed over the people gathered there, he realized that these were the people who were the dearest to him.

He hadn't been close to Honoria when they were children. But after the war, during which time she'd married a doughboy who'd promptly gotten himself killed, she asked Freddie to manage the money she'd inherited from her husband. Since then, the two had become fast friends.

Freddie had only met Ivy the previous fall, although she and Honoria had been dear friends since the war. Freddie had first liked Ivy because she was Honoria's friend. But since having come to know Ivy, Freddie had come to consider her as dear a friend as Honoria did.

It was odd, Freddie realized, that he'd known Ivy almost as long as he'd known his mother as someone other than a distant presence in his life. Like most people of his position, he'd been raised by a nurse and then a tutor. He had spent very little time with his parents, and as he grew into adulthood, he'd found he had little in common with them. Or thought he hadn't. The previous fall, he'd made a point of spending some time with his mother and had found the two of them were a lot more alike than not. That she'd not only accepted Kathy but Lowell, as well, amazed Freddie.

Of course, there was more detente between Gloria and Lowell than not, but that had more to do with Lowell's atrocious manners. He had been a scholarship student at Harvard when he and Freddie had formed their friendship, and for all his exposure to polite society, he had little liking for it, especially after his disastrous marriage.

Just beyond Lowell, Gam shifted. Kathy's eleven-year-old brother was struggling to be extra good. Freddie had been surprised that he had bonded so closely with the lad, but then Freddie knew the terrible secret that was behind why he and Kathy had taken him from the Kansas farm where she and Gam had been raised, to live in New York City.

Lastly, Freddie's eyes fell on Kathy, the dearest of them all. The two had met when she edited his first novel for the publishing house where she'd worked at the time. The relationship had grown into something much deeper very quickly. Freddie marveled yet again at how profoundly she had changed his life and made it so much better and sweeter. Without her, his relationships with even Lowell and Honoria would have remained shallow and merely amusing. Without Kathy, he would never have come to see himself as a real writer, as opposed to someone who merely wrote as a way to fill up empty hours.

Not that he had many empty hours anymore.

Gam got a nod from Ivy and cleared his throat.

"Mrs. Little, Freddie, and Honoria," he said, reciting by rote. "I would like to extend my con- con-condolences on your recent loss." He nodded and then looked over at Ivy. "Did I do that right?"

"You did very nicely, young man," Gloria said. "We'll make a gentleman of you yet."

Freddie hoped his mother missed Gam's shudder.

"I wish to offer mine, as well," said Ivy.

"That's very kind of you, dear," said Gloria. "Thank you."

"What were you all talking about?" Honoria asked.

"People from the party," Kathy said. "Apparently, your cousins Wilfrid and Constance, and Aldrich left early."

Honoria frowned. "No. I saw them leaving just

after Father…" She blinked her eyes. "I remember seeing them as I ran for you and the stairs. They left out the front, and they had their coats on."

"Then they were getting ready to leave when things happened," said Lowell. "I saw them at the same speak shortly after Miles and Lovey Johnson came in."

"The Johnsons are such tiresome little people," Ivy said.

"They were at the party last night," said Lowell. "They left early and wound up at the speak I was at, having a terrible fight."

Honoria waved a dismissive hand. "Those two fight so often, the gossip columns aren't bothering to report it."

"Lowell seems to find them amusing," Kathy said.

"In a tragic way, of course," Lowell put in.

"There is nothing tragic about those two," Ivy said. "Especially if you are forced to work with them."

"Unfortunately, Lovey has decided that she's a Broadway genius," Lowell explained to the others. "And since that idiot Miles buys her everything she wants, he's bought her a few plays to produce. One did rather well a season or two ago, but by all accounts, working with her was pure hell."

"It was," said Ivy, who was an actress. She'd started out in film but had managed to get a major lead role on Broadway that winter. She'd gotten the night before off to watch Gam while the others were at the party. "The problem is, Lovey does have a good sense of what the public likes, which is why Love in Bloom, that was her first play, did so well. Sadly, it went to her head, and with her next two plays, she has been a complete harridan. She has her fingers in everything, including telling John Barrymore how to do his role and which side is his best side."

"I didn't know Barrymore was coming back to Broadway," Lowell said.

"He didn't," Ivy replied. "He left the show. Miles Johnson was furious, even made some rather nasty threats. Barrymore laughed at him and went to London to do Hamlet."

Gloria frowned. "You said you saw the Coates brothers at the speak?"

"Yes," said Lowell. "They are an odd pair of ducks. I can never remember which one of them is married to Constance and which one is divorced."

"There's a reason for that," said Honoria.

"Honoria!" Gloria said, glancing at Gam.

"I never got on with them," Freddie said with a slight shudder at the memories. "They're not very nice fellows."

"Oh, who cares about them," sighed Honoria.

"I think Lowell was trying to cheer us up," Kathy said, reaching over and patting Honoria's hand.

"I think we need to be finding out who killed Father," Honoria said.

"Honoria, the police have it well in hand," said Freddie.

Honoria folded her arms across her chest and snorted.

"But you guys are really good at solving crimes," Gam blurted out. "Better'n the police."

Gloria's eyebrow lifted and she glared at Gam.

"You'd better not let your Uncle Dan hear you say that, young man," Kathy told her brother. "And there were extenuating circumstances with the police in Kansas."

"Come along, Honoria," Ivy got up. "You, too, Gammers."

"But—" Honoria began.

"Darling, we're all feeling a little nervy," Ivy said. "I agree with Freddie. Best to let things drop for the time being. Who knows? Maybe the police will find the killer in the meantime and we won't be bothered."

Honoria looked around the room. "I'm sorry."

Kathy got up and hugged her sister-in-law. "It's all right, Honoria. It's been perfectly horrible and we're all understandably upset. If we let things settle for a few days, our minds can get nice and clear and then we can look at where things stand and do things logically. If we go off half-cocked, we'll be that much more likely to get into trouble, and we don't want that."

"You're right." Honoria sniffed.

"Come along, darling," Ivy said, gently taking Honoria's arm. "It's your turn to cry. We'll go up to your apartment and you can let loose until I have to leave for the theater."

"And you can go back to Mrs. Davies," Freddie told Gam.

Gam looked at Kathy. "Do I hafta?"

"Yes, you have to," Kathy said firmly. "Mrs. Davies says you're horribly behind on your English grammar and I don't believe for a minute that you made any progress last night."

"Tell you what," Freddie said. "If Mrs. Davies gives me a good report on you this afternoon, we can go over the Wall Street Journal together tonight."

Gam brightened. "That'd be swell." He shrank back. "Uh, sorry."

He ran from the room, as Freddie winced and Kathy tried not to laugh.

"Oh, dear," said Gloria calmly, watching the door close behind the boy. "Rome was, indeed, not built in a day. Freddie, you have your work cut out for you."

"Why would a boy his age want to read the Wall Street Journal?" Lowell asked.

Freddie flopped onto the couch. "It is completely unaccountable, but he is fascinated by stocks and finance and all that. The frightening thing is, he's very good at it. He catches things, and he's getting pretty good at reasoning out what they mean. He's given me more than a few good tips."

Gloria suddenly took a deep breath and stood. "That's all very well and good, but if you boys are going to talk about business, I, for one, would rather be elsewhere."

Freddie scrambled to his feet. "Of course, Mother."

"Kathy, will you come?" Gloria asked.

"Actually, Mother Little, I would find business talk rather soothing at this point."

"Perfect," Gloria said. "Freddie, I appreciate you bringing me over here, what with the police all over my home. But I've changed my mind and I do believe I'd be more comfortable there."

"I'll get my coat," Freddie said promptly, in spite of how surprised he was.

"Don't bother, darling. I'll have Taylor call the car." Gloria's smile was more brave than happy and she suddenly frowned. "Now that I think about it, I do believe I want a bit of time to be by myself. I dare say, we've a number of trying days ahead of us and I'd like to prepare myself for them."

"Of course, Mother." Freddie pressed the button hidden under the end table for his valet, Roberts, then kissed his mother's cheek.

"Are you sure you don't want to stay with us?" Kathy asked, getting up. "We're perfectly happy to have you."

"I'm sure you are," Gloria said. "And I appreciate it. Truly, I do. But sitting here, chatting aimlessly... I should be better at that and yet..." She sighed deeply. "I somehow feel as though I could be better occupied at home. Freddie, darling, it was so sweet of you to bring me over here. I know you intended the best. I simply..."

She sighed again and didn't say more.

Freddie looked at Kathy, who very slightly shrugged.

"Well, if that's how you feel, Mother," Freddie finally said. "Then by all means."

Freddie and Kathy walked his mother out to the foyer, where Taylor and Roberts were both waiting. Taylor announced that the car was waiting and the elevator had arrived. Freddie and Kathy each kissed Gloria's cheek and sent her on her way, not entirely noticing that Taylor had slipped into the servants' quarters rather than going back to the Little mansion.

As soon as they were alone, Kathy sighed and frowned.

"Are you all right?" Freddie asked anxiously.

"As well as can be," Kathy said. She gazed at the front door. "You know, it's odd. While we were sitting alone in the living room, your mother seemed... Well, not nervous, but as if she didn't want to be sitting there doing nothing. And now she says she can be better occupied at home than here. Funny thing is, even as close as we've gotten these past few months, your mother has always seemed to be convinced that whatever she was doing was what she should be occupied by."

Freddie also looked at the door, thinking. "You know, you're right." He sighed. "However, I have no idea what, if anything, to make of it. I suppose the best thing to do is let her go."

"I suppose you're right." Kathy sighed. "It's not as though we don't have other matters to occupy us."

"Indeed, my darling, one of which is sitting in our study drinking up all our whiskey, if I know him."

"And smoking your cigarettes," Kathy said with a chuckle, "He's lucky he's such a good friend."

Freddie smiled softly. "Yes, he is. Well, shall we attempt to stave off being drunk out of house and home?"

"Let's." Kathy took his arm with the soft smile that still sent his heart racing every time he saw it.

He patted her hand and the two headed for the study. But Freddie glanced back at the front door, where his mother had been. He didn't doubt his mother had other things to occupy herself, and there really wasn't anything he could do about it.

CHAPTER FOUR

The funeral was held the following Monday. It was a somber affair, interrupted by the swarms of reporters, first outside the church, and then outside the graveyard. Sheltered by the police and their limousines, the family escaped answering questions as they rode back to the Little mansion. While it had seemed as though the entire Four Hundred of New York society had shown up at the church, Gloria had made a point of inviting only the relatives and a few old family friends to the gathering at the mansion. Mr. and Mrs. Lewton were there, as were Mr. and Mrs. Marston, Mr. and Mrs. Hudson, and Mr. Terence Carter, a widower who, Freddie noted, kept watching Gloria with keen interest.

Sometime after luncheon, Kathy slid up to Freddie's side with a worried frown on her face.

"Is something wrong?" Freddie asked her.

"I don't know," Kathy said softly. "It looks like people are taking things and pocketing them. I even saw Aunt Miranda wrapping something rather long in an afghan from the game room."

Freddie looked around and there were several small art objects missing from various surfaces, and even an old portrait of his great-grandmother had disappeared from the wall. After reassuring Kathy, Freddie found his mother in the drawing room and pulled her aside.

"It looks like the pilfering has started," he whispered to her.

Gloria shrugged somewhat listlessly. "I'm not surprised. And Thelma was complaining last month that half of the contents of your grandfather's Long

Island estate had disappeared after his funeral. Perhaps she's hoping to get something back. She did say the drawing room at the estate was looking rather empty."

"Are she and Stephen still living there?" Freddie asked. "I thought they were going to move out last month."

"Thelma said that they didn't want to leave the estate empty." Gloria discreetly rolled her eyes. "The truth is they don't have anywhere else to go."

"Doesn't Stephen have a place in the city?"

"That burnt down years ago, when you were at Harvard," Gloria said. "Oh, good. Looks like your cousin Victoria got that ugly Dresden shepherdess from the mantle."

Freddie looked as his cousin slid out of the drawing room holding her coat close to her side.

"I rather liked that one," he said. "I think I picked that up at Great Uncle William's funeral when I was in prep school. Poor Kathy is utterly scandalized."

"It does seem a bit ridiculous. But people will want their mementos. I should probably reassure Kathy that I already put anything I truly want in the carriage house and locked it. With spring cleaning coming up, I will probably leave most of it there until we're done."

Spring cleaning occurred the week before Easter, and every room in the mansion was emptied, the room scrubbed, and everything gone over before it was returned.

Freddie nodded as Mr. Marston, a balding man of medium stature, blatantly picked up an antique silver cow creamer and looked it over with an appraising eye.

"Oh, please take it," Gloria muttered as she turned toward Freddie and pretended not to see.

Kathy tried not worry as Freddie's relatives picked up and slid the small art objects into their pockets and under jackets and the like. It seemed as though everyone felt entitled to take something, and apparently, they were. The problem was keeping track of who was taking what. The items seemed small and trivial and Freddie had reassured her that it happened at every funeral in his family. But Kathy couldn't help but wonder if one of the relatives doing the pilfering had, in fact, provided the opportunity by killing her father-in-law in the first place. She tried to think who had been in the ballroom when she'd left and who hadn't. As she stood in the hall, she noticed Mr. Carter coming from the game room with one of Father Little's rifles. Kathy watched him leave, then went into the game room, herself. There were two other empty slots in the gun cases that had been filled the morning after the party.

Back at home, she compared what she'd seen taken to the list of people who had left their wraps rather than face the police on the night of the party.

"You see, Freddie," she explained in the study after Gam had gone to bed. "Anyone who left his or her wrap probably did not want to deal with the police simply because one doesn't like having to. But it could also mean that he had just shot your father and had good reason not to want to speak to the police."

"I understand, Kathy, but that has nothing to do with the pilfering," he said, wearily lighting a cigarette.

"But what if someone really wanted something and felt he'd been done out of it?" Kathy looked up earnestly from her knitting. "Wouldn't causing a funeral create the perfect opportunity to get that item?"

Freddie shrugged. "It might seem so, but nothing that was pilfered was anything of significant value. It never is. The whole point is to take a memento and nothing more."

"I find it extremely hard to believe that no one has ever taken gross advantage of the custom," Kathy snorted.

"Naturally," Freddie said with a laugh. "I remember after Great Aunt Sarah's funeral, Aunt Thelma made off with Aunt Sarah's best silver coffee urn, which was supposed to go to one of her cousins, I forget whom. But it was in Aunt Sarah's will."

"What an odd custom."

"It is, perhaps," Freddie said. "It supposedly started after my great-great-grandfather, Jedediah Little, died. His widow, Mary, unintentionally, but very publicly, caught someone taking something. So, to spare that particular relative embarrassment, my great-great-grandmother said it was all right, that everyone could have something from the estate. Then one of the aunts did the same, and by the time my great-grandfather died, it was well-known that as long as one was reasonably discreet, anything that could be pocketed was there for the taking. Mother made sure that anything of significant value was locked away."

Kathy sighed. "I suppose killing your father just to make off with a china whatnot is a bit weak as a motive. Still, I did see that Mr. Carter taking one of your father's guns, which seems pretty suspicious, especially since he was one of the people who left his wrap the night of the party. And there were two other empty spaces in the gun cabinet."

Freddie nodded. "Yes. Mr. Lewton and Mr. Hudson. Mother told me that she'd told both of them and Mr. Carter to each take one of Father's guns, as they went hunting with him more often than anyone else."

"Oh." Kathy frowned. "It would probably make more sense for the killer to leave the gun behind so that he wouldn't be connected to it."

"I guess." Freddie frowned as well and stubbed out his cigarette. "Still, how could the police connect the killer to the gun unless someone saw the killer using it?"

"They could take fingerprints off the gun and then match them."

"But wouldn't they have to know which gun to fingerprint and which person to match them to?"

Kathy sighed, defeated. "That's true."

"And the police didn't fingerprint Father's guns," Freddie said. "They were all in place and the cases locked. The killer wouldn't have had enough time to return the gun to the gun case and relock it. I might also add that none of those men seems to have a motive. They were Father's friends. That's why Mother offered them the guns." He paused as he noticed Kathy's glare. "However, I suppose it wouldn't be a bad idea to ask them a few questions."

But Freddie's best intentions were thwarted by a telephone call that came in while he ate his breakfast. It was from the law firm that handled his family's business. He made the appointment for later that morning and returned to his meal feeling quite out of sorts.

Because he was feeling out of sorts, he made a point of walking to the law offices on Lexington and 43rd rather than driving or taking a taxi. It was a fair morning, with the sun making the occasional appearance over the buildings. Freddie breathed in the cool air and let it out again with deep relief. Alone, at last, among the crowds on 5th Avenue, he gazed about him, not really seeing the shops or caring. The days before had been so full, between receiving condolences and helping his mother go through his father's various offices, he'd not had more than a few minutes at a time for solitude. The walk relaxed and refreshed him and he began thinking more about the next scene that he wanted to write, rather than dealing with his grandfather's probate and print runs and an over-active young brother-in-law.

At 42nd he smiled at the lions in front of the great library and debated stopping in. He loved the huge old reading room with its polished wood beams and dark tables and chairs, worn smooth from years of use. It remained one of his favorite places to hide. But as tempting as hiding was at that moment, he did have his appointment at the family's law firm. So he continued walking down to 43rd and turned toward Lexington.

Mr. Edward Carstairs, the attorney who usually handled the family's affairs, had recently been made a partner in the firm, Mr. Carstairs' father having retired. Mr. Carstairs was somewhat older than Freddie, who had recently turned thirty. His dark hair was beginning to show flecks of silver and he needed spectacles to read. Freddie knew him as an unusually jovial fellow for a lawyer.

But that morning, as Freddie entered the office filled with bookshelves, rich red velvet curtains and overstuffed chairs in front of the huge teak wood desk, Mr. Carstairs was filled with gravitas.

"Good day, Mr. Little," Mr. Carstairs said, shaking Freddie's hand and motioning him to take a seat. "Would you like a cigarette?"

"Yes, thank you." Freddie got himself seated and the offered cigarette lit as Mr. Carstairs settled himself behind his desk.

The lawyer shuffled a couple of papers, then looked up at Freddie. "Do you know what firm your father planned to use to contest your grandfather's will?"

"I'm sorry?" Freddie asked.

"I'd heard that your father and your uncles were going to contest your grandfather's will, and we could not possibly represent your father and uncles in that regard, being the firm that drew up the will and that is currently representing you as executor."

"Oh." Freddie frowned. "When I last spoke with Uncle Stephen, I got the impression they hadn't gone so far as to secure another firm. I think Uncle Stephen was planning on using the firm his family uses."

Mr. Carstairs nodded. "Yes, Berger, Wineman, and Smith. I know them well. That is good news. You see, there's a possibility that what I have as your father's last will and testament may not, in fact, be the last one. If your father saw fit to engage another firm to handle contesting your grandfather's will, and I have reason to believe it is not Mr. Smith's firm, it is possible that he used that firm to make another will. The one I have is rather old."

"How old?"

"It's dated November twelve, eighteen-ninety-five." Mr. Carstairs looked morosely at the papers he held in front of him.

"What?"

"Your father made the will shortly after you were born and never updated it," Mr. Carstairs said. "I remember advising your father to update his will about a month ago, and he told me he wanted to see what kind of man you would be."

"Oh." Freddie sighed.

"He never mentioned to me that he had any intention of contesting your grandfather's will. In fact, I asked him about it directly, and he said that his brothers-in-law had suggested he should, but he hadn't made up his mind. He didn't think he had much of a case. Which he didn't."

"I wonder what changed," Freddie said.

"I suspect it was your uncles continuing to put pressure on him." Mr. Carstairs lit a cigarette of his own. "But that is based on hearsay, not actual evidence, mind you."

"Well, there was nothing unusual in his papers," Freddie said. "My mother and I checked the house here in the city, his office at the corporate headquarters, and his office at our Yonkers factory. Those are the places he went most often. But we even went up to his office at our primary factory in Poughkeepsie and looked there."

"I would advise looking through his accounts, then, to see if there's a draft or other sign that he's engaged another firm. As far as Mr. Coates' firm goes, I had lunch with Mr. Smith yesterday, after your father's funeral. We've been friends and rivals for many years now. I can't discuss the particulars, you understand. But he as good as told me that your father had not engaged his firm. Which means that the will I have should be the standing one, and it is in good order, in spite of its age."

Freddie nodded. "Then I suppose we should set a date for the reading and gather the beneficiaries."

"That is what we're doing now," Mr. Carstairs said. "You are the only beneficiary."

"But what about my mother and my sister? His sisters?"

"Well, your sister wasn't even born when this was made. As for your mother, we are to presume that you will take care of her. Or Mr. Coates, who was named as your guardian, should your father die before you came of age. The will also names our firm as executor."

"Well, at least I have that off my hands," Freddie said, grasping for the one bit of good news in what the lawyer had told him.

"I will see to filing this with the probate court in the morning unless you have any reason to delay."

"No, I don't. Actually, the sooner it's filed, the sooner we'll find out if Father made a newer one."

"I've not seen any evidence of a filing, and you would think, given the unfortunate publicity, someone would have seen to it promptly."

"There is that." Freddie sighed as the full weight of his father's will suddenly dawned on him. "I get it all?"

"Well, what the government doesn't take." Mr. Carstairs flashed a smile more in keeping with his usual humor.

Freddie sighed again, this time even more deeply. "This is damned inconvenient."

Mr. Carstairs looked at him in surprise. "How do you mean?"

"To the uninformed, it would appear that I had good reason to want my father dead, which I most certainly did not. Losing one's father is hard enough, and whatever conflicts there were between us these past weeks, I still loved and revered him. But even besides all that, this couldn't have happened at a worse time, what with Grandfather's will still in probate and my own little publishing company in its formative stages. There are several very good people looking to me to help bring it into the world and I can't let them down. Nonetheless, because my father was unhappy about Grandfather's will, there are certain members of the police force who believe I had reason to want Father dead, and now, with me turning up as his only heir, I am certain they will believe I had even more reason."

"That is damned inconvenient." Mr. Carstairs puffed thoughtfully. "But I thought the police said that an arrest was imminent."

"They always say that." Freddie stubbed out his cigarette and accepted another from Mr. Carstairs. "Last I heard, they didn't have any evidence, which is probably why we're not doing this in a jail cell." Freddie shuddered at the memory.

"It will come to nothing, like that other incident last summer," Mr. Carstairs grinned. "I truly enjoyed Mr. Eckert's account of the whole incident. He had some very interesting things to say about your wife, by the way. He was astounded by how sharp-witted she was."

Freddie smiled. "She is, indeed. Now, is there anything further regarding my father's will?"

"None at all."

"And regarding grandfather's will?"

Mr. Carstairs shrugged. "We're just waiting for the judge, and for enough time to pass. Fortunately, your grandfather didn't have any debts. That always complicates things. And his affairs were in excellent order." Mr. Carstairs paused. "I fear the same will not be said of your father's probate."

"Given the date of his will, I would not be surprised," Freddie said.

"It's not just that." Mr. Carstairs sighed. "Given that your grandfather and your father are both dead, it is not technically a breach of confidentiality for me to tell you, I suppose."

"Tell me what?"

Mr. Carstairs winced. "I drew up your Grandfather's last will. In his previous wills, he had intended that your father receive the bulk of the inheritance with the stipulation that you receive almost all of the company shares when your father passed. After your father and uncles insisted that your grandfather retire, the old man still kept an eye on things, you might say. He was not happy with how your father was running the business. Or not running it, rather. I'm not sure what did or did not happen. I do know that after your father became chairman, every so often we would receive complaints about unpaid invoices. One worker wanted to sue for back wages. That sort of thing. We didn't have any problems covering the oversights financially. But they shouldn't have happened in the first place. Not to mention the extra costs of soothing the ruffled feathers involved." Mr. Carstairs sighed. "I know you to be fairly astute when it comes to business, so when your grandfather wished that he could leave it all to you instead, I told him there was no reason he couldn't."

"I see." Freddie's finger beat a tattoo on the chair's arm. "I have you to thank for that."

"Maybe not directly." Mr. Carstairs flashed a grin. "I was trying to serve my client's best interests. And the only reason I'm telling you this now is in those same interests. It's only fair to warn you, not to mention give you a chance to find out what's going on and hopefully correct it before it's too late."

"I see." Freddie sighed as he pulled a small black diary and pencil out of his jacket pocket. He made a note. "Well, I suppose I have my work cut out for me. How much can I legally do while everything is still in probate?"

"That is a good question. If the other shareholders are not opposed, you should be able to appoint a temporary chairman, even yourself, just to keep things going. Your uncles should agree to that, even if they still want to contest your grandfather's will. After all, it's to their benefit to make sure the company doesn't languish during probate. In the meantime, I'll see if I can get a conference with Judge Titus about the matter. Since he's overseeing your grandfather's probate, he should be able to give us some guidance on how to proceed."

Freddie nodded. "I'll make that argument, then. I was thinking of asking my Uncle Stephen to take over as chairman. Is there any legal reason why I shouldn't?"

"It might give him something of an edge if he contests the will, although I think we can make a solid argument that your intent is to make peace with him. Other than that, there's no legal reason why you can't."

Freddie stood up. "Well, that's that. Thank you, Mr. Carstairs, for your time."

"Of course." Mr. Carstairs rose also. "And, eh, Mr. Little, you might want to show more interest in the business right now. I know you have your own venture, but there are those who would take advantage of that and argue that you shouldn't be involved in overseeing your family's interests. You could try to make up to your uncles. Stand them to dinner at the Union Club. Play some golf with them. You might even let them win."

Freddie chuckled grimly. "I won't have to let them win. But it's not a bad idea."

The two shook hands and offered their final goodbyes, then Freddie left the office.

At the Little mansion on West 59th and Madison, Gloria Little was busy finishing a note in her diary. Briggeman slipped into the doorway of the small study on the second floor where Gloria did most of the tasks related to the part of her life that participated in polite society. Fortunately, Gloria saw the aging butler before he could startle her. She hated embarrassing the poor man, but it was an awkward problem that the two continued to dance around even though Briggeman had been with the family for close to thirty-four years and in his current position for at least half of them. Gloria would become absorbed in some bit of writing or reading and Briggeman would need to attract her attention for one reason or another and would accidentally startle Gloria out of her absorption.

"Yes, Briggeman?" Gloria asked, shutting her diary and removing the glasses she only wore when alone.

"The car is out front, Ma'am."

"Excellent. Thank you, Briggeman."

After hiding the glasses in her desk, Gloria picked up her handbag and pulled on her gloves. She took a quick look in the small mirror behind the study door just to be sure all was as it should be. It was, more or less. The smooth curves of her youth had filled out considerably, but one expected that when one had passed one's fiftieth birthday. Hair that had once been light brown was now streaked with gray which she tried to tell herself looked distinguished. At least, she'd been able to convince Parker, her lady's maid, that she did not need to be wearing her widow's weeds, even if her understated polished cotton jacquard day dress was black. Gloria twisted sideways. The black was rather dreary, but it was also quite becoming. She had chosen a black hat with a fairly wide brim and some veiling, which was still appropriate to her recently bereaved status, but not the dreadful full veil she'd worn to the funeral the day before.

She headed out to the car with her eyes starting to fill again. It was annoying. She liked to think she had better control over her passions. Nonetheless, it was disconcerting how much she missed her husband. Theirs had never been a passionate relationship. Still, she had appreciated him and liked to think that he had been fond of her, his many infidelities notwithstanding. One expected that of men. And it was true that Fred had been more distant than not of late. But he had been at her dinner table almost every night. He indulged her various fancies and even occasionally listened to what she had to say. It wasn't the passion and partnership that Freddie shared with Kathy, yet what Gloria had shared with her husband was better than what many of her peers shared with theirs.

Van Schuyler, the chauffeur, was waiting on the sidewalk in front of the mansion, holding the door open to the Packard automobile that Fred had preferred to drive when he'd decided to drive rather than be driven. It was what Gloria chose to ride in when she wanted to be inconspicuous. Van Schuyler sometimes teased her that the long cream-colored car was hardly inconspicuous, but even he conceded it was more discreet than the Rolls Royce limousine Gloria usually used.

"Where to, Ma'am?" Van Schuyler asked, in a low cultured voice.

"We have another secret mission today," she said.

"Dat's what I love to hear." Van Schuyler's voice shifted into his native heavy Bronx accent.

He was a small man whose face and stature bore a rather unfortunate resemblance to a weasel. Some years before, Gloria had caught several of Van Schuyler's colleagues remarking unkindly on the chauffeur's appearance.

"It don't bother me none," Van Schuyler had told her. "Fact is, I do kinda look like a weasel."

"Well," Gloria had paused, feeling nonplussed for a moment. "Actually, with your nice, white shirt, you remind me more of a Martes Americana or American pine marten."

"What's that?"

"A tree-dwelling relative of the weasel,"

"Now, dat would be my cousin Louie."

Gloria smiled at the memory as she settled herself into the car's back seat. Van Schuyler quickly shut the side door and scurried to the front and got behind the wheel.

"So, what do we have on de agenda today?" he asked, starting the engine.

"We're going to my husband's hunting lodge."

Van Schuyler turned to her with a worried frown on his face. "You sure you're up for dat?"

Gloria sighed. "No, I'm not sure. But I don't have much choice. My husband was murdered and I must do my best to see that the miscreant is brought to justice."

She thought she saw a smirk on Van Schuyler's face as he started driving.

"I heard da cops was tinking your son done it," Van Schuyler said. "On account of the old man's will. I told 'em dat was nonsense. Mr. Freddie wouldn't hurt a fly."

"Your loyalty is commendable, Van Schuyler." Gloria sighed. "However, I have heard about Detective Crowley's suspicions. One can hardly blame him, either. If one applies the basic logic of cui bono, that is, who benefits, then from an outside perspective, it does appear that Freddie benefits the most from his father's passing. We who know Freddie are the ones who understand that Freddie doesn't see himself as benefitting in the least. Which is why we're going up to the hunting lodge. My late husband may have left something there that would help us uncover the guilty party."

"And if dere just happens to be something the cops might find incriminatory, we can take care of it."

"Heavens, no! We will not do anything that utterly unethical." Gloria paused. "We might, however, let Freddie explain it before handing it over to the police."

"Dat's what I meant, Ma'am."

Gloria seriously doubted that. But, perhaps, that was to be expected. Over the six years that Van Schuyler had been part of the staff, no one except herself had found out about the chauffeur's misbegotten past. Or as Van Schuyler referred to it, his unfortunate tarriance at the Hotel Sing Sing. Briggeman had known about it when he hired Van Schuyler, and apparently had hired other reformed criminals, as well.

Gloria occasionally wondered if she should have been more concerned when she had found out about Briggeman's odd sympathy for former criminals. But there had been no problems with either criminal activity or the quality of the service. If anything, Gloria's friends commented on the uncommon excellence and loyalty of her staff. Gloria had seen no reason to question Briggeman's decisions. And the skills Van Schuyler had acquired during his sojourn with the criminal element had proven useful on occasion.

She had forgotten how long it took to get to Fred's hunting lodge, and it was getting quite late in the afternoon when they drove up the drive lined by pine trees. It was a relatively small house, only nineteen rooms in two stories. Even though Gloria had always loved the quiet beauty of the surrounding woodlands, she had never understood why Fred had loved such a small place. He'd always said there was enough room for the two of them, completely forgetting that even a minimal staff would be forced into cramped quarters there.

Van Schuyler stopped the car near the front porch. Gloria saw that the porch furniture had been cleared of its winter coverings, but that no cushions had been set out. It was the compromise the caretaker had made in keeping the lodge almost ready so that it took a minimum of time to set it to rights. Fred had taken to going up to the lodge on the least whim and without warning. Gloria had tried explaining to him that the caretaker and his wife needed some notice to get the lodge ready, but Fred had merely laughed at her. He really hadn't had the least idea of what it took to keep a place livable.

It was but a moment before Van Schuyler had the car door open and was helping Gloria out. The air was filled with the chill of early spring and rich with the smell of pine. Birds sang raucously, a melody punctuated by the cawing of a crow or the screech of a blue jay. Squirrels chirruped to each other and one plump fellow sat on the porch looking curiously at the car.

Van Schuyler walked behind as Gloria mounted

the porch stairs and went to the door. Her eyes filled again and she shut them tight to prevent any tears. Shaking her head to clear it, she stepped up to the door and turned the handle. It didn't move. She shook it.

"It's locked," she said, surprised. "That's odd. Briggeman said it was open as usual when I asked about the key this morning."

Van Schuyler shrugged. "Maybe it's just the front."

But it wasn't. The whole lodge was locked quite solidly. In addition, the caretaker and his wife were not at home. Gloria sighed deeply as they returned to the front porch.

Van Schuyler grinned. "What an unfortunate turn of events. And you come such a long way, too."

Gloria looked at him with the barest hint of a smile.

"Am I to suppose that you can find a way into the house even though it is locked?" she asked, wondering if she should be encouraging him.

"Well," Van Schuyler said. "Dat was my specialty before New York's Finest decided I should become a guest of the state, if you know what I mean."

"You know very well that I do."

"It ain't breaking and entering if it's your own place." Van Schuyler paused. "I tink."

"It's certainly breaking and entering since you do propose to break the lock in order to for us to enter," Gloria said. "But whether it's illegal or not, I would have to assume that it isn't, since, as you pointed out, it is my lodge. Oh, go ahead."

Van Schuyler hurried to the trunk of the car and rummaged around for a minute. He pulled up a ring that held several thin pieces of metal, most no longer than a hand.

"I probably shouldn't carry dese," he said, coming back up to the porch. "A copper finds dem on me and it's back to Sing Sing. But dey do have deir uses apart from criminological pursuits."

"Indeed."

After taking a quick look around, Van Schuyler knelt in front of the door and had it open in a few moments. He got up and stepped back.

"After you, Madam," he said with a bow.

Gloria entered the huge front room. Rustic leather and wood furniture sat scattered about and a tall rock fireplace and hearth took up the larger part of one wall. There were only a couple of stuffed heads of deer on the walls. A few stuffed fish were also mounted on plaques and hung. Even her own poor attempt at stuffing a squirrel, mounted sideways on a good-sized board, still hung from the wall. In a corner next to the fireplace, a huge stuffed bear stood in a frozen snarl. Fred had bagged the animal on a trip out West and had been quite perturbed when the taxidermist had stood the animal in its angry pose, rather than a more natural, four-legged one. Fred's lion was at the other end of the room, posed as it would have been walking about the African Veldt. There was a tiger skin on the floor as a rug, but the other two tigers were scattered about the lodge, posed more naturally. Fred, who had loved nature, had donated any number of his trophies to the Natural History Museum.

Gloria wasn't sure what she was looking for. Her eyes swept the room but did not find anything out of place. She slowly made her way through the house, lifting pillows, opening drawers. In the small study, it did look as though someone had gone through what few papers Fred had left in the small desk. Gloria went into the bedroom next door. She tried the drawer in the table next to the bed but didn't find anything beyond some stomach powders and some candy wrappers. She opened the armoire and found not only a good business suit but all manner of hunting clothes. Two pairs of well-worn boots sat next to the armoire.

Gloria found herself shaking her head and smiling. If Taylor had seen the boots, he would have been humiliated, as any proper valet would be upon seeing his master's boots uncared for, let alone left out.

However, Taylor almost never went to the hunting lodge. Gloria had managed to convince her husband that he didn't need a valet when he was there.

It had been extremely easy to do. Fred had always liked to pretend he could manage without servants and had been prone to making unreasonable demands of them in the fond belief that he could manage the task just as easily. So while the staff was, in fact, uncommonly loyal to her, it had been next to impossible to keep a valet for Fred employed for any length of time. The fact that Taylor had lasted almost two years was probably because Fred had spent so much time at the hunting lodge. Gloria had arranged for a couple of young men interested in learning to become valets to unobtrusively see to keeping Fred's clothes in order when he wasn't at the lodge. The lodge's caretaker looked after the grounds and had his wife do the cooking and some of the housekeeping, with some local girls taking care of the rest when Fred was back in town.

It had been the perfect solution and Gloria wished she'd thought of it sooner. Her visits to the lodge had become few and far between over the past decade or so, and she was the one whose insistence on a well-kept household had made a larger staff necessary. Perhaps if she'd been more willing to rough it, as Fred called it, she'd have spent more time with him there.

They had spent a fair amount of time there when the children were still too little to go. But then, as Freddie had gotten older, Fred had insisted on taking the boy out on a deer hunt. Gloria shivered at the memory. The poor child had only been about four or so and Gloria had told Fred that he was too young. But Fred, as he often did, had gotten it into his head that the boy was ready and there was no talking him out of it. Freddie had survived the sounds of the guns going off, but had hated the cold, wet forest and had been completely traumatized by the dead deer. Worse yet, Fred had insisted the lad watch as the animal was skinned and butchered in the lodge's small abattoir.

Freddie had gotten over his trauma but had never picked up his father's love of the sport, going only when he was expected to.

Gloria sighed again and tried to clear her mind of the flood of memories. Odd how a couple pairs of boots could do that to her. Given that so much of psychiatry seemed to be tied up in memories, she couldn't help wondering if that relatively new science was behind what was happening to her. But then she wrenched her mind back to the task at hand and noticed something rectangular and white just under the armoire. She was about to get down on her knees when she thought better of it and instead nudged the mysterious item free with her foot. It was a small book bound in dark green leather. The white she'd seen was the edge of the pages. Fortunately, she did touch her toes twenty times every morning, so picking up the small volume was no trouble.

It was Fred's diary. It was more of an appointment book than a journal, but it did contain the few things that Fred did not want to forget. Gloria remembered hearing Fred berate Taylor the night before the party over some lost item. And Fred had only returned that afternoon from the hunting lodge. Ergo, the diary must have been the missing item.

"Mrs. Little!" Van Schuyler called from the bottom of the stairs. "I found someting."

Gloria hurried to the landing, holding up the diary. "So have I. What did you find?"

"Mr. Little's safe."

"A safe?" Gloria came down the stairs. "Why would Fred have a safe here?"

"Dat's a good question," Van Schuyler said. "Dere wasn't anyting in it."

"You opened it?"

"Uh, yeah. My former career, you might say."

"Oh, that's right. You keep telling me you were rather good at it."

"I was da best!" Van Schuyler puffed himself up

with some pride. "And let me tell you, it was no trick to find it. Though I must be honest, cracking it took a bit of doing. Dat is one premium safe."

Gloria looked around the room, then spotted the open wall safe. It had been hidden behind the plaque with the badly-stuffed squirrel on it, which Van Schuyler had set on the floor just underneath.

Gloria was about to ask another question when there was a loud pounding on the door.

"Cheese it!" Van Schuyler hissed, pushing Gloria toward the back of the house.

"What?"

"Open up!" a voice outside demanded.

"Let's go." Van Schuyler pushed harder. "Dat ain't de caretaker's voice."

CHAPTER FIVE

As Freddie stepped into his apartment, he could hear Kathy's voice coming from the study. Freddie looked at Roberts as the valet took his overcoat, gloves, and hat.

"I presume that she is speaking on the telephone," Roberts said, anticipating Freddie's question. "We've had no visitors."

Freddie glanced at the telephone sitting on the hall table. They had installed another telephone on Kathy's desk in the study, as the fledgling publishing company had no offices as yet.

"Freddie! You're home!" Gam came running into the foyer from the back bedroom that had been made into his schoolroom.

"Yes, Gam." Freddie smiled even though he did not feel like dealing with the boy.

Mrs. Davies, fortunately, came to the rescue. She was a tall, full-figured woman, with an authoritarian bearing that made her all the more formidable. It was, perhaps, just as well, Freddie often thought, as Gam's lively curiosity and unrelenting energy made him something of a hand-full.

"Young Master Briscow," Mrs. Davies announced in her full-bodied voice. "I should think that someone who can name as few capitals as you would be ashamed to be seen in public."

"It's geography," Gam told Freddie in a slightly lowered voice. "It's really boring."

"I agree," said Freddie. "But how are you going to understand shipping and bills of lading if you don't know where places are?"

Understanding brightened Gam's face. "Oh.

Yeah!”

Mrs. Davies sniffed. “And don’t use slang. Come along, young man.”

Mrs. Davies did not approve of Freddie’s methods. But the fastest way to interest Gam in his schoolwork was to apply it to business, and even Kathy conceded it was worth doing.

Freddie sighed. He could hear Kathy’s voice getting tight with annoyance as she tried to speak pleasantly.

As he entered the study, she was pacing around her desk with the handset to her face.

“Mr. Cavendish, I do appreciate the difficulty of your position,” she said, not seeing Freddie as she glared at her desk. “But there really isn’t anything we can do about it. As I told you last month, it was your choice to make. Now that you’ve made it, we can’t be held liable because it did not turn out well, especially when we encouraged you not to make that choice and I have the copy of the letter to prove it.”

The man on the other end of the line did not seem to be mollified. Freddie winced. Kathy had wooed author Aldous Cavendish almost before the ink was dry on the incorporation papers for Signature Books, Inc. Unfortunately, the company that had fired her the previous fall, Healcroft House, had also wooed Mr. Cavendish and had made a substantial offer that Kathy had not wanted to meet. Having championed Mr. Cavendish’s work while she’d still been working there, Kathy knew that Mr. Thaddeus Healcroft was not in the least interested in the novel and had suspected that he’d wooed Cavendish purely to spite her and the other authors that had left Healcroft House to form Signature Books.

“Well, I agree that your best course of action would be to discuss this with a lawyer,” Kathy said, finally. “However, and I’m sure he’ll tell you this, you’re better off aiming your ire at Mr. Healcroft since he’s the one who has caused you harm. Now, if you’ll excuse me, I must hang up now.”

She sighed as she placed the phone in its cradle, and then turned and jumped.

"Oh! I didn't know you'd come back." She gave Freddie a quick peck on the cheek before flopping onto the sofa. "What a miserable mess!"

"They're sitting on the novel after all?" Freddie looked longingly at the crystal decanter of whiskey on the credenza next to the door.

"It would appear so," said Kathy, rubbing her face and her eyes. "And since Cavendish won't get any money until the book is published, he's beginning to think they never intended to publish it."

"And we told him that would likely happen, didn't we?" Freddie sank into his chair.

"Of course, we did." Kathy glared at the floor then looked over at him. She gasped. "Freddie, you look completely used up. What's happened? Did your father disinherit you or something?"

"If only he had," Freddie said with a snort. "No. I get everything. Mother and Honoria are not even mentioned. The only reason Uncle Stephen was mentioned is that he was to be my guardian if Father died before I came of age."

Kathy looked puzzled. "You've been of age for a good nine years now. That doesn't make sense."

"It did when I was an infant, which is when Father made the will."

"Oh, dear. I hope that doesn't mean there will be any trouble with the probate."

"Right now, my darling, I couldn't possibly care less if there is." Freddie sank back and rubbed his eyes. "That is the one good part. I don't have to execute the will. Father assigned that miserable business to the law firm." He sighed again. "And it is going to be a very miserable business. According to Mr. Carstairs, Father appears to have left his affairs in a mess. The firm has gotten dunning letters for unpaid invoices and there are rumors of worse. I'm going to have to get involved, too, whether I want to or not. If I'm not, then my uncles have an excuse to contest grandfather's will on the basis that I'm not interested in the business."

"And the irony is, you're not really interested, are you?'

Freddie frowned. "I do enjoy business as an occupation. It's all this family strife that's so unmanageable. If it weren't for you or mother or Honoria, I would sell the whole enterprise, lock, stock, and barrel and be perfectly happy. But, alas, your fortunes and welfare are tied to the family business, so I must take care of it."

"Poor darling." Kathy pulled herself up off the sofa and sat on the chair's arm next to Freddie, pulling him close. "You've spent your entire life not having to be responsible for anyone and now you've got all these people depending on you."

"That's exactly what it is." Freddie nestled his head into her bosoms. "I don't like it. Or rather. I don't mind the responsibility, but I don't like having it all dumped on me at once with all the rancor and fussing."

Kathy kissed him on the top of his head. "You'll manage, darling. And I'm here to help."

"I can't tell you how much I appreciate that." He released her. "Now, tell me all about your day."

"It's not been bad," Kathy said. "Even with Mr. Cavendish. Oh, and I did have a most interesting meeting at luncheon."

"You did? With whom?'

"Mr. Steven Fiske."

Freddie thought. "The name sounds familiar."

"One of my fellow junior editors at Healcroft House." Kathy grinned wickedly. "It seems the atmosphere at Healcroft House has gotten pretty awful of late and he's looking for a new job."

"With us?"

"Yes."

Freddie creased his brow. "Could it be another dirty trick on the part of your former employers?"

"It could, indeed, although I don't think so." Kathy

landed on the couch again. "It doesn't matter. Until we've got some steady revenue, we shouldn't be hiring anyone."

"Being undercapitalized isn't a good idea, either."

"Even then, we still need an office and a couple good stenogs and typists first."

Freddie nodded. "Tell you what. Why don't we make up a list and we'll go over the finances with the board sometime next week?"

"That sounds like an excellent idea. Now, Mrs. Washington has cooked us a lovely lamb stew for dinner tonight." Kathy suddenly yawned widely and deeply. "Oh, excuse me."

Freddie looked at her with a frown. "You had another nightmare last night."

Kathy looked panicked. "Did I wake you?"

"No."

"Then all's well." Kathy smiled and got up.

"Kathy—"

"I'll get over them," Kathy turned and glared at him. "I told you, it's happened before and they eventually go away. They won't get any better by coddling me."

She turned and left the study. Freddie shook his head.

The nightmares had started the night after his father's death. It had made sleeping very difficult for both of them. Kathy, however, had made it clear that she did not want to worry Freddie and refused to wake him when she had one. And that worried Freddie even more than if she'd bothered him.

Kathy, for her part, was furious with herself for letting the yawn escape. The last thing Freddie needed was to be fretting over her silly weak-mindedness. She hurried to the bedroom, hoping that Freddie wouldn't follow her.

True, there were moments when all Kathy wanted was to wrap herself in his arms and howl until she couldn't anymore. There would be time for that later.

Freddie needed her to be strong, so strong she would be.

She sighed. It was odd that he, an incredibly curious person under normal circumstances, seemed so uninterested in finding out who had killed his father. Or it would have been odd, except that the most logical suspect was Kathy's mother-in-law.

As Kathy was fast learning, there were two very different sides to Gloria Little. She remained very much the society matron she was and presented herself as to the world. Still, there was the other side, the one that was filled with surprises. The one that read F. Scott Fitzgerald and Somerset Maugham and let out odd hints of other activities and interests not at all in keeping with her public side. Was it also a side that could murder a man in cold blood?

Gloria could have been the person she saw on the terrace. Although it didn't make sense that Mr. Little would have demanded what she was doing up there. After all, her bedroom was right there. Perhaps he was wondering why she wasn't in the ballroom attending their guests.

Kathy went into the bathroom and washed her face. The worst of her suspecting Gloria of the murder was how to talk to Freddie about it. He was still clearly grieving his father's death, not to mention feeling all the family strife and responsibility. How could Kathy add to the poor man's misery by asking him whether he thought his own mother could have killed his father? It occurred to Kathy, at that moment, that Freddie was possibly just as suspicious of his mother, which, on one hand, could make it easier to talk about her concerns. On the other hand, perhaps fears of Gloria's guilt were what was keeping him from looking into the murder. In that case, talking about it with him would only confirm his worst worries and make it that much harder to investigate.

Kathy left the bedroom for the study only to find Freddie in the foyer talking on the phone and smoking.

"I agree completely," he was telling the person on the other line. "There's a little place in the Village,? run by an Italian... Yes, that's the one. One tomorrow then..?" Freddie nodded as he snubbed out his cigarette. "Excellent. I'll look forward to it... Good-bye."

He hung up and looked over at Kathy.

"I've an appointment tomorrow with your Uncle Dan," he said.

"Oh?"

"Yes. I'm hoping to find out what the police are thinking about my father's case." Freddie paused to light another cigarette. "I'm sure they must suspect me, but if I'm the one who tells them about Father's will, then maybe that will give them less reason to do so."

Kathy smiled. "One can certainly hope so. Is it time for dinner yet?"

As if in answer to her question, Gam came running out from the back of the apartment with Mrs. Davies following him, her purse in hand.

"Freddie!" Gam yelled. "I got all the capitals of Europe named! I even got Africa."

"Indoor voice, Master Briscow," Mrs. Davies said.

"That seems like excellent progress," Freddie said, smiling.

Kathy smiled, too. For all Gam's energy and restlessness, he was doing very well with his schoolwork. It seemed a pity that Mrs. Davies never seemed pleased with his progress.

"It will do for now," Mrs. Davies sniffed as Roberts brought her gloves, coat, and hat.

That was high praise from Mrs. Davies.

"Freddie, can we read the Journal together tonight?" Gam asked excitedly.

"I don't know. Mrs. Davies?"

"He passed his arithmetic test well enough for him to begin algebra," Mrs. Davies said. "He did, indeed, name his capitals correctly, and can name the organs of the body competently. However, his grammar remains quite atrocious, and his last essay…” She shuddered. “I have set him some extra sentences to diagram.”

Gam kept his face straight, but as soon as Mrs. Davies had her back turned, he stuck his tongue out at her. Kathy pretended not to see.

“We’ll work on his sentences tonight,” Kathy said quickly.

“Indeed, we will,” said Freddie, whose grip on Gam’s shoulder told Kathy that he had seen the tongue. “Thank you once again, Mrs. Davies. And we’ll see you tomorrow.”

“Tomorrow then,” Mrs. Davies said with a sniff.

Roberts held the door open for her and the household watched as she stepped onto the elevator. Mr. Elroy, the old Negro man who operated the conveyance, spotted Gam and winked at him. Gam waved back. Kathy wondered what mischief the boy had planned with the aging elevator operator.

“Hey, Freddie, how much time do we have before dinner?” Gam asked once the front door to the apartment was closed.

“Hay is for horses,” Freddie said. “And I’m not sure. But we probably have enough time to write your parents. They are overdue for their weekly letter.”

Gam made a face. “But what do I write about your pa?”

“Oh, that’s right,” Kathy said. “That happened after last week’s letter. I haven’t even had a chance to write, myself. All right, Gam. I’ll write the letter with the news and you can add your usual letter at the bottom.”

But the letter never got written. Kathy’s words had barely escaped her mouth when the hall phone rang. Kathy reached for it, but somehow, Roberts got to it before her.

“Little residence,” he said solemnly and listened. “May I ask who’s calling..? Indeed. I’ll put him on immediately.”

Roberts handed the phone to Freddie. “It’s the

police in Phoenicia, sir. They have Mrs. Little there."

"What?" Freddie grabbed the receiver.

The conversation was relatively short and mostly one-sided in favor of the other end of the line. Freddie agreed to get there as fast as he could.

"What's happening?" Kathy asked as Freddie hung up the phone.

"Mother's been arrested," Freddie said. "She was caught breaking into Father's hunting lodge."

"What?" Kathy asked. "Why would the police care if she was going into her husband's lodge?"

"I don't know." Freddie picked up the phone again and dialed. "All they said was that she was with a disreputable character." He paused for a moment while the other line picked up. "Briggeman, it's Mr. Freddie here. Do you know what plans my mother had for today..? I see... Yes, there does appear to be a problem, but I'm going up to Phoenicia to straighten it all out... She's not been hurt, as far as I can tell... Thank you, Briggeman, but I think we can handle it... I will convey your concern to my mother when I see her."

"What did Briggeman say?" Kathy asked the second Freddie pulled the phone from his ear.

Freddie thoughtfully laid the phone in its cradle. "Not very much, I'm afraid. She left just after lunch with the chauffeur. She'd asked earlier that morning about Father's hunting lodge but did not say that was where she was going nor when she intended to be back." He sighed. "I'd better get going."

"We're going," Kathy said.

Freddie stopped. "You don't mind?"

"Of course not. Now get the coats and the car while I call Honoria to see if she can watch Gam."

"I wanna go!" Gam protested. "I'm always left out of everything."

"Gamaliel," Kathy said. "This is not the time."

However, when Honoria expressed the same sentiment as Gam, it was quickly decided that she would join Freddie and Kathy, with Lowell driving Ivy and Gam. Why Lowell had been visiting with Honoria and Ivy at that moment, and why Ivy was not working that night, Kathy could only guess, but it had turned out to be darned convenient.

They were on the road in minutes. Kathy had a small flashlight so that she could read the roadmap, not that Freddie particularly needed it. He knew the way to his father's hunting lodge and knew that the town of Phoenicia was on the same road. However, Kathy preferred to focus on the map since Freddie was driving very fast.

"I hope the local police don't think we're rum runners," Kathy said once when they skidded around a rather sharp curve.

"If we were rum runners, we'd be going the other direction," Honoria said.

Freddie ignored her but did slow a bit. Nonetheless, he made what was normally a three-hour trip in less than two hours.

The Phoenicia police station was a small one-room affair. There was a counter separating the larger part of the office from the front. Gloria was sitting rather stiffly between a battered desk and the jail, in which Van Schuyler was sitting.

Freddie rushed to the edge of the counter. "Mother!"

The police officer stepped up to the desk, effectively blocking Gloria off from view. He was a little taller than average with broad shoulders, a jutting jaw and a nose that had probably been broken more than once.

"This is your ma?" he asked Freddie.

"Yes. Mrs. Frederick Little, Senior," Freddie said. "That's her chauffeur in jail."

"You don't say," the officer growled. He looked back at Van Schuyler, then leaned forward over the counter toward Freddie. "I know your ma seems to like that fellow, but he's, uh, not the sort I'd want driving my mother around, if you get my meaning."

"I'm afraid I do not, sir," Freddie said coldly. "My

mother is a sensible woman. If she says she can trust Mr. Van Schuyler, then I have no reason to doubt her."

"Yeah, but…" The police officer frowned. "Look, Mr. Little, I seen a lot in my day, and I can tell a felon when I see one. And that fellow in there is a felon."

"Be that as it may, officer, I also trust my mother's judgment," Freddie said, suddenly not at all sure he could.

"Well, the safe was open and empty when we found them." The officer looked back at the jail, then back at Freddie. "I've seen cases like this before. Some fellow kidnaps this old lady and she falls for him."

"Officer, this man has been driving for my family for several years now," Freddie said. "Now, if you will let me speak with my mother, I'm sure we can get everything straightened out."

As Freddie was let around to the back, Gloria looked up, filled with righteous indignation.

"Thank God, you're here," she hissed. "That officer is the most stubborn, rude, completely idiotic fellow I've ever met. He wouldn't listen to a word I said. Van Schuyler most certainly did not kidnap me. I've never heard anything so ridiculous in my life! He drove me up to the hunting lodge because I asked him to."

"But why did you go up there?" Freddie asked.

"Never mind that. Just get us out of here."

Freddie looked over at the officer, then back at his mother. "He's worried that Van Schuyler is a felon."

"Whatever happened to innocent until proven guilty, I ask you?" Gloria snorted. "The police found no evidence that he'd committed a crime. I had every right to be there and to have the safe open. Unless they've suddenly changed the laws and it's now illegal to visit one's own property."

Freddie sighed. It was definitely not the time to let his mother know that the lodge was now Freddie's property, technically, instead of hers.

"Will you get us out of here, please?" Gloria asked. "It's past time for dinner and I'm quite starved. Not to mention poor Mr. Van Schuyler."

"Yes, Mother." Freddie sighed again.

He looked around the tiny police station. Honoria looked like she was about to give the officer a piece of her mind. There was an additional commotion as Lowell and Ivy arrived with Gam. Fortunately, the officer looked a little overwhelmed and Freddie took full advantage of it to get Van Schuyler released to his custody. Freddie also got the use of the phone to let Roberts know that it was likely that the group would be spending the night at the lodge, only to find that Roberts had anticipated this. The valet had not only telephoned and had a message sent to the hunting lodge's caretaker but was sending up a footman and a maid with night things and such for everyone. In addition, the caretaker's wife had been asked to prepare dinner for everyone.

There were greetings and kissed cheeks all around, which made it hard for Freddie to explain that everything was waiting at the lodge. Still, once he did, it was generally agreed that this was an excellent course of action, especially since they would have to go there to get the family car that had been left behind. As the crowd made their way outside to their cars, Gloria held Freddie.

"Freddie, dearest," she said just loudly enough for the now-abashed police officer to hear. "Tomorrow morning, I want you to contact Mr. Carstairs. I plan to file suit for false arrest."

"I will, Mother," Freddie said, gently pushing his mother out the door.

CHAPTER SIX

With Honoria, Lowell, Ivy, and Gam in the other car, Freddie seated Kathy and Gloria in the back seat and Van Schuyler up front. An icy silence reigned for the short drive to the lodge.

All was in readiness, although the safe was still open, with the stuffed squirrel's plaque still underneath. It didn't matter. The rich smells of meat cooking and bread baking filled the cabin.

Kathy winced at all the stuffed animals, but Gam was fascinated by them. Kathy hissed at him not to touch anything.

After everyone had taken off their hats and coats and laid them on the front room sofa, Freddie led the group to the small dining room behind the front room. The table had already been laid and the caretaker's wife, presumably, bustled out of the kitchen with a large tureen of soup. Gam looked at it nervously.

"Just eat some bread, dear," Kathy told him quietly.

Learning new table manners had been difficult for the boy and eating soup without slurping was not a skill he'd mastered yet. Still, the boy took some soup, made a monumental effort and managed to avoid slurping expect once or twice.

As soon as Gam was done, Freddie nodded at Kathy, who insisted it was well past time Gam was in bed and pushed him upstairs to where a room had been prepared.

Freddie barely waited until Kathy had returned and seated herself before glaring at his mother.

"Miss Saint James," Gloria jumped in quickly. "How is it you are not working tonight?"

"Prohibition violation," Ivy said. "The theater is closed this week."

Freddie cleared his throat and glared again at his mother.

"I hardly know where to begin," he said. "What were you doing up here? And why is that police officer so sure your chauffeur is a felon?"

"I was trying to find out who might have killed your father," Gloria said. "I thought I could look around here and see if there was anything missing."

"Do you know what was in the safe?" Honoria asked quickly before Freddie could remonstrate.

"I didn't even know the safe was here," Gloria said. "Thank God for Mr. Van Schuyler. He found it for me."

Freddie's eyes narrowed. "If you didn't even know it was here, then how did it get opened, pray tell?"

Gloria winced and sighed. "It is the answer to your second question. Mr. Van Schuyler is a reformed felon. He has been on the straight and narrow since before he came to us, and before you ask, Briggeman is perfectly aware of his criminal past. He has made it his mission to help such unfortunate souls. We've had absolutely no problems with theft and our servants are uncommonly loyal. So, we've done rather well that way. In addition, Mr. Van Schuyler's felonious skills came in rather handy today. Not only was he able to open the safe, but he got us into the lodge, in the first place. It was locked up tighter than a drum. Which is probably the first thing we must investigate."

Freddie struggled not to gape. "Investigate? What?"

"The lodge was supposedly open," Gloria continued calmly. "Briggeman assured me it was this morning. I must ask the caretaker if he was the one who locked it. Or was it you, Freddie?"

"I never came up here," Freddie said.

"Well, somebody came up here and searched the place," Gloria said. "Some of your father's papers were disturbed."

"But who would search here?" Honoria asked. "There's not even a telephone, so Father couldn't have been doing business here."

"Except for the fact that your father was here a great deal." Gloria frowned. "I did not find any evidence that he'd brought any of his liaisons here, and there was absolutely nothing pertaining to business except his diary. I found it almost under the armoire in his bedroom. I hope to read it tonight and perhaps discover a clue."

"Mother," groaned Freddie. "You can't simply take off and start investigating."

"Whyever not?" Gloria said, unperturbed. "You aren't. I know you have a great many different things to work on now, but you aren't doing a thing about your own father's murder."

"She has a point, Freddie," Kathy said with a sigh. "We've done it before."

"Yes, but we didn't have an alternative then," Freddie said. "Besides, that last time, we all nearly got ourselves killed. Do you really want to risk that?"

"But we didn't die, Freddie," Honoria said.

Ivy cleared her throat. "And things might not have gotten as far out of hand as they did if we had been working together."

Kathy put her hand on Freddie's. "Perhaps, darling, getting this solved will be what you need to restore order to your life."

Freddie sank back into his chair in defeat. "I suppose so." He sat up straight, his mind suddenly buzzing with thoughts. "Very well, then. We'll need a plan. With all of us working, it will be too easy to duplicate our efforts, or worse, work at cross purposes. We also need to figure out what we know and what we do not know. Has anyone some paper and a pencil or two?"

Kathy, Honoria, and Ivy had small notepads and pencils in their purses and produced them. Then Gloria remembered that there should be a portfolio in her car and Van Schuyler was summoned from the kitchen to fetch it. As it turned out, there was not only the leather portfolio containing a writing tablet, there were several additional tablets and sufficient pencils and pens for everyone.

As Van Schuyler distributed the writing materials, Freddie watched him carefully.

"Is that everything?" Van Schuyler over-pronounced his "th" sounds, as he usually did when not alone with Gloria.

"Just a moment, Mr. Van Schuyler," Freddie said.

"Freddie," Gloria said in a warning voice.

"It's all right, Mrs. Little," Van Schuyler said, again lapsing into his native Bronx accent. "If you was my ma, I'd be worried, too." He turned to Freddie. "But I swear, Mr. Little, I am on the upright and true, and I take care of your ma as if she were my own. She's a great lady, your ma. I would cut off my right arm sooner dan do anyting to hurt her."

"I don't think we need to be quite that drastic," Freddie said, feeling reassured in spite of himself.

"Mr. Van Schuyler, why don't you join us?" Gloria asked. "I'd like to question him about the safe, anyway."

"Oh, dat," Van Schuyler sighed, but remained standing.

"Did you know it was here?" Gloria asked. "Perhaps you saw Mr. Little put something in it."

"As you know, he preferred to drive himself here," Van Schuyler said. "So, I did not have much occasion to notice his activities. I did not know dere was a safe here. I only surmised it."

"Then how did you know to look for it?" Gloria asked.

"Oh, dat was easy," Van Schuyler grinned. "In my former life, and I do mean my former life, Mr. Little, I learned dat when people want to hide tings, dey don't want to forget where dey hid dem. So dey make it easy to see. Dat squirrel over dere. All de other stuffed animals are big ones. Dat's de only small animal. And, if you'll forgive me for saying so, it's not done too well."

Gloria sighed. "It was my first attempt at taxidermy."

"See?" Van Schuyler puffed himself up. "And a sentimental choice at dat. So, I figure dere's gotta be someting behind it. And I took a look. Dere it was. And since I figured Mrs. Little would want to peruse de contents, I went ahead and got some practice opening it. Cracking safes is an art, you know, and a handy skill to have if you know someone who don't remember combinations so good."

"An excellent point," Lowell said, sighing as he shifted in his chair. "I shall have to have you come to my place and open mine."

"But there was nothing in it," Freddie said. "At least, that's what the police said."

"Not a ting, as I live and breathe," Van Schuyler said.

"Perhaps someone else opened and emptied it," Honoria said. "But who?"

"Someone who is a master of de art," Van Schuyler said. "Or who had de combination. Dat's a very strong safe you got dere."

Honoria frowned. "Could Uncle Stephen have gotten the combination? If he were behind this, it would be worth his while to be sure that there was no evidence here."

"Why did Father Little have a safe here, in the first place?" Kathy asked. "Isn't there one back at the mansion? Why would he need two?"

"I remember," Gloria sat up and gestured with her index finger. "It was several years ago. The lodge needed some repairs after that very bad winter we had. When was it..? Oh, never mind. In any case, Fred said that he was going to have it rebuilt so that we could live here full-time. A preposterous notion, of course, but that was what he eventually wanted to do. Then your grandfather retired and Fred took over the chairmanship of the company and even he agreed we couldn't live so far out here while he was chairman of the board."

Freddie saw Kathy sighing and stepped in. "That's all very well, Mother, but what does all this have to do with the safe?"

"It must have been installed when your father had the lodge rebuilt," Gloria said. "He would need one if he were living here full-time. And it would also explain why it was empty. He didn't need it just yet."

"Unless Uncle Stephen got the combination and emptied it," grumbled Honoria.

"What could possibly have been in it?" Gloria asked. "Some cash? All the family jewels are at home. And we've accounted for all the important papers, I believe."

"Not necessarily," said Freddie. "There could have been Father's last will. According to Mr. Carstairs, the only one we have is the one father made shortly after I was born."

"The one your grandfather insisted he make," said Gloria with a nod. She frowned. "He didn't update it?"

"Apparently he didn't see any reason to," Freddie said. "At least, that's what Mr. Carstairs thinks. The passage appointing Uncle Stephen my guardian was only relevant while I was in my minority."

"Was there a reading already?" Honoria asked.

"Uh, yes, this morning," Freddie said. "As you weren't even born at the time the will was made, Honoria, you were not mentioned."

"Oh."

"Why was I not notified?" Gloria asked.

Freddie sighed deeply. "You weren't mentioned, either, Mother. Just myself and Uncle Stephen, and the only reason he was mentioned was that I would need a guardian should Father die before I achieved my majority." He paused. "I'm apparently the sole heir."

"Oh," said Gloria softly. "Oh, dear."

"I'm sure it was just an oversight, Mrs. Little," Ivy said.

"It probably wasn't," Gloria said. "Fred's father insisted on the will because I had gotten nowhere insisting upon it, myself. That's just the sort of thing Fred would have done to spite me." She took a deep breath. "Nonetheless, I do find myself in a rather awkward position."

"No," said Freddie sharply. "Absolutely not. Mother, you need not worry. I will take care of you. In fact, I will do my best to see to it that your life does not change."

"Yes, of course, you will, darling." Gloria sighed and blinked. "It was just that I was hoping that... Oh, never mind."

"That, at last, you would have some autonomy," Honoria said. "The chance to order your affairs as you see fit. Is that right, Mother?"

"Yes," she said softly.

"Then we'll fix it so you can," said Freddie. "I don't know how yet. And it is entirely possible that Father left another will. We just haven't found it yet. But no matter what happens, I will do right by you, Mother. You will have autonomy and support and whatever you need. I insist."

Gloria smiled. "You are a good son. I suspect your father would be proud. I know your grandfather would be. In any case, this is not getting us any closer to our stated aim this evening, of sorting out what we need to know and who will find it out. Now, shall we start with who benefits the most from your father's death?"

"That would be Freddie, wouldn't it?" Lowell asked.

"I don't feel as though I'm benefitting," Freddie grumbled.

Ivy tapped her pencil on the table. "But it does make sense to consider it from the point of view of the police. Not that you did it, Freddie. However, we don't want to be blinded by our own prejudices."

"Indeed, not," said Freddie. "Still, I was in the ballroom the whole time. I was never alone for a minute."

"I suppose you could have paid somebody," Lowell said. "But why have your father shot at the party? The odds against catching him alone at just the right minute have to be phenomenal."

"That's what Detective Crowley said the next day," Kathy said. "That it was a crime of opportunity. Someone saw the chance to shoot and did. Which would negate Freddie paying someone to do it, as that would have been a planned murder."

"Why not Uncle Stephen?" Honoria said. "He might have thought that with Father out of the way and Freddie preoccupied with his publishing company, he could get more control of the business."

"But didn't he and Aunt Thelma stay at the party after Father Little was killed?" Kathy asked.

"He could have brazened it out," Honoria said. "And I didn't see him in the ballroom much that evening. Or Aunt Thelma, either."

"She was in the drawing room gossiping," Kathy said. "At least, that's where I found her before I went outside. And Mother Little was upstairs when it happened."

"Really?" Freddie asked. "What were you doing up there?"

Gloria blushed. "I was..." She paused as she noticed the suspicious looks around her. "Well, I'm not that young anymore and I had to... To..."

"You were using the necessary," Ivy said, smiling.

"Exactly," said Gloria. "I went upstairs to my room. It's simply more comfortable there."

"Did you see anyone on the terrace?" Kathy asked.

"No. I didn't see a thing. I didn't even think to look when I heard the shots." Gloria frowned. "I thought it was a car backfiring. After all, one doesn't expect to hear gunshots from one's own terrace."

Kathy squeezed her eyes shut for a moment. Freddie reached over and took her hand.

"It's all right," said Kathy. "I'm sorry. I didn't see

where the shots came from."

"Nobody expects you to, darling," Freddie said.

Kathy shuddered. "It's so frustrating! As bad as it was, the worst is that I didn't see enough to help us. I was simply so shocked. The only thought I had was to try and find the person on the terrace."

"So, we're back to where we started," said Freddie. "Trying to figure out who would benefit from Father's death. And there really aren't that many people who would."

"I would," said Gloria. "Or I could be considered to benefit, as I would have had a reasonable expectation of support."

"Don't be ridiculous, Mother," Freddie said, almost too quickly. "You wouldn't be up here looking for the killer if you had done it."

"What about any enemies?" Ivy asked. "He had to have had some."

"Aside from his sisters and their husbands, I can't think of any," Gloria said, then shook her head. "But Fred kept me so shut out of much of his life. He could have an army of people who hated him and I'd never have known."

"It is a place to look, though," said Freddie. "Why don't I question Uncle Stephen and Uncle Thomas? Maybe one of them will let something slip. I need to get on their good sides, anyway, assuming they are innocent. I'll play a couple rounds of golf with them, maybe stand them to a luncheon."

"As for enemies," Ivy said. "Perhaps that's where Lowell and I can be most useful. People would want to spare the family their feelings, but they're usually happy to gossip with a stranger."

"True," said Honoria. "And I can talk to Aunt Thelma and Aunt Miranda. They mostly seem to like me."

"I shall read Fred's diary and see if I can make anything of it," Gloria said.

"I suppose I can keep tabs on the police through

Uncle Dan," Kathy said.

"That's right. I'm having luncheon with him tomorrow," said Freddie. "Would you like to join us?"

Kathy smiled weakly. "I'll have to see."

"Somebody might want to talk to de Phoenicia police," Van Schuyler said. "Dey got to de lodge a lot quicker dan if someone out here had called dem. Dey'd have to go into town to do it, on account of dere's no phones here."

"I must speak to the caretaker, as well," said Gloria.

"But how did the caretaker and his wife get the message that we were all coming?" Kathy asked.

"Dey take a message at the general store in town and run it out here," Van Schuyler said.

"Then I should probably talk to the police officer in the morning," Kathy said. "It would be interesting to know how the police were summoned and why they thought Mother Little was kidnapped or breaking in."

Freddie finished furiously scribbling some notes then nodded. "Well, it would appear that we have our plan. Why don't we meet in a few days to see if anyone has found anything?"

He was answered by a loud snore. Lowell had fallen asleep in his chair.

"How grotesque," Gloria said. "Nonetheless, an excellent reminder that it is getting quite late and I, for one, would like to get some sleep. Shall we?"

It was agreed, Lowell was awakened, and the group went on to their assigned rooms and beds. Kathy did take time to check on Gam.

He was in bed, snoring loudly. Kathy chuckled.

"You're not asleep," she said, coming into the room.

"I'm asleep," Gam said from the bed, where he was lying on his side facing away from his sister.

Kathy went over and pushed him onto his back. "So I see. You were spying on us, weren't you?"

"I don't see why I can't help," Gam grumbled. "No one pays any attention to me and I hear things, you know?”

“Oh?”

“Like I heard that Mr. Taylor? Mr. Little’s valet that won’t leave?”

“What’s he still doing at the apartment?”

Gam shrugged. “Well, he says that Mrs. Little suggested he stay there to help Freddie, I guess. After all, there isn’t anyone for him to work for at Mrs. Little’s mansion.”

Kathy pondered this. “I wonder why Roberts didn’t say anything to me about it.”

“I guess ‘cuz of Mr. Little dying,” Gam said. “I heard Roberts tell Mr. Taylor that he was going to talk to you and Honoria after the funeral about him staying. But I heard something else. Mr. Taylor was telling Roberts how mean Mr. Little was.”

“It seems you’ve been doing quite a bit of sneaking around.” Kathy ruffled Gam’s hair. “I don’t doubt you know how to find things out, young man, but I’d rather you stayed out of this. There’s murder involved and if someone is desperate enough to kill once, he can do it again. Do you think I want to face Pa if I let anything happen to you?”

“I won’t let anything happen to me, Kathy.”

“You may not have that choice,” Kathy said. “Listen, Freddie’s got enough to worry about. It will only make him worry more if he finds out you’re sticking your nose into this. Can you please behave for his sake?”

Gam grimaced. “I’ll do my best.”

“That’s my boy,” Kathy said, smiling. She hugged her little brother. “I know it’s not any fun being left out. I’ll try and keep you up to date on what’s going on, okay?”

“Sure, Kathy.”

“All right. Good night, Gammers.”

“Good night, Kathy.”

Kathy left the room, a huge yawn almost breaking her jaw.

The next morning, she awoke feeling better than she had in days.

"Wow," she said, softly.

Freddie stirred and rolled over next to her. "Is everything all right? Another nightmare?"

"No, Freddie," Kathy said, sitting up with a smile. "It's morning. I didn't have one."

Freddie yawned, then sat up as well, blinking. "You're right. Could it be we're past it?"

"I don't see why not," Kathy said. She swung her legs off the bed and got up. "And I smell bacon cooking. Looks like we're going to have a busy day. Best get up and at 'em."

Freddie grumbled. As pleased as he was that Kathy was feeling better, he really didn't care for mornings. Worse yet, the early part of the day was when Kathy was most cheerful. At least, he had finally convinced her that she didn't have to be up before the first light of dawn.

Honoria, Ivy, and Lowell were still asleep when Freddie came downstairs to breakfast. Kathy had already served herself and was reading a newspaper as she ate. Gloria and Gam were just returning from an early nature walk.

"Freddie, your ma knows all sorts of swell stuff about nature," Gam announced running up. "And I caught a frog! We're gonna dissect it later and look at its innards. Won't that be corking!"

He held up a large mason jar bearing the amphibian. The lid had been pierced multiple times and there was a small pool of water and some greenery in the bottom.

"Watch the slang, young Master Briscow," Gloria said sternly, then looked up at Freddie and smiled happily. "He has the most inquisitive mind."

"Yes," said Freddie, smiling at Gam, who was admiring his frog and eating a huge pile of scrambled eggs. "We know."

Kathy looked up from her newspaper. "We have

to talk to the Phoenicia police today, Freddie, and you need to be back in New York well before one to meet Uncle Dan. Mother Little, did you get a chance to speak to... What's the caretaker's name?"

"Williams," said Gloria, helping herself to eggs and bacon. "And, yes, I did. He saw Uncle Stephen up here on Saturday and assumed he was here on our behalf. So, when Uncle Stephen had him lock the place up, he didn't think anything of it. Stephen also told Williams to ask the police to keep an eye on the place in case some of our more rapacious relatives tried to remove property they weren't entitled to."

"Well, that would explain why they got here so fast," Kathy said. "They were already watching."

"And it makes sense that the most rapacious of all the relatives would be the one to worry the most about someone getting something to which they weren't entitled," said Freddie.

"At least, we no longer need to question the police," Kathy said. "That will save a stop this morning." She checked her watch and got up. "Good lord, it's almost eight. I'd better get our things packed so that we can be on the road right away."

Kathy hurried out and upstairs.

"But, dear Kathy, Mrs. Williams will see to it," Gloria called after her.

"Let her go, Mother," Freddie said, setting his own breakfast plate on the table. "Keeping her occupied will give me a chance to eat."

"Gamaliel!" Kathy called from upstairs. "Come get your things!"

"Coming!" Gam swallowed the last of his eggs. "Freddie, will you watch my frog, please? Make sure nobody lets him go?"

"I will."

Gam ran off.

Gloria looked at Freddie. "They do quite a bit of shouting, don't they?"

"I suppose." Freddie shrugged as he ate. "I think

I'm getting used to it. And I have to admit, while it is occasionally unpleasant, it does seem to work better than enforced silence. I seldom have to wonder what Kathy is thinking about me."

"There is that." Gloria grew pensive. "And yet, it always seemed as though it was when I spoke up that your father was most difficult. When I was quiet, he seemed quite content to let me pursue my own interests while he pursued his." She sighed. "It wasn't a bad way to live."

"I'm sure it wasn't, Mother." Freddie smiled at her. "I've merely found a different way and it seems to suit me. That's all."

There was the rumbling sound of Gam pounding down the stairs.

"Where's my frog?" he asked as he careened into the dining room.

"Deportment, young Master Briscow," Gloria said with a smile. "And your frog is right here where you left it."

"Sw-" Gam stopped and held himself up straight. "Thank you, ma'am."

"Freddie, are you finished with your breakfast?" Kathy asked as she came into the room, her coat, hat and gloves in hand.

"Just a moment more," Freddie said.

CHAPTER SEVEN

Freddie ended up going to the luncheon with Uncle Dan by himself. Upon arriving at their apartment in New York, Kathy found that the printer needed her attention, and the owner of the bindery did as well, besides which two of their authors had burning questions that needed resolving, another needed soothing, and the typist that they had hired, Elsie Quinn, was waiting at the apartment with twelve letters for Kathy to sign and a question about a manuscript that she was typing.

Freddie quickly excused himself and found a taxi waiting for him on the street. Uncle Dan was waiting outside the restaurant when the taxi pulled up.

"I apologize for my tardiness, Uncle Dan," Freddie said as the two shook hands.

"I wouldn't worry about it," said the older man. His black hair was flecked with gray, and there were a couple of veins beginning to show on his nose. He was of medium build with a small paunch that his brown wool suit failed to hide.

The two men got themselves settled, their hats on the post next to their table, and quickly ordered. The waiter looked at Freddie, clearly not wanting to ask if the man he was with was a cop, and if the man was a cop, was he one of those who frowned on the usual tendency to flout Prohibition?

"Is there a problem?" Uncle Dan asked.

"I don't know," Freddie asked. "How do you feel about Italian red wine?"

"It goes very well with lunch," Dan replied.

Freddie nodded at the waiter. "My usual tea, then." He leaned over to Dan once the waiter had left.

"I'm not sure where the restaurant's owner finds the grapes, but he does make a very nice wine. I've heard it's still legal to make some for yourself."

"That, and the churches need it, you know," Dan said. "For communion."

The two continued to chitchat until the waiter had brought their lunches and a teapot filled with red wine, which they poured into teacups.

"Well, now that we're settled," Uncle Dan said, digging into his pasta and red sauce. "I'm guessing you want me to tell you what's going on with your father's case."

"That would be helpful since I understand that Detective Crowley seems to find me interesting as a suspect," Freddie said, cutting up a veal cutlet.

Dan shrugged. "He does seem to think you have the most motive but can't find any way to pin it on you. You're lucky you were in the ballroom the whole time. They were able to get some boot prints off the terrace, not as that's a help. A couple reporters got up there the next morning, so it's as likely as not that the boot prints are theirs. At least, we know he was probably shot from the terrace."

"How do you know?" Freddie asked.

"The path of the bullets into the body," Uncle Dan said and paused. "It's not the most pleasant topic for over lunch, though I don't mind. For my sins, this job has toughened me to it."

"Say on," Freddie found himself growing more curious than disgusted.

"Well, if he'd been shot straight on from the conservatory, perhaps, the bullets would have hit him in the chest and lodged near his back. But when the autopsy was done, one bullet went through his heart, then into his liver and guts. And the other landed next to it. If it's any comfort, he was probably dead before he hit the ground."

"So, he was shot from above." Freddie frowned. "Then it's likely that Kathy saw the man who shot him?"

"It's possible," Uncle Dan said with a shrug. He chewed thoughtfully. "We'd still like to find out who your father was talking to when he left the conservatory. Just to be thorough, you know. Several folks were in there at one point or another. We even found some evidence of a couple different trysts, you might say."

Freddie rolled his eyes. "That always seems to happen. I have no idea why the conservatory is so popular that way."

"In any case, Crowley is looking at a young man whose brother was killed in your father's factory. Ronald O'Hare. He's been active with some Socialists here on the Lower East Side. O'Hare and another fellow, Edgar Watson, were questioned then let go by one of the harness bulls near your family's place about half an hour after the shooting. We haven't found them yet, but we will. We just have to hope we find a gun on them."

"What good will that do?"

Dan's eyes sparkled with lust. "There's a new twin microscope that can compare two bullets and prove that they were shot from the same gun."

"How does it do that?" Freddie asked.

"Well, a pistol or a rifle has that rifling in the barrel to keep the bullet going straight, right?"

"Yes."

Dan swallowed a bite, then smiled. "Well, as the bullet goes through the barrel, the rifling marks the bullet, and each gun marks the bullet in its own unique way. No two guns will mark a bullet the same. You can tell by looking at it through a microscope. And now there's one that lets you look at two bullets side by side. If we find that O'Hare or Wilson have a gun or two, assuming we can use the microscope, all we have to do is shoot a bullet from whatever gun they have, then see if it matches the bullets from your father's body, and if they match, we'll know O'Hare and Wilson did it. They're using the microscope for the Sacco and

Vanzetti shooting. The only problem they're having is getting the results admitted as evidence. Of course, I'd have to convince the Captain that your father's case warrants getting the inventor to let us use his device."

"Your department doesn't own one?" Freddie asked.

"Not yet," Dan sighed. "It is amazing the wonderful things that scientists are coming up with these days. It won't be long before a crook won't be able to get away with anything. But for now, those microscopes are damned expensive and the lawyers don't always trust the results. Even if it didn't help the court case, it would be wonderful to have a place to look."

"For Heaven's sake, why didn't you just ask me?" Freddie said with a smile.

Dan almost looked affronted. "What do you mean? I'm not going to be coming to you and beg every time I want something. I have my pride, you know. And we'll have one soon enough. It's just a matter of time."

"Well, let me help in this case," Freddie said calmly.

"You'd really buy us a microscope?" Dan looked puzzled. "Why? Most of you swells complain pretty loudly when they get asked for something. The captain has tried a couple times, you know."

"I'd like to think I'm not like most swells," Freddie said. "But, after all, it was my father who was murdered. And to prevent your captain from thinking he can simply push you into hitting me up every time he wants something, I'll make the donation anonymously. Would that work?"

Uncle Dan laughed greedily. "That would be a grand thing. Might even make old Michael jealous enough to cough up a bit more often."

"Truth be told, Uncle Dan, I don't really mind buying things for people," Freddie said. "It's when they start taking advantage and become demanding and angry that I start balking. Not everyone has their pride, you know."

"I'll do well to remember that." Dan looked him over carefully. "That's a very kind thing you're doing for us."

"As I said, it is my father's murder," Freddie said, shifting uncomfortably. "I'm hoping that the sooner we get the killer found, the sooner Kathy will get over her nightmares."

"She's been having them, has she?" Dan shook his head. "It happens that way, sometimes. It's kind of like the boys who were shell-shocked in the war. It does fade with time. And keeping her occupied, you know."

"I've heard in Britain, they're doing some interesting work helping the lads there," Freddie mused. "But it all sounds very drastic. Kathy isn't nearly that badly off."

"She'll get over it," Dan said.

"And she didn't have one last night and last night was the first time we really talked about who might be the killer,"

Dan glared at him. "You're not going to try to find him yourselves, are you?"

"My mother is already on the hunt," Freddie sighed. "I'll have to look into what I can if only to stay one step ahead of her and, hopefully, keep her out of trouble. The Phoenicia police caught her yesterday breaking into my father's hunting lodge. They weren't quite convinced that she was there innocently." Freddie shuddered.

"Was she?"

"Of course, she was," Freddie said. "She may even have found a clue, my father's diary."

"Did she see anything on the terrace, perchance?"

"I'm afraid she didn't see anything. In fact, she thought the shots were a car backfiring."

"What was she doing up there, in the first place?"

"Eh, answering nature's call," Freddie said, flushing a little. "Her own bathroom was more comfortable."

"Oh, right." Dan smiled and shook his head. "I told

Crowley there was a logical reason for her to be there. He's a good man, but a bit earnest. Wants to make captain before he's thirty."

Freddie chewed thoughtfully, then swallowed. "I can't entirely blame Detective Crowley for wondering about Mother. Not that I would say so to him but were one to make certain reasonable assumptions about her and her expectations, she would have had more than one motive to kill Father."

"You mean besides-" Dan suddenly coughed.

"My father's infidelities?"

"You knew about that?"

Freddie nodded and shrugged. "It is rather expected among my set, I'm afraid, especially among the men. I have no idea how the women deal with it, generally, but certainly my mother knew about it. However, what could she have done about it? Her social status and support were entirely dependent on my father. And now she is entirely dependent on me."

"What do you mean?"

Freddie frowned as he lit a cigarette. "The main reason I asked you to lunch. I wanted to tell you that my father left everything to me. He didn't provide for my mother. She wasn't even mentioned. Nor was my sister. Fortunately, Honoria has her own support."

Dan shook his head. "It's a good thing you came to me with that bit of news. It gives you a motive."

"Superficially, yes." Freddie gazed at the last of his cutlet. "But that's assuming my father's wealth means anything to me. Or control of the family business, which I have or will have, once Grandfather's estate gets out of probate. My father's estate only means more work for me."

"Surely some extra money would help with your publishing company."

Freddie shrugged. "It won't hurt, but that's assuming there is extra money. Sadly, my father did not leave his affairs in good order. And I have..." He sighed and flushed. "Uncle Dan, most of my wealth is actually my own. Over the years, I've gotten any number of bequests, a small portion of shares of the family business, and I've done a fair amount of investing. Some with my grandfather's help. Some on my own. I may have started with a great deal, but instead of spending it willy-nilly, like some of my peers, I have been making my money work for me. So, my father's wealth may add to my own, but it would hardly make much of a difference in how I live or what I do, even with the publishing company. Believe me, I would not be funding that venture if I did not believe I could make a significant profit from it. Fortunately, I do not have to execute my father's will, but apart from the grief of losing my father, his death couldn't have happened at a worse time. My mother would have had a better motive, especially if you assume she could have expected to have been well-provided for, in spite of the loss of her social status."

"You're right. That does give her a motive." Dan picked up his teacup and held it in both his hands as he thought.

Freddie took a sip from his cup, as well. "Even so, it isn't all that much of one. She pretty much runs her life as she pleases and as a widow, her social status would diminish considerably. The problem is, we can't think of any enemies Father had."

"We've found a few. That O'Hare fellow, for starters. A couple of your father's friends."

"May I ask who?"

"No." Dan chuckled sadly. "I hate to say this, but if I had friends like your father's, I'd be watching my back a whole lot more closely."

"I'm not surprised," said Freddie. He winced. "Real friendship among our set is the exception rather than the rule. I don't know why that is. You would think that people with social status would have the least to prove. And yet, everyone is completely conscious of who has what and how much more or little one has than someone else. Nor are they very introspective. A few are, but not many."

"Well, Freddie, it isn't much different among the hoi polloi. Everyone is struggling to get ahead and God forbid you get in anyone else's way."

"I dare say it's human nature," said Freddie.

"It is and it keeps me employed." Dan grinned then finished off his wine.

Honoria got home a little after one o'clock to find Roberts, Freddie's valet, waiting for her, alongside her secretary, Mrs. Grant, a large woman of nervous mien. Mrs. Grant had a long list of calls for Honoria to return, five letters that needed signing, plus a stack of letters that needed answering. Roberts had only one problem, but it was significant.

"I'm sorry, Mrs. Grant," Honoria told her secretary. "That business will have to wait. I'll be along shortly."

She then turned to Roberts and had him follow her downstairs to Freddie and Kathy's apartment.

Kathy was in the study, talking on the phone and signing letters.

"I understand, Mr. Woodson." Kathy looked up at Honoria with a panicked frown. "But we ordered the mahogany leather bindings for a reason. If there was going to be a problem, you should have told us weeks ago... No, I don't care to pay any more for them because I have a signed contract that says mahogany leather and that is what I expect to see on those books at the rate we agreed to last January. Now, will I have to contact our lawyer about this matter..? Very good... Good-bye."

Kathy hung up the phone with a disgusted sigh, then looked up again at Honoria.

"Please tell me I haven't forgotten some crucial party or something," Kathy said.

"No, nothing like that," Honoria said with an off smile. "But we do have a slight problem vis a vis the domestic staff that we should be able to clear up quickly."

Honoria saw the pained look on Kathy's face and debated settling the issue, herself. She had been overseeing the servants by herself ever since she and Freddie had moved into the building shortly after the War. It had been an ideal situation. Honoria and Freddie each had their own apartment, with Honoria's on the floor above Freddie's. Because Freddie managed her money, Honoria managed his calendar and the servants for the two apartments.

Or she had until a few weeks before when the cook had taken ill and been forced to quit. Because Honoria was frequently elsewhere at mealtimes, Kathy had had the most contact with the cook, so she had tried to hire the new one. But it had not gone well because Kathy had no idea how to handle servants. Worse yet, both she and Honoria were getting so busy with their respective businesses that neither really had the time. So, the two had agreed to work together in regards to the domestic staff, which they mostly shared, anyway.

Kathy got up from her desk and followed Honoria into the foyer, where Roberts waited.

"Okay. Who has quit now?" Kathy asked.

Roberts looked over at Honoria, who chuckled.

"Nobody, darling," Honoria told Kathy. "Actually, we have one more servant than we need."

"It's Mr. Taylor, Ma'am," Roberts said. "The senior Mr. Little's valet"

"Oh, right," Kathy groaned. "Gam told me last night you were going to talk to me about it soon."

"Yes," said Roberts. "He's been here since Mr. Little passed away."

"Here?" Honoria asked. "Why didn't he go back to the mansion?"

"He said that Mrs. Little suggested he remain since there was no one at the mansion with need of a valet."

"But doesn't he work for Mrs. Little now?" Kathy asked, with that frantic look she got on her face every time she was confronted with what she called living like a rich person.

"He wishes to transfer his employment to our household," Roberts said. His face was bland, but Honoria caught the implied plea. Roberts clearly did not want to hire Mr. Taylor.

Kathy thought. "If we promote you, Roberts, to butler, then can't Taylor work as valet? You've been doing both for so long, I imagine it would be a relief not to have to do so much."

Roberts hesitated.

"That's the problem, Kathy," Honoria said. "Freddie is not going to want to change his valet."

"Oh, that's right," Kathy said. "He doesn't need that right now. Does this mean we tell Taylor to hit the bricks? Or do we have to find him another job?"

Roberts coughed slightly. "The problem, Ma'am, is that I do not feel that I could provide a good recommendation for Mr. Taylor."

That surprised Honoria. "Whyever not, Roberts?"

Roberts kept his face bland, but Honoria could tell it was a bit of a struggle.

"Nothing I can prove, Mrs. Wentworth," Roberts said, finally. "He has a reputation as less than discreet to the point of discussing the senior Mr. Little's affairs. In addition, since he has been here, a few small items have disappeared. A few pieces of silverware are all, and as I said, I have no proof. However, the timing is suspicious, especially since the disappearances stopped as soon as I questioned Taylor about them. Oh, and the pieces have mysteriously reappeared elsewhere in the apartment. I guess that we are to believe that the silverware was misplaced."

"That does sound pretty suspicious," Kathy said. "So, I guess he doesn't get the job." She looked at Honoria. "But we can't fire your mother's servant, can we?"

"Mr. Briggeman will see to that," Roberts said, then paused. "I have been made aware that you now know about his crusade to help the less fortunate.”

“Yes,” said Honoria. “What a wonderful thing to do. Oh, wait. Taylor wasn’t...”

“No, Mrs. Wentworth. Taylor is not among those Mr. Briggeman has helped to gainful employment.” Roberts sighed again. “He would have been more trustworthy if he had been, I’m sure. No. You may not be aware of this, but the senior Mr. Little had great difficulty keeping a valet. I do not know the particulars. However, he managed to keep Taylor in his employ longer than almost anybody that I know of, which was odd when you consider how little regard Taylor had for Mr. Little.” He sighed again. “I would not disparage your father, Mrs. Wentworth, but I gravely fear that your father had secured Taylor’s ongoing employment by less than honorable means.”

Kathy gasped. “Roberts, could Tayler have killed Mr. Little?”

Honoria gasped also, then realized Kathy had a point.

Roberts’ shoulders lifted in the barest hint of a shrug. “I cannot say, Ma’am. I have no proof, nor any real reason to believe so other than that Taylor has been quite open about disparaging Mr. Little.”

“That would make him less likely to have done it,” Honoria said. “After all, if he had, wouldn’t he be more likely to hide his dislike?”

“You would think so,” said Kathy. “However, based on some of Uncle Dan’s stories, most criminals aren’t that smart.”

“Hm.” Honoria checked her wristwatch. “I should probably talk to Mr. Taylor. Maybe if we let him think we might want to take him on...”

“But would he talk frankly to you about your father?” Kathy asked. “Even if he thinks he might get a job out of it?”

“There is that problem.” Honoria smiled. “But it’s no secret that my father and I did not get along. I could use that, and the fact that I’m not even mentioned in his will."

"That could work," said Kathy.

Honoria checked her wristwatch again. "Very well. Roberts, is Mr. Taylor staying here for the time being?"

"Yes. He's in the servants quarters down here even now."

Honoria nodded. "Then go ahead and send Mr. Taylor to me in about two hours. That will give me some time to catch up on my work first. Oh, and, Roberts, please do not say that we are thinking about taking him on, but if Taylor happens to think so, don't correct him."

A corner of Roberts' mouth just barely twitched up. "Very good, Mrs. Wentworth."

Honoria waited while Kathy scurried back to the study then went upstairs to her own where Mrs. Grant awaited her. Honoria found that two more calls had come in, so Honoria decided to take care of the letters first, found mistakes in two of the letters and had to ask Mrs. Grant to re-type them. Looking at the letters that needed answering, Honoria wondered if it would be worth it to learn how to type. She'd seen Kathy dash off letters when the matter was too urgent to wait for her typist to come to get them, type them, then bring them back. Instead, Honoria sorted the letters that Mrs. Grant could answer for her and those that she'd have to dictate. However imprecise Mrs. Grant's typing was (and it wasn't all that bad), she was a whiz at stenography, which was why Honoria had hired her.

Honoria turned to the calls, returned the few that really needed returning, dictated the letters that needed answering, and by that time Roberts arrived at the study door with Taylor in tow. Honoria dismissed Mrs. Grant and Roberts, shuffled some papers on her desk, then looked at Taylor.

His sour face was looking almost cheerful, his dark hair was slicked back and the smell of his pomade almost made Honoria sneeze. It also reminded her of her father's smell.

"Well, Taylor, I understand from Roberts that you'd like to come work in this household," Honoria began slowly.

"Or the one downstairs, Ma'am," Taylor said, his voice rich with a British accent. "I dare say Mr. Freddie could use an extra valet."

Honoria worked hard at smiling. Freddie barely used Roberts' services as it was. If Taylor had been staying at the apartment since the murder, then he should have known that.

"But why stay here?" Honoria asked. "I would imagine that a British valet of your experience would have no trouble getting taken on somewhere else."

"Yes, Ma'am, but I have developed an affection for your family."

It was the opening Honoria needed and she took it.

"I can't imagine why," she said. "My father was extremely unpleasant. If I were you, I couldn't get away fast enough."

Taylor winced. "He was difficult, to be sure."

"He was dreadfully unkind to me," Honoria said.

"That he was, Ma'am. He could be quite cruel to me, as well."

"How so?"

Taylor glanced behind him. "I shouldn't like to be indiscreet."

"Oh, please. I don't mind." Honoria let out a nice, flirty giggle. "I'd love to know what skullduggery my poor old father was up to. Might help me in the fight over his will."

"Fight, Ma'am?" Taylor suddenly seemed even more interested in Honoria.

"You know Father didn't even mention me or Mother?"

"No, Ma'am, I did not."

"Well, Mother and I are going to contest the will. Mother has to do something for her support, you understand. If Father was cruel to you, it will help." Honoria wasn't at all sure it would make a difference if she had been inclined to contest the will. But if Taylor thought so, that was all that mattered.

"Well, he was mostly prone to making unreasonable demands and then bellowing at me when I couldn't meet them. For example, the night before he passed, he had lost his diary and screamed at me for some time, as if it were my fault that he had lost it."

"Oh, dear. That's terrible. But why would you stay on if he was that way? As I understand it, most of his valets left."

Taylor sighed and again glanced behind him. "You must understand, Ma'am, that I was completely blameless. However, he threatened to tell his colleagues that I had taken liberties with Mrs. Little, your mother. I most certainly had not. I would never do such a thing. However, in my profession, one's reputation is one's calling card, so to speak. It would have ruined me."

"Oh, no! But I'm sure somebody would have believed you."

"I did not feel I could take that chance."

"I understand. I wouldn't want to, either." Honoria thought for a moment. "And, yet, you say you have developed an affection for our family."

"Yes, Ma'am. Mr. Litttle, your brother, has been most kind to me," Taylor said.

"Really?" Honoria tried not to purse her lips. "That's odd. I wasn't aware that my brother even knew you were here."

"I've been helping him dress every morning."

"Every morning?" Honoria asked, wondering why Taylor was telling such a flimsy lie, especially when it was well known among the limited staff that the reason Roberts had so little to do was that Freddie dressed himself and always had.

"Except for this morning when he was out," Taylor said. "He has been most complimentary about my service."

"Well, that is very interesting," Honoria said. "What does Mrs. Kathy think about it?"

"She has expressed her confidence in me."

"That's odd." Honoria glared at him and folded her arms. "When we were discussing your remaining here earlier, she seemed perfectly happy letting you go. In fact, she was rather worried about some silver that turned up missing."

Taylor's face soured even more than usual. "I had nothing to do with that, Ma'am. It would appear that the silverware in question had merely been misplaced and it was not by me. I never touched it."

"I also know that you have not been helping my brother dress. He dresses himself. Not to mention that he has, and always has had, complete confidence in Roberts and I can't imagine him wanting to change valets at such a tumultuous time in our lives." Honoria stood up behind her desk. "That's what bothers me, Taylor. I don't doubt my father was very unkind to you and screamed at you. But you're not being honest, either. I'm afraid I'm going to have to send you back to my mother's home to be dealt with there."

"I wouldn't do that, Ma'am," Taylor said. "I have learned things about this family and I've seen things. I can keep secrets. That is what a good valet does. But if I am to be impugned in this manner, I could arrange for a great deal of harm to come to his family."

"Are you threatening me, Taylor?" Honoria glared at him.

The man shifted. "Not as such. But given that my honesty has been challenged, I must find a way to defend myself."

"That's all very well and good. Just remember that I do not respond well to threats. And if any harm comes to any member of this household, I will consider whether you might be personally responsible." She pushed a button on her desk and Roberts appeared a moment later. "Roberts, would you see to helping Mr. Taylor gather his things and sending him off to my mother's, please?"

Taylor appeared to have spotted the tiny hint of

glee in Roberts' eyes but could not say anything. As the two left the study, Honoria released her breath, then pulled her diary from her desk drawer and made several notes.

At the Little mansion, Gloria was feeling quite nonplussed. Having arrived home and taken a soothing bath, she had gone to her second-floor study to look over the mail with a perfectly lovely glass of Bordeaux and some very nice pate. It would have been a most soothing snack were it not for Briggeman's report.

"Burglars broke in? Here?" Gloria asked, the mail abandoned.

"Yes, ma'am. Last night. According to what Dimbly overheard, they were looking for a ruby," Briggeman said.

"A ruby? I don't have any ruby jewelry. Oh, wait. I do have that ruby parure, but that's quite a few rubies, not one. And I haven't worn it in ages."

"I believe it may have been the one Mrs. Kathy was wearing for the presentation party."

"Oh. Yes. That would make sense. Why would they look for it here?"

"Dimbly didn't say. He only heard the one remark before attempting to apprehend the two burglars. They, sadly, escaped."

Gloria frowned. "Did they get anything else?"

"No. We are quite fortunate that Dimbly was so alert."

"Indeed. See to it that he receives a nice bonus, please."

"Thank you, Ma'am." Briggeman withdrew.

Gloria stared at the small pile of letters. Most of them were condolences and she was getting quite tired of thanking people for their kind concern in her hour of grief. She appreciated the kindness but suspected most of it was as rote as the thank you notes she returned.

But someone had broken into the mansion looking for a ruby. A single ruby rather than the parure, which really wasn't nearly so spectacular as the necklace Kathy had been wearing. The necklace Gloria should have been wearing if only Fred hadn't tried to sell it all those years ago. Her father-in-law had been furious when he found out and Fred had blamed Gloria that he had.

Gloria shut her eyes and sighed. It was all over and done with and had been for many years. Kathy certainly deserved her chance to wear the gem and Gloria did not want to begrudge her the opportunity.

Gloria sighed and pulled out her husband's diary. She had tried reading it the night before but had not been able to make much of the cramped writing. Her eyes were not what they used to be. Sighing, she fished around her desk and pulled out the eyeglasses few knew she had. It was, perhaps, silly to be so vain. She could and often did carry a lorgnette for the opera. The eyeglasses were absolutely necessary if she wished to read. But then, she didn't particularly like letting people know that she read as much as she did.

The glasses helped, but only so much. Fred had written in an odd form of shorthand, randomly dropping vowels and sometimes whole words. Even once she deciphered the writing, the diary did not reveal much. It was mostly made up of notes about appointments and other things to do. Fred, sadly, had not been prone to introspection or observation.

One of Fred's notes suddenly made Gloria sit up. Almost two weeks before Fred's death, he had noted that he needed to fire "Wtsn" as an example to the rest of the company. She found her current diary on her desk but then realized she'd just changed over to a new one, having filled the other up. She'd given up on buying dated diaries years before. Her thoughts seldom ran to just the one page provided by the dated ones.

She took the one remaining bite of the pate, then a good solid drink of the Bordeaux, and then rifled through her desk, hoping that the older diary hadn't been moved to the carriage house yet, where all her other diaries and correspondence were currently waiting for spring cleaning. Fortunately, she hadn't moved the older diary to the shelf by the time of the presentation party, and she found it at the back of the desk drawer.

It didn't take long to find the pages closest to the date of Fred's note. Her diary only noted that Fred had seemed to be in an unusually ill temper at dinner the night of February 17. Gloria re-checked Fred's diary. His note was made on the page for the 15th of February, but that didn't mean that he'd necessarily made the note on that day. His ill-temper implied that he must have done the firing earlier in the day on the 17th. Gloria frowned. There must have been an unpleasant scene at the factory. Otherwise, she could not imagine that Fred would have cared that much about firing somebody.

She took off her glasses and thought for a moment. She wasn't sure she wanted to speak with Detective Crowley, not when the man seemed far too interested in arresting either her or Freddie. But then she smiled. She hadn't met Kathy's relatives when her parents and family had visited over Christmas, but Gloria knew who all of Kathy's aunts and uncles were, even the one married to the Jew. Gloria sighed as she looked over her library. Perhaps it was time to start thinking more democratically. In any case, it was time to make use of her new connections.

Briggeman saw to calling Sergeant Callaghan, who showed up quite promptly. Gloria met him in the drawing room and invited him to sit down.

He sat on the silk-upholstered sofa rather gingerly, fidgeting with the bowler hat that he had kept in his hands rather than let Briggeman take it. His suit was of a lesser quality of brown wool, but still kept neat and pressed. Gloria thought she saw hints of Kathy's face in the man, especially around his blue eyes, even though Kathy's eyes were brown. Both his and Kathy's eyes were alert and it would be hard to slip something past either one of them.

"It's a pleasure to meet you at long last, Sergeant Callaghan," Gloria said from her own favorite chair by the fireplace. A small fire burned quietly, although it was almost warm enough to do without.

"Likewise, Ma'am," the sergeant said. "Your man said you had something for me?"

"Indeed." Gloria handed him Fred's diary. "This is my late husband's diary. I have marked the page with the relevant entry. It's a note reminding himself to fire a Watson somebody. At least, I believe that's the name. My husband used a rather peculiar form of shorthand. The note implies that the intent was to make an example of the man."

"Watson, you say." Callaghan's eyebrows lifted. "An Edgar Watson was questioned outside your home the night of the…"

"The murder, Sergeant." Gloria sighed. "I am quite hardened to it. But thank you for trying to spare my feelings."

Callaghan chuckled. "You've got the moxie, Ma'am. I can see why you and our Katie-girl get on." He opened the diary and held it out so that he could see it. "You know, I think you're right. We'll have to call the factory to confirm that he did fire the man. But that's rather interesting. There's also a Ronald O'Hare whose brother was killed at the factory."

Gloria thought, then shook her head. "The name means nothing to me. I'm afraid, Sergeant, that my late husband was rather determined to shield me from his affairs. Perhaps you have done better with some of his friends and associates?"

Callaghan sighed. "No. They're not talking to the likes of Crowley or me. Complaining that we haven't brought the killer in already, yes. But give us an idea of who he might be? No, can't be bothered." He stopped suddenly. "I beg your pardon, Ma'am."

"Actually, Sergeant, no apology needed. In fact, I should probably apologize to you. My son told me not too long ago that he'd had no idea how narrow-minded he'd been as a young man until he formed his friendship with Mr. Winters. I didn't quite understand what he meant, but I think I do now." Gloria frowned. "I understand Detective Crowley suspects me, as well."

Callaghan nodded. "He does have reason."

"Of course, he does, never mind that my expectations did not fulfill themselves. It would have been perfectly reasonable for me to have believed that my husband had seen to my support. And that I was quite fed up with dealing with him. I won't say that Fred couldn't be difficult. He was, quite often. But he mostly left me to my own devices and I was content." Gloria suddenly found herself blinking back tears. "I'm actually rather surprised at how much I miss him."

Callaghan quickly pulled a handkerchief from his breast pocket. "It's clean, Ma'am."

"Thank you, I have mine." Gloria blinked and pulled hers from her pocket. "I apologize for that unseemly display."

"You're newly bereaved, Ma'am. I'd be more worried about you if you weren't upset about it."

Gloria sniffed and quickly wiped her eyes. "That's very kind of you, Sergeant. Well, you have the diary. If you would be so kind as to return it to me when you're finished with it, I would appreciate it."

"Sure and I will." Callaghan got up. "Thank you for calling us."

"And thank you for coming so quickly."

"Well, I just had luncheon with your son. He cleared up your motives, you know. He's a fine gentleman, he is."

Gloria beamed. "Isn't he? It doesn't do to say so, but I'm very proud of him. Have you read his book?"

"I've been working my way through it." Callaghan smiled. "But, for my sins, I've got plenty to keep me busy today, so if there's nothing else, I'll take my leave."

"Please do. And please feel free to call on me and let me know what's happening with the case."

Callaghan's eyes narrowed. Gloria swallowed.

"I do have an interest in seeing that my husband's killer is brought to justice."

"As long as you're not the one trying to do it. Or your son and my niece. We are perfectly capable of finding the killer ourselves."

"Naturally, Sergeant. And if we happen to find information you can use, you will be the first person we call."

Callaghan broke into a grin. "You do that. Good day, Ma'am."

As soon as the sergeant was gone, Gloria rang for Briggeman and had him bring her glass of wine and another small slice of pate. It wasn't, perhaps, the best thing for her figure, but at that moment, it was the best thing for her soul.

The information from the diary proved to be very useful. Two days later, the police announced that they had arrested Ronald O'Hare and Edgar Watson for the murder of Frederick Little, Sr.

Daniel Callaghan had confided to Kathy and Freddie that Watson, when questioned, had ratted out O'Hare's location and that a small rifle had been found in O'Hare's possession. In addition, Watson's boot matched a footprint Detective Crowley had found at the mansion. Both had admitted to being at the mansion the night of the party but swore that they hadn't killed Mr. Little and had only gone upstairs.

"Not that it matters," said Uncle Dan.

He, Freddie and Kathy were seated in the apartment living room, late that afternoon, sipping tea and nibbling on biscuits. Dan had stopped by to bring the news.

"We've gotten the new microscope," Dan continued. "With many thanks to you, Freddie. If a bullet from the gun they found matches the ones taken from your father's body, then all we'll have to do is build a case. Oh, and here's your father's diary. Your mother asked if we could return it. We've got photographs of the important page and plenty of eyewitness testimony that Mr. Watson did not take his firing quietly."

"So, I've heard," said Freddie, taking the small book. "At least, for the time being, we were allowed to appoint my Uncle Stephen as chairman of the company until my grandfather's will finishes probate."

"Well, that's that, then," Dan said, getting up.

"Thank you for everything," Freddie said, rising also.

"'Tis I who should be thanking you," Dan said, shaking Freddie's hand.

Kathy rose also and gave Dan a peck on the cheek.

After showing the older man out, the two returned to the study and looked at each other, both feeling vaguely out of sorts, as if they should be happy the matter was finished but somehow wondering if it really was.

Nonetheless, they hosted Gloria, Lowell, and Honoria at dinner the next night. The mood was oddly restrained for a celebration.

"I suppose we should be grateful," said Gloria with a small sigh after Gam had been sent to bed. "Now we can put all this behind us and get back to our normal lives."

"Yes," said Freddie, uncomfortably aware that his life would never be what he'd considered normal again.

"I don't know," sighed Honoria. "I somehow thought seeing justice served would be more... satisfying, I guess."

"It does seem rather anti-climactic," Lowell grumbled.

"One almost feels sorry for the poor fellows," Honoria said. "Did you know that one had a brother who died in the Yonkers factory and left behind a widow and four children? And no one from the factory gave them any charity. No one."

"How dreadful," Gloria said.

"Uncle Stephen probably thought it was their own

fault," said Freddie. "And Father never noticed."

"That's still no excuse," said Kathy.

"No, it's not," said Freddie. "But I can't help how they behaved."

"But we can help how we behave," said Honoria emphatically.

Freddie saw his mother pursing her lips and, wishing to avoid a potentially unpleasant debate, he scrambled to his feet and raised his glass.

"Nonetheless, may I propose a toast?" he asked, smiling at the people at his table. "To justice served."

"To justice served," the others murmured.

"And to the end of our investigation," Gloria added, taking another sip of wine.

CHAPTER EIGHT

"Fore!" Uncle Stephen Coates' deep voice blasted through the mid-morning air.

Freddie took a deep breath and set up his swing. He pulled the club back, twisted his torso just so, rotated through the swing and watched as his ball hooked to the left and into the rough near the tenth hole.

Stephen, a medium-sized man with blonde hair and an athletic build, laughed raucously around the cigar he'd freshly lit and kept clamped in his teeth.

"That's looking better, Freddie," Stephen announced.

It wasn't anywhere close to better and Freddie knew it. He only played golf because it was expected of him. He particularly hated playing golf with Uncle Stephen, who was extremely good at it and so relentlessly competitive that he played all manner of tricks, such as jumping in to "help" Freddie just as he was about to take a swing or padding Freddie's score.

But that morning, two weeks after the funeral for Freddie's father, Stephen hadn't played one trick. He was also encouraging Freddie instead of "helping" him. That meant only one thing. Stephen wanted something, and Freddie profoundly hoped he wouldn't have to play all eighteen holes before finding out what it was. He'd already tried asking.

Stephen pulled the cigar from his lips and took a deep breath. "Nothing like a good morning on the links, eh, Freddie."

"No, there isn't," Freddie said, picking up his cigar from the top of his golf bag and puffing quickly.

Stephen stuck his cigar back between his teeth and teed up. A minute later, his ball sailed onto the putting green.

It was a glorious morning, still, and just enough chill in the air that the argyle sweater and plus fours that Freddie wore were quite comfortable. Not so far away, Freddie could hear the sharp cracks of the target shooters' guns. His Aunt Miranda was supposedly among them, according to her husband, Uncle Thomas. Thomas had begged off the round of golf, claiming his dyspepsia was bothering him and that he'd be waiting for Miranda in the lounge. But thanks to an odd look on Stephen's face, Freddie had guessed that Stephen simply didn't want Thomas around for some reason.

The caddies, two freshly washed young boys who probably should have been in school, waited for Stephen's nod, then each grabbed a golf bag.

"I'm glad you came out with me today," Stephen said, clapping Freddie on the shoulder.

"I appreciate the invitation," Freddie replied as the two ambled toward the rough where Freddie's ball had landed. It utterly failed to surprise Freddie when Stephen "found" the ball just at the edge of the rough closest to the putting green.

Trying not to let his sigh show, Freddie pulled his chipper from his bag. Surprisingly, he landed the ball not far from the green. Another chip shot and his ball was on. Stephen's ball had landed barely five feet from the hole.

"Let's see if I can land this eagle," Stephen said, grabbing his favorite putter and spinning it in his fingers.

Seconds later, Stephen's ball rolled obediently into the hole. Freddie pulled a putter and set up his shot. It only took two more strokes for him to get his ball into the hole. Stephen continued chatting about what a great day it was and how some stock he particularly liked was doing. As they walked to the next tee, Stephen suddenly looked pensive.

"You've been pretty quiet, Freddie," he said after taking a steady pull on a hip flask.

Freddie finished the sip he was taking from his own. "I suppose."

"Still getting over your father's death, eh?" Stephen nodded. "That was one hell of a shock, I tell you. Too bad your sister and your mother are contesting his will."

Honoria had told him and Kathy about her conversation with Mr. Taylor. She said she'd purposely dropped the tidbit that she and her mother were going to contest Mr. Little's will. After all, Mr. Taylor's pathetically weak lies could only mean that someone was paying him to spy on Freddie and Kathy. Freddie had expressed some skepticism. But the fact that Uncle Stephen was remarking on something they'd told no one else meant that, to Freddie's chagrin, Honoria had probably been right. Freddie silently thanked God that his father's murder had been solved and that Freddie need not suspect Stephen of anything worse than his usual manipulative skullduggery.

"Where did you hear that?" Freddie asked.

Stephen chuckled. "I have my ways. Have to keep on top of what's going on in the family. In your Aunt Thelma's best interests, of course."

"Of course," Freddie said.

"As a matter of fact, that's something I wanted to talk to you about,"

Freddie braced himself, but what he heard next could not have rocked him harder.

"We're taking the company public," Stephen said.

"What?" Freddie gasped.

"Freddie, Freddie," Stephan said, patting Freddie's shoulder. "You need to get with the times. We need to capitalize. Miles Johnson, the banker, he's all set to buy in and he's got a whole crew of others who are interested. Your father and I and Thomas had it all worked out."

"I can't believe my father was going to let total strangers take control of the family business," said Freddie.

"Nobody is taking control, Freddie." Stephen paused and looked around quickly. "Although you may not want to let Johnson know that. Nah, we just sell a few of the shares and make sure the family has a controlling interest. Your tee."

They had reached the tee for the eleventh hole. Freddie forced himself to concentrate on teeing off for the time being and narrowly missed a sand trap. Stephen's drive landed his ball somewhat closer to the green, but not on it.

"That's why we had to contest your grandfather's will," Stephen said, his tone matter of fact, although his eyes glanced quickly at Freddie as they walked toward their balls. "Since your father was already with us, we had to keep him in charge to pull this off."

Freddie stopped Stephen with a hand on the older man's arm. "And what is going on at the business that you need capital so badly for?"

"Freddie! I thought you understood business," Stephen pointed. "There's your ball."

Freddie suddenly felt as though he were five years old and Uncle Stephen was once again making fun of him. He fought the feeling back and concentrated on hitting the ball. By some miracle, the ball not only sailed onto the green, it fell right into the hole.

Stephen stepped back. His chip shot landed on the green, but it took two putts to get it in the hole. Freddie let him mark the score, then stopped him once again.

"I do understand business, Uncle Stephen," Freddie said, glaring at his uncle. "Which is why I am asking why our family business needs capital so badly that you want to sell shares of it to total strangers."

"I thought you trusted me," Stephen said, gesturing at the caddies.

"I do. I suggested that the Board appoint you chairman. Now, what is going on?"

"Nothing." Stephen snarled, then got a hold of himself. "There is nothing going on that shouldn't be. We just want to grow the business is all. Capital is necessary for expansion. It's in everybody's best interest. Well, what do you know? We've got a party of ladies immediately ahead of us. Do you want to play through?"

The four young women were in their early twenties and three of them were apparently more interested in gossiping than playing. The fourth, a brunette with broad shoulders and gray eyes, glared at them, then smiled at Stephen, who returned the smile.

Freddie looked at the tee then shook his head. He didn't want to but finished the round because it was expected. Stephen continued to expound, in a rather vague way, about the benefits of going public while Freddie, in an effort to shut him out, concentrated on his game. As a result, he played his best game ever, never mind what Stephen said his score was.

He begged off going to the club's lounge for a drink and headed for the front of the building, his caddie following behind with the bag of clubs. Near the door, Freddie turned to take the bag. The caddie was a year or two older than Gam with an eager face capped off by unruly brown hair.

"Thank you, young man," Freddie said, then paused. "Why aren't you in school?"

"Can't," he said.

"Oh?"

The boy flushed. "My English is not good."

"That shouldn't keep you out of school."

"Must work." The lad's accent seemed Russian to Freddie. "Father died in factory accident. Mother work but is not enough. I help."

"And you're a good lad for doing so," Freddie said. He pulled a five-dollar bill from his billfold and handed it to the boy. "What's your name?"

"Mikh— I mean, Michael."

"Thank you, Michael." Freddie smiled as the boy ran off.

It was odd, Freddie thought, how he was so much more conscious of lads like the caddies than anyone else among his peers. He was happy to credit Lowell Winters and Kathy for that. Whether it made him a better person, he could not say. But Freddie certainly felt better about himself when around most of his peers, such as Uncle Stephen, who only knew the names of the caddies he preferred and woe to the lad who made even the most innocent of mistakes.

Freddie arrived back at the apartment just in time for luncheon, and Kathy made a point of leaving the study long enough to eat with him and Gam. Freddie dutifully pecked her cheek, then sat down and glared at the cup of bouillon in front of him.

"Well, you're in a mood," Kathy said acerbically.

Freddie looked at her and sighed deeply. "Oh, I am so sorry, Kathy. I'm afraid I've had a very trying morning."

"I'm not surprised." Kathy laid her napkin on her lap and took a sip of her soup. "You've been complaining about having to play golf with your uncle all weekend." She stopped and smiled gently at him. "So, he was that terrible?"

"Worse," said Freddie, still staring at his bouillon. "He and Father and Uncle Thomas had plans to take the business public."

"That doesn't sound so bad," Kathy said.

"That's awful!" Gam blurted out, then sat back repentantly.

"You're right, Gam, it is," Freddie said. "It's our family business. It is meant to stay in the family."

"So why take it public?" Gam asked.

"Uncle Stephen said it was necessary to expand," Freddie said.

Gam frowned. "Well, I s'pose you'd need capital to do that, but sounds kind of fishy to me."

"To me, too," said Freddie. "Especially since Uncle Stephen refused to give me any details."

"Uh-oh," said Gam.

"Do you think he's hiding something?" Kathy asked.

“I'm fairly certain of it.” Freddie took a sip of soup, then sighed. “Which means I'm going to have to hire an independent accountant to go over all of the books. I just hope I can convince the probate judge to let me make the decision to do an audit before probate is finished. Because if I have to convince the rest of the board to do it, Uncle Stephen and Uncle Thomas will be sure to block it and Uncle Albert does whatever they want.”

“Oh, dear. That does sound miserable,” Kathy said. “But I do have some very good news for you.”

Freddie looked up. “I could use some.”

“The Covenant,” Kathy said. “It's selling like hotcakes.”

“It is?” Freddie smiled.

There had been a party for the release of Signature Books' debut novel, The Covenant, by Harold T. Mennerly, the Friday before. Most of the crowd had bought copies of the new novel, but Freddie had expected that. He'd been pleased by the reviews in the New York papers, which had been very complimentary. Still, even good reviews did not mean the book would sell.

“It's gotten excellent reviews across the country,” said Kathy. “And I've got telegrams from Boston, Miami, San Francisco, and Chicago, all asking for more copies. One more telegram and I'm going to have to schedule a second print run.”

Roberts appeared in the doorway of the dining room. “Mrs. Little, pray forgive me for interrupting, but there's another telegram.”

He handed her the yellow envelope. Kathy grinned as she opened it.

“And here it is,” she announced waving the paper inside. She bounced up. “Freddie, will you please excuse me? I absolutely must call Mr. Trimble immediately to place the order, then I'll come right back.”

Freddie and Gam both scrambled to their feet as Kathy left. She proved true to her word and returned quickly and luncheon passed pleasantly until Mrs. Davies emerged from the back of the apartment to fetch Gam for his afternoon lessons.

Later that evening, Freddie got a call. The information was dire and as soon as he hung up, he hurried into the study.

"Kathy, I've got to go to the hospital," he said. "Uncle Stephen has been shot and Aldrich says I should come."

"What?" Kathy dropped her pen on her desk and leaped to her feet. "No, wait. I'll go with you."

Roberts had their coats ready and the car called. Freddie scrambled behind the wheel of his Cadillac barely waiting for Kathy to be seated.

"What do you think—" Kathy began.

Freddie waved her off. New York traffic was hard enough to negotiate. Trying to get to the hospital as fast as he could while dodging buses and flivvers meant that speculation would have to wait.

Neither of them was entirely surprised to see Kathy's Uncle Dan in the hospital's patient ward, sitting in the corridor along a row of rooms. They were surprised to see Gloria sitting with Aunt Thelma outside Uncle Stephen's room on the wooden chairs polished to a high gloss with extensive use. Uncle Stephen's two sons, Wilfrid and Aldrich, paced the corridor. Aldrich was the older of the two, although both looked very similar, with athletic builds and blond hair. Wilfrid, however, carried himself as if he was perpetually furious with the world and all its inhabitants. Wilfrid's wife, Constance, a willowy brunette with a hard look about her, sat a short distance away, reading a magazine.

Nurses slid quietly in and out of the rooms and back and forth along the hallway. Among them was one tall older woman who carried herself with certain authority and glared at the visitors in the hall as if they were only there to wreak havoc among her patients.

With a disdainful sniff, she quietly slid into Uncle Stephen's room

"I came as soon as I'd heard," Gloria said as Freddie and Kathy approached.

"And she has been quite the rock," Thelma said with a sniff. "I had to send Miranda home. She was worse than useless."

Gloria winced but didn't say anything.

"How is he?" Kathy asked.

Thelma shrugged. "He made it through surgery. They're settling him now. If there aren't any complications, the doctors think he will recover."

Freddie nodded. It wasn't the best news he'd ever heard, but there was room for some optimism.

The tall nurse came out of the room.

"Mrs. Coates? You can see him now," the woman said, holding the door open. Her brown hair was perfectly placed under her starched cap. "Please don't excite him. He needs complete rest."

Aunt Thelma meekly nodded and hurried into the room. The nurse silently shut the door behind Freddie's aunt, then glared again at the group gathered in the hallway. Wilfrid glared back and Freddie had to admit he was happy to see the nurse slightly discomfited.

As the nurse moved off down the hall, Freddie looked at Uncle Dan.

"What happened?" he asked.

"Well," Dan said. "It looks as though someone was waiting for him to leave the country club. He was shot in the jaw and in the chest. No one saw anything. We're looking at O'Hare and Watson just to be sure."

"But they're in jail," Freddie said.

"Not as of last week," Dan said. "The bullet in the gun they had didn't match the one that killed your father, so they had to let them go. I just found out about it today."

"Matching bullets?" Gloria asked. "How can you match bullets?"

"It's from the rifling on the inside of a rifle or

pistol," Dan explained. "There's a new microscope that will let us look at two bullets side by side to see if the markings match. It's unique to each gun. They caught Sacco and Vanzetti that way, you know."

"No, I didn't," Gloria said. "But it sounds fascinating." She suddenly checked herself.

The nurse returned to the room and a moment later, shooed Aunt Thelma out.

"I told you not to agitate him," the nurse snapped and slid back into the room and silently shut the door.

Thelma pulled herself up imperiously. "I wasn't agitating him. He wanted to tell me something."

She sank into a chair. Sniffing, she pulled a handkerchief from her pocket and blinked back her tears.

"What did he want to tell you?" Gloria asked gently.

Uncle Dan slid ever so slightly closer.

"I think he saw who shot him," Thelma said. "He kept muttering, 'He had Fred's gun, his favorite one.' And something about the ruby. Poor Stephen was slurring so much, I could barely understand him."

The nurse emerged again and Dan got up and spoke softly to her.

"Certainly not!" she snapped and swept off in high dudgeon.

Sighing, Dan returned to the little group.

"She's not going to let me question him," he said softly to Freddie and Kathy. "I suppose it will be all right to wait since they expect him to make it."

A minute later, Honoria and several other cousins arrived. They spent the evening attempting to be soothing to Aunt Thelma, but when one of them began passing a flask around, the angry nurse attending Uncle Stephen sent all but the immediate family away.

Gloria had Van Schuyler waiting with her car and Honoria opted to ride back to her apartment with her mother. Freddie offered Uncle Dan a ride to his home and Dan accepted. Once Kathy and Dan were settled on the front seat beside him, Freddie pressed the starter and the engine roared to life.

"Uncle Dan," Kathy said the second Freddie had pulled away from the curb. "With O'Hare and Watson eliminated as suspects, does this mean Father Little's killer is still out there?"

"That depends on whether you believe they've been eliminated," Uncle Dan said with a shrug. "Detective Crowley still seems to believe they're guilty. He simply doesn't have enough evidence yet."

"And what do you think, Uncle Dan?" Freddie asked.

Dan sighed. "I do not want you two to think that I'm giving you permission to go haring off on your own after this fellow. But, no, I don't think O'Hare and Watson killed your father, Freddie. For one thing, I watched Crowley question the two of them. They both admitted that they were at the mansion and had climbed onto the terrace looking for your father. But they said that they didn't want to kill your father, just hurt him. Now, most guilty people won't even admit that much, and Crowley went after them pretty hard. But they wouldn't change their story, no matter how hard—" Dan cleared his throat. "Well, you know what I mean."

Freddie didn't say so but he didn't understand the implication. It was clear from Kathy's face that she did. He made a mental note to ask her later.

"In any case," Dan continued. "They may have been guilty of trespassing, but I don't think they're guilty of murder."

"And now we have Uncle Stephen getting shot," Kathy said. She frowned. "Could it be related to Father Little's death?"

"Of course, it could," Dan said. "In fact, I'm inclined to believe it is, given what your aunt said about what he told her. I'm glad I told the doctor to give me the bullets he got."

"Well, we should know very soon, then," said

Freddie. "Once Uncle Stephen recovers enough to tell us who shot him."

"That we will," Dan said, suddenly sounding very weary.

They left him outside of his brownstone in Hell's Kitchen. Freddie waited just long enough for Dan to slowly mount the stoop and go inside.

"What did Uncle Dan mean when he was talking about interviewing O'Hare and Watson?" Freddie asked as he turned the car around to go back uptown.

"That they got the stuffings beaten out of them." Kathy looked at him.

"The police beat them?" Freddie was shocked.

"You didn't know that?" Kathy asked.

"No, I didn't."

Kathy shrugged. "They don't exactly advertise it, and, of course, someone of your privileged status would never get hit. But it happens quite frequently. Sometimes, it's the only way to get a killer to confess."

Freddie shook his head. "So, what are we to make of this evening's events?"

"I have no idea, but I'm sure we'll know more tomorrow."

There wasn't that much more to be said, so the two talked briefly of their day until they got home.

Honoria and Gloria were waiting in Freddie's living room when they got there.

"So, what did Kathy's uncle say?" Gloria asked quickly before Freddie could ask why she was there.

"That he didn't think O'Hare and Watson were guilty and given what Aunt Thelma said, it seems likely that Father's killer also shot Uncle Stephen," Freddie replied.

"The we merely have to wait for Uncle Stephen to tell us who shot him," Gloria said as the telephone rang in the hallway.

Roberts appeared a moment later. "Excuse me, Mr. Little, Mr. Aldrich Coates is on the phone."

Freddie took the call, then returned to the living

room shaking his head.

"What is it, Freddie?" Kathy asked anxiously.

"There was a complication," Freddie said. "Uncle Stephen just passed away."

CHAPTER NINE

Horrified, Gloria hurried off to be with Aunt Thelma. Freddie, Kathy, and Honoria continued discussing over and over why Stephen would have been shot, presumably with one of their father's guns and possibly the same gun that had been used to kill their father.

"But who would benefit from killing both Father and Uncle Stephen?" Honoria groaned, yet again, as the clock on the living room breakfront chimed half-past eleven.

"I have no idea," Freddie snarled, sipping on his fourth whiskey. "And continuing to ask the question again and again is not going to change that!"

"That's enough," said Kathy firmly. "We're already overwrought, as well we might be, and it's getting late. We're not going to make sense of anything if we're both overwrought and exhausted. We'll have to take this up tomorrow between all our other engagements and doing what we can to help with arrangements for Uncle Stephen. Honoria, why don't you ask Ivy if she has been able to find out anything about Father Little's enemies?"

"That's something, at least," Honoria snapped, then sniffed as she left the apartment.

But the next day between appointments and helping out Aunt Thelma, there wasn't time to speculate on who might have killed both Freddie's father and Uncle Stephen. And, if Freddie were completely honest with himself, he had little interest in doing so.

"The worst of it is," he explained to Kathy as they got into bed that night after a very long day and dinner with the Coates family. "I feel as though I should be doing something. Bothering your uncle or something. But I simply do not want to. It's as if I cannot take any more strife. I am full up."

"I don't doubt it, darling," Kathy said, sliding up next to him. "It has been traumatic enough on the surface of it, without all the unpleasantness from your relatives."

"Yes. Aldrich seemed quite put out with you this evening at dinner."

Kathy snorted. "He tried to make time with me! And I gave him a piece of my mind. Imagine. Trying to make time with a married woman, let alone a relative during a time of grief."

Freddie suddenly laughed out loud. "So, that's what he meant by you being cold and unfeeling."

"What?" Kathy glared at him.

"He took great umbrage at your refusal," Freddie said, still chortling. "He apparently couldn't understand why you didn't find him irresistible."

"He did? What a miserable excuse for a human being." Kathy shuddered. "I'm sorry, Freddie. I know he's your cousin."

"But he is also a miserable excuse for a human being. Which is why I generally avoid him and his brother."

"You don't think he could have killed your father?"

Freddie shrugged. "I could understand him killing his father, perhaps, but not mine."

He yawned deeply.

"Oh, dear," said Kathy reaching over to turn off the bedside table light. "I guess it is time we went to sleep."

"Well, maybe not immediately," Freddie said with a chuckle.

Late the next morning, he dragged himself into the study.

"Kathy, my darling, if you will forgive me for touching on an otherwise taboo subject, I dare say your brother is the single most potent argument in favor of us avoiding procreation," he proclaimed. "Assuming we can,"

Kathy looked up as her husband sank into his favorite chair next to the study fireplace.

"Oh, dear," Kathy said. "What has he done now?"

"It was not so much what he did as the debate that ensued when his infraction was brought to my attention." Freddie rubbed his eyes in exhaustion. "Roberts had caught him playing mumblety-peg in the servants' hallway. So, when I confronted young Gamaliel about it, the scamp pointed out that it was causing minimal harm to the floor, which is already quite scuffed, that we had not forbidden him to do so, and that with the complete lack of grass or dirt in the near vicinity, he didn't have any other option. Not to mention the lack of like-minded young men with which he could socialize."

Kathy smiled weakly. "He does have a point or two."

"I know," Freddie groaned. "Which is why I did not confiscate his pocket knife again." He rubbed his eyes then looked back at Kathy. "But good lord, I have met philosophers and lawyers who couldn't argue so well. It utterly terrifies me to think what our combined progeny would be like."

Kathy chuckled as she got up from her desk and kissed the top of Freddie's head. "I know, my dear. That's why I'm taking precautions. But I do appreciate you taking Gam in hand."

Freddie looked up and realized she had her purse in her hand. "Are you going somewhere?"

"Yes. I promised to eat luncheon with your mother today. She called this morning to let me know that she would not be occupied with caring for your Aunt Thelma and that she would dearly love some company."

"Oh. Well, I've got a meeting with Mr. Ames at the Yonkers factory at..." Freddie suddenly sat up and pulled his pocket watch from his vest. "Good lord. I'd better hurry.”

“And I will be on my way, too.” Kathy gave him an affectionate kiss, then left the apartment.

As usual, there was a taxi waiting for her. She got in and during the ride to her mother-in-law’s, Kathy wondered if she’d ever get used to riding everywhere in taxis. Or, worse, limousines.

The front entryway of the Little mansion was as cold and imposing as always. The banisters on the sweeping marble staircase shown with pearlescent luster. Portraits of stern relatives looked down from the walls. Kathy shivered as Briggeman took her hat and coat.

“Mrs. Little is waiting for you in the drawing room,” Briggeman told Kathy.

Kathy took a deep breath and went into the room. Gloria was ensconced, as she so often was, in her favorite chair next to the fireplace. A small fire burned cheerfully. She stared at her book, held at arm’s length, with a frown on her face, but snapped it shut the moment Kathy walked into the room.

“Hello, Kathy, dear,” she crooned, setting aside the book and rising.

“I hope I didn’t catch you at a bad time,” Kathy said after kissing each of Gloria’s cheeks.

Gloria settled back into her chair and laughed. “Good heavens, no. In fact, you’ve saved me. I thought a little Thomas Hardy would be suitably somber for the day. But, no. He’s merely depressing.”

Kathy chuckled as she slid onto the sofa. It had been placed at a right angle to Gloria’s chair with a small whatnot table between. Kathy sat at the end closest to Gloria.

“I know. I find Hardy very dreary,” Kathy said.

“And yet, I keep going back to him, thinking I’m going to enjoy him more than I do.” Gloria rolled her eyes. “I’m so glad you could come, darling. It’s gotten dreadfully boring all of a sudden. Thelma doesn’t want me around. All my friends are avoiding me. I’m not sure if it's their not wanting to intrude on my bereavement or their fear of a lusty widow going after their husbands." She sighed. "I do hope it's the former."

Kathy's grin grew wicked. "Do they have reason to fear?"

Gloria laughed out loud. "None in the least. I even have a widower chasing me, one of Fred's old friends, Mr. Terrence Carter. I'm not at all interested and am even considering hinting at my impecunious state in an attempt to drive him off."

"It would be very telling if that plan didn't succeed."

"Yes, it would." Gloria suddenly blinked back tears and took out her handkerchief. "I'm so sorry. These things catch me at the oddest times."

"That's quite normal, I'm told," Kathy said, and tried to hide a yawn. "It catches Freddie, too, especially since his uncle was killed." She watched as Gloria's face grew wistful. "Mother Little, why do I get the feeling that there's more to your tears than grief? Especially since we were talking about scaring off Mr. Carter by telling him you have no money."

"Why else would he want me?" Gloria said.

"What do you mean?" Kathy was aghast. "Mother Little, you are a delight! You're intelligent, witty, wonderfully curious about everything."

Gloria chuckled ruefully. "Alas, my darling, those are not traits valued amongst the Four Hundred, especially in a woman."

"Now that you mention it, it's not just the Four Hundred," Kathy grumbled.

"The problem is that the very people you would think are not going to be interested in how well-positioned one is are the most conscious of it. I suspect that it is because there are certain scoundrels who will try to win the heart of an heir or heiress solely for his or her position in society." Gloria sniffed.

Even though Gloria was not speaking about wealth or money, Kathy understood that was what she meant. Since the subject of money was grossly vulgar, one spoke about one's position in society, specifically New York's famed Four Hundred, instead.

"Which happened to you, didn't it?" Kathy asked gently.

Gloria nodded. "He was a young professor of literature, a poor cousin of one of our more notable families. We met at some cotillion or other and began a correspondence. I was so completely in love that I was about to run away with him." She sniffed again. "Father found out that he was courting me and told me in no uncertain terms that if I married the fellow I would be cut off from the family and would not receive a penny as an inheritance. I told my intended what Father had told me and that was it. He returned my letters and I never saw him again."

"Oh, dear. No wonder you were so adamant that Honoria and Freddie marry one of your own." Kathy reached over and held Gloria's hand.

"Oh, yes. It's why I'm so very glad that you clearly love Freddie so much, and in spite of his position. But it's also why I accepted Fred's courtship soon after. There were several fellows seeking my favor, and he was the least objectionable. I'd always liked his father, as well." Gloria sighed. "It wasn't that Fred and I didn't get on. We were very companionable. There simply wasn't any spark. Poor thing. He was merely doing what was expected of him, as was I. And we did have a friendship, of sorts. We both loved nature. He wasn't quite so bombastic in those days. Well, not often." Gloria chuckled. "He was dreadfully spoiled. Not only was he the youngest child, he was the only boy and the only child of Father Little's second wife, Eugenia. She died just after Fred and I were married. Father Little had been forced to work in his father's business day and night from his youth on and did not want his son to be forced to do the same. But then Fred's mother let him run wild, so when Fred achieved his majority, Father Little could not get him interested in the least in the family business, which is why Father Little eventually turned to Freddie."

"And why Freddie has a stronger sense of duty to the family," Kathy said.

"Quite probably. But it wasn't as though Fred didn't want to please his father. He simply didn't understand business the way Freddie does innately. That's why Fred spent so much time making friends with self-made men. He was hoping to learn something and prove to his father that he was competent at running a business. At least, that's what I've gathered from listening to Stephen, Thomas, and Uncle Albert talking in their respective drawing rooms before dinners and the like."

Kathy grinned again. "When they thought you weren't listening."

Gloria smiled as well. "Precisely. One thing I had learned to do over the years was to manage Fred into doing what he needed to be doing. And to know what that was, I had to keep an ear out, if you know what I mean."

"I think I do." Kathy shuddered. "I much prefer the direct method."

"Which is just as well because Freddie does not like to be managed." Gloria laughed. "I remember one young woman, lovely thing, well-positioned and perfectly suitable. She almost had Freddie shortly after he returned from the Army. But then she tried to manage him out of his love for cars and airplanes. She might have had a point, but all she achieved was managing herself out of a husband."

"Luckily for me." Kathy paused. "Was she the one Freddie always regretted?"

Gloria's eyes lit up. "You mean the one from his novel? You know, I have been wondering who she was from the moment I read it."

Kathy fidgeted. "So have I. Well, since I realized that his character Meaberry was based a lot on him. Did you know in the first version I saw, Meaberry married her and they lived happily ever after."

"Oh, that's telling, isn't it?" Gloria suddenly gasped. "Oh, dear. You mustn't worry, darling. I'm very sure he's gotten over her by now, whoever she was. And he's much happier with you than I've seen him with anyone else."

"Thank you for the reassurance, Mother Little."

Briggeman appeared in the doorway. "Luncheon is served, Ma'am."

"Do you mind eating in here, Kathy?" Gloria suddenly asked.

"Not at all," Kathy said.

"Briggeman, please have Brighton bring our luncheon in here."

"Yes, Ma'am."

The young footman brought in a small table, then brought in plates, silverware, napkins and tea things. As he returned the final time with a lovely chicken pie, Kathy reached for some tea and accidentally knocked Gloria's book off the whatnot table. She swooped down to get it, and in doing so, couldn't help reading the title. She waited just long enough for the footman to leave before looking at her mother-in-law.

"This isn't a novel by Thomas Hardy," Kathy said, setting aside her silverware and opening the book. "In fact, this isn't a novel at all."

"Eh, no," Gloria said with an embarrassed sigh.

"'Relativity: The Special and General Theory,'" Kathy read off the title page. "Albert Einstein. I don't think I've ever heard of him."

"He's positively brilliant. It's about the speed of light and how force changes based on the size of the object, which is the theory of special relativity and then in general relativity, he adds the effects of gravitational pull. It's why our planets orbit around the sun, rather than float off into space."

"Oh."

Gloria winced. "I am explaining that rather badly. I much prefer chemistry to physics."

"I don't think any of us had the least inkling that

you understood science at all, let alone enjoyed it."

"It's not something I let get out. It would have the most deleterious effect on my social standing." Gloria took a slice of pie with a slightly injured sniff. "But what else does one do when one has nothing but time on her hands? I visit and do charity work, but it doesn't fill nearly as many hours as one might think. Nor is it very interesting. So, I read science texts, in addition to novels. I've managed to do a few experiments here and there, published a paper."

"You what?"

Gloria giggled guiltily. "It's my greatest secret. I'm in correspondence with a great many scientists. In fact, it was Dr. Hubble, in California, who recommended that I read Dr. Einstein's book. But they all think I'm a man. Mr. G. Derby. I was doing some research into polymers and discovered a rather neat equation, based on some work with Dr. Billings, at the Massachusetts Institute of Technology. He insisted I submit it for publication, which I did, and it was published."

"And to think Freddie was astounded to find that you read Fitzgerald."

Gloria sniffed. "Well, I do have my social standing to consider. Can you imagine the scandal it would cause if anyone found out?" She paused and looked a little frightened. "I do hope you'll keep this in strictest confidence."

"Of course. Did Father Little know?" Kathy focused on eating her slice of pie, trying to hide what she feared.

"Of course not. I think he understood that I took a more than ladylike interest in the natural world. But it would never have occurred to him that I was capable of understanding anything so masculine as business and science. Not surprising when you consider how difficult it was for him to grasp those ideas." Gloria studied her for a moment. "Why did you ask?"

"Well, Mother Little, if Father Little disapproved, it would give you motive for..." Kathy sighed.

"Darling girl, I have plenty of motive even without that, which, by the way, I discussed with your uncle not too long ago." Gloria frowned. "Still, he seems to have changed his mind about Mr. O'Hare and Mr. Watson. Something about what Aunt Thelma said Uncle Stephen had told her?"

"Oh, that." Kathy all but groaned. "I was going to tell you after dinner, but then Aldrich... I'm sorry, Mother Little, but his behavior toward me was utterly dreadful."

"Oh, dear. I thought I saw him eyeing you." Gloria snorted and took a sip of tea. "Well, he probably got everything he deserved."

"I'm glad you think so," Kathy glared at her bit of pie.

"I'm sorry you had to deal with him. I've always thought Thelma should have used a stronger hand with those boys, but it was not my place to say so." Gloria rolled her eyes. "You should have heard him teasing his Aunt Miranda about rum runners lying in wait on the street to shoot at each other and hitting her. She was terrified. Anyway, you were going to tell me something?"

"Well, remember when Aunt Thelma came out of Uncle Stephen's room saying that he'd been trying to tell her something?"

"Yes, she thought he'd seen who shot him."

"Apparently, he said the killer had Father Little's favorite gun and something about the ruby." Kathy fidgeted with her fork. "Anyway, Uncle Dan confirmed yesterday afternoon that the bullets from Uncle Stephen were shot from the same gun that killed Father Little."

"Which means if Thelma heard Stephen correctly and he recognized the gun, then he was shot by Fred's favorite rifle." Gloria sat back surprised. "But it's here. I saw it in the game room the morning of the funeral when I went in there to pull the guns for Mr. Carter, Mr. Hudson, and Mr. Lewton."

"Are you sure?" Kathy looked at her closely. "There were so many people taking things."

"I suppose, but I didn't see anyone with it." Gloria closed her eyes. "And I wouldn't have given it away. It was very special to him. His father had bought it for him when he was a boy. It didn't have a special rack space, though. In fact, he tended to leave it lying about where he could play with it. But it did have a special case. The servants, when they saw it, would simply return it to the case and put it back in the bedroom, I believe."

"I remember the night of the party he was polishing a rifle with gold inlaid into the muzzle," Kathy said. "Could that be it?"

"Most definitely." Gloria looked over their empty plates. "Would you like another slice of pie or should we investigate?"

"By all means. Let's look."

The room, with its collection of stuffed animals, had felt uncomfortable enough when Kathy had first seen it. Empty of her father-in-law, it took on a rather chilling aspect. Even the overstuffed chair facing the dartboard looked as though someone was about to sink into it with a half tumbler of whiskey.

Kathy walked over to the billiards table and touched the rail of the table. "This is where he left the rifle when we were talking to him."

Gloria was looking around behind the chairs and along the edges of the cabinets. She came around the other side of the billiards table and bent.

"Here's the case," she said, holding it up. "And it's empty."

Kathy looked over at the end of the room, where there was a door. "Where does that door lead to?"

"It's a servants' hall." Gloria gazed at the door thoughtfully. "The conservatory is directly on the other side of the hall, and there's another door from the conservatory to the public hallway near the ballroom."

"So, anybody could have come in here, picked up

the gun and gone upstairs.”

“Or followed Fred through to the conservatory. He frequently went from here to the conservatory rather than walk around.”

The two women looked at each other.

“That could also include O’Hare and Watson,” Kathy said. “And they might know how servants halls work better than, say, someone from your crowd.”

“Indeed.” Gloria’s eyes narrowed as she thought. “And yet, your uncle does not believe that they are guilty.”

“No.” Kathy bit her lip. “Actually, he said they… Uh, didn’t act guilty when they were questioned. They even admitted being here and wanting to hurt Father Little, but that is, apparently, all they intended.”

“Yes, there is that,” Gloria said. She looked at Kathy. “Now what?”

Kathy shrugged. “I don’t know.” She thought for a moment. “Honoria hasn’t said whether Ivy or Lowell discovered any possible enemies. But with everything so topsy-turvy at the moment, we haven’t really had a chance to do more than say hello to each other.”

Gloria thought. “We should probably have another meeting of the minds, as it were. Dinner tonight is too soon. Oh, blast! Freddie’s Aunt Wilma is coming up tomorrow from Washington for Stephen’s funeral and Thelma is insisting that Wilma stay with me.”

“Well, maybe you can have a dinner for her and Aunt Miranda and Uncle Thomas, and learn something from them,” Kathy said.

Gloria’s eyebrows lifted. “Yes. Maybe I can. And perhaps I can convince Miranda to look after Wilma on Saturday and we can have our meeting then.”

A deep yawn escaped Kathy.

“Oh!” she gasped. “I’m so sorry, Mother Little!”

“You’re forgiven, darling. But haven’t you been sleeping?”

Kathy shook her head. “It’s nightmares. I’ve had them before when that crazy woman tried to kill

Freddie and me and shot her brother. They eventually went away. It took a few months, but they did. I've just been having them again since Father Little was shot. They were easing off, but I had another last night and the night before."

"It's probably the shock of Uncle Stephen getting shot," said Gloria soothingly.

"It probably is."

"You poor thing." Gloria reached over and pulled Kathy to her side. "You've been so very brave about poor Fred's passing. I can't imagine it hasn't had an effect on you."

"Thank you, Mother Little."

Gloria released her. "Well, in any case, we now have something to investigate. It will either cement the case against O'Hare and Watkins or reveal the true killer."

"Yes, and I must get back to work. Thank you so much for the luncheon." Kathy wiped her eyes quickly and stuffed her handkerchief back into her dress pocket.

Freddie stepped away from the roar of the looms and into the hallway leading to the offices in the Yonkers factory.

"As you can see, sir, everything is in fine working order," said Stanford Ames, the Vice President in charge of Operations at Little and Sons Manufactures, Incorporated.

He was a trim-figured man with dark hair slicked down and a trim pencil-mustache. His suit was perfectly tailored to his build and his vest sported a dazzling gold watch-chain with a shark tooth fob.

"It certainly appears so," Freddie said, going into the office that had been his grandfather's and his father's.

He winced at the stuffed rabbit sitting on the edge of the desk. It was otherwise empty except for a blank blotter pad and a telephone. A portrait of the company's founder and Freddie's great-great-grandfather, Jedediah Little, glowered from the wall behind the desk. Facing it, on the opposite wall, was John Gordon Little, Freddie's great-grandfather. Freddie's grandfather hadn't thought to include a portrait of himself on the office walls and Freddie's father hadn't bothered.

The room, painted a calming green, also featured several bookshelves and dark oak paneling. A Tiffany lamp lit up the desk, in addition to the wall sconce lamps on either side of Jedediah's portrait. Unlike the other offices in the Yonkers factory, there was a ceiling fan in this office.

"Very well, then," Ames said. "It's probably time we headed back to New York, isn't it?"

"I haven't seen the accounting room yet," Freddie said. "Or the warehouse."

Ames smiled weakly. "Yes, of course."

The accountants and computers all seemed very busy over their ledgers and adding machines. Freddie made a point of stopping to talk to the head accountant. It was a pleasant enough conversation, but Freddie couldn't escape the feeling that Ames' presence was keeping the accountant from saying anything of substance.

The next stop was the warehouse. Men went back and forth, many carrying huge rolls of fabric. Others wrapped the rolls in burlap before putting them on trucks parked at the open warehouse door. However, in one corner near the back, Freddie saw shelves filled with other rolls with red tags on them.

"Isn't that the place where we put rolls refused by the clients?" he asked Ames.

"Well, yes," Ames said. "If I may direct your attention this way to our foreman."

"No," said Freddie. "That space for the refusals looks exceptionally full. Why were all those rolls refused?"

Ames rolled his eyes. "A simple misunderstanding,

sir. I'll send the contracts around to your office first thing next week. Now, the foreman, sir?"

The foreman, a big burly fellow with a lit stogie clamped in his teeth, shuffled forward.

"Why is that cigar lit?" Freddie asked, glaring at the man. "I hardly think we can afford any more refusals because the fabric stinks."

"It's lit?" The man pulled the stogie from his teeth and looked at it. "Sorry, sir. I forgot that it was. I was in the office, figuring hours."

"Mr. Simpson, is it?" Freddie asked and got a nod in affirmation. "I think we shall have to be more careful in the future, won't we?"

"Yes, sir."

Freddie nodded and wandered around the warehouse for several minutes more. There wasn't much else to see. Yet the way Ames had been dogging his every step had Freddie wondering. Ames had been with the company in various jobs for at least seventeen years, but he'd only risen to his present rank under Freddie's father.

Freddie's grandfather hadn't spent a lot of time with Freddie going over employee issues, although Freddie had heard the occasional complaint or two. Still, something was not quite right with Mr. Ames and Freddie was at a loss as to how to approach it. He drove Ames to the train station, but then drove the rest of the way home by himself.

He left the car in front of his building. But as he turned to enter, he suddenly found himself tackled by the small, but scrappy doorman while three loud cracks echoed in the street.

"What?" Freddie gasped as the man kept him pinned.

"Sorry, sir," the doorman gasped, then coughed. He lifted his head gingerly, then rolled off of Freddie. "You all right, sir?"

Freddie eased himself into a seated position. "I believe so, but what in the name of all that is holy did you do that for?"

"Someone was shooting at you, sir. There was a car and I saw the gun."

Freddie's jaw fell open. "And you risked your life to save mine."

The man shrugged and coughed. "Not much risk in diving for the sidewalk."

Freddie struggled to his feet, then reached out to help the man up. "Then I am profoundly grateful that you chose to dive in my direction."

A police whistle shrieked and grew closer. The harness bull hurried up, with another not far behind. There wasn't much Freddie could tell them. There were no bullet holes in his car and only chips where the shots had ricocheted off the building and sidewalk. The doorman had little more to add, only that he'd seen the gun poking out of a car window and dove for Freddie and the sidewalk. A sergeant in uniform had driven up at that point and talked to the other two officers.

"Must have been bootleggers," the sergeant concluded. "Not much we can do here."

Freddie refrained from saying anything. He dreaded going upstairs and worrying Kathy. The only thing worse would be not telling her and having her find out anyway, which she would. That was not a tongue-lashing that Freddie wanted.

However, when he got upstairs, Kathy and Mrs. Davies were having it out in the foyer of the apartment.

"But he also needs fresh air and activity," Kathy was saying as Freddie walked in.

"He is grossly behind in his studies," Mrs. Davies said, her full chest puffed up in annoyance. "He is not going to catch up gallivanting about in the park."

"He can't learn the names of plants?" Kathy demanded. "Won't it be easier to teach him his botany if he sees the actual plants rather than pictures?"

"That's assuming I can keep his attention focused long enough. It's hard enough to keep him at his lessons here."

"Because he's cooped up all day in here with you!" Kathy groaned. "It's no wonder he's causing trouble. This time of year back home, he'd be spending half the day outside."

Mrs. Davies sniffed.

"Are you suggesting you're not up to dealing with a boy with Gam's energy?" Kathy glared at the tutor with her arms folded across her chest.

"I am merely suggesting that young Master Briscow is not going to improve in his studies if he does not apply himself."

"And I am saying that if he does not get out and get some fresh air and exercise, he is not going to be able to apply himself at all. Now, if you will not add a daily walk or two to his schedule, I will find someone who will."

Mrs. Davies sniffed again, then looked at Freddie in mute appeal.

"I agree with Mrs. Little," Freddie said. "In fact, if she hadn't, I was going to request the same, myself."

Freddie glanced around, then nodded at Roberts.

"I'll fetch Master Briscow's hat," Roberts said. "And Mrs. Davies' things as well?"

"Yes. Thank you, Roberts."

Kathy disappeared into the school room at the back of the apartment and there was a loud whoop of joy. Seconds later, Gam burst into the hallway. Mrs. Davies accepted her hat, coat, and purse with disdain, but did not say anything.

Kathy returned to the foyer as the two left.

"What did he do now?" Freddie asked her, following her into the study.

Kathy sighed. "Just a little spring fever. He was watching the birds outside the window and sassed Mrs. Davies when she objected. I fear she is not going to be around much longer."

Freddie winced. "I would never have imagined that finding a suitable tutor would be so difficult."

"Ma said he's been a handful at school. Playing

hooky and getting into everything and still staying ahead of everybody in his class. Pa thinks he was bored.”

“That makes sense. Pity he couldn’t be content reading something salacious under his desk.”

Kathy’s grin grew wicked. “But, my dearest, not everybody is as good as you.”

Freddie found himself chuckling as she kissed his cheek. Looking down at the dust on his suit, he suddenly quailed, then pulled himself together.

“Darling,” he said slowly.

Kathy turned and a worried frown creased her face. “Oh, dear. You look as though something terrible has happened.”

“Not quite.” Freddie shrugged and wriggled his back to alleviate some of the residual soreness from his fall. “I don’t know if it was simply terrible bad luck or an actual attempt to harm me, but there was a shooting outside on the street. The doorman saved me.”

“The doorman?”

“Yes, short, spindly fellow with a nasty cough.”

“Carruthers. He got gassed in the War.” Kathy looked thoughtful. “He got moved from evenings to days last month.” She suddenly pressed her lips together. “You got shot at? But why?”

“I haven’t the faintest idea.” Freddie shook his head. “Normally, I would say that we’re getting close to someone, but we haven’t been investigating anything.”

Kathy sighed. “Are we sure that Watson and O’Hare killed your father and uncle?”

Freddie sighed and frowned. “Your uncle seems fairly sure they didn’t. And I can’t imagine what they’d have against me.”

“Then it must be somebody who needs all three of you dead,” Kathy said.

“Or wants revenge on us. But for what?”

Kathy gasped. “Your Uncle Thomas. Maybe he wants control of the company.”

“But he can’t get control of the company,” Freddie

said. "Even if I'm dead, you get the bulk of my fortune and Honoria gets the shares from the business. I have to keep those in the family. I believe I assigned the family shares to a couple of my cousins if neither you nor Honoria lives, but they're both Wilma's sons."

"Wait a minute. What about what your uncle said in the hospital? Something about the ruby. Or is there another ruby in the family besides the necklace your grandfather gave you?"

Freddie sighed. "None that I've seen. But, again, how would killing my father and uncle and me get this person the ruby? It's a family heirloom. It could only go to a relative."

"Maybe the thinking is that your Smith cousins would be more amenable to selling it."

"I seriously doubt they would be. It's why, after Honoria, I left everything to them."

Kathy shrugged. "I have no answers. But we should probably call Uncle Dan. He'll want to know."

"Yes, I expect he would."

CHAPTER TEN

As it turned out, Daniel Callaghan had been apprised of the shooting and did not agree that it was the result of bootlegging, but he was not able to say more than that until he saw them. Kathy, with Freddie's approval, invited her uncle for luncheon the next day.

Then Freddie told her all about his factory visit and his uneasiness. Kathy asked if there was a way to have someone from outside the company try to find out what was going on, and Freddie remembered that he'd been intending to do just that and decided that he would simply go ahead and do so.

The next morning, he'd barely arranged for the accountant to go over the books when Uncle Dan arrived for luncheon. Gam had been invited to the table so that he could spend some time with his uncle, but the lad's presence definitely put a damper on the conversation. It wasn't until Gam had gone back to his tutor that the three adults were finally able to talk about what they needed to talk about.

"It's getting worse," Dan sighed. "We were able to pick up a couple of the bullets that were fired at you yesterday, and they definitely came from the same gun that killed your father and uncle."

"Could it have been O'Hare and Watson?" Kathy asked.

"Why would it have been them?" Freddie asked. "They have no motive to shoot me."

"Unless they want revenge on your whole family," Kathy pointed out.

"They might," Uncle Dan conceded. "But if they do, they have someone helping them. Crowley was up in Yonkers searching both their houses yesterday, looking for that gun of your father's. And O'Hare and Watson were there the whole time."

"And obviously Crowley didn't find the gun," Kathy said. "How likely is it that O'Hare and Watson have help?"

"Not very," said Uncle Dan. "We've been asking around and it would have gotten out. For all we talk about killing someone when we're angry, very few people actually would try to, and those people don't talk about their plans. It'd be too easy to get caught."

"So, we're probably looking at someone else," Freddie said with a sigh.

"We are," said Uncle Dan. "I can't fault your doorman for hitting the ground and taking you with him, Freddie, but if he'd gotten a look at the license plate on the car, we might have an idea. The only thing your man said was that he thought it might be a Model T."

"In other words, a black car in a sea of black cars," Freddie sighed.

"And he couldn't be certain of that." Uncle Dan rolled his eyes. "The question is who would benefit if they got rid of you, your father, and your uncle?"

"No one," Freddie said. "Except Kathy and Honoria, and they clearly are innocent. Kathy will inherit my personal wealth and Honoria gets the family shares of the business. Those cannot be willed out of the family, and I've already seen to it that the most reliable of my relatives will inherit those shares if Honoria doesn't survive me. Or the shares that will be mine once Grandfather's will gets out of probate."

Kathy frowned worriedly at her plate. "Maybe someone thinks that if they let Honoria or your cousins inherit, they can buy into the company?"

Freddie shook his head. "But Stephen and my father wanted to take the company public. Why kill them? I'm the one who won't sell the shares."

"I don't understand," Dan said.

"My uncle wanted to sell some of the shares in the company as common stock," Freddie explained.

"You mean in the stock market?" Dan asked.

"Yes," Freddie said. "It would be a way of raising money, Uncle Stephen said, but never explained why we needed to. In any case, he told me that he didn't want to sell enough that the family wouldn't still have the majority of the shares, and thus, control of the business. It doesn't matter. Nothing could have been done until Grandfather's will gets out of probate, at which time, I will have over seventy percent of the shares and control of the company. And I would never do something like that."

"Hm. It would almost make sense for you to have killed your father and uncle," Uncle Dan said.

"That's just it," said Freddie. "Grandfather willed the shares to me, not my father. Father was chairman of the company because he and my other uncles had convinced Grandfather to retire a couple years ago. But he would never have been able to take over because I will have the controlling interest."

"I imagine that did not make him very happy," Dan said.

Freddie sighed. "It didn't. It put considerable strain on what was never a very good relationship."

"Ultimately, Uncle Dan," Kathy said. "Looking for who could get control of the business probably won't get us very far, since most of Freddie's relatives knew that killing Freddie's father and uncle would not get them that control."

Freddie suddenly began rapping his finger on the table. "On the other hand, disrupting the business might be a benefit to someone."

"But to whom?" Kathy asked. "Another textile mill?"

"Possibly," said Freddie. "There are those among my family who think we should be the only people selling textiles in America. It stands to reason someone else might think they should be the only ones."

Dan shook his head. "Well, you know more about this business stuff than I do. However, I do know criminals, and I've seen darned few who would kill just to hurt someone else's business. I have seen plenty of them kill for revenge. I would start by looking at who has something against your family."

Freddie and Kathy looked at each other.

"We'll have to see if Ivy and Lowell have found anything," Kathy said.

Dan's eyebrow quirked up.

"They agreed to ask about people who might have something against Father," Freddie said quickly. "The theory was that those people would not say anything to Honoria, Kathy, or me, but might to a casual acquaintance. And you did say that many of my father's peers would not talk to you."

Dan grumbled but had to concede.

As her fifth client that afternoon left the grocery store's back room, Honoria began to doubt the wisdom of going back to her former career as Madame Krichevsky, gypsy fortune teller. She had mostly given up the business after Kathy had found her out the previous fall. It didn't help that the speak that she had used as her base of operations had been raided and closed shortly after that. Honoria had returned to the role only sporadically, usually when a previous client had begged (via a letter sent to a local grocer). At the funeral for Honoria's father, Aunt Miranda Wilson had confided to Honoria that she was quite unsettled about something personal and had asked if Honoria knew any good spiritualists. It had been too tempting an opportunity. After some letter writing, Miranda, or "Mrs. Smith," had agreed to visit the little grocery store in Greenwich Village that afternoon. Unfortunately, it had gotten about in the neighborhood that Madam Krichevsky was in and available for consultations, and Honoria had found herself besieged by lovelorn young girls and weeping matrons, all trying to sort out the kinds of problems that, Honoria thought, could be better solved by a little common sense rather than a mystical seer.

Honoria sighed and checked the pocket watch that swung from the gold chains girdling the brightly colored skirt she wore. Aunt Miranda was late again. Or rather, "Mrs. Smith" was. Honoria had not been entirely surprised her aunt had used a pseudonym but thought the lack of originality rather appalling. She'd almost dismissed the first letter that Mrs. Smith had sent, but then recognized her aunt's handwriting.

Honoria was almost ready to give up on her aunt when the curtain to the back room parted and Aunt Miranda slipped through. Honoria was reasonably sure that Aunt Miranda would not recognize her with her dark wig and many veils. But a bit of theater, as Ivy would have called it, couldn't hurt, either.

"Shah!" Honoria announced in a deep voice and bad approximation of a Russian accent. "I see a woman who has seen great sorrow. A cloud of death has hovered over her."

"Oh!" Aunt Miranda trilled. "It has! It has! My brother and my brother-in-law, both dead within weeks of each other."

"An evil spirit has caused their deaths. I smell murder."

Aunt Miranda gulped "How do you know that?"

"Madame Krichevsky sees much." Honoria paused. She didn't really want to do a séance but would if Miranda asked. She was not going to suggest it. "But what is here? Why do I see the letter W? It floats above your head."

"Oh, dear." Aunt Miranda flushed, seemingly relieved. She smiled as if to ingratiate herself. "That's my real name. Wilson. I'm… I'm afraid I made one up. Is that all right?"

"Madame Krichevsky does not share secrets. But she does not like being lied to."

"Oh, no!" Aunt Miranda squeaked. "I promise. I

won't lie to you."

"I will know if you do."

"I won't. I promise."

Honoria pointed to the rickety wooden chair next to the small round table covered with a red cloth. A crystal ball sat in its base on top.

"Sit," she ordered.

Aunt Miranda scurried to the chair and adjusted the jacket of her black day suit around her ample curves.

"Now. Tell me what you want to see," Honoria said, swooping into her chair on the other side of the table.

"But I thought you would know that."

"I know many things. But for you to hear what you most need to hear, you must tell me your intentions."

"Oh. Well." She paused to gather her thoughts. "Well, I have a problem. There was a gift my mother promised me when I was a little girl. Only my father gave it to my brother, who is now dead. It is mine, and always should have been."

"Then why do you not ask his wife for it?"

"Oh, she doesn't have it anymore. It went to… to someone else."

"Then ask this person for it. If you are kind and respectful, this person should listen." Honoria sighed again. Another problem solved by common sense. "After all, you should have what is rightfully yours."

Aunt Miranda actually shuddered, then sat up straight. "You are right. That is absolutely what I should do. My goodness. You are the best spiritualist I have ever consulted. Most of them just talk about dark, mysterious men and ask for money."

"They are false. You come to Madame Krichevsky. She has the Second Sight. She knows." Honoria reeled off the sentences. "But do not forget to feed the Sight. Silver is good, gold is better."

"Oh, of course." Aunt Miranda dug into her purse and pulled out a coin. She placed it on the table and got up. "Thank you so much!"

"But the murders in your family. You are not worried?"

The older woman paused. "They are terrible. But they have nothing to do with me. I mean, it's been dreadful. Still, I can't imagine what to do about it."

"You are not afraid of evil spirit?"

Aunt Miranda suddenly paled. "Should I be?"

"That is for you to answer."

Aunt Miranda shrugged, then left.

As she slipped through the curtain, Honoria sighed. She had hoped Miranda would reveal something about her father's death, or at the very least, let something slip that she knew more than she should have. And all it had been was a petty dispute over some silly trinket. She picked up the coin and noticed that it was a twenty-dollar gold coin. Honoria shook her head. All that money for simple common sense.

Late that evening, Ivy St. James slid into her dressing room at the theater and shut the door firmly. Her wig had been removed by her dresser just off stage and she slid out of her costume and tossed it aside so that it could be cleaned. She enjoyed acting, as a rule, but it was exhausting work. It wasn't until she'd sunk onto the chair in front of the makeup table that she noticed the huge vase filled with red roses.

"Oh, no," she sighed, then plucked the card off the vase's rim.

It was from Donald Marston, another socialite. It wasn't the first time one of Honoria's set had become a stage-door Johnny. Nor the first time that the fellow in question had been as old as Honoria's father. Ivy generally put the flowers out into the theater's green room and ignored the invitations. However, she realized that Honoria had introduced her to a Mr. Marston at some point or another. They'd run into him at a restaurant or something. If it was the same Mr. Marston.

In fact, it was the same Mr. Marston. He was waiting at the stage door as Ivy emerged, freshly washed and dressed again. He was of medium stature and balding. What was left of his hair was mostly dark, but with flecks of gray.

"Oh, Miss St. James, your performance tonight was simply heartrending," he sighed. "Simply heartrending."

"Thank you, Mr. Marston," said Ivy.

"Did you get the flowers?"

"Yes. The cast is quite grateful." Ivy smiled. "Is Mrs. Marston well?"

"Miss St. James, could I interest you in a drink tonight?"

Ivy sighed inwardly but smiled again. "That does sound nice. Tell you what. There's a lovely speak right around the corner on 31rst. Why don't I meet you there?"

"Oh. Well. I..." Mr. Marston looked a little nonplussed, but apparently decided he would take what he could get.

It was Ivy's intent that he would not get much at all, but perhaps she could get something from him. For once, she was glad that Honoria had hired a driver for her. He dropped her off in front of the speakeasy. Ivy went down the steps to the basement under the millinery shop. It was one of those rare speaks near Broadway that was relatively quiet, with no band playing. Just good booze served at small tables where people could have a good conversation.

The quality of the speak was the only redeeming part of the evening. Ivy desperately wanted to go home and sleep. It felt as though she'd worked a matinee and was now beginning the evening performance, without the nap in between.

She handed her mink coat to the hat check and debated lighting her own cigarette. Letting Marston do it might give him some hope and therefore gain her more information. On the other hand, giving him some hope might make things more difficult when she eventually gave him the brush off. Sighing, she pulled her cigarette case and holder out of her purse. She barely had the cigarette fitted into its holder, a small mother of pearl one, when Marston appeared with lighter in hand.

"Thank you, Mr. Marston," Ivy said.

"My pleasure." He slid out of his overcoat and handed it to the hat check girl.

He waved at the maitre d' and the two were seated immediately.

"I must compliment you on your excellent choice of speakeasy," Marston said, after ordering a pair of martinis.

"Well, I'm afraid that unlike many of my colleagues, I prefer a little less pandemonium after a performance." Inside, Ivy suddenly quailed. But then, she pulled herself together, remembering that Marston would misread her intentions no matter what ambiance she had chosen.

"I don't doubt it," Marston said. "You were so life-like. Are you a student of Master Boleslavsky?"

Ivy quirked an eyebrow. "I haven't had the opportunity yet, although I'm very intrigued by his process. How is it that you are familiar with him?"

"I quite like the American Laboratory Theatre. Some very lovely ladies working there." Marston ignored the waiter setting the two martinis on the table.

"I see," Ivy smiled and took a sip of her drink.

So, Marston only wanted to impress her with how much he supposedly knew. As it happened, Ivy did want to take acting lessons with the much-lauded Richard Boleslavsky and Madame Ouspenskaya and learn about the methods created by Master Stanislavski. However, Marston had obviously charmed more than one young actress into his bed with his "inside knowledge" of the theater world.

"If you want to take lessons there, I could help you

get in," Marston said. "I live to further the arts, you know."

"I don't doubt it," Ivy said, wondering what she would have to do to further her art, had she been interested. "However, my schedule is quite over-booked for the time being. How did you come to be so interested in the theater?"

Marston recognized his cue and rambled on about coming to the theater as a boy and being entranced and all the usual things one said.

"You know how it is among my set," he said, finally.

"Yes, I do, actually," Ivy said. "My dearest friend is Mrs. Honoria Wentworth, and I've certainly seen quite a bit."

Marston chuckled indulgently. "Oh, dear little Honoria. What a radical she turned out to be. Quite gave old Fred fits. If the bastard hadn't been gunned down, I'm sure she would have driven him to apoplexy."

"That was some unfortunate business." If Ivy hadn't already had a good idea of Marston's opinion of her, swearing in front of her would have made it clear. No gentleman swore in front of a lady.

"For me it was." Marston gulped his martini and waved at the waiter. "The son of a bitch owed me a small fortune. He'd pay me off just often enough that I'd still play cards with him."

"If he was so unreliable in his debts, I'm surprised that you kept your acquaintance with him."

"Well, you know how it is. It's expected. He wasn't all that bad a fellow. Very full of himself, but I'm told I can be, too." Marston laughed heartily. "He even promised me, the week before he died, that he'd remember me in his will."

"And did he?" Ivy asked.

Marston glowered, the rage suddenly turning his face red. "He did not. Welshed in death, too. And I can't send a thug to break his knees, either."

The waiter appeared with two more martinis. Ivy realized she hadn't finished her first one. Marston gulped one and waved at the waiter again, all the while talking about something else unrelated to Mr. Little, his rage having disappeared as quickly as it had appeared.

Ivy looked at her watch. "Oh, dear. Is that the time?" She stood and Marston staggered to his feet. "Well, it was lovely chatting with you, Mr. Marston, but I'm afraid I have an early appointment tomorrow."

Ivy swept from the room. Fortunately, she was known at the speak, and the hat check girl had her mink ready when Ivy entered the foyer. Ivy slipped her a dollar and hurried to her car.

She arrived home to the apartment she shared with Honoria to find everything in a tumult. Every picture on the foyer wall was askew. Virginia, the lady's maid, was wearing her wrapper, nightgown and hair net, as she paced the foyer frantically, her perpetually sour face even more worried than usual.

"Good heavens! What's happened?" Ivy asked the servant.

"Burglars, Miss." Virginia cried. "We could have been murdered in our beds!"

"I can see that. But how would a burglar have gotten in here without waking anybody? Where's Mrs. Wentworth?" Worried, Ivy took off her coat and hat.

"Downstairs, Miss." Virginia continued pacing and missed Ivy handing her the coat and hat. "It's even worse down there."

"Where was she when this happened?" Ivy asked, ignoring the fallen coat.

"Here, asleep," Virginia said. "We could have been murdered."

"But you weren't." Grimly, Ivy hurried to the servants' stair, which was the quickest way between the apartments, and scrambled down.

Freddie was furious. Not a room in the apartment was untouched. Paintings were tossed from the walls, drawers emptied, and every book in the study was on the floor. A lovely Impressionist landscape lay on the foyer with a huge tear in the canvas. The worst was the horrible realization that all had happened while they'd been asleep.

At least Kathy and Gam were all right, as was Honoria. The three stood in the foyer looking frightened as they watched him smoke too fast. Ivy hurried in from the servants' stairs and stood agape at all the damage.

"The police should be here any moment," Roberts announced. He, the cook, and the young girl who helped with the cleaning, all stood nearby in their nightclothes.

Freddie was too upset to say anything. He stubbed out his cigarette into shreds and lit yet another.

"I saw the damage upstairs," Ivy whispered to Honoria. "Are you all right?"

"Well enough," Honoria said, shuddering a little. "But we're all at sixes and sevens here."

Freddie strode to the phone on the hall table and dialed. The phone seemed to ring endlessly, but eventually, it was picked up.

"Little residence," announced Briggeman's voice.

"Briggeman, Mr. Little here. I need you to send Mr. Van Schuyler over here right away." Freddie noticed Kathy shaking her head.

"Mr. Van Schuyler, sir?" Briggeman asked.

"Yes. Van Schuyler. I need to speak to him now," Freddie demanded.

"I trust you do not believe he has violated your trust, sir?" Briggeman's voice took on an odd quaver. "He has been here all night."

"No, no. But I need his expertise and I need it now."

"Yes, sir."

As soon as Freddie had put the phone down, it rang again, with the front desk announcing the arrival of a Detective Crowley.

The detective's face looked even more hang-dog than usual. He shook his head as he looked at the damage.

"What happened?" he asked.

"What do you mean 'what happened?'" Freddie snapped. "Burglars broke into the apartment looking for something! That's what happened! One was going through our bedroom when my wife awoke and scared him off."

"He got into the back bedrooms?"

"Everywhere," Freddie said. "I don't know how they did all this without waking us. There must have been a whole crew of them. And upstairs in my sister's apartment, too."

"That one didn't get very far, there, though," Honoria said. "Just the front rooms."

"Roberts tried to stop him," Kathy said. "The rest ran down the servants' steps."

Crowley turned on Roberts. "What did you see?"

"Not much, sir. It happened quite quickly. The men were wearing black suits, gloves, hats. And they wore masks."

"Gloves. Terrific. No chance of fingerprints." Crowley swore under his breath, then glared at Freddie. "Looks like someone wants something from you."

Freddie glared back. "We have already come to that conclusion, Detective. The question remains what and why."

He snubbed out another cigarette.

Crowley looked around the foyer and his eyes settled on Ivy.

"You're still dressed," he said.

"Yes, Detective," Ivy replied, holding her ground. "I am an actress. The play I am in ended somewhat after eleven. It was probably around midnight when I finished cleaning up and dressing to go home. I did, however, meet with a gentleman claiming to be a fan. One must, you know, as they are the ones who buy the tickets. However, I was able to leave fairly quickly and arrived just a short bit ago to find all the to-do going on here. Being concerned for Honoria, who so very kindly allows me to share her apartment, I came downstairs immediately."

"An actress?" Crowley said.

Honoria glared. "Detective, it is not your place to question whom I chose to make part of my life. Ivy has been my bosom friend since I was a young girl, long before she took to the stage. If I choose to share my apartment with her, it is none of your business. Are we clear?"

Freddie was a little puzzled by the vehemence of Honoria's response, but whatever the cause, the detective clearly needed to understand what his position was.

Crowley turned to Freddie. "All right. What time does everyone go to bed around here? That is my business to know so that I can find out who did this to you."

"My young brother-in-law retired at 9 p.m." Freddie nodded at Gam. "I presume he was asleep by the time my wife retired at ten-thirty."

"Not quite," Kathy said.

Gam had the grace to look a little abashed.

"I also checked on him right before I went to bed near midnight," Freddie continued. "And he was asleep then. The staff goes to bed around ten, as well."

"We do, sir," Roberts said.

Crowley looked at Honoria.

"I went to bed around midnight," Honoria said. "I sometimes wait up for Ivy, but I was reading in bed and fell asleep."

There was a buzzing sound from the servants' quarters. Roberts looked at Freddie, who nodded affirmation, and Roberts slipped back to the servants' quarters. Crowley wandered into the study and stood looking at the mess, shaking his head.

"Nothing," he grumbled. "Absolutely nothing."

He wandered into the servants' quarters and then came back, his hat in one hand and tugging at his hair with the other.

"So," Crowley said, finally. "Anyone have any guesses as to what this person wants or who it might be?"

"I do!" Gam piped up.

"Gam, hush," Kathy said.

"No. Let the kid speak." Crowley tried to smile at the boy. "Who do you think it was?"

"That valet guy from Mr. Little's mansion," Gam said. "He came over with Mrs. Little the day after the shooting and when she went home, he stayed. He kept snooping around the whole time he was here."

"And how long was that?" Crowley asked.

"Just under a week," said Roberts, who had silently returned to the foyer. "The senior Mrs. Little had given him leave to remain here after her husband's death, as there was no one for Mr. Taylor to serve at the mansion. However, as there was no one to serve here, either, he was dismissed. In addition, he, ahem, proved less than honest."

Crowley snorted. "You don't say."

"What do you mean, Detective?" Freddie asked, suddenly curious.

"He kept swearing he hadn't seen anybody go upstairs the night your father was murdered," Crowley said. "But we know at least four people did."

"Watson and O'Hare," said Kathy.

"Them," Crowley said. "Plus the senior Mrs. Little and Mrs. Everett Lewton. And the killer, of course. The problem is, the only clear footprints we found on the terrace were nowhere near the edge where the killer was. And besides that one that matched Watson's boots, there were a couple that came from a lady's shoe. But those were most likely from the senior Mrs. Little or Mrs. Lewton."

"Lenore?" Honoria asked. "She was up there?"

"Yeah," said Crowley. "Why do you ask?"

Honoria flushed. "No reason, really. It's just that she and Mr. Lewton both left their wraps at the party. We believe the killer might be among those people because presumably they left their wraps behind rather than speak with the police."

Crowley shrugged. "Interesting timing, but we surmised that she was up there answering the call of nature, if you will."

"That's odd," Honoria said. "I didn't think she and mother were on the sort of terms where she'd go to the private part of the house without asking. And why would she go out on the terrace?"

"Old ladies," Crowley said with a shrug. "What can I say?" He yawned loudly all of a sudden. "Well, excuse me. I suppose there's nothing more I can do here tonight." He put his hat back on. "Call me if you think of anything else. In the meantime, I'm going to have the boys keep an eye on this building."

"Thank you, Detective," Freddie said, holding onto his temper.

The detective left and Freddie looked at Roberts. The valet nodded and disappeared into the servants' quarters, reappearing a second later with Van Schuyler in tow. The man's small, sharp nose was twitching as he looked around the apartment.

"Yeah," he said softly. "Dis here was a professional job."

"Which is why I asked you here," Freddie said. He held up a hand. "Not to accuse you. Briggeman was quick to point out that you'd been at home all evening."

"Dat I was, sir."

"However, you might be able to tell us something about who did this."

"Dey was pretty ballsy." Van Schuyler started as he saw the women. "Begging your pardon, ladies." He looked around again. "I, personally, would not have gone into an apartment like dis with people in it." He saw the painting and sighed. "I would also venture to argue dat dey did not find what dey was looking for. Somebody got angry."

"I know it seems likely there were more," Kathy said. "But I only saw the one man."

Freddie and the others followed Van Schuyler into the study.

"Dere was a whole team of 'em," Van Schuyler said. "Had to be. Look at all dese books. Takes hours to get that many off the shelves nice and quiet-like. You come into a place, 'specially with people in it, you don't know how much time you got. And with people asleep right on the same floor, you gotta be nice and quiet-like. So I figure dey brought three or four guys. I saw da door downstairs dat goes up to da servants' quarters. Someone picked da lock. Did a nice job, too. Not too many scratches. Yep. Dese guys were no slouches. Knew dere business. Dey's da kind you hire when you want someting specific."

"Do you have any ideas who they could have been?" Freddie asked.

Van Schuyler winced. "Could be. I don't wanna be no snitch, you understand. 'Course, da guys I knew coulda done dis, dey's in Sing Sing, I tink. It's been a while since I been in da game."

"And what are the odds they could tell us who hired them?" Kathy asked.

"Pretty lousy, if you ask me," Van Schuyler said. "And even if dey did know, dey wouldn't say nothin'. It ain't good for business if it gets around dat you snitch to da police or anyone else."

Kathy looked at Freddie. "And what we need to know is who paid these people to try and rob us."

Freddie went over to the sideboard and got a glass and decanter. "Does anyone else want a drink?"

"Always," said Ivy with a smirk.

"You've more than earned this one," Kathy said.

Freddie felt the pleasant warmth of the liquor fill his mouth, then swallowed.

"Well, I don't think it would be wise for Mr. Van Schuyler to compromise himself with little chance of a payoff," Freddie said, finally, as he handed Ivy a glass of whiskey.

"Dere is one possibility," Van Schuyler said.

"See, da ting is, it ain't cheap to hire four guys of dis professional capability. And most of de men on de street, so to speak, know who dose fellows are. I gotta figure someone is feelin' more dan a little flush and someone is bound to remark upon it. I could keep my ears open amongst my former associates and see what I pick up."

"But wouldn't that put you in danger?" Freddie asked. "Or my mother?"

Van Schuyler frowned and looked around at the mess. "Nah. Besides, like I told you before, I would cut off my right arm rather dan let someting happen to your ma. And if it's getting close to you, it's getting close to her. Guys who pull jobs like dese, dey don't play nice, if you get my meaning. If finding out who was behind dis job will keep you and Mrs. Little safe, and I tink it might, den I will find out."

"Mr. Van Schuyler," Honoria said, coming over and placing her hands on his shoulders. "We can't thank you enough. But please, please be careful."

"I will, Mrs. Wentworth." Van Schuyler suddenly smiled. "Now, what do you suppose dese fellows were looking for? Someting you might expect to find in a safe. Which, by the way, I do not see one of."

Freddie forced himself to keep looking at Kathy, at Gam, at Honoria and Ivy, anywhere but the shelf next to the fireplace.

"I have one," he finally conceded. "But I do not keep much in it."

"The ruby necklace," Kathy said suddenly. "What was it your uncle said? Somebody wants the ruby."

"That is at the bank," Freddie said.

"But who would know that?" Kathy pressed. "That is certainly not something you are prone to bruiting about."

"Good Heavens, no."

"The ruby necklace?" Honoria asked, looking rather frightened. "The one you wore that night, Kathy?"

"Are there any other rubies?" Kathy asked.

"Well, Mother does have a rather nice ruby parure," Honoria said, her mind clearly on something else.

"But Aunt said ruby, in the singular," Freddie said. "That would seem to eliminate a parure, by definition."

"Oh, I get it." Van Schuyler said. "By definition. A parure being a set of matching jewels, rather than a single piece of jewelry. Dat's clever."

Freddie shot him a warning glare and the man, wisely, became quiet.

"Never mind all that," Honoria said in an annoyed tone. "It's a long story, but Aunt Miranda came to me asking about how to get back something that her mother had promised her, but that Grandfather gave to Father, instead. I told her to simply ask the person who had it. And that she should have what is rightfully hers."

"Could Aunt Miranda believe that the ruby should be hers?" Freddie asked.

"I wouldn't have thought so," Honoria said.

"I would," said Kathy, suddenly. "She told me at the party that it was good to see the old family ruby again, but I got the impression that she did not mean it was good to see me wearing it."

Freddie felt his gut tighten. Aunt Miranda's behavior was not surprising, but Freddie could not help feeling guilty at having exposed Kathy to it.

Gam suddenly let out a huge yawn.

"Oh, good heavens!" Kathy gasped. "Look at us, yammering away, and we all need to go to bed and get some sleep."

"Yes. That would be an excellent idea," Freddie said.

CHAPTER ELEVEN

The next morning, Kathy woke up quite late and Freddie even later. Freddie ate his breakfast alone as Kathy remained occupied by telephone calls and dictating letters to Elsie Quinn. Then Ivy came downstairs with what she'd learned from Donald Marston.

"Did he say why Father wouldn't pay?" Freddie asked Ivy.

"Oh, dear. I didn't think to ask," Ivy groaned. "I should have. I did ask Mr. Marston why he remained on friendly terms with your father when he had such a bad habit of welshing, and Mr. Marston merely said that it was expected and that your father wasn't such a bad fellow otherwise. But Mr. Marston was very angry about the money."

Kathy came out of the study, her purse in hand. "Freddie, it's time to go."

Freddie thanked Ivy, got Kathy's coat from Roberts and helped her on with it, then got his own coat and hat from the valet.

Given the success of Signature Books' first release, Kathy had set up a meeting and early luncheon at the Plaza Hotel for the author partners that morning. The mood was celebratory and it was quickly agreed that what was most needed was an actual office, with secretaries and even perhaps another editor or two, as the fledgling company was inundated by manuscripts to be read from would-be authors, each hoping to be the next Ernest Hemmingway or F. Scott Fitzgerald.

Lowell Winters insisted that Freddie and Kathy start looking for office space that very afternoon and volunteered to go with them.

"I do have a novel that I'm trying to finish," Freddie complained as the taxi took them down 5th Avenue.

"Just a couple prospective properties," Lowell promised. "Besides, I have some information for you."

"About what?" Freddie asked.

"About your father's murder," Lowell said. "I wasn't going to say anything at first. After all, the police had arrested the presumably guilty parties. But since it appears they weren't guilty, you might as well know. I ran across a certain gentleman late last week who had some interesting things to say about your father. Turns out, Fred Little was not a popular fellow in various gambling halls in the city."

"Why?" asked Kathy.

"I can't imagine he had that much trouble covering his debts," Freddie added.

"That wasn't the problem," Lowell said. "He, apparently, was something of a sore loser. If he lost a bet, he would accuse the establishment of cheating him. Most of the establishments simply ignored him, partly because he didn't spend much time in them."

"Hm," said Kathy. "That also fits with something Ivy told Freddie this morning before we left. Fortunately, she'd gotten up early enough to tell us. Father Little had welshed on several gambling debts to Donald Marston."

"Marston?" Lowell sat back and chortled. "That little fop? Who wouldn't?"

"Ivy said he seemed very angry about it," Kathy said.

Freddie frowned. "Quite frankly, I can see him being quite angry about a great many things. He is not treated well by the others in our set. His brothers have the business, although he has a role in it. His wife seems to have him completely under her thumb."

"I wonder if he and his wife left their wraps at the party," Kathy said.

Freddie shrugged.

Fortunately, the rest of the afternoon passed

pleasantly, although neither of the proposed offices was suitable. Freddie did put his foot down as they left the second office and insisted that he and Kathy had to get back to their apartment.

"It's ridiculous," Freddie sighed as they rode the elevator up to their home. "I haven't been able to write a word since Father died. I was so looking forward to spending some time working on the novel."

They left the elevator and entered the foyer.

"I'm getting very close to finally finishing it," he continued and hurried into the study.

Roberts was leaving with the coats and hats and Kathy was checking her diary to see which call she needed to make next when Gam burst into the foyer from the servants' quarters, where the building stairway was.

"I'm here!" the boy yelled, gasping heavily. "I got kidnapped! They grabbed me and tied me up, but I got away."

Kathy was about to reprimand him for making a very poor joke when she saw the look on Gam's face.

The telephone rang and Roberts quickly appeared and picked it up.

"Gam, are you serious?" Kathy asked, still in shock, as Freddie returned to the foyer.

"This is he," Freddie told the person on the other end of the line. "Oh… Indeed…" He looked over at Gam with a puzzled frown.

"Yeah!" Gam hissed at Kathy, struggling not to disturb Freddie's call. "I got myself untied and everything."

"That is all very well," Freddie told his caller. "But I do not have a son and I am looking at the only boy in residence here right now… Yes, well, I think your sense of humor is in exceedingly bad taste. Good day."

Freddie hung the phone up and looked at Kathy.

"What was it?" she asked.

"A ransom demand for Gamaliel," Freddie said.

"I know!" Gam said, bouncing up and down. "I was

kidnapped! They threatened to kill me, but I got away."

"Gam!" Kathy stumbled into the living room and sank into the nearest chair.

Gam scurried to her side. "I'm all right, Kathy. They didn't hurt me."

"I can see that," Kathy said, her heart still beating hard. She grabbed her brother and held him. "But that they thought they could." She shuddered, then looked over at Freddie, who was smoking very fast again. "What did they want?"

"The ruby," Freddie said. "I'd like to know where Mrs. Davies is."

"I don't know." Gam suddenly looked anxious. "We were walking in the park when the men grabbed me. It wasn't really her fault. I heard one of the men yell that she'd bit him, then clobbered him with her purse."

A couple minutes later, the downstairs desk called to let two police officers upstairs.

The harness bulls arrived a minute later and Roberts ushered them into the living room. They seemed nervous.

"I'm O'Reilly," the one said. "We got a complaint that a young man at this address has been kidnapped."

"I was!" said Gam. "They tied me up and put a gag on me. But I wriggled my hands loose and got my pocket knife out and cut the rope. I ran all the way back here."

"What?" O'Reilly asked. Both the bulls looked relieved.

"His tutor appears to be missing, however," Freddie said.

"No, she's in the hospital," O'Reilly said. "They found her in the park, knocked out cold. She was pretty worried about the lad, but they wouldn't let her call us until they were sure she would be okay."

"We just got a ransom demand a few minutes ago," said Freddie. "It seemed like a particularly mean joke until Gam told us about the kidnapping and that he was okay."

"We'd better call Uncle Dan," Kathy said as the phone in the hall rang again.

Roberts appeared in the living room doorway. "Sergeant Callaghan is on his way up."

Dan stormed into the apartment a minute later. Kathy was glad she wasn't the two young police officers. Even though she couldn't see what the officers had done wrong, Daniel still gave them a tongue lashing for the books before sending them back to their beat. The older man's eyes were still blazing when he turned on Freddie and Kathy, but they softened when they saw Gam.

"So, I hear you escaped," Dan said at last with surprising gentleness.

"I did, Uncle Dan," Gam said. "I held my hands like they say to in the adventure books, you know, side by side instead of my wrists flat against each other. Then I got my pocket knife from my sleeve and cut the ropes from my feet. And then I yelled for the one guy and when he came in, I clobbered him over the head with the chair."

Kathy looked at him. "You didn't say anything about that last bit."

Gam looked a little abashed. "Okay. I snuck up on him. But I did hit him. He was blocking the door and I had to get out of there."

Dan went on to question Gam about everything that had happened, but there wasn't much to be learned. Sadly, Gam didn't know the city well and by the time he'd left the tenement where he'd been held, he'd been too afraid to do anything more than run. The only reason he hadn't gotten lost was that he knew Freddie's address and had seen the street numbers increasing as he ran across them.

"Well, you're not only a brave lad, you're a smart one, too," Dan said finally.

Kathy hugged her little brother. "I'm so proud of you, Gam. Thank God you weren't hurt."

The next order of business was to visit Mrs. Davies

in the hospital. Kathy made sure the tutor had a large vase of flowers. Mrs. Davies, lying in a white gown with a bandage wound about her head, smiled weakly when she saw the flowers.

"I don't deserve them," she sniffed. "They got away with him."

"It's all right, Mrs. Davies," Gam said. "I heard one of them yell that you'd bitten him and that you'd hit him with your purse. They were awful big, too."

"Awfully big," Mrs. Davies said. "And you were very brave to fight." She blinked back tears. "It was a most terrifying experience. And yet, all's well that ends well."

"I concur," Gam said, standing up straight and looking at Mrs. Davies.

Mrs. Davies did agree to let Gam have a holiday for the rest of the afternoon but insisted that the next day he finish diagramming a full page of sentences, not to mention work several math problems and draw a map of New York state.

Gloria had a headache. Although it didn't do to say so, she felt certain that this one had Mrs. Thelma Coates written all over it.

"Thelma was always one for theatrics," said Mrs. Wilma Little Smith, echoing Gloria's thoughts. "Briggeman says he'll have your aspirin in a minute."

"Thank you," Gloria sighed.

They were comfortably settled in the upstairs sitting room. Wilma, the youngest of Fred's three older sisters, had the same family height and spare figure. Her hair, however, was brown, with sections of gray at her temples. Gloria and Wilma had become close friends soon after Gloria had made her debut, even though Wilma was seven years older. It was Wilma who had introduced Gloria to Fred.

"I know how Thelma is," Gloria continued. "But I am trying desperately to be charitable. And she has good reason to be distraught."

"She had no reason to imply that you should be mourning her Stephen more than your own dear Fred," Wilma sniffed. "And she is, by no means, the first woman to have lost a husband. Good Heavens, Honoria showed more aplomb when she lost... What was his name again?"

Gloria had to think about it. "Henry, I believe. His family was out of Virginia, or one of the Carolinas. I had thought they had a cotton plantation, but they didn't have any connection to our family at all and have never tried to make any. Anyway, Honoria didn't know poor Henry long enough to have any real attachment. And she was mostly trying to get away from home as it was."

"What a scandal that was," Wilma said with a chuckle. "If you'll excuse me for bringing it up."

"I suppose I should mind, but I couldn't care less at the moment," Gloria said. She paused as Briggeman entered the room, the aspirins and a glass of water on a silver tray. "Thank you, Briggeman. Oh, would you wait a moment?"

"Yes, ma'am."

Gloria swallowed the aspirins with a solid gulp of water, then turned to Wilma.

"Darling, I am utterly done in. Would you mind not dining tonight? We can have something nice on a tray in here and be comfortable for a change."

"How utterly inappropriate!" Wilma tittered. "I love it! In fact, I was going to beg off dinner and have a tray in my room. But your idea sounds much nicer."

"Done. Shall we start with some oysters?"

"Oh, yes."

Gloria turned to Briggeman. "Oysters, please? And some Chablis. Better yet, do we still have a bottle of that lovely Macon Villages?"

"We have a case, ma'am," Briggeman said. "However, you did ask me to remind you that you wanted to save it for your next dinner party."

Gloria sighed. "If only it weren't so hard to lay

hands on it these days. Prohibition is such an utter nuisance. Well, one of the lesser Chablis, then, and we'll wait until it's properly chilled."

"Yes, ma'am."

"That's what I've always loved about visiting you, Gloria," Wilma said as Briggeman left. "You do have an excellent nose for the best in food and wine."

"Thanks to you and my mother," Gloria said, resting her head on the back of the chair. "Mother had developed quite the reputation for the best and was terrified that she wouldn't be able to show her face if everything wasn't absolutely top notch. She always insisted that learning to appreciate the best in food and wine was the best way to be sure that you actually had it. Anyway, what were we talking about? Oh, Honoria's scandal."

"And I do apologize for bringing it up. That must have been deeply embarrassing."

"It was." Gloria shuddered. "It was months before I could face anyone and years before they stopped whispering behind my back."

"You've survived it well. And to think, our mothers were so sure that the least scandal was tantamount to a slow, torturous death." Wilma sniffed. "Then it suddenly dawned on me that was because the only things our mothers did was visit and gossip about each other."

"We do, too," Gloria pointed out.

"Very true. I think that's how I came to that conclusion. I realized that it was all terribly dull and that I really didn't care who was doing what, or even who had taken whom as a lover. And once I realized that, I realized I no longer cared what anyone thought of me." Wilma smiled and sat back on the satin sofa. "It's been an enormous relief."

Gloria thought about it for a moment, then blinked. "It would be."

In the hallway, the front doorbell rang.

"I don't know if I could give up my good name,"

Gloria continued.

"Oh, I would not go that far," Wilma said. "I do prefer discretion."

Briggeman appeared in the sitting room doorway. "Mrs. Wilson is here to see you, ma'am. She says it's urgent."

"Miranda?" Wilma asked. "What could she want?"

"She's your sister," Gloria said. "Oh, go ahead and admit her, Briggeman, but please wait on the oysters until she's gone. And you might want to have an ice bag for my head once she is."

"Certainly, ma'am."

A moment later, Miranda Wilson swept into the sitting room and sat down on the chair across from Gloria without waiting to be asked. She wore a black day suit with a wide-brimmed hat and sat with her spine erect, the high dudgeon wafting off of her in waves.

"I've come to have the ruby necklace returned to me," Miranda announced. "You may not be aware of it, but my mother promised it to me before she died."

"Good heavens, Miranda!" Wilma snorted. "Are you on about that nonsense again? You got Grandmother's diamond collar and bracelet, which were older and finer."

"But Mother promised me the ruby!" Miranda snapped.

"No, she didn't," Wilma said. "I know that because Thelma insists that Mother promised it to her. And it wasn't Mother's to give, anyway. It was Father's, from his father, and he gave it to Fred."

"Fred got everything." Miranda sniffed.

"He most certainly did not," Wilma said. "Thelma got the emerald parure, you got the diamonds. I was left with the sapphire tiara."

"And earrings," Miranda said. She turned on Gloria. "Gloria, darling, that necklace should have come to me. Now, I would appreciate it if you'd give it to me."

“I don’t have it,” Gloria said. “Father Little gave it to Freddie before he died. How he got it back from Fred, I do not know. But that’s how Kathy came to be wearing it, which she fully deserved to.”

“I concur,” said Wilma. “Honestly, Miranda, you have plenty of jewels, no less spectacular than the ruby.”

“Mother promised it!” Miranda wailed. “I deserve it.”

“Not acting like that, you don’t,” Wilma muttered.

“Now, now, Miranda,” Gloria said quickly. “You know I wouldn’t mind giving it to you. But I simply do not have it. You’ll have to talk to Freddie about it.”

“Freddie?” Miranda said. “Oh, good Lord, he’s as stubborn as Father. It’s just not fair.” She sniffed and stood up. “I can see that I’m not going to get any help from you. Good day!”

As she swept from the room, Wilma chuckled.

“Poor Miranda,” she said. “How’s your head, Gloria?”

Gloria sighed. “Not so bad. I think the aspirins are starting to help.” She frowned, then dismissed the thought. “Which means it’s time for oysters and Chablis.”

Honoria and Ivy looked at the crowd of brownstones lining 34th Street, just east of Lexington.

“Which one is it?” Ivy asked. She was wearing a burnt orange suit with a tan cloche and dark brown kid gloves.

Honoria’s suit jacket was green over a plaid pleated skirt that fell to just below her knees. Her cloche was a matching plaid, and her gloves, shoes, and purse matched her jacket. She pointed.

“That one,” she said. “At least, that’s the address Mr. Taylor gave to the agency when he signed on. He must have just moved there. I hope he’ll talk to me.”

“He’ll talk to me,” Ivy said with an impish grin, as they mounted the stoop.

"Maybe I'll wait in the hall," Honoria said.

"No. Come on in. It will be harder for him to squirm out of something with the two of us there," Ivy said.

They found the apartment on the third floor. Honoria stepped up to the door and knocked.

Samuel Taylor, the former valet, opened the door, saw who was there and would have shut the door, except that Ivy had already shouldered her way inside.

"What are you two doing here?" Taylor demanded.

"Getting the truth from you," Honoria said, folding her arms across her chest. "You were the only person I talked to about contesting Father's will. I'd like to know how my Uncle Stephen found out about it. I'd also like to know why you lied to the police about who was upstairs the night my father was killed."

"I— I— I was protecting the family," Taylor said, backing up further into the tiny apartment.

There seemed to be little more than the one room. Honoria could see a small icebox under a short counter at the back. A hot plate sat on above the ice box, plugged into the wall next to it. A chair and lampstand were precisely placed in the mostly empty space in front of a huge cabinet backed up against the wall. A radiophone cabinet stood under a window with several magazines strewn across the top.

"By lying to the police when my mother was in her bedroom for perfectly circumspect reasons?" Honoria asked.

"We didn't know that at the time," Taylor said.

"Oh, for Heaven's sake, Mr. Taylor!" Honoria snapped. "You've been with the family for at least two years. You should have been able to figure it out. Instead, you make my mother look guilty by lying."

"Well, she wasn't the only one up there, and I did not think it proper to mention the second lady."

"You mean Mrs. Lewton, who was also using the washroom, I understand."

"I seriously doubt that, Mrs. Wentworth," Taylor smirked. "She was in your father's bedroom. You can see why I would not want to divulge that to the police or to your mother.”

Honoria pressed her lips together. She had known about her father’s dalliances more in theory than anything else, assuming that he, like most men she knew, kept mistresses and had affairs. It was a bit of a jolt to be confronted with evidence of the reality.

“That still does not answer how my uncle knew about something that I had told only to you,” Honoria said. “Kindly explain that.”

“I was looking out for the family,” Taylor said, pulling himself up straight. “Mr. Coates made it quite clear he is only interested in the family’s well-being, and that anything I told him was in complete confidence.”

“You were spying for him!” Honoria said. “How dare you?”

“It wasn’t spying,” Taylor said.

Ivy chuckled. “It certainly sounds like spying to me.”

“Especially when you lied trying to get me to keep you on as Freddie’s valet,” Honoria added. “How much was Uncle Stephen paying you?”

“Not enough,” Taylor grumbled.

“And what did you tell him besides me fighting my father’s will?”

“Nothing much to tell, I’m afraid.” Taylor snorted. “Nor was there much opportunity to hear anything except business and publishing. If you want to tick me off for spying, you should also look at that young scamp your sister-in-law has taken in. Talk about listening at keyholes.”

“Oh, we know,” said Ivy with another laugh. “The important difference is that he is not selling what he hears to other members of the family. You did.”

“As I said, Mr. Taylor, if any harm comes to anyone in my family as a result, I will hold you personally responsible,” Honoria said. “And someone did break into my and my brother’s apartment last night. You’d best expect a visit from the police.”

"I didn't do it," Taylor snarled. "I had nothing to do with it. I told you, I was only looking out for the family's best interests when I talked to Mr. Coates. I haven't talked to anyone else. I haven't even said anything about the gun."

"What gun?" Honoria demanded.

Taylor sneered. "I thought that might catch your attention. Shortly after the shooting, I saw your father's favorite gun on the bed. It wasn't on the bed earlier when I saw Mrs. Lewton. But there it was. You can imagine the first thing the police would have thought, so to protect your mother, I hid the gun away in the butler's pantry, then put it in its proper place the first thing the next morning."

Honoria caught Ivy's warning glance and held her tongue

"That only implicates you further, Mr. Taylor," Ivy said.

"I guess we'll just have to see what the police find when they do their search here," said Honoria, sweeping her gaze over the room. "Doesn't look like there's much room to hide something, but you never know."

She glanced at Ivy, the two turned and left the apartment.

"Are you all right?" Ivy asked as they got onto the sidewalk.

"A little shaken is all," Honoria replied. She looked back at the apartment. "Funny thing is, I believed him when he said he only talked to Uncle Stephen, and about the gun."

Ivy hailed a taxi. "I have to agree with you. But that doesn't help much, does it?"

"Even him having hidden the gun," Honoria said with a sigh, as the two got into the taxi. "It certainly makes it likely that the killer used Father's gun to kill him and Uncle Stephen, but Taylor seeing it on the bed doesn't tell us much about who the killer was. It might help if we could figure out why Uncle Stephen wanted to know what was going on at the apartment." Honoria shook her head. "Maybe we'll get an idea when we have our meeting tomorrow afternoon."

The meeting was held that Saturday at Freddie's apartment. Gloria had left Aunt Wilma to console Aunt Thelma and arrived early for luncheon with Freddie, Kathy, Gam, Honoria and Ivy. Lowell showed up at the same time and got the desired invitation. Gam got to tell Gloria and Lowell about his kidnapping, although the tale had grown somewhat in the telling. Nonetheless, Gloria and Lowell proved to be a most appreciative audience, with Gloria gasping in all the right places and Lowell chortling in approval.

But then Gam was sent back to the schoolroom to work on his grammar and spelling. Honoria shared what Mr. Taylor had told her and Ivy the day before, nicely omitting what the valet had said about Mrs. Lewton being in her father's bedroom, with its nasty implication. It was generally agreed that finding the gun in the bedroom did not offer much illumination as to who had used it for the murder.

"Unless Mr. Taylor was the one who killed Father and Uncle Stephen," Freddie said. "He does seem to have the most motive."

"Why would he have wanted to kill your uncle?" Lowell asked.

"Maybe Uncle Stephen tried to renege on paying him," Honoria said. "And he might see Freddie not taking him on as sufficient injury, especially if he's doing this because he's unbalanced."

"But he doesn't seem to have any interest in the ruby," Gloria said. "If we are to believe that Thelma reported Stephen's words accurately, that is what is driving the murders."

"I'm wondering if we aren't dealing with two different criminals," Kathy said. "Consider, there are two different types of crime. One is the direct murder of Father Little, Uncle Stephen and the attempted murder of Freddie. All of them shootings and from the same gun. The others are a burglary and a kidnapping both perpetrated by presumably hired criminals. There doesn't seem to be any benefit to the murders, especially if you include the attempt on Freddie, so it seems likely that spite is behind those. Whereas, the burglary and the kidnapping were direct attempts to get the ruby necklace."

Gloria suddenly gasped. "There was a burglary at my home, as well."

"What?" gasped Freddie, his face growing even more worried.

"It happened the night we were all at the hunting lodge," Gloria said. "I was aghast, at first, but didn't think much about it afterward. After all, Dimbly, the footman, frightened the burglars off before they could take anything. But now that I think about it, Briggeman said that Dimbly had overheard them talking about a ruby."

"Well, who do we know that wants the ruby?" Freddie asked.

"Aunt Miranda," said Honoria, sitting up suddenly. "The day of the burglary, I, uh, had a chance to speak with her. She mentioned something that she thought should have been hers and wanted it back."

"Oh, she wants the ruby," Gloria said. "She demanded it from me the day before yesterday. But would she know how to go about hiring criminals? I certainly wouldn't and I know a former criminal."

"But Aunt Thelma wants it, too," said Freddie. "And it's just as unlikely that she would know how to hire criminals, as well."

"I wonder if Mrs. Lewton would know how," Kathy said, thoughtfully. "She was certainly interested in the necklace the night of the party. And that banker... Miles Johnson. He told me that Father Little had offered to sell it to him."

"And he would not only know how to hire thugs," Lowell said. "He has the money to do it."

Gloria cleared her throat and shook her head at

the vulgarity of mentioning someone's money.

"I wonder if Father offered to sell the ruby to anybody else," Freddie said thoughtfully.

"Well, then, I guess that is our next line of inquiry," Gloria said.

It was happening again and Kathy was powerless to stop it. The ball was in full swing, she could hear the band playing. But she was trapped in another room, a room filled with guns and mounted animal heads on the walls. A madwoman had a pistol trained on Freddie. She turned and there was Kathy's father-in-law, in white tie and tails. The woman saw him, too, and screamed. Bright red blotches opened up on Father Little's white shirt and vest.

"You could have stopped this," he told Kathy and fell.

Kathy tried to run and couldn't. The madwoman aimed her gun at her and Kathy woke with a start. The darkened room did little to soothe her. Freddie lay on his side, snoring gently. Out in the hallway, the grandfather clock chimed three times. Kathy lay back but soon realized that she was not going to get back to sleep.

Sliding out of the bed, she got her wrapper and slippers on and slid out of the room and went to the kitchen. This wasn't the first night she'd taken refuge there. She knew where the pans and cups and milk were kept. She even knew where the can of cocoa was so that she could add it to her milk. But as she put the pan on the stove and poured the milk, she heard the door open behind her.

She jumped and turned. Gam was standing in the doorway, in robe and pajamas, blinking curiously.

"Gam! You scared me." Kathy put the milk on the work table. "What are you doing up?"

He shrugged. "Couldn't sleep. I had a bad dream."

"Oh, dear. About being kidnapped?"

"Maybe." Gam frowned. "'Bout stuff that happened

in Kansas."

"Come have some warm milk," Kathy said, picking up the milk bottle. "I'm putting some cocoa in it."

"Why are you up?" Gam asked, sliding into a wooden chair at the table.

"Bad dream," Kathy said. "About the shooting. You dreaming about what Bill Javits did to you?"

"You knew about that?" Gam looked up at her.

Kathy sighed. "Freddie had to tell me. It's why he wanted to take you in with us."

"I'm glad I'm not in Kansas, but I do miss Ma and Pa."

"I do, too, sometimes."

"You know, it's queer," Gam said as Kathy poured the milk and cocoa into a couple coffee cups. "I hated Kansas. It weren't just Bill, either. Folks just didn't care about anything interesting. I know Joshua and Gideon love farming, but I don't see how. It's the most boring, miserable, hard work in the world."

"Well, our brothers simply took after Pa, I guess," Kathy said, as she sat down across from Gam. "It happens that way in families. You, me and Abraham, we're more city folk. Joshua, Gideon and Theresa, they're more farm folk. Isaac is a bit of a puzzle because he did not do well here in the city, but he's not the farming type either."

Kathy smiled as she thought of her siblings. She was the eldest of a brood of seven. Her next oldest brother, Joshua, grew oranges in California. Abraham was getting his law degree at Harvard, where an uncle provided scholarships. Her widowed sister Theresa was taking over the town newspaper, while Gideon and Isaac were still in their teens.

"He likes painting and drawing," Gam said, then shook his head. "I used to think he was the most miserable excuse for a human being there was. He was always teasing me, you know."

"No, I didn't," Kathy said. "Isaac was still a toddler and you were just born when I left for college."

"Did you miss us when you went away?"

"Even Theresa."

"Ain't that the queer part, though." Gam took a long pull on his milk. "You'd think I'd be jumping up and down about not having Isaac teasing me and beating me up. About being someplace where I can learn stuff and look at the stock market. And I am. I really like being here. But there's just something about not being able to see the others that makes me want to all the more. I can't have it, so that's what I want, and I'd do just about anything to have it. That doesn't make sense, does it?"

"It makes perfect sense, Gam. You're just smart enough to parse it out. But I think you know as well as I do, if you'll forgive the cliche, that you can't have your cake and eat it, too. Let's just be grateful Freddie's rich enough that we can go back and visit whenever we want."

"That's right." Gam nodded sagely. "I guess that's why I'm not hankering to go. I just miss them is all."

"I know, Gam. And they miss us, too. Even Theresa and Isaac."

The two looked at each other and burst into laughter. Some minutes later, Gam helped Kathy clean up the pan and the cups and the two went back to bed and fell into dreamless slumber for the rest of the night.

CHAPTER TWELVE

Of all the threats and other problems facing his family at the moment, Freddie had to concede that protecting his mother from a masher was the easiest to deal with. That the masher in question was actually a man of mature years with sufficient social status to be a good match for his mother did not reassure Freddie in the least.

It was Palm Sunday at St. Thomas Episcopal Church. Freddie's mother hung onto his arm as she visited with her fellow parishioners in the vestibule following the services. Freddie was all too conscious of the two large footmen employed as bodyguards in the wake of the shooting and kidnapping attempt. He was grateful for the pouring rain outside which made lingering on the church stairs, out in the open, impossible.

Freddie felt his mother stiffen and when he looked up, he saw a man making the most of his medium height with almost painfully erect posture. His white hair was perfectly trimmed and he wore a monocle over his right eye. His dark suit was cut with exquisite care and he carried himself with the confidence of a man with exacting standards.

"Good day, Mrs. Little, Mr. Little," he said with a smile.

His eyes caught Freddie's for a brief second, then he focused all his attention on Gloria.

"Good day, Mr. Carter," Gloria replied with a hint of an edge in her voice. "Freddie, you know Mr. Terrence Carter, don't you?"

"We've met," Freddie said.

"Indeed," Mr. Carter said almost jovially. He was

far too elegant to be completely jovial. "But it's always a pleasure to make your acquaintance again, Mr. Little."

"Likewise, Mr. Carter."

"Terribly wet day out," Mr. Carter said, glancing at the door. "Still, might I entreat the two of you to join me for tea this afternoon?"

"I'm afraid I can't," Gloria said. "But Freddie might be able to."

Freddie bit back his retort. He'd wanted to get some writing done that afternoon but supposed he could go to tea and return soon enough to get some work done before Gam and Kathy returned from Sunday dinner at their Uncle Mike's.

"If we make it early enough, I think I can oblige," Freddie said, suddenly realizing that he did want to talk to Terrence Carter very much. "Would the Union Club suit, or would you prefer the Plaza?"

Mr. Carter looked a touch nonplussed, then smiled. "Why not say one o'clock and make it a late luncheon? And let's do the Plaza."

"Very good. I'll see you at one at the Plaza."

Mr. Carter excused himself. Just as Freddie was looking to signal the footmen to bring the car, Aunt Thelma suddenly appeared from the church's sanctuary.

"You!" she snapped when she saw Freddie. "Honestly, Freddie, I should almost blame you for what happened to Stephen."

"Thelma, darling, I know you're feeling quite troubled right now, but we are in public," Gloria said.

Thelma lowered her voice but kept her eyes on Freddie. "Everyone says what wonderful detectives you and that woman are. Why couldn't you have found your father's killer before he killed my husband?"

Freddie felt the anger rippling through his body. "I deeply wish we could have, but there's very little to go on. Even yesterday, several of us met and concluded that we hadn't found anything substantive." He debated telling her that up until the previous Monday,

Uncle Stephen was as good a suspect as any.

"You could try harder," Thelma said with a sniff.

"We're looking at those who wanted the family ruby," Gloria said.

Freddie cringed as Thelma drew herself up to her considerable full height and glared.

"That should have been mine. Mother promised."

"Miranda says the same and Wilma says you're both wrong and that it wasn't your mother's to give," Gloria said with a smile.

"The important thing right now, Aunt Thelma, is to protect the ruby from whoever is trying to steal it," Freddie said. "I've seen to it that it's being kept in a very safe place. And until we find out who wants it badly enough to kill for it, we'd best leave it there and worry about to whom it belongs later."

Thelma looked him up and down again. She couldn't quite look down her nose at him, as he was somewhat taller than her. She huffed quietly for a moment, then turned and left the vestibule.

Gloria chuckled. "Freddie, darling, I know it doesn't do to tell you just how proud I am of you, but you were magnificent just now. Quite the diplomat."

"Thank you, Mother." He looked out the door. "I see that Van Schuyler has pulled up. Shall we?"

As they left the building, he quickly put up an umbrella and held it over his mother's head, letting the rain tumble onto his silk top hat.

The rain still hadn't let up by the time he got to the Plaza Hotel tea room. Mr. Carter was already there waiting. Freddie felt slightly abashed that Mr. Carter showed no sign of having been out in the rain, while Freddie's overcoat and hat were quite wet. Freddie checked both his hat and coat and followed Mr. Carter to a table near a window.

It was a most elegant room, with white walls and pilasters decorated with gold leaf. Silver gleamed from the table tops covered in white linen. The two men ordered lunch and Freddie felt thoroughly justified in ordering two martinis. Mr. Carter had ordered the same.

"I'm so very pleased you could join me," Mr. Carter said as soon as the waiter had brought their plates.

"I appreciate the opportunity to speak with you," Freddie said.

"I think the world of your mother," Mr. Carter said.

"If you'll pardon me for being so direct, I must confess that's what I find a little odd. She does not seem to be returning your attentions."

"I haven't had much of a chance to win her over. And I understand that she is still grieving the loss of your father. But I've been quite fond of her for a good many years now. Your parents, my late wife, and I were all great friends. And I like to think we still are."

Freddie shrugged. "Mother says she does consider you a friend, but nothing more."

"I was afraid of that." Mr. Carter looked a little deflated. "Still, it's early in her bereavement. I hope that she wouldn't mind me occasionally calling on her, strictly in friendship, of course."

"I'll discuss it with her," Freddie said. He looked at Mr. Carter. "However, you should know that I have her care completely in my control."

Mr. Carter smiled. "As well you should. Now, we've cleared that up, shall we discuss something more pleasant? Golf? The current season at the Metropolitan Opera?"

Freddie chuckled and found that he and Mr. Carter had a great deal in common, at least as far as the opera was concerned. The afternoon passed pleasantly and it was a good deal later than he'd hoped when he finally arrived back at the apartment. Gam and Kathy had also returned from their Sunday dinner. They all spent the rest of the day comfortably in the study, but Freddie got involved helping Gam with the schoolwork Mrs. Davies had assigned from the hospital and writing was yet again put aside.

The next morning found him at the company headquarters near Wall Street. Freddie looked around the office his father and grandfather had occupied when each was chairman and debated rearranging things to suit himself. Assuming he decided to take the chairmanship. Or rather when he did. There didn't seem to be anybody he could turn it over to.

Freddie glanced at the desk calendar and saw a note to fire Ames written in his father's hand. But before Freddie could ponder why his father would want to remind himself to fire Mr. Ames, the secretary announced through the desk speaker that there was someone to see him.

"And who is it?" Freddie asked, depressing the button on the speaker.

"Oh," said the female voice and the speaker clicked off. A moment later, it clicked on again. "It's your accountant."

"Please send him in," Freddie said.

Mr. Sharp had dark, curly hair, wore glasses and had a rather large nose for his smallish face. Freddie was surprised to see him so soon, and said so as the two settled themselves, Freddie behind the massive oak desk, in the massive wooden chair that both swiveled and rolled, and Mr. Sharp in the nicely carved chair on the other side.

"I'm afraid we're not done, sir," Mr. Sharp said. "But we did find something and thought you'd want to hear about it sooner rather than later."

"I see.'

Mr. Sharp pulled several papers out of a leather portfolio. "It's these invoices, sir. All of them are signed by Mr. Stanford Ames for payments to a company that he appears to own. We thought something was strange when we couldn't find bills of lading for the materials that were apparently purchased. And the address on the invoice was suspect. There's an office building not far from here that offers itself as a mailing address for many less than honest businesses. There are several legitimate businesses there, as well. But when I see some discrepancy like this and that address, I become suspicious. So, I had one of my men investigate the ownership.”

“And found Mr. Ames.” Freddie sighed. “Which means he's embezzling from the company.”

“It would appear so, Mr. Little.”

“Have you any idea how long this has been going on?”

Mr. Sharp shook his head. “Not yet, sir. As I said, we're not finished.”

Freddie looked the invoices over. “These all went to Yonkers.” He looked up. “Well, Mr. Sharp, I thank you. Please continue your work. I fear this is only the first of many irregularities.”

As Mr. Sharp left, the secretary announced through the desk speaker that Mr. Edward Carstairs was on the phone.

Freddie picked up the handset. “Mr. Little here, Mr. Carstairs.”

“They said at your apartment that you were here,” the lawyer said, sounding quite pleased with himself. “I apologize for hunting you down, but I've got some good news for you. The probate will be finished on your grandfather's will as of this Wednesday. You should have your official letter at your home with the morning post. I'd called to see if you'd gotten it.”

“The post hadn't arrived before I left.”

“I know, but your wife said that you do have a letter from the court, so that must be it.”

“It must, indeed. Well. Thank you, Mr. Carstairs. Let's call a board meeting for Thursday, then, and can you see to getting the paperwork and everything in order?”

“I will.” Carstairs paused. “Are you going to accept the chairmanship?”

“I'm afraid I have no other alternative,” Freddie said with a sigh. “At least, for the time being. I'll have to see if any of the cousins show an aptitude. But I've already discovered some irregularities and fear there are quite a few more."

"Oh, dear."

"Yes. I'm afraid I'll be keeping you busy, Mr. Carstairs. Now, if you'll excuse me, I must go fire my vice president of operations. Oh, and find someone to replace him almost immediately."

"Have his immediate subordinate serve as acting vice president until you can find someone you like better," Carstairs suggested.

"An excellent idea, Mr. Carstairs. Thank you. And good day."

Freddie hung up the phone, still feeling restless. He debated calling Kathy to let her know that he'd accepted the inevitable but decided that it would be better to get the worst of it over with. He pushed down the button on the desktop box, then realized he did not know the secretary's name.

He remembered his grandfather's secretary. Mr. Osgood Ahlers, a dour man who seemed to enjoy keeping people away from Freddie's grandfather. The new secretary was a pretty young woman with blond hair and generous curves. Freddie decided he'd better get to know her, so he stepped outside the office.

"I'm sorry," he told the secretary, who was lounging in her chair behind the desk. "I don't believe we've been introduced. I'm Mr. Little."

"I'm Jeannie," she said, shifting herself so that Freddie had the best view of her blouse and what was under it.

"Well, Miss Jeannie—"

She giggled loudly. "No! That's my first name."

"And your last name is..?"

"Smith."

"Very well then, Miss Smith," Freddie said. He looked over the desktop littered with makeup and manicure tools. There was a typewriter on a small table next to the desk, but no sign of any actual work being done. The speaker box was on a corner, with the cord trailing into what was now Freddie's office. "As you may know, I am soon to take over the company. We've just gotten word that it will be official as of Wednesday. In the meantime, I may as well begin working here as of today. Let's see. To begin with, I will need proper stationery reflecting my new title." He paused. "And I would appreciate it if you would keep your desk in an orderly and businesslike manner. If someone wishes to see me, please get his name and the reason for seeing me before you let me know that someone is here, and the same when there is a phone call. Do you understand?"

The girl frowned. "Yes, sir."

"You will see to getting my new stationery, then?"

"Yes, sir."

"Thank you very much. Now, will you have Mr. Ames report to my office, please?"

"Yes, sir."

Freddie retreated into the office, found a pad of paper and a pencil and started making a list of things that needed doing. He debated adding hiring a new secretary but decided to give Miss Smith a chance to improve first. A few minutes later, her voice came through the speaker box.

"Mr. Ames is here, Mr. Little."

"Thank you. Please send him in."

Mr. Ames seemed puzzled by the summons but smiled anyway as Freddie invited him to sit in front of the desk.

"As you know, Mr. Ames, I am in the process of assuming control of the company," Freddie said. "We just received word that the probate on my grandfather's will shall be finished as of Wednesday, and I have decided to officially accept the chairmanship."

"Congratulations, Mr. Little. That's very good news, indeed." Ames smiled insincerely.

"I'm glad you think so," Freddie said. He pushed the invoices he'd been given at Ames. "These are all signed by you, there are no bills of lading to reflect the delivery of the goods in question and, according to my accountant, the company that these invoices are paid to is owned by you. Can you explain this?"

Ames went pale. "Uh, yes. Uh, it's all perfectly common practice as a way of... uh... avoiding taxes."

Freddie's eyebrows rose. "Really? I've never heard of it. I'd be interested to know how the money is returned to the company."

"Oh, that. Well, it's... it's simple." Ames gasped like a fish out of water.

"No, it's not. It's embezzlement." Freddie stood up. "As of right now, you are relieved of your position. You have one hour to clear your office of your personal belongings. Mr. Brennan, in personnel, will see to it that you do not take anything that isn't yours. In fact, wait here a moment."

Freddie had Miss Smith put through a call to Mr. Brennan, then walked Ames to his office.

"You'll be sorry you did this," Ames snarled.

"He has one hour, Mr. Brennan," Freddie told the personnel chief. "And he is not to make any phone calls during that time. We need to find some way to prevent him from emptying his bank accounts so that we might recover some of the money he has stolen."

"Yes, sir."

"And I need his subordinate in my office right away," Freddie said, and then left.

He returned to his office, remembering what Kathy had said about how hard it had been to think of his apartment as hers, as well, when they'd first married and she'd moved there. It was going to take a while before he thought of the office as completely his.

There was a crystal decanter of whiskey on the credenza behind his desk. Freddie got a glass and poured a well-deserved snort, drank it, then poured another to sip. Sighing, he spotted a ledger listing the company's real estate holdings and going through it, he suddenly thought of something.

He had Miss Smith put a call through to Kathy at the office. It took several minutes, and Freddie was about to see what was taking so long when Miss Smith announced that the call was ready.

"I'm just about to leave for an important luncheon, Freddie," Kathy said brusquely.

"I've a great deal of news, but the most important items are that I'm accepting the chairmanship," Freddie said.

"Well, we knew you would."

"And I've found a solution to our office problem."

"What?"

"I own two buildings in Lower Manhattan, and one of them, I believe, has an entire floor vacant. I'll check with my properties manager, but we should be able to move in at any time."

"That is good news. Thank you, darling. That's perfect. Oh, dear. I really must rush. I may have some interesting information regarding your father's murder."

"Oh. Good. Be careful."

"Of course. I'll have my footmen with me. You be careful, also."

"I will."

They made their goodbyes quickly. Freddie took another sip of his whiskey as Miss Smith announced Mr. Brennan.

Kathy hurried from the apartment and into the car that was waiting. She would have preferred taking the subway, but that would have been foolhardy. She didn't like being frightened about leaving her own home, but she would be damned before she would cower.

The tea room on 5th Avenue was elegant enough, with white tablecloths and a mostly standard menu. Mrs. Everett Lewton was waiting near the door when Kathy entered. She was a medium-sized woman, roughly the same age as Kathy's mother-in-law. But where Gloria was rather stout, Mrs. Lewton's curves were more defined and her hair much darker, with no gray.

The two were led to a table near the window and a waiter promptly brought tea and took their orders.

"It's very kind of you to invite me today," Kathy told Mrs. Lewton.

"Well, you are new to our little group," Mrs. Lewton said. "But I do think it's about time we got to know one another. We've been friends with Freddie's family for most of our lives."

"How lovely."

The waiter brought their lunches, a beef stew for Kathy and a bit of roasted chicken for Mrs. Lewton.

"How are you holding up after all the trouble?" Mrs. Lewton asked as she nibbled at the chicken.

"Well enough," Kathy replied. "It's been such a shock, but things are settling down a bit. Freddie, of course, is very focused on taking his grandfather's place."

"That was quite another shock, wasn't it?" Mrs. Lewton said. "You seem to be managing quite well. I assume we can count on you to help with the latest hospital gala?"

"I'll be happy to contribute," Kathy said. "But I'm afraid I really don't have time to do much beyond that."

"Oh. You're busy doing what?"

"The publishing company, of course," Kathy smiled, but she got the feeling that Mrs. Lewton was fishing for something.

"That's… Different." Mrs. Lewton smiled. "I apologize. I had assumed that once you were presented to Society that you would participate fully. After all, you turned out so nicely at the party."

"Thank you, Mrs. Lewton. It was quite an evening."

Mrs. Lewton shuddered. "Well, except for how it ended. My poor husband had been left alone in the game room right before it happened. I'm afraid we'd decided to make an early evening of it."

"I understand you were upstairs," Kathy said.

"Good heavens, why would I go up there?" Mrs. Lewton suddenly seemed very nervous. "You weren't up there, were you?”

“No. I was downstairs the whole time.”

“And looking quite splendid, I must say.” Mrs. Lewton forced a smile. “It must have been quite a treat to wear that wonderful ruby. It’s such a beautiful piece.”

“It is.” Kathy smiled warmly. “And quite a few people seem to be interested in it.”

Mrs. Lewton forced another smile. “As I said, it is particularly lovely. I wouldn’t mind owning it, myself. Fred was going to let my husband buy it, you know.”

“He was?” Kathy was surprised. “But it’s an heirloom. That’s why Freddie wanted me to wear it that night. His grandfather had given it to him.”

“Then why would Fred allow us to buy it?” Mrs. Lewton sat up imperiously.

“That is a very good question, Mrs. Lewton.” Kathy looked at her. “And how badly did you want it?”

The other woman shifted and it seemed as if she were blinking back tears. “Not that badly. It seems Fred was mistaken again.” She blinked. “It was not unusual.” She swallowed, then smiled. “Have you tickets for the next opera opening?”

Kathy smiled and said she didn’t know. Mrs. Lewton chattered on about who would be there and why Kathy would most certainly want to go and be seen. Kathy smiled and nodded, her mind elsewhere.

She had been right that Mrs. Lewton had seemed to feel entitled to the ruby. But it didn’t entirely make sense that Father Little would have offered to sell the ruby, especially to another member of Society. Nor, if the murders were, indeed, linked to the ruby, did it explain why killing Father Little, Uncle Stephen and trying to kill Freddie made sense.

Finally, Mrs. Lewton pushed aside her almost full plate and stood. “Well, this has been quite delightful, Mrs. Little, but I’m afraid I must be on my way.”

“Thank you for the lovely luncheon,” Kathy said, rising also. She checked her wristwatch. “And I see that I am once again late for my next appointment. Good day to you.”

Mrs. Lewton smiled at Kathy. “Good day!”

Kathy left the tea room slightly ahead of Mrs. Lewton and was rather surprised to find that when she got outside, the older woman was still inside and had seated herself again at the table, only now, she was eating voraciously. Kathy’s car was waiting, so she got in and headed back to the apartment.

However, instead of going to her office, she went upstairs to Honoria’s.

Honoria was eating a sandwich at her desk.

“Am I interrupting?” Kathy asked.

“Not really,” said Honoria. She wiped her mouth and sat back. “What’s all the rage?”

Kathy sank into a chair in front of Honoria’s desk. “I’m not sure. I just had lunch with Mrs. Lewton. We were talking about the night of the murder and she said... Wait. No, she implied she wasn’t upstairs that night and looked rather nervous.”

“She did?” Honoria sat up. “Oh, good Heavens! I completely forgot to tell you the part about Mr. Taylor that I couldn’t say in front of Mother. He says he saw Mrs. Lewton upstairs and in Father’s bedroom.”

“Oh.” Kathy thought it over. “Could she have just been lost?”

“Taylor didn’t seem to think so, but who’s to say he wasn’t lying?” Honoria glared at her sandwich. “I mean, when you think about it, it’s not all that hard to believe that Father had various mistresses.”

“Mrs. Lewton seemed to think that your father was going to sell the ruby to her and Mr. Lewton.”

Honoria almost gaped. “How? Father didn’t even have it. Grandfather did.”

Kathy shrugged. “I have no idea.”

“Wonderful.” Honoria pulled her diary from her desk drawer. “Something else we have to figure out. Perhaps we should ask Freddie when Grandfather gave him the ruby.”

"I'll take care of that tonight." Kathy made a note in her own diary, then got up. "Oh, and Freddie called earlier. He just remembered that he has a building in Lower Manhattan with a whole empty floor. Would you be interested in sharing offices?"

Honoria thought about it. "It might make sense."

"Why don't you come down and have dinner with us tonight and we can talk it over then?"

"Excellent."

Kathy returned downstairs just in time to get a call from Freddie explaining that things at the company were even worse than he thought and that he was going to be staying quite late while he tried to figure out what all was going on and how to fix it. Kathy sympathized and went back to work.

Freddie slipped into the apartment close to midnight, hoping against hope that Kathy had already gone to bed. Fortunately, she had, so his only task was to avoid stumbling enough to keep her from waking. He was not going to be in any shape the next morning for his uncle's funeral, either.

But he'd needed a few drinks after seeing what a shambles the company was in. His father had let everyone run amuck and Ames' embezzlement was merely the tip of the iceberg. Not only were the accountants he hired finding more irregularities, but several of the various chiefs were also quite concerned, too, and were beginning to report even more. The head accountant at Yonkers was only the start, and Freddie was beginning to wish he hadn't called the fellow that afternoon.

He slid into bed and lay, wide-awake. Kathy stirred beside him, but it was not the anguished movement that meant another nightmare. At least, she could wake up from her nightmares. Freddie felt as though he was living his.

CHAPTER THIRTEEN

Freddie woke up with a headache, a horrible, pounding, nauseating headache. The curtains were drawn, but the beams of light at the edges of the windows pierced his eyes and he shut them against the agony.

"Uncle Stephen's funeral," he muttered, as he tried to sit up.

"That was yesterday," said Kathy's voice.

She was not happy. Indeed, she sounded very angry with him.

"Oh," Freddie mumbled. "Right. I remember now."

"Really?"

It was all coming back to him. The somber church service, with his head pounding from the night before. The graveyard service, with his stomach heaving at inopportune times. Then the reception after, where he was able to get a glass or two of whiskey and finally settle everything down. Then the invite from someone, one of the cousins, he thought, to go to the speakeasy, where he freely imbibed martinis until the two footmen guarding him had to help him stumble to the car and then into the apartment.

"Do you remember throwing up all over the foyer?" Kathy asked angrily.

"Yes, actually." Freddie forced his eyes open. "I'm in the living room."

"That's where you finally landed. I decided it was just as well, as you were not going to come to bed with me."

Freddie winced as he shut his eyes again. He felt rather than heard her sigh as she sat down next to him.

"Darling, I know it's bad," Kathy said softly.

"You don't know how bad it is," Freddie groaned. "Even I don't know how bad it is."

"Getting drunk isn't going to help you fix things."

"The secretary doesn't know how to type," Freddie groaned. "She was shocked that I actually expected her to work. She said my father thought she was just fine as she was."

"Get a new secretary. They're easy to find."

"Not good treasurers and operations chiefs."

"I know, darling. You told me yesterday. You poor thing. I'm sorry it's so difficult now." She sighed. "I should probably let you suffer."

"Oh, Kathy, not now!"

"But here's your hangover cure. And aren't you lucky I'm not interested in you being miserable? You know how I feel about your drunkenness."

"I do." Freddie gingerly accepted the three aspirin tablets and glass of water.

He swallowed the pills, then drank the tomato juice concoction that set his mouth aflame and nibbled on the cabbage leaves. In his more sober moments, he agreed with Kathy that he shouldn't drink so much. Kathy left him to sleep a little longer and it only took another half hour or so before Freddie felt well enough to get up. His headache wasn't completely gone and his luncheon visitor did little to ease it.

Uncle Thomas Wilson was tall and broad-shouldered enough to strike terror in even the most hardened criminal. Or he would have been able to had he not carried himself with the timid mien of someone trying to hide just how big he was. What was left of his hair was brown and gray and he wore spectacles, which he was prone to removing from his face and polishing fervently when he was nervous.

He was nervous now, Freddie noted, as Uncle Thomas polished away with a dark red Asian print handkerchief. The older man was seated on the living room sofa, completely oblivious to the afghan bunched up at the end. Freddie sat in the occasional chair next to the sofa, wondering when Uncle Thomas would get to the point of his visit so that Freddie could go back to his luncheon.

"It's all about what a man needs," Uncle Thomas said for the third time. "And I certainly deserve it. I'm no idiot, you know."

"Of course not," Freddie said as soothingly as possible. "But what is it you want?"

That appeared to flummox Uncle Thomas for a moment. "Want?" He gaped for a moment then slammed his fist onto his knee. "Good God, haven't you been listening, Freddie? I want what every man wants. A little respect, damn it!"

"I'm more than happy to give you your due," Freddie said. "But what I don't understand is how this applies to the Board. Or anything I can do for you. Because I certainly respect you, sir."

"It was Stephen and Uncle Albert, you know. They're the ones who were behind it all."

"Behind what?"

"Selling family shares to the public. Miranda's cousins don't pay any attention to the company. Three of them are running their fathers' businesses and the fourth, he's holed up in Paris. Or dead, or something."

"So I understand." Freddie could only think of how often Kathy chided him for not getting to the point. He debated asking if Uncle Thomas wanted the chairmanship, but then realized what a disaster it would be if Thomas not only wanted it, but Freddie gave it to him. "What I don't understand is what you want from me, Uncle Thomas. Respect, I know, but in what form?"

Uncle Thomas went back to polishing his spectacles. Freddie deduced that Uncle Thomas had never actually expected Freddie to take him seriously.

"Perhaps if I deferred to you occasionally, would that help?" Freddie asked. "Maybe sought your opinion in front of the others?"

Uncle Thomas gaped for a moment, then put his

spectacles back on. "Yes. Yes. That would be very satisfactory. Yes, it would." He sighed. "I must confess, Freddie, having spent so much time being bullied by Stephen and Uncle Albert, and, sadly, your father, I had no reason to believe you would offer anything different."

"I may have to overrule you occasionally," Freddie said. "Men of good conscience can disagree, you know. But I would appreciate your wisdom."

"And you shall have it, young man. Quite good of you to see reason." Uncle Thomas stood. He paused. "Eh, you know Miranda would dearly love to have that ruby. Eh, you wouldn't be able to see your way to, eh…"

Freddie got to his feet. "Right now, I am concerned with keeping the ruby safe. There have been several attempts to steal it and until I know who is behind those attempts, then I will see to it that it is kept at the bank, where it belongs. We'll work out to whom it belongs later. I'm sure you can understand my concern."

"Yes. Yes, of course. Well, good day."

The two men shook hands, then Roberts saw Uncle Thomas out and Freddie breathed a sigh of relief.

"My, you handled that masterfully," Kathy said as they lingered over luncheon.

Gam had been banished to the schoolroom, and while his natural exuberance was starting to come out, he was still trying to prove himself to Mrs. Davies, who had fought so hard to save him and was still in the hospital.

"I still don't know what he wanted," Freddie said.

"It doesn't matter," Kathy said. "Defer to him every now and then and he will probably never disagree with you again. Now, all you have to do is find a way to soften the stone that Great-Uncle Albert calls a heart."

"Another labor of Hercules, if I recall." Freddie sighed.

"You're up to it, my darling. And you have all the shares, anyway. Great-Uncle Albert is going to have to work very hard to find a way around you." Kathy smiled fondly at him. "You're very good at this. I know it's a lot to have to deal with, and certainly finding out that all is not well is very upsetting. But you haven't told me anything that leads me to believe that it can't be saved."

"No," Freddie conceded. "We're not that far gone. Just far gone enough that if I take my hand from the tiller for a moment, we could easily end up on the rocks."

"Then be thankful 'The Covenant' is doing so well. If things keep up, we may be doing a third printing by the end of next month. Between that and Lowell's book, which I expect to do almost as well, we will have our fortunes made." Kathy smiled.

Freddie smiled back at her. From her perspective, their fortunes were made. What she didn't know, and he would never dare tell her, is that the textile business was worth far more than two books. Of course, that also meant she would be comfortable with far less than he would consider comfortable. Freddie decided that was one of the many blessings in his life that Kathy was responsible for and let it go at that.

"You know what this also means," Kathy continued. "We, perhaps, should have been looking at Uncle Thomas as a suspect."

"You've got to be kidding. Earthworms have more backbone than he does."

"But we've seen how far earthworms can go when they're pushed to their limits," Kathy said.

"True. You make an excellent point, my dear."

"I usually do."

"No need to rub it in." Freddie creased his brow as he thought it over. "Do you think that I've appeased him enough to get him to stop shooting at us?"

"Assuming it was him shooting at us, perhaps." Kathy made a face. "But then where does the ruby fit into all of this?"

"Well, as you suggested, we could be dealing with

two different malefactors. One who wants control of the business and one who wants the ruby.”

“Oh, dear. That does muddy the waters, doesn’t it?” Kathy sighed. “On the other hand, both Aunt Thelma and Aunt Miranda want the ruby quite badly. If Uncle Thomas could get both your father and Uncle Stephen out of the way, perhaps he thought he could get the ruby, as well.”

“And he did ask for it at the end of our interview.” Freddie took a last sip of coffee, neatly laid his silverware across his plate, then dabbed his mouth with his napkin. “It’s well worth considering. However, I must get back to the salt mine. My new secretary can only hold the hordes off for so long.”

Kathy’s eyebrows lifted. “Already?”

“Yes. I got the call shortly before luncheon,” Freddie said, getting up. “And she sounds as though she is going to be quite effective.”

Freddie hurried off and got to his office in good time, his two bodyguards leaving him in the lobby of the building. As he stepped into the foyer outside his own office, he noted that even the air was different. Sitting behind the secretary’s desk was a middle-aged woman, her long brown hair firmly pinned into a roll at the back of her neck. She wore a cream-colored blouse with a long chain and pendant around her neck, and she was absorbed in sorting through several letters as she talked on the phone.

“I’m afraid not,” she told the person on the other end. “Please give me your name and number and why you’re calling and I will let him know when he comes in... Yes, I understand this is quite urgent.” She grabbed a pencil and tablet from next to the typewriter. “Yes, sir... Your name..? Now, your number..? Thank you very much, Mr. Johnson. I will let Mr. Little know you called at the earliest opportunity.”

She picked up her pendant, which Freddie suddenly saw was a watch, noted the time on her note, then looked up and finally saw him standing there.

"I'm sorry," she said in a tone that said she wasn't. "The front desk did not announce you. May I ask who you are and what your business here is?"

Freddie smiled. "You most certainly may and I'm glad to hear you do so. And the reason the front desk did not announce me is that I'm Mr. Little and they don't seem to care if I simply walk in off the street."

She scrambled to her feet. "I apologize, sir."

"Please don't," Freddie took off his coat and was happy to see her right there to take it and his hat. "You must be Mrs. Putnam."

"Yes, sir."

"Excellent. And I can't imagine why you'd know me from anyone else around here since we've only spoken on the telephone."

Mrs. Putnam stood back and looked him up and down. "I dare say I should have recognized you. You look just like that portrait of your grandfather in his younger years. The one on the third floor. In the Accounts Receivables department."

Freddie raised an eyebrow. "I don't think I've seen that one. I shall have to go look at it."

"With your permission, sir, I would recommend against doing so right now. You have several calls that you might want to return, including one from Mr. Carstairs, who is very concerned about Mr. Ames' firing. And your cousin, Mr. Wilfrid Coates is waiting downstairs. He would like to see you as soon as possible. In addition, we need to set the agenda for tomorrow's board meeting. I have already assigned a photographer and have invited your mother and wife to join us."

"What an excellent idea," said Freddie going into his office. "Would you add my sister, Mrs. Honoria Wentworth, as well, please?"

"Certainly, sir. And Mr. Coates?"

Freddie briefly debated sending him away. "May as well deal with the worst of it. Please send him up. And then put through the call to Mr. Carstairs."

Freddie had barely settled himself behind the

desk when Mrs. Putnam announced that Mr. Carstairs was on the line and Mr. Coates on the way up. Freddie asked her to let his cousin wait while he dealt with the lawyer.

"He's gone, damn it!" Carstairs said after Freddie picked up.

"Mr. Ames?"

"Yes! The coppers went round yesterday and he'd run. At least we were able to get the assets frozen on that company of his. But, Freddie, do not do that again. If there is even the faintest hint of criminal liability you talk to me first before you fire someone. Are we clear?"

"Yes, Eddie. I solemnly promise. Now, is there anything that needs to be done for the board meeting tomorrow?"

"I've papers for you to go through."

"Send them to my secretary," Freddie smiled, thinking of the blissfully competent woman outside his office.

"Um, Freddie, are you sure?"

"I let my father's secretary go. I've got a new one."

"I do not understand why your father didn't have a second secretary. Half the fellows around here have two. One to look at and one to work."

Freddie was reasonably certain his father had not been only looking at Miss Smith.

"It doesn't matter now. Mrs. Putnam is quite competent and that's what matters to me."

"Oh, and speaking of your father," Carstairs paused. "I've got some bad news there."

"They found another will?"

"No, but almost as bad. The probate notice went up and we've been getting all kinds of claims against the estate."

"Are they legitimate?"

"I have to imagine some are," Carstairs said. "But it's not unusual in a case like this. People knew your father didn't have his affairs in the best of shape, so they try to take advantage of it. You expect a couple folks to make claims based on verbal promises. People make promises all the time that they intended to fulfill and weren't able to. But when you get as many claims as we've gotten, you know damned well people are taking advantage. So, if anyone, and I mean anyone, says your father owed them something, you tell them to provide a signed and witnessed document of the debt to the court. You don't pay them anything, you don't owe them anything unless the judge says so. Are we clear?"

"Of course. I wouldn't do otherwise," Freddie replied, feeling as if he were being lectured to. He had to admit his mistake in firing Ames so quickly gave Carstairs good reason to lecture.

Freddie hung up shortly after and had Mrs. Putnam send in Wilfrid. He was several years older than Freddie, but his perpetual angry sneer made him seem more like a spoiled college boy.

"It's about time," Wilfrid grumbled as Freddie offered him a seat in front of the desk and a cigarette. "That battle ax you've got out front was nothing but trouble. Kept me cooling my heels for over an hour."

"I'm sorry about that, Wilfrid," Freddie said, feigning affability. "Now, what brings you here today?"

"Tomorrow's board meeting." Wilfrid flicked the ash from his cigarette onto the floor. "It's not fair, Freddie. Aldie gets to manage Mother's shares of the company and I don't get anything." Aldie was Aldrich Coates, Wilfrid's older brother. "And Mother is going to have even more shares from Grandfather, now that he's dead."

"What about shares from your father's family business? I would imagine you'd get some of those."

"That's the worst of it," Wilfrid said. "The will was read this morning, and, yes, Aldie and I split the estate, but truth be told, there isn't much of an estate left. Mother does like to live in style, you know." He rolled his eyes. "At least, Aldie has her support on his hands. But how am I going to keep myself and my wife, I ask you? We have a position to maintain and I have no means of support beyond a few measly shares of the Coates business and limited expectations from this one.”

Freddie doubted that was entirely true. “That sounds rather awful. But why are you telling me all this?”

“You’ve got all the shares, Freddie. You can either let me have a few or find some other way so that I can join the board and get some compensation that way. Aldie’s an idiot. He’ll be of no use to you on the board. I, at least, can contribute some intelligence.”

“And being an intelligent man, I assume you’ll understand if I ask what else you can offer me for the shares?” Freddie asked.

Wilfrid rolled his eyes. “I should have known you wouldn’t be interested in helping me.”

“I did not say that, Wilfrid. I’m merely negotiating, as any intelligent person would.” Freddie snubbed out his latest cigarette and fitted another to its holder. “Tell you what. Why don’t you come to the board meeting tomorrow? I’ll see to it you have an invitation. And I’ll ask if the board is willing to make you a member-at-large. You’ll have limited voting rights, but that would be true, even if you had shares. And you will have a voice.”

“And compensation?”

“I can’t promise, but I don’t see why not.”

Wilfrid shrugged and pulled himself out of the chair. “If that’s the best I can do.”

“I could offer you a position in the firm,” Freddie said.

Wilfrid glared at him. “That’s beneath you, Freddie.”

Freddie shrugged and let Wilfrid out. Mrs. Putnam had some issue to bring before him, but he asked for some aspirin first, as his head had begun pounding again. Alone in his office, he looked longingly at the decanter of whiskey on the credenza behind his desk. Only the thought of Kathy smelling the booze on his breath kept him from taking a drink, however much he thought he needed it.

The afternoon passed quickly. Freddie met with several of the company's chiefs, took telephone calls from others, returned his other calls and went over the papers sent by Mr. Carstairs.

"We're not in the clear by a long shot," Freddie told Kathy that evening at dinner. "But at least I have a competent secretary and several subordinates I can trust. I hope. And everything is in readiness for tomorrow's board meeting."

"I'm glad, darling," Kathy said.

"The biggest problem is the inventory overrun from all the refused merchandise," Freddie said. He'd already outlined all the reasons the overrun had happened.

"It's not just the inventory," Gam said. "You'll have to fix your relationship with all the customers who are mad about it."

"Indeed, yes," Freddie said. "And I've several meetings over the next month to do just that. It will probably involve a significant dip in our revenues."

"Ouch," said Gam. "But that sort of thing is only temporary and your shareholders aren't going to vote you off the board."

Freddie couldn't resist smiling at the boy. "This is, indeed, true." He looked at Kathy. "And how was your day, my dearest?"

"At least as busy as yours," Kathy said. "Honoria wanted to know why you didn't think of your empty floor sooner."

"It wasn't empty until the middle of last month and we were rather well occupied with other things then."

"I thought as much," Kathy said. "We're measuring out the offices now. I've got three potential editors to interview, plus several typists. Elsie Quinn, thank heavens, has agreed to work as my personal secretary. And since I've been able to pay her well enough, she's now able to get a bigger and nicer apartment, which means she'll be able to keep her mother and her aunt, and they'll take care of her children while she's at work."

Freddie suddenly wondered if Mrs. Putnam had children, or a husband, for that matter. He knew Elsie, a friend of Kathy's when they'd worked together at Healcroft House, was a widow with four young children. She'd been fired by Kathy's former boss for no good reason and left to raise the children by taking in what typing she could find and helping her mother take in laundry. Kathy had good reason to be pleased.

Roberts cleared his throat at the door to the dining room.

"Yes?" Freddie asked.

"Mr. Miles Johnson is downstairs, sir. He says you invited him?"

"I returned his call and left a message for him," Freddie said. "I'm not in."

Roberts appeared a moment later. "Downstairs, sir. They say that Mr. Johnson is making something of a scene. Do you want them to summon the police?"

Freddie sighed. He looked at Kathy, who shrugged. Dinner was almost finished, anyway.

"Send him up, Roberts. We'll have coffee in the living room."

"Yes, sir."

A few minutes later, Roberts showed the stocky man into the living room.

"Freddie! Good to see you again!" He shook Freddie's hand firmly and ignored Kathy and Gam.

"Yes, Mr. Johnson. Please have a seat." Freddie indicated a chair across from the couch where Kathy and Gam were.

Johnson sat down. "I heard that probate was done on your grandfather's will, and I wanted to talk to you before your big board meeting tomorrow. You see, your father, your uncles and I, we had a deal. We are taking the company public.”

“Do you have a contract or other document spelling out the terms with my father’s and uncles’ signatures on it? Because I am not aware of any.” Freddie sat down in the chair next to the couch.

“A man’s word is his bond. We were just about to get the paperwork going. But the bottom line is, we had a deal. It was set. And I expect you to honor it.”

“You do?” Freddie glowered at the smaller man. “As I understand it from my uncle before he died, the deal was still far from set and that only a few shares would be sold. As far as honoring any deals my father made, I will be happy to do so, if you can provide a signed and witnessed contract.”

“I don’t need a contract!” Johnson sputtered. “I know what we agreed to. Are you calling me a liar?”

Freddie sighed. “No, Mr. Johnson. You may well have made such an agreement. The problem is that, apparently, my father made several such deals, so many that we have to believe that at least some of the claims being made are suspect. So, in justice to everybody, I have to insist that any claim being made involve a signed document. It’s the only fair way to do it.”

Johnson harrumphed and sat back in his chair. “You obviously don’t understand how business works. It’s based on trust and keeping your word.”

“I fully intend to keep mine, Mr. Johnson,” Freddie said. “However, it would be foolish of me to assume that everyone does. I know for a fact that your business doesn’t. A friend recently paid a debt to me with a check drawn on your bank. I could not go to your bank and simply say that a man’s word is his bond and that my friend had given me a check. I had to produce the signed check. That is how business is done, Mr. Johnson.” Freddie fought to keep his voice steady in spite of his temper rising. “In addition, any deal that my father and uncles may have made with you would have to have been clearly contingent on them obtaining sufficient shares of the family business for the rest of the board to be overruled, either by my father's expected inheritance, which did not happen, or by successfully contesting my grandfather's will, which also did not happen. So, while I do feel enough respect for my father to take into consideration his wishes and plans, I also have my grandfather's wishes and plans to consider, and one of the reasons I was made his primary heir was precisely to prevent what you are suggesting. So, I am afraid, Mr. Johnson, that Little and Sons Manufactures will not be sold as common stock while I have the majority of the shares. I am sorry if you were led to believe otherwise by members of my family who had no right to do so. If you wish to make a claim against my father's estate, please feel free to join all the others. However, I suspect you will not get very far without a signed and witnessed document. Now, will you please excuse us. My family and I have other business to attend to."

Freddie slid his finger under the end table to yet another call button, then got up and folded his arms across his chest. On the couch, Gam started bouncing as if he wanted to add something, but Kathy pushed him back with a firm hand to his chest. Johnson slowly pulled himself upright, anger shining in his eyes.

"Mr. High and Mighty," Johnson scoffed. "Your dad used to do that, you know? Made out like he was better than me just because I had to work my way up in the world."

"I'm sorry my father's attitude was so unkind," said Freddie gently. "That was unnecessary."

Johnson stepped back for a moment. "You're damned tootin', it was." He looked around as if debating what else to say.

"Roberts?" Freddie said to the valet, who appeared right away, as always. "Mr. Johnson is just leaving, if you could see him out, please? Mr. Johnson, thank you for stopping by."

Silence reigned in the living room until the front door shut. Freddie started to open his mouth when Gam waved at him and ran out of the room. He was back a moment later.

"He's really gone," Gam announced, flopping onto the couch. "Roberts said he got on the elevator, and Roberts made sure Mr. Ellroy knew to take him downstairs."

"Good Heavens," said Freddie with a chuckle. "That was exceptionally cautious of you."

Gam shrugged. "Well, with all the strange crap going on—"

"Gamaliel!" Kathy snapped. "Such language. I ought to wash your mouth out with soap."

"Sorry." Gam slumped. "But he used filthy language in front of you and you didn't get upset. I've even heard you say some things."

"I am grown up," said Kathy, who was blushing nonetheless. "You are not."

"I think we can let you off with a warning this time," Freddie said. "But I'm also afraid your point is well-taken."

Kathy shivered, then thought. "You know, Mr. Johnson was very interested in the ruby the night of the party. Said that your father had offered to sell it to him."

"That's right." Freddie looked at the front door, pondering. "So much of what he had to say differed from what Uncle Stephen had told me, I was beginning to wonder if that man could even tell truth from lies. And yet, didn't Mrs. Lewton say that Father had offered to sell the ruby to them?"

"She did. Which means your father probably offered to sell it to Mr. Johnson too. And if your father had offered to sell it to someone, then decided not to..." Kathy's brow creased in annoyance. "But I just can't imagine anyone trying to kill him over it unless someone lost his temper."

"Well, that would make sense, especially with

what Detective Crowley said about it being a crime of opportunity," Freddie said. "But that actually lets Mr. Johnson off the hook. He'd already left the party."

"Oh, that's right," Kathy said. "And if someone merely wanted the ruby, why kill Uncle Stephen over it? Maybe you were right, Freddie. Maybe we do have two different criminals here."

"Or someone like Uncle Thomas who wants both the ruby and the business," Freddie said.

"I don't think it's your Uncle Thomas," Gam said. "He didn't sound like he wanted the company all that much when he was here this morning."

The boy squirmed as he saw both Freddie's and Kathy's eyes on him.

"I see," said Freddie slowly. "Do I want to know how you came to be privy to that particular conversation?"

"Uh, probably not?" Gam smiled haplessly.

"You've been listening at keyholes again, haven't you?" Kathy said, clearly trying not to laugh.

"But I keep finding things out," Gam said.

Freddie looked at Kathy with an eyebrow lifted. True, it wasn't appropriate to encourage such eavesdropping. On the other hand, Gam was finding things out. Worse yet, simply forbidding the activity was not likely to get him to stop.

"You do realize that eavesdropping is a low habit," Freddie said.

"I'm a low person," Gam replied.

"And one of the great virtues of living in our fair land is that you do not have to remain so."

"Both of you, enough," Kathy cut in. "Gam, you know better than to eavesdrop. Freddie, you don't have to encourage him by debating it. Now, it's getting late. Gam, you will write 'Eavesdropping is naughty' one hundred times by tomorrow morning. In ink. And if you smudge, you'll get to start all over again."

Gam gasped. "No!"

"Now, to your room. And if I catch you reading instead of writing, it'll be two hundred times."

Gam slumped out of the room.

Freddie waited until the boy was gone. "That won't stop him from eavesdropping."

"Of course, it won't. But if he's going to do it, he should at least do penance for it. Besides, his penmanship is getting sloppy again and Mrs. Davies asked me today to have him work on writing with a pen."

"You are a marvel, my darling." Freddie smiled fondly at her.

"As are you." Kathy smiled warmly back. "My goodness, I was ready to shout at that odious Mr. Johnson and yet you kept your temper so beautifully. I was very impressed."

Freddie felt himself stir. "And maybe I can impress you another way tonight?"

"Oh, I think so." Kathy giggled as he got up and pulled her to her feet. "I do have to check on Gam in a bit."

He nibbled on her neck. "We'll take turns."

CHAPTER FOURTEEN

When the flashbulbs from the cameras finally stopped flashing, Kathy realized that not only had she been blinded, her eyes were watering. As her vision returned, she saw Honoria dabbing at her eyes with a handkerchief. Freddie was talking to a reporter about how the company was entering a new era or some such nonsense. The rest of the board and several of the chiefs of the company were chatting quietly amongst themselves.

Honoria pulled her gloves off and ran her hand over a huge roll of tan fabric.

"What's this?" she asked. "It's very nice."

"Not if you were expecting wool and silk," Kathy said quietly.

"What?"

"It's the worst of our problems," Kathy said as Gloria drew closer. "Our customer was told that it was a wool and silk blend. But it's really wool and artificial silk. Apparently, the chief of purchasing had made a huge viscose purchase by mistake and Mr. Ames encouraged the factory manager to use it instead of the real silk."

"Oh, dear," said Gloria softly. "I hope the customer doesn't bring charges against us. That is, technically, fraud."

"Mr. Ames, apparently, was able to pretend it was all a mistaken shipment and the customer bought the excuse," Kathy said. "But they will be looking at any new shipments very carefully from here on out. Not to mention the discount they were given on the original order. And we still have a great deal of viscose in one of the warehouses taking up space, not to mention all the rolls of this fabric that were refused. Fortunately, most of the other refusals are simply an issue of bad dye lots. Still, it's beginning to get out that quality from our mills is slipping and that is quite serious. That's why Freddie was so happy to have the reporter here today. He wants everyone to know that he is taking the reins and that things will be different."

Honoria took the end edge of the fabric and draped it across her hand. "It's a pity this was refused. It's absolutely lovely, isn't it, Mother?"

Gloria looked at it, then, after glancing around, slipped off her glove to touch the fabric.

"Yes, it is," she said. "And we have a great deal of viscose, you say?"

"Yes, Mother Little," Kathy said.

"That's that new fiber that the Federal Trade Commission named rayon about a year and a half ago, maybe two years?" Gloria said. She brightened. "Do you think our sales or advertising fellows could do some sort of campaign about the fiber of the future?"

"I don't know," Kathy said. "That's what they're calling artificial silk, isn't it? I had an artificial silk blouse once. It was a disaster. It's actually quite fragile. I put an iron to it and completely ruined it."

"We'd have to find some way to let women know how to handle it," said Gloria.

"My magazine," said Honoria. "It would be exactly the sort of article I'd use."

Their conversation was cut short as Freddie stepped to the head of the conference table and rapped a small gavel on it.

"Gentlemen, I'd like to call this meeting to order," Freddie announced. "As you can see from the agenda in front of you, we have a number of important items to discuss, but first, Uncle Thomas, would you be so good as to lead us in a quick invocation, please?"

Kathy thought that might have been laying it on a bit thick, but from the way Uncle Thomas' eyes gleamed, it was apparent Freddie had, again, managed his uncle well. Everyone bowed their heads as they stood around the table. Uncle Thomas finished the prayer, requesting wisdom and guidance, in remarkably short order and there was a great scraping and thundering as chairs were pulled from the table, sat in, and settled.

"Our first order of business," Freddie began, almost before everyone was seated, "is the request of our cousin and brother, Wilfrid Coates, to join and serve the board."

Kathy smiled as Freddie's eyes bore down on Wilfrid, who was sitting near the end of the table and as far from his brother, Aldrich Coates, as possible.

"Wilfrid is very interested in offering his wisdom and insight to speed our cause," Freddie continued, his eyes never leaving Wilfrid's. "He also has the time that many of us lack to devote to this task."

Wilfrid squirmed, but his return gaze held steady.

As Freddie asked for thoughts and comments, Kathy looked at Honoria and Gloria, asking if it was time to go. But before she could get a response, a man burst into the room.

"Mr. Ames!" Freddie yelped. "What are you doing here?"

The slender, well-turned out man gasped for a moment, then smoothed the pencil mustache on his lip.

"Mr. Little, fellow board members," he gasped. "I hope you'll hear me. I have come at great risk to my own personal safety to seek your help. As Mr. Little will tell you, I have been accused of embezzling company funds. But I am innocent. Yes, I did sign invoices that paid a company in which I have an interest, but only because my name is listed as a principal. But you'll also find, when you investigate, that funds from that business did not go to any account that I own. They went, instead, to the account of a board member, the same board member who directed me to set up the phantom company and sign the invoices."

"Do you have the documents to prove this?" asked Freddie.

“Yes. They are right here.”

Ames pulled a sheaf of papers from his small, black briefcase. Freddie nodded and held his hand out. Ames hesitated, but slowly came around the table and handed Freddie the papers. Freddie flipped through them, sighed deeply, then looked at Ames.

“Mr. Ames, you may, in fact, have been wronged,” Freddie said slowly. “And I would very much prefer to keep this situation private. However, I also remember the story you told me when I first confronted you about this situation. Now, there are many good reasons why you might lie about your involvement in this incident, even if you are innocent. And I don’t doubt that the board member you list here was, in fact, involved in the activity you describe. However, I have been instructed by counsel to turn you over to the police.”

Ames looked frantic as the board members shuffled and grumbled amongst themselves. Freddie rapped his gavel quickly.

“I haven’t finished,” Freddie said. He paused. “I think we need to find a way to keep an eye on you without turning you over to the police while we conduct a rigorous and thorough investigation. It’s not fair to us, if you are guilty, to let you escape without being able to recover some of our losses. But it’s not fair to you, if you are innocent, to force you to endure the hospitality of New York’s Finest. I think we can enlist a private detective agency to do the investigation and take care of guard duty, as long as you promise to stay at home until the investigation is finished. Is that fair enough, Mr. Ames?”

Mr. Ames gulped and nodded. Freddie turned to his personnel chief.

“Mr. Brennan, would you see to that immediately.”

“Yes, Mr. Little.” The balding heavyset man hurried from the room.

“Mr. Ames, why don’t you remain with us for the time being?” Freddie asked.

“But who is the board member?” Great-Uncle

Albert Little demanded. He had the family height and light features, but his white hair was sparse and he was hunched over.

The others echoed the statement. Freddie looked at the papers.

"Mr. Stephen Coates," Freddie said softly. "That does not, however, automatically implicate his sons."

"I didn't know anything about Father embezzling," snapped Aldrich, who was a slightly younger copy of his father.

"You can't expect Freddie to believe that," snarled Wilfrid, eyeing Freddie malevolently. "He has no proof."

"I believe the law says innocent until proven guilty," Freddie said. "It would be ridiculous to suggest that a vote would have any meaning, given my control of the shares. However, this board is important. I need your advice and collective wisdom. So. Any thoughts on whether we should include and compensate our cousin Wilfrid, and if so, what shall the compensation be?"

Gloria nodded at Kathy and Honoria and the three of them slipped out of the boardroom. Gloria suggested that they have luncheon together, and in a fit of madness, Kathy suggested a delicatessen that she and Honoria knew and liked.

"You can leave your fur in the car, Mother Little," Kathy said as they got into the back seat of Freddie's Cadillac.

Van Schuyler happened to be driving, and when he heard the address, he grinned.

"Yeah, we know dat neighborhood," he said, putting the car in gear.

Honoria and Kathy looked at Gloria.

"I don't know the delicatessen," she said. "But I have had occasion to go to the Lower East Side. Not often, admittedly, but one does."

Kathy and Honoria looked at each other, both wondering what occasion that could have been. But Gloria did not seem interested in elaborating and there was little reason to press the issue.

As the three women ate lunch, they continued to discuss the board meeting and the troubles the company faced. But whether they should offer their ideas remained elusive.

"Freddie's not stupid," Kathy said finally when the three women had eventually gotten back to Kathy's apartment. "His pride is worth something. But he will eventually want to hear what we have to say. We just have to give him room to ask for it."

"That seems optimistic," said Gloria.

"They've not even been married a year yet," said Honoria. "It's entirely possible he might ask Kathy."

Kathy checked her wristwatch. "Whether he does or doesn't, it's irrelevant at the moment. Freddie should be home any time now, and I would like to be the loving, supportive wife I'm supposed to be."

Honoria and Gloria demurred and quickly left.

Freddie was quite surprised and pleased when Kathy greeted him at the door with a passionate kiss and a cocktail.

"Darling," she explained. "It's the drunkenness that I object to, not the drink."

"Oh, I see," Freddie said as he gave in to the temptation to grope her.

"My beloved, Gam is waiting to hear all about the board meeting, and while I do enjoy your more amorous attentions, he would be..."

Freddie sighed. "Utterly appalled."

He took a good, solid drink of the whiskey and soda, kissed his wife soundly, then slid apart. Kathy yelled for Gam, and there was an extended dissection and analysis of everything that had happened at the board meeting that lasted all the way through dinner. There was, however, one issue that confused Gam.

"I don't understand, Freddie," he said as they made their way to the study, having finished eating. "I mean, it doesn't make sense to add Wilfrid to the board if they don't want him."

"Yes, they were quite clear about that," Freddie said. "Poor Wilfrid was humiliated."

"So, if you want to help him," Gam continued. "Why can't you just give him a job?"

Freddie rolled his eyes. "I did offer him one. He took it as an insult."

Gam frowned. "Why? If I were him, I'd've loved a job."

"People of our social status don't take jobs," Freddie said. "We serve on boards. Oldest sons usually end up running our families' businesses. To offer Wilfrid a job meant that I had no respect for his social status. Or he took it that way. I had gotten the impression he was more worried about his bank account than appearances. Unfortunately, I was wrong."

"Well, that's as may be," said Kathy. She picked up a note from her desk. "I got some good news this afternoon. Mrs. Davies was sent home from the hospital today. She won't be able to come to work until Monday, at the soonest, but she did give me plenty to keep you occupied, Gam, including working on your penmanship. So, I think an early night for you is in order. That way, you can be up bright and early and get to work."

Gam made a face but agreed.

The next day was quiet. Freddie worked most of it at his corporate office, while Kathy and Gam worked in the apartment study.

"It's almost been too quiet," Freddie said that night after Gam had been sent to bed and he and Kathy were relaxing in the study.

"Oh, please don't tempt fate," Kathy hissed.

The phone in the foyer rang and she glared at him before heading to the front of the apartment. Freddie followed her.

Roberts had, as always, gotten to the phone first.

"Yes, thank you. I'll inform Mrs. Wentworth, as well." He hung up the phone. "Sir, there is a fire at your parents' home. It sounds serious."

"Please get Honoria," Freddie said. He looked at Kathy. "I fear this is another attack."

"Oh, dear," said Kathy. "And even if it isn't, someone might take advantage of it. You know what? I'd better stay here with Gam. Ivy will be home in a couple hours, and we have the footmen for protection."

"I'll make sure I have another two of them with me." Freddie looked down at Kathy and his eyes filled. "Be very careful."

"You, too." Kathy suddenly hugged him. "And it may have been an accident. It may not be an attack."

"I hope so," Freddie said, holding her as tightly as she held him.

Honoria came rushing into the foyer, dressed to go out. "Are we going?"

"Yes." Freddie pulled away from Kathy and grabbed his hat and coat from Roberts.

Traffic was snarled as Freddie drove up Madison. He eventually parked the car near 57th and he and Honoria hurried up the sidewalk. A small crowd was gathered at the edge of the street. Freddie pushed through it to find several police officers holding the people back. Firelight lit the faces of the onlookers, while the fire trucks and firemen were dark shadows against the blazing mansion.

"There!" Honoria pointed to Freddie's right, where just inside the circle of officers, Briggeman and the rest of the household staff stood watching the fire. Most were dressed, but a few were still in their nightclothes.

Freddie pushed through the crowd toward the servants, then pushed past a harness bull.

"Hey, come back here!" the officer yelled.

"That's my mother's house," Freddie yelled back as he dragged Honoria toward Briggeman.

"Mr. Little!" Briggeman called.

"You recognize this guy?" asked a fireman who looked like he was the chief.

"The owner's son," Briggeman said. "And

daughter.”

The fireman waved the harness bull back.

“Where’s Mother?” Freddie gasped.

Trembling, Briggeman looked back at the house.

“No!’ cried Honoria.

“We couldn’t find her,” Briggeman said. His face was sooty and a bright red burn ran down his cheek. Several others of the servants bore similar marks. “Van Schuyler went in again.”

Above them, on the far side of the mansion, a turret exploded with a huge roar and a great ball of flame. Briggeman closed his eyes and shook his head. Freddie’s heart stopped and Honoria sobbed.

“Make way!” one of the firefighters near the front door suddenly hollered.

Several men rushed forward as two figures, clasped tightly to each other, stumbled their way out of the billows of smoke. Both were coughing furiously. Four ambulance drivers hurried forward with stretchers and two huge boxes.

“It’s Mother!” Honoria screamed and ran toward them.

Freddie scrambled after her. Gloria was, indeed, coughing and waving off the ambulance men.

“Take care of Van Schuyler,” she kept yelling, even though the other pair of ambulance men had the chauffeur on a stretcher and were putting on him a mask hooked up to the large box they carried.

“Mother, let the men help you,” Honoria ordered.

Gloria sank down onto the stretcher and was given a mask from the other large box. Freddie knelt beside her.

“Mother, are you all right?” he asked.

She nodded and he and Honoria held her hands until she pushed them away and pulled the mask from her face.

“How is Van Schuyler?’ she demanded, coughed, then put the mask back on.

“I’m fine, Mrs. Little,” the small man croaked from

his stretcher.

An ambulance man touched Freddie's arm. "We need to take them to the hospital now."

"We'll ride with her," Freddie said, indicating Honoria.

"No, Freddie." Gloria coughed. "You ride with Van Schuyler. He saved my life."

The two were loaded up, Honoria and Gloria in one ambulance and Freddie and Van Schuyler in the other. Freddie sat watching the man as he coughed. His hair was a little singed, but he seemed otherwise unhurt.

"Thank you, Van Schuyler," Freddie said. "Mother says you saved her life."

Van Schuyler pulled the mask back. "Who wouldn't. I always said I'd cut off my right arm."

"Well, you made good on that tonight, several times over."

"I knew where she was, is all."

As it turned out, neither Gloria nor Van Schuyler was hurt much beyond having breathed a fair amount of smoke and a few superficial burns. Freddie called Kathy from the hospital, then conferred with Honoria. Honoria called Kathy back and Kathy agreed to let Gloria stay in her apartment. Briggeman arrived at the hospital and was able to reassure Gloria that everyone had gotten out of the house unharmed and that everyone, including Van Schuyler, had someplace to stay for the night. Freddie got a ride back to 57th, where he'd left his car, with a police officer, and by the time he returned, Gloria was ready to leave the hospital.

The next morning, after an emergency order of fresh clothes from B. Altman's had been made and received, Freddie and Kathy took Gloria to the mansion, where some of the staff were already trying to sort out what could and could not be salvaged. The front of the house still stood. Except for the hole where the turret had been, the only hint of the fire were the streaks of smoke marks outside the windows on the upper floors.

Gloria looked up at what was left of the turret and her tears spilled silently onto her cheeks.

"It's all gone," she said, softly. "All my research. Gone."

Freddie looked at Kathy curiously and Kathy shrugged. Briggeman walked up.

"Ma'am, the carriage house was untouched," he told Gloria.

"It was?" Gloria sighed with enormous relief. "All my diaries and correspondence are in there. Spring cleaning, you know."

Freddie did know. Normally, the cleaning staff moved about the house all but invisibly, waiting for rooms to empty before going through with their mops and feather dusters. But spring cleaning, the week before Easter, was the big exception. Every room in the house was emptied, thoroughly cleaned, and everything gone over and put back. Gloria supervised the effort personally. She would never say why, but Freddie suspected it was because all the things she'd mislaid over the course of the year were suddenly found. At least, he'd always remembered her talking about all the things that had been found each spring cleaning.

"And the household safe did not burn," Briggeman said. "We are assuming the contents are intact."

"What about the wine cellar?"

"We are trying to determine the extent of the damage," Briggeman said. "The bottles are all intact, but alas, the heat has damaged much of the contents."

"The Macon Villages." Gloria blinked back tears. "Oh, blast. Wilma and I should have drunk one of those when we had the chance."

"Mother, we can replace the wine," Freddie couldn't help giving her shoulders a quick squeeze.

"I know." Gloria dabbed at her eyes with her handkerchief, then coughed and glanced up at the turret. "I suppose I can even recreate some of the research. But I was so close!"

"Close to what?" Kathy asked.

"Developing a polymer fiber," Gloria said as if that explained anything. "That's why I was up in my laboratory last night." She nodded at the turret. "I was finalizing an experiment. I didn't smell the smoke because the coal tar smelled so strong. Thank God Van Schuyler found me. I suppose it was getting warm, but I was so busy, I really didn't notice. By then, it was so smoky, I would never have made it out. Van Schuyler took me down the side servants' stairs. We got blocked by the fire near the ballroom, but Van Schuyler found a way to the front door and we were able to get out."

"A laboratory?" Freddie asked, incredulous.

"Yes. It was my respite." Gloria dabbed at her eyes again. "I loved that room."

"Your mother enjoys chemistry," Kathy told her husband.

"I am a dedicated amateur chemist," Gloria said, holding her chin up. "I even have a paper published." She shrunk into herself a little. "I never told anyone because I do have to maintain my social position. If people found out, it would ruin me."

"Mother, I had no idea," Freddie said.

"Of course not! You weren't supposed to." Gloria sniffed again. "It was my little secret and I loved having it."

"There, there, Mother," Freddie said with a sigh. "We'll build you another secret laboratory and you can research poly-whatever they are to your heart's content."

"I wouldn't be so dismissive of my work, if I were you," Gloria growled. "If I am successful, it will be the next biggest thing in textiles. It could completely revolutionize the industry."

"I apologize, Mother. I'm afraid it's all been a bit much to deal with on top of everything else. The most important part to me is that you are safe and unhurt."

Gloria smiled at her son. "Freddie, you are such a dear thing." She dabbed at her eyes once more, sniffed, then put her handkerchief into her purse.

"Now, enough sniveling. There is work to be done. Let me think. The first thing to manage will be the staff. I know Briggeman found them a refuge last night, but we can't assume that will stand for the long term. I suppose I can send most of them to the summer home."

"Is that where you want to live, Mother?" Freddie asked.

She sighed. "If I have no other option." She looked at Freddie. "I am reminded that I am dependent on you for my support."

"Do whatever you want, Mother. You can rebuild the mansion even bigger and better than it was if you like." Freddie said.

"You are a good son." Gloria turned back to the servants and took Briggeman with her.

Freddie went to follow, but Kathy held him back.

"Let her go," Kathy said quietly. "It'll be the best thing for her."

Once Gloria had settled what would happen with the servants for the time being, she returned to Freddie.

"Darling boy, it suddenly occurs to me that I should have thought about where I will stay," Gloria said. "I don't know why we didn't discuss this earlier, but would you mind terribly if I stayed at your place for the time being? I know it might be quieter at Honoria's, but she seemed terribly put out last night. Not that she said so, of course. I'll need my lady's maid, Briggeman, and Van Schuyler, of course."

"Of course, you're welcome, Mother Little," Kathy cut in. "We'll get everything worked out when we get there."

"Well, Briggeman said that it is going to take all day and then some to sort out what can be salvaged and what can't, and suggested that I leave him and the others to it," Gloria said.

"Do you know if they've figured out what started the fire?" Freddie asked.

"I don't believe the fire department has," Gloria said. "But someone had better speak to them. The fire was, without question, started deliberately."

Freddie squeezed his eyes shut while his gut tightened. "How can you know?"

"The ballroom has the worst damage," Gloria said. "I believe someone piled a bunch of rags under one of the curtains and lit it. You can see the streaks on what's left of the wall. And I smelled kerosene."

"Couldn't someone have been using it to clean something?" Kathy asked.

Gloria shook her head. "The ballroom was cleaned the first part of the week. The smell would have dissipated by now. This smell is far too strong. I asked Briggeman to have someone sift the ashes just in case something can be found. But it makes sense. It's a room that's almost always empty. One can get to it easily from the street. And, thanks to the draperies, it would burn fairly easily and before drawing much notice. Thank Heaven, my staff is unusually alert and went straight to my bedroom to fetch me. I just wasn't in it and they couldn't get past the flames to the turret room."

Freddie nodded and saw a fireman approaching the house. Leaving Kathy and Gloria, Freddie went over and told the man what his mother had told him. The fireman thanked Freddie and moved on to the house.

Gloria shook her head as Freddie walked up.

"A lot of good that's going to do," she said.

"It's the best we've got," Freddie said. "Would you like to come back to the apartment now, Mother, or do something else?"

"Let's go back to the apartment," Gloria said, a little sadly.

Once they got there, they found that Honoria was waiting for them.

"Mother, I've taken a few liberties," Honoria confessed as Roberts collected coats and hats. "I called your favorite dressmaker while you were out. She's going to send some additional intimates and dresses for you this afternoon. Fortunately, you already had a couple on order, so it was no trouble. But if you like, I can take you shopping now for shoes and anything else you might need right away.”

“That’s so sweet of you, Honoria,” Gloria all but staggered into the living room. “I’m so muddled right now, I can’t even think of where to begin. There’s so much to replace. I don’t even know where I’m going to live. Or how I’m going to live.”

The older woman finally broke down, sank onto the couch and began sobbing. Honoria and Kathy flew to either side of her. Freddie stood nearby, feeling utterly useless. Fortunately, Roberts slipped up to his side and whispered in his ear.

“I think I will see him,” Freddie replied, not that he particularly wanted to speak with Donald Marston at that moment, but the visit would get him out of the living room. “Please send him to the study.”

When Marston entered the study, Freddie was ready and offered his father’s old friend a fresh cigarette and a glass of whiskey. Marston took both. Freddie gestured to the occasional chairs and made a point of sitting in his favorite.

“I’m so glad you could see me,” Marston said, his voice taking on a slight whine. “Your father’s death is, of course, quite upsetting to you, so I haven’t wanted to bother you. But since it’s been a month or so, I thought I might now.”

“Very good of you,” Freddie said, lighting his own cigarette. He’d made a whiskey and soda for himself. Kathy wouldn’t approve of him drinking so early in the day, but he needed a drink and it would be rude to make Marston drink by himself.

“I don’t know if you’ve heard,” Marston said, looking at his cigarette. “But your father owed me quite a bit of money. Gambling debts, you know.”

“I have heard he was not terribly prompt about paying his losses.”

“He didn’t pay them at all!” Marston snapped.

"I don't really need the money, but it's the principle of the thing, don't you know? He even said that he'd remember me in his will, as if that would make things better."

"He may have intended to once he made a new will," Freddie said, trying to be conciliatory. "I was told he was about to but didn't quite get to it."

"It's too late now," Marston grumbled. "But that's why I'm here. Forced to grovel for what's rightfully mine. Can you think of anything more humiliating?"

"I suppose not." Freddie thought for a moment. "And to spare you any more, why don't you make a claim against his estate? I'm sure the judge will take gambling debts into consideration."

Marston grimaced. "Why can't you just help me out now?"

"I've been advised by my lawyer not to," Freddie said with a wan smile. "It's incredibly inconvenient, I know."

"It most certainly is." Marston slammed his glass down on the end table. "It's not fair, Freddie."

"I'm afraid it isn't," Freddie said, summoning Roberts with a quick hit of the hidden call button. "But there really isn't anything I can do at this point. I'm sorry, Mr. Marston."

Marston got up and made his goodbyes. Freddie stayed in the study, sipping his whiskey as he mulled over an idea. He had Roberts put in a call to Mr. Carstairs and when the lawyer was on the line, Freddie moved into the hallway.

"Eddie, is there any reason Mother can't sue Father's estate for her support?" Freddie asked.

"What? Don't you want to support her?"

"It has nothing to do with that," Freddie said. "You may have heard about the fire last night. She's lost everything. It would do her a world of good to be able to recover some money and manage her own affairs as she sees fit without feeling she must defer to me all the time."

"Well, there is the tradition that a widow is entitled to a third of her husband's estate," Carstairs said, musing. "If you don't mind losing that much of the estate, that is, then get her a lawyer."

"As I said, I couldn't care less how much of the estate I get." Freddie paused. "Will there be enough left to keep my mother in her accustomed style?"

Carstairs chuckled. "It depends on her accustomed style, but I'd say so. Most of the folks making claims don't have any documents to support them. And even if your father was prone to letting things go, he wasn't a spendthrift, so most of his investments have done well. A lot will depend on how the judge rules on the claims."

"And I've just sent another his way," Freddie said. "Gambling debts. Well, thank you, Eddie. I appreciate your time."

Freddie hung up and was happy to discover that his mother was still in the living room with Kathy and Honoria.

"I've got some news," he said. "I just spoke with Mr. Carstairs, and we believe it should be worth it to sue Father's estate for your support, Mother."

"What?" asked Gloria, looking a little flummoxed.

"Sue the estate—" Freddie said.

"I know what you're talking about," Gloria snapped. "I just didn't realize I could. But why couldn't I? Hm. We can't have Carstairs do it, can we?"

"I'm afraid not," Freddie said. "He's the executor. But we'll find another good lawyer for you."

Gloria turned. "Kathy, darling, please add find lawyer and file for my share of Fred's estate to our list." She settled herself pleasantly. "Freddie, I know it doesn't do to presume a victory. However, would you mind terribly if I, shall we say, borrowed a sufficient sum so that I may get a suite at the Plaza?"

"Of course, Mother," Freddie said. "I've already said—"

"I know what you've already said and I appreciate it." Gloria smiled. "Even though I wanted to stay here,

I'm afraid I've changed my mind again. I would much rather be on my own. This is working out better than I hoped."

Roberts appeared in the doorway. "Mrs. Everett Lewton is here to see the senior Mrs. Little."

"Oh." Gloria looked less than pleased. "I was hoping somebody else would come by to visit. Well, if nothing else, then we shall get some news. I'm in, Roberts."

Some minutes later, Lenore Lewton bustled into the living room. "Gloria, darling, I came the very second I heard. How terrible. I'm just glad no one was hurt."

"As am I, dear," Gloria said, indicating the occasional chair.

Roberts appeared with tea and cakes as Mrs. Lewton settled herself into the occasional chair.

"But I'm told you've lost everything," Mrs. Lewton. "Or almost everything."

"I was very fortunate in that some important keepsakes had been removed to the carriage house, which was not touched," Gloria said.

"Your jewelry?" Mrs. Lewton's eyes danced with interest.

"That was in the safe, which did not burn," Gloria said. "We are waiting to see if the contents were not harmed."

Mrs. Lewton smiled smugly. "Were you aware that there's a rumor going around that the fire was deliberately set?"

"Oh?" Freddie asked. "Who's saying that?"

"Mrs. Henry," Mrs. Lewton said, giving him an odd look as if he didn't belong there. "She lives on the corner across from you, doesn't she, Gloria?"

"Yes. Directly across the street from the front of the house," Gloria said.

"Well, she said she was told by one of her servants that the firemen were sifting through the ashes. Although, I think we both know that she was watching through her windows again," Mrs. Lewton said. "She called me this morning to ask if she should talk to the police. Or if her servants should. Apparently, they saw something last night that could be most incriminating."

"What, in Heaven's name?" Gloria asked.

"One of the Coates boys was watching the fire with the rest of the crowd. I believe they're your nephews, aren't they?"

"Yes, they are," Gloria said.

"Why would that be incriminating?" Kathy asked.

Freddie caught the looks between Mrs. Lewton and his mother.

"It's only an ugly rumor," Gloria said, dismissively. "And there's plenty of traffic along Madison. There's no reason why one or other of those young men wouldn't have stopped to watch, and that's assuming what Mrs. Henry saw was accurate."

"There's always that, I suppose," Mrs. Lewton said and checked her lapel watch. "Oh, my! Is that the time?" She popped up and Freddie summoned the valet with the hidden call button. "I'd best be running. Do let me know about the state of your jewelry, Gloria, when you find out. I may be able to loan you a piece of mine if you need it."

"Very kind of you, Lenore."

Roberts was already at the door to the living room and showed Mrs. Lewton out. Freddie looked at Gloria.

"Why did you dismiss that rumor about Aldrich and Wilfrid?" he asked. "And while you're at it, what is the rumor?"

Gloria sighed. "Darling, do you remember when you were about seven and Aldrich and Wilfrid kept lighting matches and putting them in your face?"

Freddie frowned. "Vaguely."

"Well, that's why I didn't let you spend a lot of time with them," Gloria said. "They were so much older, anyway. I was quite put out with Thelma over the incident and even more so with Stephen, who insisted we were coddling you. What they refused to see was that it was not simply boys being boys. And there have been other small fires. In fact, one of the reasons Thelma and Stephen moved into your grandfather's place on Long Island is that their place burned down. It was almost ten years ago, and you were at Harvard, so I don't know if you remember it, Freddie."

"I remember that," said Honoria. "You told Father something about not being surprised if one of the boys was behind the fire and Father told you to hush and not speak of it."

"Honoria! How did you find that out?" Gloria looked shocked.

"I listened at doors," Honoria said irritably. "Miss Jennings would tell me to go to bed, then go to her room. And I almost never went. I didn't listen to you and Father that much. You weren't terribly interesting."

"Well, I can't imagine we would have been to a young girl," Gloria said. "As for quashing the rumor, I simply felt that Thelma has been through enough these days. And it's not as though the police will be able to prove anything. So why give Lenore the opportunity to make trouble?"

"She'll do that," grumbled Honoria. "I wonder why she was so interested in whether your jewelry survived the fire? I can't imagine it was because she wanted to loan you anything."

Gloria let out a dignified sound that in anyone else would have been a snort. "I don't believe that for a moment. She probably just wants something to gossip about."

"Or maybe she wants the ruby," Kathy said. "She told me as much at luncheon on Monday. She said Father Little had offered to sell it to her and Mr. Lewton."

"Father wouldn't have done that," Freddie said.

"He most certainly would have," Gloria said angrily. She sighed deeply and looked at her two children. "I haven't wanted to say anything to diminish your respect for him. But your father did, in fact, try to sell the ruby. I'm not sure why. I suspect it was to spite me or your grandfather. Your father had told me it was stolen. And that was the last time I saw it. Your grandfather did tell me that he'd gotten it back from Fred and that he was going to keep it secure. That's why I was so shocked when I saw you wearing it, Kathy." Gloria looked down at her hands. "I would have loved to have worn it at least a few more times, but it wasn't safe in Fred's hands."

"Then why would Father tell someone he was going to sell it to him?" Freddie asked.

Gloria looked away. "Your father found the combination to your grandfather's safe a few months ago. I don't think he stole anything. I only happened to overhear him bragging about it to one of his friends. He seemed to think that since it would be coming to him eventually, it didn't matter if he took things out of it. This was after your grandfather's fall when it began to look like he wouldn't recover."

"Sounds to me like Father Little wanted to get even," Kathy said as the phone in the hallway rang.

"It does, doesn't it?" Freddie sighed.

Roberts appeared in the living room doorway. "Mr. Terrence Carter is here to see the senior Mrs. Little."

"How many times does that make it today?" Gloria asked. "He came by twice this morning before we left to see the house, didn't he?"

"At least twice," Kathy said.

Freddie looked at her, puzzled. It was disconcerting to have visitors coming that he knew nothing about.

"He also came by when you were gone," Roberts added.

"I'm not in," Gloria said.

"Yes, ma'am."

Gloria re-settled herself. "Let's see. What else do we need to attend to?"

Freddie smiled. His mother was still feeling the shock of the loss of her home but was determined to go on.

CHAPTER FIFTEEN

That Sunday, Easter, passed quietly. The whole family walked 5th Avenue in the annual celebration, but then parted ways. Gloria to her suite at the Plaza Hotel, Honoria to spend the day at home, and Freddie, Kathy and Gam to have dinner with Kathy's Uncle Mike, a prosperous lawyer and the family patriarch.

The next morning started quietly enough, with Freddie getting up early so that he could be at the office in good time. Gam and Kathy had almost finished their breakfasts when Freddie arrived in the dining room and picked up his paper. He kissed Kathy's cheek, patted Gam on the head, then got a cup of coffee and looked over the front page of the paper.

"Good news, darling," Kathy said. "Mrs. Davies is coming today."

Freddie looked up and smiled. "That is good news." He grinned at Gam. "I take it there will be exemplary behavior today?"

"I'll do swell," Gam said, grinning.

Kathy pointedly ignored him, then looked up as the door to the apartment buzzed. "That should be her."

Freddie got up long enough to greet the tutor and see Gam on his way. Kathy went to her desk in the study and Freddie settled back down at the dining room, intending to enjoy his coffee and a good, solid breakfast while reading the newspaper. What he read, however, had him cursing like a sailor. Kathy came running in.

"Freddie! What's wrong?"

"This!" Freddie shoved the paper at her and pointed to the offending story.

"Little and Sons shares to be offered to the public," Kathy looked up at him. "But I thought you weren't going to sell any shares to the public."

"We're not!" Freddie yelled. "This is some sort of sick joke." He hurried to the telephone in the hall and clicked to reach an operator. "I'm calling Carstairs and then I'm going to fire Mr. Brennan."

Kathy left him to it.

When Freddie arrived at the office not long after, Mrs. Putnam took his coat and hat.

"I must confess, we were all surprised by the news, Mr. Little," she told him.

"So was I," Freddie said. "I'll need to dictate a letter to be sent to the newspapers immediately."

"We've been getting quite a strong response."

"Actually, I'll need to dictate a letter to the other board members first. And I need to find out who released this story to the news."

"I seriously doubt it was anybody here," Mrs. Putnam said, scrambling after Freddie into his office. "Everyone seems quite surprised. I'll have the switchboard take messages, sir."

Freddie grumbled and complained while Mrs. Putnam spoke with the switchboard. He was so furious, it was hard to know what to do first, but Mrs. Putnam helped him order his thoughts. Another hour and several letters later, Freddie held a meeting with the various company chiefs, then went to a conference room filled with reporters, where Freddie made it very clear that company shares were not going to be sold publicly.

"My grandfather, who handed the control of this company to me, as his father and grandfather had handed it on before, did so, trusting that I would keep it in our family and make sure that it would support all of us for generations to come. This is a sacred trust to me. I appreciate it that so many people think highly enough of us that they are eager to buy our shares. And I understand that there are those who think we'd be better off selling them. However, not only I but several family members, beg to differ and I would not want to betray their trust in me."

The reporters tried to ask more questions, but Freddie refused and left the conference room quickly.

He was not happy to see Donald Marston in the foyer to his office. He was about to send the man out, then thought better of it.

"Wonderful news, Mr. Little," Marston said as he followed Freddie into his office.

"It's not true," Freddie said, shutting the office door.

"But, Mr. Little, this is perfect!" Marston said, bubbling over. "Give me first chance to buy some shares and it will cover your father's debts."

"The company shares are for family members only," Freddie said. "The story in the Times was a complete fake."

"No! The Times wouldn't print a false story."

Freddie turned on him. "Were you counting on that when you gave them the story?"

"What? Gave them..?" Marston fumbled. "What, in Heaven's name, are you talking about?"

"The story in the Times," Freddie said. "I want to know if you gave them the story in an attempt to force me to sell the shares."

"No!" Marston gasped. "I would never..." He paused. "You thought... Actually, I wish I'd thought of it. But, no. I didn't give them the story."

"Do you know who did?"

"Somebody who wants your company?"

Freddie took a deep breath. "Yes. That would seem obvious."

"You could still sell me a few shares, just on the side, you know."

"You're not a family member, and I strongly suspect your wife would object to any attempt on your part to marry one."

Marston flopped into one of the two chairs in front

of Freddie's desk. "My wife. Do you know how hard it is to support a society woman these days?"

"I can imagine," Freddie said quietly.

"The demands are endless. Whatever one of them has, the rest of them insist they need it, too. Do you know what mine is demanding? A ruby like the one your wife has. I'm sure I'm not the only one being forced to think about our position and what the others will say. It's ridiculous, I tell you. And I can't divorce her. Can you imagine the settlement?" He shuddered.

"I'm sorry you're having such a difficult time." The phone on Freddie's desk rang. "Now, if you'll excuse me, Mr. Marston, I believe I have a very busy day ahead of me."

Freddie's day only got marginally better, but he found he was able to soothe several large customers and even gain their sympathy regarding the bad news release. He ended up working late, and managed to avoid all but a couple drinks and felt quite sober when he got home.

Kathy was full of news about her day, listened quite patiently to the story of his day, then the both of them found themselves laughing quite heartily over dinner at Gam's description of his day.

"It's quite surprising, really," Freddie told Kathy as they got ready for bed that night. "Poor old Mr. Marston, complaining about how all the society ladies now want a ruby like yours, or something just as showy, and I couldn't help thinking how I do not have to worry about things like that."

Kathy's grin grew just a touch evil. "You don't?"

"For one thing, you already have the ruby and you were utterly terrified when you wore it." Freddie grinned back. "And I can't imagine you caring what those other women think of you, anyway."

"I didn't think I did." Kathy frowned. "I suppose some of it is that I don't want anyone thinking badly of me. But I also worry about how their bad opinion affects you and your business."

"Fortunately, my business interests are not dependent on the good opinions of the Four Hundred," Freddie said. He sat down next to her on the bed and pulled her close. "I suspect we'd have been bankrupt before my grandfather's time if that were the case. As for the rest of society..." He sighed. "I used to think it was all terribly important. But these days, it all seems very shallow. I used to hate going to the opera or concerts because it was all about being seen. Nowadays, you and I go to actually see and listen to the opera, and I'm beginning to truly love the art in a way I never could before. We get to have dinner with Lowell and Mrs. Parker and Mr. Benchley and Mr. Kaufman and even Mr. Marx, and it's all delightful fun. It's stimulating and thoughtful and far more entertaining than a fancy dinner with my so-called peers. I could never understand why Honoria was always trying to avoid doing what was expected of her and now I know why. She was utterly bored, and she has had fewer opportunities to exercise her intellect than I have had." He squeezed Kathy even closer to his side. "My darling, darling Kathy, Heaven forbid I ever lose you, but if I ever do, my life will still be better than it was before I met you. You saved me from what I was supposed to be and gave me a chance to be the man I really am."

"And you genuinely believed in me and what I can do." Kathy sniffed. "I do not want to think about losing that, or you."

"Then everything will be all right," Freddie said.

He kissed her tenderly, and the tenderness soon melted into a deep want and need.

Gloria looked at the tarnished and charred silver cigarette lighter, then at Briggeman. They were in the sitting room of her elegantly appointed suite at the Park Plaza hotel. It wasn't quite as comfortable as her own home had been, but she was able to keep her most trusted staff members nearby.

"And where was it found, again?" she asked.

"Right under the window you indicated as the possible starting point for the fire," he said.

"You are absolutely certain of that."

"Yes, ma'am."

"Thank you, Briggeman. It does lend considerable weight to our theory that the mansion was burned intentionally." Gloria paused. "However, I think we should keep this just between us for the time being."

"Perfectly understandable, ma'am."

"There are certain legal ramifications, you understand."

"I do, ma'am."

Gloria put the lighter into her purse. She had been quite disturbed the day before about the news of company shares being sold to the public and very relieved when Kathy had called that morning to reassure her that Freddie had done no such thing. The Tuesday paper had featured a picture of Freddie at the start of their business section. It didn't do, but she couldn't help feeling a great deal of pride in her son. And he was going to meet her at the hotel restaurant for luncheon that very day. She smiled and couldn't help wondering how many of her peers had such a fine date to be seen with, and all the better because Freddie was actually an interesting person.

She went downstairs a touch early to leave some letters for the concierge to mail and then found a comfortable chair in the hotel lobby to wait for Freddie. She was not happy to see Terrence Carter coming her way, but there was no way to avoid him.

"Gloria, I'm so glad to see you," Terrence said. "I'd heard you were stopping here for the time being."

"I am. How are you, Mr. Carter?"

He winced slightly at the formality. "Quite well. May I join you?"

"I'm waiting for my son," Gloria said. "We're going to have luncheon together. Just the two of us."

"Oh." Carter waited for a moment. "Then I suppose we can have a nice chat while we're waiting for him."

Gloria sighed. "Terrence, I'm not sure what is behind your attentions, but haven't I made it clear that they are not welcome?"

"You misunderstand, Gloria. I am not seeking another wife."

Gloria smiled. She did not believe him for a second.

"I'm sure you're not. But I can't imagine you find me all that scintillating."

"Ah, but you are." Terrence smiled. "I've often thought so. Your smile is quite dainty and your grace is so charming."

Gloria frowned. "But what have we to talk about?"

"We can talk about the opera. It's quite a fine season, don't you think? I believe last November's Tosca was possibly the best thing I've seen in years. Although I did see it again a couple weeks ago, and I must say, I am quite fond of Madame Easton."

"I haven't been to the opera this past month, Terrence." Gloria debated whether she should tell him that she found the opera an enormous bore.

"Hello, Mother." Freddie suddenly appeared in front of her. "Hello, Mr. Carter. I hope you don't mind. My mother and I have a luncheon date."

Carter scrambled to his feet. "So she said. And I'll happily hand her off to you."

Gloria glared at him quickly and accepted Freddie's hand up. Freddie, fortunately, had the good sense not to say anything until they were seated in the restaurant and had ordered.

"You did not seem very happy with Mr. Carter," Freddie said.

"Oh, he's not bad," Gloria sighed. "Just not terribly interesting."

"Really? We got on fairly well. He's quite the fan of the opera."

"And you're most emphatically not."

"I am."

Gloria glared at him. "As many times as I've had to practically twist your arm to get you to show up at an opening.”

“That was different.” Freddie smiled. “That was about being seen. I’ve been going with Kathy, and she loves the music and the pageantry and we’ve had a wonderful time. She loved hearing Madame Jeritza sing Tosca last November. It was quite enthralling.”

“Hm. And to think I find all that shrieking terribly dull. And I know just enough French and Italian to get snippets of it, but not enough to actually follow the story.”

“But to get back to Mr. Carter.”

“Him.” Gloria sighed heavily. “I can’t imagine what he sees in me.”

“Your wit, your intelligence.”

“My smile and my grace.” Gloria shuddered. “He’s looking for another fawning female to listen to him. He talked his first wife, Alice, into an early grave.”

“He thinks you’re putting him off because you’re still grieving Father.”

Gloria paused as the waiter placed their lunches in front of them.

“I was afraid of that. I put it to him quite clearly just before you arrived and he merely said he was not looking for another wife.” She glared at the teacup filled with red wine in front of her. “He said I misunderstood him.”

“I doubt you misunderstood him,” said Freddie. He looked at her thoughtfully. “But how do I say this? I do not wish to imply that you wouldn’t be worth a great deal of extra effort to win. However, you seem to have made it clear that a three-legged horse could win the Belmont Stakes sooner than he could carry you off.”

Gloria had to laugh. “I tried to.”

“So why is he pressing his suit? I’ve already let him know that I have control of your support, so I can’t imagine that’s why he’s chasing you.”

“He could have heard that your father’s gun collection largely survived the fire,” Gloria said. “He always envied it.”

"Did the collection survive?"

"Only half the room burned, which was surprising when you think about all those moldy stuffed heads in there. Briggeman said that most of the guns survived, as well. At least, they weren't visibly burnt or melted. He's seeing to it that they get cleaned. Did you want any of them?"

Freddie shuddered and shook his head. "No. I really don't care for hunting."

"I know, darling." Gloria felt the sigh rising up from the soles of her feet. "Of all the things that we lost, I can't believe that it was your father's guns that survived. At least, I still have my diaries and correspondence."

Freddie reached forward and touched her hand. "Mother?"

Gloria shook her head. "I'm fine, Freddie. Now, what were we talking about? Oh, yes, the unaccountably persistent Mr. Carter."

Freddie suddenly frowned. "You don't think he could have shot Father, could he? To get the guns or to get you?"

"Oh, that's ridiculous!" Gloria suddenly stopped, her heart in her throat. "Or is it? I wouldn't imagine that having either your father's guns or me would cause him to murder your father. And yet..."

Freddie thought it over. "I'll start with asking Honoria whether he left his coat that night. We are supposing that those who left without claiming their outerwear meant that they wanted to avoid the police, possibly for good reason." He paused. "And would you do me an enormous favor?"

"Of course, my dear."

"Please do not go trying to find out if he did shoot Father, Mother. I do not want to be worrying about you."

Gloria smiled. "I understand, dear. The only thing I am trying to find is how to make useable fibers out of petroleum distillates. Or maybe I should look for another base polymer., They've done some very interesting things with cellulose-based materials, besides the viscose."

Gloria laughed as she watched Freddie trying not to roll his eyes.

"That all sounds very fascinating, Mother."

"No, it doesn't. Except to me, of course." She smiled fondly at her son. "I'll spare you the details. Oh. And I've just now remembered." She picked up her purse from the side of the table and opened it. "Briggeman said they'd found this in the ashes. Under the very window I thought was where the fire started."

"I've seen this before." Freddie took the small silver cigarette lighter and ran his thumb over the bas-relief design on the front. "I think I gave out several of these at Christmas a year ago. He flipped the lighter over to look at the engraving on the back. "AGC. Aldrich Gordon Coates?"

"I wouldn't be a bit surprised," Gloria said. "Yet, I've always considered Aldrich to be merely a bully. It's his brother Wilfrid that has always worried me. Not that I would have said so to Thelma."

"She does dote on her boys, doesn't she?" Freddie gave her the lighter back. "But even if it is Aldrich's, it's not really proof he started the fire. He could have lost it. Or perhaps someone stole it and used it to make Aldrich look guilty."

"I would think it would give you a place to look."

Freddie nodded. "It does, I suppose. All right. I'll look into it."

"I knew I could count on you." Gloria smiled.

Freddie left the luncheon feeling more than a little worried. He did not trust his mother's promise to not go questioning Terrence Carter. He also wondered how and when he would be able to talk to his cousin Aldrich. He looked at the slip of paper in his coat pocket. It contained a message from Lowell Winters, carefully written in Mrs. Putnam's exacting handwriting. Freddie knew the place referred to in the message. It was a nice little speak just east of 5th and 42nd. Lowell often went there, ostensibly to write, when he could no longer bear looking at the four walls in his apartment. Never mind that Lowell's apartment had at least seven rooms, let alone four walls. The odds were even that Lowell was actually writing in the speak. The odds were even lower that Lowell could say something that would ease Freddie's mind about his mother, but relatively decent that Lowell could find something cheering to say.

The speak, hidden in the basement of a bookstore, was dimly lit and in spite of its trade in illegal liquor, it was a quiet place, with a well-polished bar and several well-used tables scattered about. Lowell was ensconced in a far corner, under one of the few lamps hanging from the wall. He was scribbling something on a tablet of some sort and several broken pencils lay on the ground around his chair. A large glass of beer sat in front of him and a cigarette burned next to him, the lit end hanging off the edge of the table. Lowell finished something with a flourish, leaned back, his gaze fixed on the tablet in front of him. His hand found the glass of beer and he took a good swallow. With a nod, he looked up and finally saw Freddie and waved.

Freddie walked over, slipping out of his overcoat. "Am I interrupting?"

"No more than usual," Lowell said. "Miserable things, novels."

"Yes, I know," said Freddie, sitting down across from his friend. "But another novel? I thought you had enough to keep you busy providing your usual tripe for Life and some of the others."

"I do." Lowell took a long drag on his cigarette. "But this novel nonsense. Once you've gone and done it, the form gets under your skin. I blame you and your literary pretensions."

"Of course," Freddie looked over at the bartender and gestured. A moment later, he had a glass of beer, as well.

"I do have some news for you, though," Lowell said. "Donald Marston has announced that he's suing your father's estate to cover his gambling debts."

"I know. I was the one who suggested that he do so." Freddie fitted a cigarette in its holder and lit it. "There was no point in not doing so. I seriously doubt he has anything written to back up his claim."

Lowell took another drag on his cigarette. "He doesn't. Your father was very smart about not giving anyone his marker. So Marston is looking for witnesses. He may be able to find a few, too. He even approached me, presumably because of my connection to you."

"Are you going to testify?"

Lowell shrugged. "I might not have a choice if I get summoned. However, that seems unlikely. I told Marston that however just his cause, I was not going to commit perjury so that he could further it. And I've never gambled with your father. As you can imagine, I was beneath his notice."

"I'm sorry about that," Freddie said softly.

Lowell snorted. "I was perfectly happy to be. I saw how he treated those self-made men who tried to be friends with him. Very pleasant and democratic while there was something to be learned from them. But then, he made it very clear he was better than they were." He looked at Freddie. "I haven't disillusioned you too badly, have I?"

"No." Freddie felt his face tighten as he frowned. "I've always known my father was not a very kind man. I don't enjoy being reminded of that and hope that it does not reflect badly on me. I think right now, however, I'm more bothered that you seem to know my father's habits better than I do."

"I wouldn't say that." Lowell shifted as he dropped the butt of his cigarette on the floor and squashed it out with his toe. "It's as was said earlier last month. People make comments around me that they would never make in front of you. I dare say if we were ever foolish enough to visit Indiana and my hometown, people would tell you things about the miserable bastard that was my father that they would never say to me."

"It seems a terrible thing to hate one's father," Freddie said.

"It seems a terrible thing to ignore one's son, or in my case, beat the tar out of him at every opportunity." Lowell shifted. "It's why I have no interest in becoming a father. I can't imagine I'd do any better." He looked at Freddie. "Are you looking at joining the ranks of fatherhood?"

"Not so far," Freddie said. "Kathy doesn't want children. Well, she's not said she won't, but she very much doesn't want to get pregnant."

"It's just as well, then. We've got books to release and to be edited. How's your novel going?"

"It's almost done," Freddie said with a sigh. "But I haven't worked on it since my father died."

"Then why don't you find some time to work on it?"

"I don't have time. I've a company to run. In fact, I should be getting back to the office."

Lowell laughed loudly. "Never thought I'd hear that from you, my indolent friend. So, how do you like being yet another working stiff?"

Freddie sighed. "I suspect I'm about to be paid back for every ridiculous thing I've ever said about working for a living." He shook his head. "Yesterday's newspaper story was bad enough, but it's not nearly as bad as some of the goings-on we've uncovered. And you heard about Mother's house."

"Yes, that was terrible." Lowell leaned back in his chair.

"Mother found a cigarette lighter with Aldrich Coates' initials on it right where she thinks the fire started."

"Hm. Not surprising, I suppose, although I would have expected it from Wilfrid sooner."

"That's what Mother said. I tended to avoid them when I was growing up. How do you know them?"

"Carlotta, my ex-wife's older sister. You remember her, don't you? She married into that family. I see her now and again at various speaks. In fact, I saw her with Aldrich on Friday night."

"The night the fire started?" Freddie's eyebrows rose. "What time?"

"Let me think. I came in early for the nine o'clock show, so maybe eight, eighty-thirty and they were already there. By the time I left at midnight, they were still there. Personally, I think she's set her cap for Aldrich."

"That's right. He's been divorced for several years now."

"And she was widowed about a year ago, maybe less."

"I remember now. It was a house fire, wasn't it?"

"Oh, yes." Lowell shifted and lit another cigarette. "They couldn't prove it, of course, but Carlotta said she was certain that Wilfrid had started it. She got drunk one night last summer and told me all about it. And her miserable marriage. And the fact that she really thought she was entitled to a better settlement from the Coates family, given that she'd produced three heirs and two girls to marry off. And now that Aldrich is coming into his inheritance, I'm guessing she's decided to try getting her hands on their money once again."

Freddie nodded. "I suppose even the risk of your brother-in-law burning you up again would be worth it. Are you certain it was Aldrich you saw?"

"Oh, yes. Carlotta stopped by my table and introduced him."

"Then someone must have stolen or found his lighter. Or maybe it just happened to fall where the fire had started and wasn't actually used."

"Or maybe Wilfrid started the fire using his brother's lighter."

Freddie snubbed out his cigarette on the floor. "That is definitely a possibility, especially since there is no love lost between those two at the moment."

He looked down. His glass was empty and he briefly debated ordering another, but checked his wristwatch, instead. "I'd better get going."

"Yes, you should." Lowell leaned back in his chair and glared at him. "Seriously, Freddie. You need to find some time to work on your book. You look worse than you did when we got stranded in Philadelphia after that all-night toot when someone stole your car."

Freddie frowned as he picked up his overcoat. "We were in Washington, DC, when the car got stolen. Philadelphia was when the truck hit us."

"Are you sure that wasn't the trip to Miami?"

"No, the car getting stolen wasn't the trip to Miami. We were driving home from Miami when the truck slipped on the ice and hit us in Philadelphia. And the car theft was in DC."

"My god, that Miami trip was a week." Lowell shuddered. "One we're not likely to try again too damned soon. More's the pity. Explains why you looked so bad. And you look even worse now. So take my advice, old man."

"I will." Freddie smiled and left. He wasn't sure he'd be able to take Lowell's advice, which was, as usual, quite good.

That evening, as he washed up before going to bed, he looked at himself in the bathroom mirror. His face was drawn and there were decided bags under his eyes. He sighed deeply.

"Darling," he said, going into the bedroom. "Please be honest. How bad do I look these days?"

Kathy looked like she was about to say something merely soothing, but then she stopped.

"Freddie, you do look awfully exhausted," she said, finally. "I have been worried about you, but don't really know what to do about it."

He sank onto the side of the bed. "I don't, either."

"Why don't we pay a call on your cousin Wilfrid tomorrow?" Kathy suggested. "Maybe if you get that bit of nastiness out of your brain, you can write."

He had told Kathy most of his conversation with Lowell and she had insisted that he take some time to work on his novel after dinner and had banned herself and Gam from the study. But the words had not come. Freddie had gotten distracted by a report on the business and before he knew it, the evening had fled without a single word being written.

"I suppose that's possible," Freddie said.

They crawled under the covers and held each other for a long time before Freddie finally fell asleep.

CHAPTER SIXTEEN

Wilfrid Coates received Freddie and Kathy in the living room of his apartment, which was a couple blocks north on Park Avenue. He had a cut crystal glass of whiskey in his hand but did not offer any to Freddie or Kathy. The three remained standing.

"So, you've come to me," Wilfrid remarked idly, swirling the ice cubes in his glass.

"We're simply looking for information," Freddie said.

"Oh, you want me to help you when you wouldn't help me," Wilfrid said.

"I gave the board every encouragement to accept you."

"You could have out-voted them."

"Yes. But why would you have wanted to be the only person in the room besides me who wanted you there? And there are other ways that I might be able to help you, Wilfrid. But I do need some information, first."

"Such as..?"

"Where you were Friday."

"Ah." Wilfrid chuckled, a soft sound, utterly devoid of mirth. "So that's what this is about. There's a fire and everyone looks at me." He glared at them. "Do you think I haven't heard the rumors?"

"Obviously, you have," said Freddie, quietly. "And for the record, I am not assuming it was you."

"Then why aren't you talking to Aldie?"

"Who's to say we haven't?" Freddie's forefinger began beating a tattoo on his leg.

"And there are others who could be involved," Kathy said. "Maybe you know something we don't."

Wilfrid turned a tight smile on her. "I know a lot of things you don't." He glanced over at Freddie. "But I don't have to tell you anything." He took a long sip of his whiskey. "I will, however, say this. You might want to look for something Aldie left behind. He's been complaining about missing his lighter."

"Thank you, Wilfrid," Freddie said. "I'll look into it."

"Fine. But before you make any accusations, Freddie, consider this. You have to prove it." Wilfrid swirled the ice in his drink. "That's why I can do whatever I want. You may want to remember that." He took a long look at Kathy, then glanced over at Freddie and went back to his drink.

"Thank you, Wilfrid," Freddie said and took Kathy's arm as they left.

In the foyer of the building, Freddie made sure the footmen were close by. He hurried Kathy into the waiting limousine.

"Well, at least we know Wilfrid set the fire," Kathy said.

"He never said so." Freddie sighed and looked out the window at the mid-afternoon traffic on Park.

"Then why did he bring up the lighter?" Kathy asked. "I'm sure he wants us to think Aldrich did it. But we know where Aldrich was that night and that he couldn't have done it. And who else would have known about the lighter?"

"Well, almost anyone who had heard Aldrich complaining about losing his lighter. Still, it could be pushing the point."

Kathy turned Freddie's head toward her. "Freddie, dearest, yes, the problem is that we can't prove it yet. But at least we know where the fire is coming from. I wouldn't be at all surprised if Wilfrid killed your father and his, as well. It would give him a chance to get something he wouldn't otherwise be entitled to."

"You're right, Kathy." Freddie shuddered. "I just hate the way he looked at you."

The car stopped in front of their building.

"I didn't like it, either," Kathy said. "But forewarned, forearmed, right? Now, I've got my meeting to go to. Why don't you take a nap before going back to your office? Get some rest, you'll be able to think clearly and then we'll get this resolved in no time."

"Yes, dearest." Freddie kissed her softly before getting out of the car.

He didn't dare tell her that he wasn't in the least reassured. She'd had another nightmare that night and neither had gotten much sleep. Luncheon had been hurried because they wanted to talk to Wilfrid before going back to their respective work.

Freddie glanced all around him as he hurried into his building. He was getting very tired of feeling exposed all the time, wondering which direction the next attack would come from. He felt somewhat safer once he walked into his apartment. Roberts was there to take his hat and coat. There were several messages from Mrs. Putnam. Freddie called her quickly, explained that he would probably arrive very late that afternoon, and she reassured him that he did not need to come in to the office at all. Freddie decided he wouldn't. He'd work on his book. He'd mull over all the different people who could be attacking his family and the company. He might even take a nap.

Kathy had been right, as she so often was. Allowing himself to get to the point of utter exhaustion was not going to help him think straight and solve his father's murder.

He became vaguely aware of raised voices coming from the living room. Sighing, he went there to look.

"All I asked was for you to attend one small meeting!" Gloria snarled at Honoria.

"I told you I didn't want to go!" Honoria snapped.

"No, you didn't. You made up some cock and bull story about needing to talk to Lenore Lewton. And what happens? I run into Lenore and she says she hasn't heard from you in several days."

“I also told you I didn’t want to go, but you didn’t hear me!” Honoria’s eyes were brimming over.

“What is going on here?” Freddie demanded, horrified by his mother’s and sister’s raised voices.

“We are having a difference of opinion,” Gloria said, pulling herself taller.

“But why are you having it in my living room?”

“I went to Honoria’s apartment, but she was down here, playing with Gam.”

“Where is he?” Freddie asked, looking around.

“In his schoolroom, where he should have been,” Gloria said.

“I was having luncheon with him while Mrs. Davies has her afternoon rest,” Honoria said. “We do it all the time. And then Mother bursts in here with all her accusations and demands. It’s not fair, Freddie. She expects me to take up all her social duties because she’s in mourning. And I happen to know for a fact that it’s just as much because she doesn’t want to go!”

Freddie gulped. He knew Honoria had little interest in social obligations, but to hear her confronting their mother in such a fashion was more than a bit much.

“You wouldn’t grant me some relief?” Gloria shot back.

“Why do we have to keep things up in the first place?”

“Think of our position. Think of the family’s business!”

“I think about them all the time!” Honoria screamed. “I’m tired of thinking about them. And it doesn’t make a damn bit of difference to the family business if we are represented at this gala or not.”

“She does have the justice of it, Mother,” Freddie said, at a complete loss for how to manage the argument.

“But you lied to me,” Gloria said, ignoring Freddie.

“You wouldn’t listen!” Honoria’s tears began streaking her mascara down her face. “I only lied when you wouldn’t listen. And how dare you chastise me for lying to you when you’ve been lying to me my entire life. A scientist? With a paper published?"

Gloria sank down onto the couch, finally defeated. "I didn't want to embarrass you. No one understood. I had to be what everyone expected. I didn't want you to be ashamed of me."

"Mother!" Honoria screamed in utter confusion. Sobbing, she sat down next to her mother.

Completely undone, Freddie went for the credenza under the window, where several decanters stood, and poured himself a stiff one.

"Mother," Honoria said, "I didn't want you to be ashamed of me. You just seemed so much happier when I lied to you. I tried to tell you I couldn't be what everyone expected of me."

"And I was terrified you'd get your heart broken by some horrible man only interested in your position," Gloria explained. "Or that someone would find out about me and you'd be shamed in front of everyone. I only wanted you to be happy and all I knew was that doing what was expected of you was supposed to make you happy."

"But it never made you happy." Honoria sniffed.

"It did. It really did," Gloria got her handkerchief out and dabbed at her eyes. "Maybe not as happy as I was in my laboratory, but I was happy."

"And I was miserable."

"I thought that was because you were fighting it so hard. And then, after Henry died, you seemed to settle down and were happy. Mostly. I did worry about your friends, though. Socialists, dear? Why, that sort of thinking is so dangerous."

Freddie sighed deeply, wondering how he could politely leave his own living room.

"Is it safe to assume you do not want to know about my double life?" Honoria asked

Gloria nodded. "Maybe not just this instant."

"I need you to listen to me, Mother, and really hear me." Honoria dabbed at the mascara streaks on her cheeks. "Not just turn deaf ears to me when it's something you don't want to hear."

"I suppose that's fair." Gloria fidgeted with her handkerchief, then looked Honoria in the eye. "But no more lying and no more saying things just to shock me?"

Honoria nodded. "Fair enough."

"Good," snarled Freddie. "I'm glad you've both got it all cleared up."

"Oh, dear, you are overwrought," Gloria said, getting up.

"Yes, I am overwrought, over-worked and very much over-tired." Freddie snapped, pouring a second drink. "And all I want right now is peace and quiet. I simply want to be left alone. No more invasions. No more family. No more murders or fires. Just leave me alone!"

"I'll get Gam and Mrs. Davies," Honoria said quietly.

Freddie leaned over the credenza and stared out the window as they left. His second glass of whiskey was empty, so he poured another.

Several hours later, he heard the elevator and Kathy coming into the apartment.

"Freddie!" she called. "I've got news!"

Freddie debated whether he wanted to answer her or not. He knew he was drunk and at the moment, all he wanted was to get drunker. The shock of the argument between his mother and sister had been bad enough. But between the very uncomfortable interview with Wilfrid, all the problems at the company and not being able to write, he felt as though his entire world was collapsing on top of him and he didn't have the least idea of what to do about it, never mind that everyone seemed to expect him to not only know but have some great insight as to the best course of action.

Kathy came into the living room, saw him sprawled on the couch and frowned.

"You've been drinking," she said, simply.

"Yes, and I don't want to hear about it."

She glared at him. "Freddie, I know Wilfrid was upsetting, but getting drunk is not going to clear your head."

"I don't care about clearing my head," Freddie snarled. "I'm tired and overwrought and I do not need a lecture on demon rum. Now, damn it. Leave me alone!"

"I see." Kathy pressed her lips together and blinked her eyes.

"And I'm sleeping in my own bed tonight."

"Then do not expect to find me in it." Kathy turned and left.

He could hear steps running and the hum of the elevator. Terror seized him and he realized he did not want her to go. He stumbled into the foyer in time to see the elevator door close on her.

Suddenly sober, he scrambled down the servants' stairs. He barely made it to the building vestibule when he saw Kathy leaving the building without a footman anywhere near. He dashed after her.

He saw the flash of late afternoon sunlight on the gold filigree of the dark stock as it poked from the window of a large black car parked across the street. There were two shots. Freddie looked up and Kathy was on the sidewalk, blood pooling beneath her head.

CHAPTER SEVENTEEN

Freddie sat in the chair in the waiting room at the hospital trying not to shiver and wondering why hospital chairs had to be so blasted uncomfortable. Kathy's relatives had shown up in force. Uncle Dan was there, his wife, Aunt Beth, in tow, as well as Uncle James, a sour old priest who glowered as he prayed his rosary beads, and Aunt Mary, a rather jovial nun, also praying a rosary. Uncle Mike paced the floor while his wife, Aunt Marian, knitted. Uncle Patrick, the doctor, was talking to the charge nurse in the ward. Uncle Thomas, who owned a speak in Hell's Kitchen, paced alongside his wife, Aunt Jane. Aunt Bridget had dragged along her husband, Uncle Morris Klein, and even the bum, Uncle John, was there, the stale booze wafting off of him.

On Freddie's side, Honoria held Gam, with Gloria and Ivy on either side. Lowell sat next to Freddie.

Another doctor came out of a nearby doorway and Uncle Patrick, an average-sized man whose girth almost matched Lowell's, went over and talked to him. Freddie got up.

"It's good news," Patrick announced. "Two wounds, but the head wound was just a graze and the leg wound was in her calf and didn't touch the bone."

The rumble that erupted was just short of a cheer, as all the aunts and uncles made the sign of the cross across their chests.

"Can I see her?" Freddie asked.

Patrick smiled at him. "Of course. Gam, you'll go second. The rest of us will have to take turns."

Freddie glanced apologetically at his mother and sister. The argument over who would see Kathy when was already starting.

"Gam," Freddie hissed, pulling the boy close to him. "Make sure Mother and Honoria get early turns, please."

Gam looked a little frightened but nodded. Freddie followed the unnamed doctor to the room where Kathy lay. Her head was bandaged, but her eyes were open and mostly alert.

"Freddie," she murmured.

"Hello, darling. I'm so glad to see you're all right." Freddie slid into the chair next to the bed. He took her hand and kissed it. "I'm so terribly sorry about this afternoon."

"I'm sorry, too." She blinked and sighed. "Think they gave me morphine."

"That's a good thing, my darling. It won't hurt so much."

Kathy snorted. "What happened?"

"You were shot. I think I may even have seen my father's gun."

"Why keep using it?"

"I don't know. I'll have to think about it."

"Good. Have you sobered up?"

"Almost immediately, my love. And I'll do my absolute best to be a very good boy from here on in."

Kathy's smile was sincere, even if Freddie got the impression she'd noticed that he hadn't promised never to drink again.

"Gam?"

"He'll be in next, and hopefully, Honoria and Mother, after that. Most of your aunts and uncles are here, too."

Kathy muttered something that sounded remarkably vile.

"I'll see to it that they don't stay very long."

"Want to sleep," Kathy muttered.

Freddie left the room shortly after that. Uncle Mike had gotten his unruly siblings in order, and Gam, then Gloria each got a chance to look in on Kathy, who had fallen fast asleep. Or at least was feigning sleep soundly enough that her relatives did not question it.

Honoria, Gloria, Gam, and Freddie all crowded into a taxi shortly after.

"What an amazing family," Gloria said. "I'm not quite sure what to make of it."

"It's like this," Gam said. "My ma, Katie Marie, ran off and left all of them to go marry my pa in Kansas. So, when Kathy came back to New York, they all felt 'sponsible for her. And now me, too."

"Apparently, Uncle Mike feels the responsibility particularly keenly," Freddie said. "He'd been given charge of Mother Briscow, and she managed to give him the slip."

Gam started laughing. "'Member when he met Pa last Christmas? I thought he was like to have near killed him for tempting Ma away."

Freddie couldn't help smiling at the memory. "There was some tension, yes. But they patched it up and became quite friendly afterward."

"But why did someone shoot at Kathy?" Honoria asked, suddenly frowning. "Uncle Dan— Excuse me, Sergeant Callaghan thought it was connected to Father's murder."

Freddie's smile died. "I can't be certain," he said. "But I thought I may have seen Father's rifle being pointed out of a car window. Uncle Dan said that the street cops had recovered one of the bullets. If they're a match to the bullets that killed Father and Uncle Stephen, we'll have a pretty good idea that it was Father's gun used in both killings."

"That's right. They have that new microscope," Gloria said. "I would love to see that." She stopped suddenly. "Or perhaps I shouldn't."

Honoria groaned. "Mother, I'm sure you can find a way to look at Sergeant Callaghan's microscope without alerting the Four Hundred. And I still don't see why you care what they think, anyway."

"It's all I've ever known, darling," Gloria said,

sounding a little testy. "Wilma and I were talking about that before Stephen's funeral. She pointed out that scandals and having others talking about us are not nearly as deadly as we'd been raised to believe. However, I'm finding that old habits die hard."

"Yes, I suppose they would," Honoria said. "I'm sorry I snapped, Mother."

"Apology accepted, darling."

Freddie looked at them crossly. "What is going on between you two? All of a sudden, it's as though you're at each other's throats at the least provocation."

"I don't know," Gloria said. She looked at her daughter. "Honoria, what do you think it is?"

"I don't know," Honoria said. "We've always argued, maybe not in front of anyone."

"But we've never said plainly to each other what we were thinking," Gloria said. "Or, rather, I haven't." She sighed deeply. "It's as though my entire world has been turned upside down and I find myself questioning things I've always taken for granted. It's all very unsettling."

"I imagine it is," Freddie said.

"Pa told me that it's always scary when things change," Gam suddenly said. "Like when I came out here to live. But Pa said if you never want things to change, you're going to have a pretty boring life."

Gloria smiled at the boy. "Gam, I do believe you're right."

Freddie spent the next day at Kathy's side, until the middle of the afternoon when she finally banished him. She took a short nap and when she awoke, she was pleased to see Gloria poking her head in the door.

"Hello," Kathy said, brightening.

"I didn't wake you, did I?" Gloria asked.

Kathy yawned. "I was just waking up. Please come in."

"Thank you." Gloria shut the door behind her and sat down in the chair next to the bed. "And how are you feeling?"

"The headache comes and goes," Kathy said. "And my leg is awful sore, but fine otherwise."

"That's good." Gloria looked around at all the flowers scattered about the room. "My, you've gotten some lovely tributes."

"Mostly yours and Freddie's relatives," Kathy said with a smile. "Each bouquet keeps getting bigger."

"Yes. They all seem to know who sent what and want to be sure they're sending the biggest and best."

"My relatives are all competing to see who can take the best care of me," Kathy said. "They're all furious with Uncle Patrick because he's the doctor and can trump them all."

"Oh, dear. Sounds frightening."

"It's how it is on that side of my family. They'll be fighting to the death, then completely making it up five minutes later." Kathy looked away, trying to fight the deep sadness she felt.

"You look as though something is troubling you," Gloria said.

"Freddie and I have made it up, but..." Kathy gestured at the bandage on her head. "It's how I ended up this way."

"He told me you'd had words."

"He was drunk again." Kathy tried not to cry.

"Ah. He gets that from my side of the family. Although I must confess, when you don't have much to do but drink and carouse, one does tend to overdo it."

"That's what Freddie said one time." Kathy winced. "But this time it's different. It's as though he's trying to escape. And he's so unbearable when he's drunk. He gets nasty or does stupid things."

Gloria sighed. "Freddie is a big boy. He can take responsibility for any weaknesses of his character."

"He hasn't been able to write, what with worrying about the factories and our publishing venture and getting shot at. No wonder he's been drinking like a fish. And all I've been doing is punishing him for it."

"Well, someone must." Gloria reached over and patted Kathy's hand. "That's what we women do. Now, being Freddie's wife is both an advantage and a disadvantage. You're close enough to him to let him know how badly he's hurting himself, but also one of the last people he wants to hear it from. As his mother, I'm in the same position but differently. He doesn't want to be babied, but I know him better than just about anyone. So, between the two of us, we'll get him back on the tracks. Don't worry, darling. Freddie loves you so very deeply, I would not be surprised if he gave up drinking for you."

"I wouldn't ask that of him."

"Well, we'll see. In the meantime, you need to build up your strength. Freddie needs you, and..." Gloria paused and blinked back tears. "So do I."

Kathy smiled at her and the two wept freely for several minutes. Then they recovered themselves and Gloria read Kathy an amusing article by Mr. Benchley.

Gloria left the hospital still feeling overwhelmed. At least, she knew what to do about Freddie. She had Van Schuyler drive her to his apartment. Freddie was in and agreed to see her. She found him slouched over his desk in the study, glaring at a decanter of whiskey on the top. She settled herself in a chair next to the desk.

"I remember when you were a little boy, and Honoria was just a little baby. She got sick and you went about the house, wearing the weight of the world on your shoulders."

"You and Nurse Pritchett told me that as her older brother, I was to take care of her." Freddie briefly glared at her, then toyed with one of the papers on his desk.

Gloria shrugged. "We had no idea you'd take it so seriously. Or when some of your playfellows were upset, you'd take it upon yourself to try to fix things, and if you couldn't, you were miserable for days. Even your grandfather was worried about the way you took responsibility for everything."

"I thought that was a good thing." Freddie's eyes, filled with resentment, briefly took in hers.

"Yes, but, Freddie, darling, you do tend to take on the cares of the world. When Honoria was in trouble last fall, you immediately stepped in. And Gam is here now because it was you that offered to take him, not Kathy. And if I understand Kathy, one of the reasons you two fell in love is that you decided to play white knight and take care of her during some trouble or other."

"I'm trying to do the right thing, Mother." Frowning, Freddie toyed with the decanter.

Gloria noted to herself that there was no glass on the desk. "Of course, you are. And it's a very good thing that you do. Except when you don't take care of yourself and let all your worries mount up and mount up. Kathy tells me you haven't been writing."

"I tried the other night, but there was this report that needed my attention." Freddie's glare rested on the decanter in front of him.

Gloria got up and picked up the decanter. "Well, this won't help you make the decisions you need to make." She put the decanter on the nearby credenza and picked up a stack of notebooks and some pencils. She slapped them onto the desk. "These will."

Freddie groaned. "I have no time to write!"

"You have no time not to. Freddie, look at me." She waited as Freddie lifted his head. "I know there are a lot of people expecting a lot out of you. And, yes, the family business is important and so is your publishing company. And so is finding out who is attacking us this way." She tapped the notepads. "But this is your most important work. And I know it is important the same way I know how important my research is. My time in my laboratory is what makes all the rest of what is expected of me bearable and sometimes even enjoyable. When I don't get time to spend there,

I become miserable and irritable. It's the same with you. You didn't write your first book because you had nothing better to do. You wrote it because that's what you do and who you really are. Cut yourself off from that part of you and you might as well cut off a limb."

"But how am I supposed to find the time?" he all but wailed.

"Do a little bit every day. Get up early and write first thing in the morning. Eat luncheon alone and write then. Or perhaps after dinner. You simply have to develop some discipline is all. But you have to write. If you don't, you won't be able to do anything else at all. Now, I shall have dinner with Gam, and have Roberts bring your dinner in here on a tray. I expect to see pages written by the time I leave. Are we clear?"

Freddie shook his head and laughed bitterly. "Yes, Mother."

The next day, Freddie arrived at Kathy's hospital room smiling and with a portfolio in hand. Kathy's eyes lit up the second she saw him.

"You look wonderful, Freddie!" she said, trying to sit up a little.

"And I have something for you," he said, handing her the portfolio.

Kathy opened it and her eyes filled. "You've got pages! I knew you weren't writing, but I didn't want to say anything. I didn't want you to feel even more pressure."

"I know, darling." Freddie smiled warmly at her. "But Mother let me know in no uncertain terms that it was what I most needed to be doing. She took away my bottle and put the paper in front of me and would not let me out of the study for dinner. And she read the pages, too, to make sure I wasn't simply writing lines."

Kathy laughed. "I wish I'd thought of that."

Freddie sat down next to her and took her hand. "Kathy, my dearest, I am so sorry I resorted to drink to solve our problems." Kathy started to say something, but he held up his hand. "If I do not want to promise that I will never do it again, it's only because I'm so very afraid of what would happen if I broke that promise. And I'm afraid I won't be able to avoid it at one time or another."

"You are only human, Freddie," Kathy said. "Which is just as well because I really don't care to be married to a demi-god. And I owe you an apology, too. I still don't like it when you're drunk. But I could have been kinder about it, especially since you are under so very much pressure right now."

"You have every right to be angry about me getting drunk. I'm not a very pleasant person when I am. And to show good faith, I will be on my best behavior and will not use being under pressure right now as an excuse to get blotto."

"Good. Thank you." Kathy looked at him, her heart filling with love for him. "Now, to address our other problem. Uncle Dan came by this morning—"

"I know. I spoke with him also."

"Did he tell you—"

"Yes, Kathy, he told me he was questioning Wilfrid Coates about the fire at the same time you were shot. If Wilfrid's behind everything, then he is obviously paying someone to do the shooting. However, we are not going to talk about theories or make plans until you are fully recovered."

"But, Freddie..."

Freddie shook his head. "As dangerous as it is for this killer to be loose, it would be far more dangerous for us to be chasing him before you're recovered. Now, your Uncle Dan and I have looked at the attacks, and each time the killer failed, he ran to earth. We believe that he's simply waiting until we let our guard down each time. Because nobody can keep their guard up constantly, there is considerable urgency to get this bastard caught. We simply have some breathing room, is all."

"But the longer we wait, the better the chance is

he'll get desperate and really do something terrible."

"That's the risk we'll have to take. I don't like it, either, but your safety and recovery are the most important thing right now. And not only is your uncle continuing to investigate, Detective Crowley is, too. They took it personally when you got shot. Now, Honoria and Mother are waiting outside. Honoria says she has a surprise for us."

Freddie went to get his sister and mother. Honoria insisted that there be enough chairs to seat all three of them and Freddie found a nurse who could provide the chairs. Honoria took the chair closest to the door, then bounced up again.

"I'm sorry to invade your hospital room, Kathy," she said. "But I wanted all of you here to applaud when I save the factory."

"What?" asked Freddie, laughing.

"Especially you, big brother." Honoria made a face at him. "You will never poke fun at my wardrobe again."

"I haven't poked fun at it in years," Freddie said.

"And you never will again," Honoria opened the door a crack. "Come on in, Ivy."

Ivy St. James slipped into the room wearing a dark-colored fall coat that had just a touch of sheen to it and a sable collar.

"Feel the texture, Mother, Kathy," Honoria said. "Isn't it nice? Now, Ivy, show them the dress underneath."

Smiling, Ivy slipped the coat off, dropping it in Freddie's lap, to reveal a sweet dress in a coordinating color, with a pleated skirt and satin collar.

"That's quite a charming outfit," Gloria said. "But how will it help save the business?"

Freddie was rubbing the coat's fabric between his fingers. "Wait a minute. This is that refused fabric, the one that had been labeled silk when it wasn't."

"Yes!" Honoria said. "I had some of it dyed and made up into Ivy's outfit. It's going in the magazine, too. By fall, you won't be able to make enough to keep up with the demand."

"But Honoria, we can't sell it as silk and wool," Freddie said.

"We're not going to," Honoria replied. "We're going to sell it as what it is, wool and rayon, the fiber of the future. It's what most people are calling artificial silk. You do have to be a little careful ironing it, but the rayon keeps the wool from shrinking, so you can wear the coat in the rain and it's a lot easier to wash. And the wool keeps the rayon from melting and tearing so easily. Mother was talking about doing an advertising campaign and I thought an article on how to handle artificial silk would be good for the magazine. But then I started thinking that the only thing that was wrong with the fabric was that the client was told it was something else."

Freddie rubbed the coat's fabric again. "You know, this could work."

"Of course, it will," said Kathy. "It's lovely stuff. Honoria, you're a genius."

"And Ivy and I will be wearing it for the rest of the spring." Honoria giggled. "I even plan to have a summer wrap made up so that I can wear it to a couple of the end of season galas next month."

"Brava, Honoria!" Gloria said. "Why don't you have a coat and dress made up for me, too? Perhaps a couple of them. After all, I do need some new clothes."

"I'd like a couple suits, please," Kathy said. "Or would that be too much?"

Honoria thought. "As long as we're not all wearing the same fabric at the same time."

Freddie smiled. "I am impressed, Honoria. Now, if you can figure out how to get back the money that Mr. Ames embezzled, restore order to at least three factories and convince the rest of our customers there will be no more mislabeled and/or badly dyed fabric, then I'll let you be chairman."

Gloria laughed. "Oh, don't be silly, Freddie." She

stopped when she saw Ivy, Kathy, and Honoria all glaring at her. "I suppose it wasn't quite that silly an idea. In fact, it wasn't silly, at all."

CHAPTER EIGHTEEN

It was a little over a week later before the doctors at the hospital decided that Kathy had recovered enough to go home. By that time, she was almost raving mad with boredom. Still, she needed a cane to walk as her left leg was still sore from the bullet wound. The stitches had been removed, but she still wore a bandage over the wound. Fortunately, the bullet that had grazed her scalp had done so along her hairline above her eyes. Honoria had brought a stylist in to shape bangs over the scar, once it had scabbed over and the bandage was removed. Kathy was quite relieved that it didn't show much at all.

"I don't care if I'm still limping," Kathy snapped at Freddie as he drove her home. "It's time we went after whoever is doing this to us. I'm going screwy with boredom as it is, not to mention all the worrying. I'm sure worrying isn't helping me recover."

"Yes, my darling." Freddie sighed with a smile. "Your point is well-taken. Everyone will be at the apartment for luncheon, and we can discuss it then."

"Really?"

"Yes, really." Freddie chuckled. "Mother and Honoria have been hounding me all week. Gam has been reading the papers and drawing all kinds of ridiculous conclusions. And I know that you have been bothering your Uncle Dan for more and more information, not to mention sending Ivy and Lowell on errands to find things out."

"Not that they've found much," Kathy grumbled.

"Sadly, no. But we do have some excellent suspects and once we pool our knowledge, we should be able to come up with a plan," Freddie said.

Everyone was waiting in the foyer of the apartment when Kathy and Freddie walked in, even Mrs. Davies, who promptly left, however. Gam was to have a holiday, but with several penmanship exercises, three chapters of geography to read, two pages of math problems and a new list of sentences to diagram by the next day, it wasn't much of one.

Still, he joined Freddie, Kathy, Honoria, Gloria, Ivy, and Lowell at the luncheon table, determined to keep quiet so that he didn't get sent back to the schoolroom.

They had finished their bouillon and were eating sole meuniere when Freddie more or less called the meeting to order.

"I think the best thing to do would be to consider each of our suspects, discuss the likelihood that any one of them is the killer, and then decide what we need from each suspect," Freddie said. "Now, one thing we have good reason to believe is that our killer most wants the ruby. Does that sound right to everybody?" Freddie paused while the rest of the table murmured their assent. "All right, then. Who wants the ruby? Why don't we begin with Aunt Thelma?"

"She keeps saying it was promised to her," Honoria said. "She and Uncle Stephen did stay after Father was shot, but she was over-loud in her grief over father. It could be she was acting more anguished than she really felt."

"I'd say it was more than likely," Gloria said. "However, her own husband was killed two weeks later, and while she has expressed interest in the ruby, she hasn't been at all forceful about it. Miranda, on the other hand, keeps sending me notes asking for it."

"And Aunt Miranda and Uncle Thomas left their wraps at the party," Honoria said. "Which probably means that they left quickly to avoid talking to the police."

Lowell shifted. "What I find curious is that the people who were most vocal about the ruby actually being theirs are the people who seem the least likely to get it. Yes, they are family members, but wouldn't they have to kill an awful lot of people to have any expectation of inheriting it?"

"That is an excellent point," said Freddie

"Perhaps they're thinking they can steal it from us while we're grieving, which seems unlikely," Kathy said. "Then there is Mrs. Lewton, who said that Father Little would sell it to her."

"She and Mr. Lewton also left their wraps," Honoria said.

"And the erstwhile valet said that she was in Father Little's bedroom," Ivy added. "Begging your pardon, Mrs. Little."

"Maybe she was just looking for the necessary," Kathy said quickly.

"She wouldn't be up there for that," Gloria said, her face growing grim.

"Mother…" Freddie began.

"Oh, don't worry about sparing my feelings," Gloria said, even though she was clearly annoyed. "Your father made no secret of his infidelities. Sometimes he would throw them in my face when he was angry enough. I do not know if Lenore Lewton was among his paramours. When we were young, she was so very sure Fred was going to marry her and then he went and married me. As I recall, they'd had some spat or other. And your grandfather didn't like her. So he encouraged Fred to marry me, as I was encouraged by my father to marry Fred. Lenore has made the occasional insinuation over the years, but I have no idea if she was actually having an affair with Fred or if she was simply jealous."

"The problem is, while she was seen in the right place, it wasn't necessarily at the right time, nor was she seen with Father's rifle," Honoria said.

"However," Ivy said. "While I can see her shooting Mr. Little out of anger, why would she have Mr. Coates killed, as well?"

"That brings us back to Freddie as a suspect,"

snorted Lowell. “The problem is that of all our suspects, Freddie is the only person for whom both Stephen Coates and Fred Little presented a problem. Did they ever determine if the gun that shot Kathy was the same one again?”

“Yes,” said Kathy. “Uncle Dan got the bullet examined and all of them were shot from the same gun. I can’t imagine why the killer is keeping it.”

“Why not, if he doesn’t know that bullets can be identified as coming from one gun or another?” Gloria said. “I had no idea that was possible until this situation came up.”

“And it’s not as though the Sullivan Act does much to stop gangsters from carrying concealed weapons,” Lowell added.

“If I saw it correctly, and it is my father’s favorite one, then it is a nice gun and worth keeping,” Freddie said.

“And I remember him polishing it in the game room right before the party started,” Kathy said.

“Oh, dear,” said Gloria. “That probably means he left it out in the game room and anyone who went in there could have taken it and gone upstairs to shoot him.”

“Could there be more behind all this than just trying to get the ruby?” Kathy asked.

“Spite would account for going after both Father and Uncle Stephen,” Honoria said. “And it would account for keeping the gun.”

“And Wilfrid is certainly spiteful enough,” Gloria said. “We’re almost certain he set my house on fire. He had reason to resent his father. I’m not sure why he would be angry at Fred, but he has always resented Freddie for some reason, so that would also account for why Freddie and Kathy have each been attacked, and possibly for Gam’s kidnapping.”

“And they were in their wraps,” Honoria said. “Aldie, Wilfrid, and Constance. Remember? The day after the party, I told you that I’d seen them going out the front of the house with their wraps on. So, one of them had either just killed Father or they just happened to be leaving when it happened."

"The trick will be proving it," Freddie said, shuddering as he remembered Wilfrid's implied threat.

"And we do have two other suspects to consider," Gloria said. "Mr. Terrence Carter, who does not seem to understand that I do not wish to marry him, and Mr. Donald Marston, who has claimed that Fred owed him a significant amount of money in gambling debts."

"How much is significant?" asked Ivy.

"I believe it's to the tune of one hundred thousand dollars," Lowell said. "At least, that's what he said when he tried to recruit me as a witness for his cause."

Even Freddie gasped at that amount. "Good Heavens! But why would killing Father increase his chances of recovering that much, especially since Marston did not have markers from him?"

"Apparently, your father was supposed to have remembered him in his will," Ivy said.

"Oh, good heavens," groaned Gloria. "He couldn't possibly have expected a bequest from Fred. He's not even related to us."

"Nor does Mr. Marston's ire account for Uncle Stephen's murder. Unless..." Kathy frowned. "What if Uncle Stephen had seen something?"

"It's possible," Freddie said. "Aunt Thelma seems to think that he saw who shot him."

"Which means it wouldn't matter if Uncle Stephen was in somebody's way or not," Kathy said. "He would have proved himself a danger just by having seen something."

"Which means Terrence Carter might not be after my mother's affections," Freddie grumbled.

"Well, that seems obvious," Gloria said.

"Actually," said Ivy. "He may, in fact, be after exactly that. It would be a very good reason for wanting your husband dead, Mrs. Little. And if Mr. Coates saw something, that would be reason enough to kill him."

"But it doesn't account for the attempts on Freddie and Kathy's lives," Honoria pointed out. "Unless he thought, for some reason, that the ruby would revert to Gloria if they weren't alive."

"What about that odious Miles Johnson?" Kathy asked. "He clearly wants the company."

"But is only tangentially interested in the ruby," said Freddie. "Oh, wait. Not only did he leave the party before the shooting, why would he kill Father and Uncle Stephen? He needed them to get what he wanted. It makes no sense to kill them."

"Could it be somebody we haven't thought of yet?" Gloria asked. "Perhaps somebody at the company who felt that your father was not treating him well or something. There was that one fellow that your father fired in front of everybody."

"I suppose that's a possibility, but, again, does not account for the attacks on us," Freddie said. "Nor would he likely be that interested in the ruby, assuming he even knew it existed."

The faces around the table fell as each considered this new possibility. Freddie took a deep breath.

"I suppose we do have to consider Mr. O'Hare and Mr. Watson," he said. "But for the time being, why don't we focus on the other suspects we have until we have determined that they could not possibly have committed the crimes? Now, what do we need to do next and who will do what?"

There was a certain amount of discussion and back and forth, but it was soon decided that Gloria would call on Aunt Thelma in the hope that she would let something slip about the ruby. Honoria would take on Aunt Miranda, hoping for the same, as Honoria had a slightly better relationship with that aunt. Ivy would speak to Mr. Marston about Mr. Little's debts, as Mr. Marston had been leaving flowers for her again. Lowell would speak to Everett Lewton since there was a decent chance the two would cross paths in some speak or another. Freddie happily decided to take on

Mr. Carter, as he wanted words with the man, anyway. Kathy would find a way to speak with Mrs. Lewton since she already had.

The group went their separate ways as soon as luncheon was cleared, except Kathy and Gam. But as much as the boy protested, Kathy insisted that he was to work on his schoolwork and would supervise it from the study. Kathy made a phone call to Mrs. Lewton, then she and Gam worked peaceably for about an hour, when Kathy got a call from downstairs. She told Roberts to send the lady up, then glared at Gam.

"You are absolutely not to move from this spot," she told her brother. "I want your promise, Gam. Solemn word of honor."

"Kathy!"

"Solemn word of honor."

"I promise not to…" His face scrunched up with the effort to think of a way to leave himself a loophole.

"Gam. Promise not to leave the room or listen in on me."

He sighed with all the depth of an ocean. "Solemn word of honor, I promise not to leave the room or listen in on you. But you better tell me everything that happens as soon as you're done."

"I will," said Kathy. "I promise."

Kathy got her cane and was just barely settled on the living room couch when Roberts ushered in Mrs. Everett Lewton.

"Mrs. Lewton, so good of you to come," Kathy said.

"Oh, darling, please. Let's be friends. Call me Lenore," said the older woman as she settled herself, in turn, on the occasional chair across from the couch.

"Thank you, Lenore. Please call me Kathy." Kathy smiled, not entirely sure she wanted the woman as her friend.

"I'm so glad to see you looking so well in spite of your recent injury," Lenore said. "What a horrifying experience it must have been."

"It was, but I'm much better now."

Lenore waited as Roberts brought in tea and cakes.

Kathy smiled at the valet. "Thank you, Roberts." She turned to Lenore. "May I pour you a cup?"

"Oh, please." Lenore also took several small cakes.

"Sugar? Milk?"

"Just a bit of sugar, dear."

Kathy smiled as she poured and added sugar to the teacup and handed the cup and saucer to Lenore.

"I was once shot, you know," Lenore said, then sipped.

Kathy finished adding sugar and milk to her own tea. "You were? I'm sorry. It's a ghastly experience. What happened?"

"Hunting accident," Lenore said. "As a matter of fact, it was your own dear mother-in-law who shot me. The gun had jammed, I believe."

Kathy's heart froze, but she smiled and sipped. "She had mentioned there was a bit of rivalry between you two."

"Oh, that's over and done with. She was always so smug about carrying Fred off, but I do believe I got the better end of the bargain."

Kathy couldn't help grinning. "Really? Was that because you only had to put up with him as your lover rather than a husband?"

"Well, ye— What?" Lenore's eyes gaped wide open. "How did you..? I mean, we were friends. Only friends."

"Lenore, darling, I understand," Kathy said. "After all... Perhaps I shouldn't say more. But lovers are much easier to deal with than husbands."

Lenore looked at her for a moment. "Well, yes. They are. I wish my own dear Everett understood that. So like a man. Thinks nothing of taking lovers and mistresses, himself, but went completely apoplectic when I took one. And I've only had Fred as my lover. He brought me the ruby once. Said I could have it as soon as his father died and he got it." Lenore blinked back tears. "But even that did not happen. He was so cruelly mistreated."

"I've thought so," Kathy said.

"I didn't tell Everett that we were still having our little affaire de la coeur, although he must have suspected."

"Were you planning a tryst the night of the party? As I understand it, you were seen upstairs in his bedroom."

Lenore sniffed again. "No. I was up there to have it out with him regarding the ruby. I saw you wearing it and couldn't help myself. Not that I begrudge you for it. You couldn't have known what Fred promised me. And then he never came up. I went back downstairs and found Everett outside the game room. I didn't hear the shots, but then we both heard the commotion and Everett said we had to leave immediately, which rather puzzled me. He seemed more nervous than usual, too. We even left our wraps. Your dear sister-in-law was so good about seeing to it that we got them back."

Kathy smiled blandly, her thoughts spinning. Lenore had little more to say, but Kathy noticed that the older woman had eaten all the cakes.

Freddie was glad that the tea room downtown actually served tea. He checked the wristwatch he'd recently taken to wearing. Mr. Carter was several minutes late. As Freddie tried to figure out how much longer he would wait, the older gentleman arrived. He seemed a little nonplussed that there was real tea on the table but took it with grace.

"Good to see you again, Freddie," Carter said, sitting down and draping his napkin across his lap.

"I appreciate you stopping by," Freddie said. "I've some questions I'd like to ask you."

"And I have one for you, but please, ask first."

"No, please, go ahead."

Carter smiled and took a deep breath. "I'd like your permission to propose marriage to your mother."

"What?" Freddie could scarcely avoid gaping. "You

are aware that it has been only a little over a month since my father died.”

“And you are aware that your mother and I are not getting any younger.”

“Mr. Carter—”

“Please, call me Terrence.”

Freddie swallowed to avoid his eyes. He did not want to be on that kind of intimate terms with the man but did still need information from him.

“Terrence,” he said, finally. “I do not understand why you insist on pursuing your suit when Mother has done everything to discourage you.”

“Isn’t it obvious?” Carter said. “I’ve been in love with her for years. She’s such a beautiful and graceful woman. Absolutely majestic.”

Freddie sighed. “You don’t seem to know her very well.”

“What do you mean?” Carter sat back in surprise. “We’ve been friends for years.”

“All right. What books would you talk to her about?”

“Books?”

“Yes. My mother loves to read. So what books would you discuss with her?”

Carter smiled. “Well, I suppose I could engage in a little light reading to indulge her.”

“Good. Although I wouldn’t call Somerset Maugham, F. Scott Fitzgerald, and William T. Mennerly light reading.”

“Oh.”

“Those are just her modern favorites. My friend Mr. Winters and she had an extended debate over Aristotle’s Poetics last winter. And I assure you, she is equally conversant regarding Shakespeare, Dickens, Hawthorne, in fact, most of the great classics of literature.”

“I— I had no idea.” Carter swallowed. “We could talk about opera.”

“She hates opera and only goes because it is

expected of her."

"Oh." Carter frowned. "Actually, that does make sense. I've always had the feeling that your mother and father were not all that well matched. I suppose they had a better marriage than many of us, but Fred..." He looked up at Freddie. "I mean no disrespect regarding your father."

"I know. My father was not the kindest of men."

"He could be rather mean, in fact, as I suspect you know."

"I do."

"It was the oddest thing," Carter said. "Last January, your father had joined us at some club or other. There were several self-made men there, as well, and your father was showing off that family ruby that your new wife was wearing at that fateful party. He said that he would sell it to the highest bidder once he inherited it. The worst part, though, was that he told me later that he was only toying with his business friends. It was as if he had to remind himself that he was their better, for some reason." Carter winced. "I say that not to disparage your father, you understand, but to point out that I am not the same kind of man and would be a better husband to your mother."

Freddie took a deep breath. "Terrence, I have pointed out to you that my mother has no interest in or affection for you. She has pointed out to you that she has no such feelings for you. I have also pointed out that the two of you have almost no interests in common. So, what is it that you actually want?"

"Your mother's hand in marriage," Carter said, bewildered.

"She does not want to marry you," Freddie said. "So why do you keep persisting in your suit? I can only assume that you want something else from us, but what, I have no idea."

"You can't convince her?" Carter asked softly.

"I don't want to convince her. Are you hoping to get the ruby?"

"I have a better one," Carter said. "And it's your wife's necklace, isn't it?"

"Then shares in our company?"

Carter shrugged. "I understand that she doesn't have any, although I wouldn't say no if you made a wedding present of some. But to marry a woman on that faint a hope makes no sense. No. I have merely been in love with her for a long time. My position in our family's business is solid. I can be kinder to her than your father was. Why wouldn't she want me?"

Freddie couldn't help smiling. The poor man's hubris was both utterly amazing and understandable at the same.

"Mr. Carter," he began, smiling inwardly as the older man's face fell. "I cannot encourage you. I know you mean well, and I believe your feelings are sincere. However, you and my mother would be more badly matched than she and my father were. They may have differed in temperament and that may have caused some distance at the end. But they did have a number of interests in common, which you and she do not. I'm sorry to break the news to you this way, but I must ask you to drop your pursuit of her. She does not want it."

Carter fidgeted with his teacup and looked around. "Well, Freddie, and I do hope we may remain on terms of friendship." He blinked several times and nodded. "I do understand and I appreciate your being so very clear and for letting me down as kindly as you could."

"Thank you, Terrence, for understanding." Freddie nodded at the back of the room. "There is a speak back behind the kitchen there. It's very nice and an excellent place to drown one's sorrows. Oh, and my Aunt Thelma was recently widowed."

Terrence shuddered as he rose from the table. "I think I will visit the back, if you don't mind."

Freddie rose also and shook Carter's hand. "And, those self-made men and the others you mentioned when you were talking about my father showing off the ruby, who were they?"

Terrence listed several names. But only one, that of Miles Johnson, piqued Freddie's interest.

When Gloria attempted to telephone her sister-in-law Thelma at the family estate on Long Island she was somewhat surprised to be told that Thelma was staying in the city with her oldest son, Aldrich. After tracking the mother down at the son's dwelling, Gloria was even more surprised when Thelma wanted very much to talk to her. So, Gloria invited Thelma to visit in Gloria's suite at the hotel.

"Aldie insists that I should think of his apartment as mine," Thelma said, once the two women were settled in their chairs, with pate and Burgundy between them, in the living room of the suite. "However, I simply do not feel at home there. I have no idea what I'm going to do. I really don't want to stay on Father's estate at Freddie's suffrage."

"I know what you mean, dear," Gloria said. "Both Freddie and Honoria have been very kind about offering me rooms in their apartments, but I do feel very much in the way."

Thelma sighed and looked at Gloria. "I assume you asked me here to make some accusation or another."

"Regarding Wilfrid?" Gloria asked.

"I'm sure you're wondering about him and the fire," Thelma said, pulling out her handkerchief. "You might as well say it. You told me so."

"Thelma, I wouldn't for the world cause you any more pain. There's nothing that can be proven, so there is no point." Gloria paused. "I am more concerned that Wilfrid may have been involved in shooting both Fred and his father."

"How could you think such a thing?" Thelma snapped, then sniffed sadly and put up her hand. "No, don't tell me. I know how you could be thinking such a thing." She choked back a sob. "Between Wilfrid and his love of fire and Aldie being so angry all of the time, it's a wonder they haven't killed somebody by now. They've been such a trial to me. However, Wilfrid was with me when his father was shot, and he was completely surprised when we heard. And Aldie was in the conservatory right before Fred was shot. So was Constance."

"Dear me. Were they having a tryst?"

"Sadly, Aldie has been having an affair with Constance almost as long as Wilfrid's been married to her," Thelma said. She paused and twisted her handkerchief in her hands. "But Fred had been flirting with Constance all evening. I suspect neither Aldie nor Wilfrid took that well, never mind that the little minx was flirting back."

"But why are you telling me all this?" Gloria asked.

Thelma broke into sobs. "I'm so afraid! My darling boys and they're such monsters. Aldie hit me last night. It was only a slap, but he was so angry, I was terrified that he'd do far worse. That's why Ernestine divorced him, you know. I only wish I'd had the strength to divorce Stephen."

"Stephen?" Gloria tried not to gape.

Thelma nodded. "He was always so apologetic every time he did. I think he really did love me."

"And now Aldie." Gloria shook her head and took a deep drink of wine. "I can almost understand a man resorting to such brutishness to discipline his wife under some circumstances. But for a son to strike his mother. I must say, Thelma, my heart is with you. Such a terrible burden." Gloria put down her glass. "Now, we must see to your care. And to make sure nothing worse happens, you'd best tell me everything that was going on with Fred and Stephen. If we can find some proof that your sons were involved in killing them, maybe we can put them in jail and you'll be safe. That's the most important thing, right now."

"Oh, but the scandal! It's why I haven't said anything, not to the police or to you. The scandal would be terrible."

"The scandal won't kill us. Aldie and Wilfrid,

however, can. Now, how badly did they want the family shares and did they want the ruby, as well?”

“Oh, the ruby!” Thelma sniffed. “Fred teased them about it, you know. How he was going to get everything and they couldn’t do anything about it. That’s why Stephen wanted Fred to contest Father’s will. Stephen could manipulate Fred into doing almost anything, even selling shares to the public. Only Stephen would never have done that.”

Gloria’s eyebrow lifted. “Except that Freddie told me that Stephen had tried to push him into selling shares, as well.”

Thelma shrugged. “Maybe he was serious, after all. I don’t know anything about business. I had thought Stephen was saying so to that nasty Mr. Johnson only to get rid of him. At the party that night, I heard Stephen tell Mr. Johnson he’d get him the ruby, as well, which was ridiculous. I have a much better claim to the gem, and someone must have said so. I think that’s why Mr. Johnson and that little tart of his went off in such a huff. I saw Briggeman giving them their wraps and coat shortly after that.”

“Yes, we know they left the party before everything happened.” Gloria ate a bite of pate. “What happened after that?”

“Stephen went back to the ballroom and I went to look for Aldie and Wilfrid. I’d seen Constance going into the conservatory and Fred following her.”

“Kathy said you’d been talking to your friends about Freddie,” Gloria said.

“That was all before that. We were in the drawing room, and once Kathy stormed out, that’s when I went to go back to the ballroom and heard Stephen and Mr. Johnson talking in that hallway leading to the conservatory.” Thelma frowned. “Then, back in the ballroom, I saw Constance, followed her, and saw Fred.” She nodded suddenly. “That’s when I went to look for Aldie and Wilfrid.” She shuddered. “I was afraid something terrible might happen. They have such tempers." She sniffed. "Mr. and Mrs. Lewton were leaving through the front of the house without even waiting for their wraps, although they weren't the only ones. I wanted to ask them if they'd seen my boys, but they were too rushed."

"Do you think Constance could have seen anything? Such as who went upstairs?"

Thelma frowned. "Now that I think about it, no. I saw her in the ballroom just before the shots were heard. Oh, dear. I'm getting this all muddled. I went back to the ballroom, saw Constance and Fred go into the conservatory, then Constance came out, and then I heard the shots. And so I went to the front hall to find Aldie and Wilfrid and that's when I saw Mr. and Mrs. Lewton."

Gloria couldn't help thinking that Fred had had one very fast tryst, even for him. She declined to say so, however.

"I was so afraid that my boys had done something terrible," Thelma continued. "I still am."

Which, Gloria thought, explained why Thelma's grief had been so over-loud, and again, she decided not to say so.

"Hm." Gloria thought it over. "I will be dining with Freddie and Kathy tonight. But right now, we must see to your safety. You absolutely must not go back to Aldie's apartment."

"But where am I to go?"

"Why don't you stay here? There's plenty of room. I'll send Van Schuyler for your things and tell the desk that they are to only admit him or me and that if your sons show up, they are not to be admitted under any circumstances. In addition, I'll have Mr. Briggeman summon a couple of our larger footmen."

Thelma began weeping again. "But I want to see my boys."

"Thelma, look at me," Gloria said, sternly. "I am dining with Freddie and Kathy tonight because we are very close to finding out what happened to both Fred and Stephen. If your boys are involved, and I hope that they are not, then it would be very dangerous for you to spend any time with them. Please think about your own safety. We'll manage any scandal, and it's entirely possible there won't be any. But if something terrible happens to you, then there will be nothing but scandal. You don't want that, do you?"

"Oh, Heavens, no!"

"Then do exactly as I say and we'll have everything taken care of soon. Now, shall we have another glass of wine and some more pate?"

When Honoria had called right after luncheon to invite her Aunt Miranda to tea, Miranda had been very enthusiastic, even to the point of insisting that Honoria join her at her home. Honoria might have wondered at it, but it was hardly the first time she'd invited an older relative to a meal only to have the older relative insist on playing hostess instead. What annoyed Honoria at that moment was that Miranda was not at home when Honoria arrived at the appointed time.

Then again, Honoria reflected, she should have known better. Aunt Miranda's chronic tardiness had been the family scandal for a number of years until Miranda had finally gotten old enough that it was regarded as an endearing quirk. At least, the drawing room was comfortable, with plenty of over-stuffed chairs and a sofa upholstered in soft blue and green silk. Honoria sighed. If she had to wait, then she could try to take advantage of it. She pulled her diary from her purse and began making notes.

Aunt Miranda breezed into the drawing room at least twenty minutes late.

"Honoria, darling, I apologize a thousand-fold," Miranda said, pulling off her gloves. She was dressed in a sporting suit of tan and green plaid. "You cannot possibly imagine the drama. And all over whether or not I should compete in the target shooting tournament when I am on the committee. How ridiculous! One hits the target or one doesn't. How should that disqualify me, I ask you?"

"I have no idea, Aunt Miranda," Honoria said diplomatically.

Miranda handed her gloves and hat to her butler, then settled herself in a chair across from the sofa.

"Isn't this lovely?" she proclaimed as a footman came in with tea and sandwiches. There was a pause as the footman distributed cups and plates, then withdrew. "I am so glad you were able to stop by, Honoria."

"Thank you, Aunt Miranda." Honoria smiled. "But it was I who invited you."

"Don't be silly. I wouldn't have dreamed of troubling you, especially since I wish your help in a matter."

"You do?" asked Honoria, trying hard not to sound as flummoxed as she felt.

"Yes," Miranda said with a self-satisfied smile. "You're the only one who can make Freddie see sense. About the ruby. After all, I don't actually expect him to know or even understand the real story."

"What real story?"

Miranda got a misty look in her eyes as she sat back into her chair. "When I was a little girl, there was nothing I loved more than watching my mother dress for the evening. She was a beautiful woman, my mother, the very height of elegance. She loved wearing the ruby, and why not? It is a most spectacular piece. And when she'd have her dressing maid bring it out, she'd always let me wear it for a few minutes, then remind me that I, too, would have a turn at wearing it to parties and operas and the like. I was only six years old when she died." She sniffed and blinked back tears. "It was barely a year later when Father married my stepmother. She was all right, I suppose, and Father really was worried that his three little girls would not fare well without a mother." A hard look came over Miranda's face. "But then Fred was born. The only boy. Everyone began doting on him, and I..." She dabbed at her eyes with a handkerchief. "I was mostly forgotten. My stepmother never let me in her dressing room, let alone occasionally put her jewels on me. It was devastating when I saw her wearing Mother's ruby."

"Oh, dear," said Honoria. "That must have been terrible. I'm so sorry."

"Well, now you see why it belongs to me? I'm only hoping that you can make Freddie understand."

Honoria bit her lip. "I'll do my best. But why don't you ask Kathy to talk to him?"

"Oh, she wouldn't understand." Miranda sat up straight. "She's not one of us."

"I don't know why you say that," Honoria said, biting back angrier words. "Kathy is very sympathetic, vastly more than, say, some of our relatives."

Miranda harrumphed. "If you were speaking of some of the men, I might agree with. Like that dreadful Stephen Coates. I told Thelma she was making a mistake when she married him. She's well rid of him."

"I didn't know you didn't like Uncle Stephen."

"How could I? He all but beat the life out of her. She thought I didn't notice, but I did. And those dreadful boys. He always thought they were so amusing when they were playing with fire or hitting kittens with golf clubs."

"How terrible!" Honoria gasped. "I knew they could be cruel, but kittens? And Uncle Stephen beat Aunt Thelma?"

"Horribly. She's well rid of him, I say." Miranda settled back into her chair. "Now, we have the rest of the season to plan. I've been told you're not interested in helping with the museum gala."

"Actually, I can't," Honoria said and looked at her wristwatch. "And is that the time? I'm afraid I really must run, Aunt Miranda. Thank you so much for the lovely tea."

She escaped shortly after and hurried back home, her stomach in knots thinking about how cruel her cousins really were.

CHAPTER NINETEEN

Freddie couldn't say he'd been looking forward to spending his afternoon meeting with the manager from the Yonkers factory, but he'd been putting off Mr. Sims since shortly after Kathy had been shot and could no longer avoid it. Freddie arrived at the office shortly after his meeting with Mr. Carter. Mr. Sims was waiting for him in the foyer to his office with two men in clean shirts, pants, and ill-fitting jackets. One had dark black hair and spectacles on his freckled nose. The other's hair was brown and he kept sniffing.

"Ah, Mr. O'Hare and Mr. Watson, I presume?" Freddie asked, opening the door.

The men nodded and muttered in affirmation.

Freddie smiled in what he hoped was a friendly way. "Well, why don't you two men come inside so that we can have a little chat. Mr. Sims, I'll call you when we're done?"

"Yes, Mr. Little," said the manager.

Freddie turned to the two men. "Please, have a seat."

They looked at each other, clearly surprised, and shuffled into the two chairs in front of Freddie's desk. Freddie slid into his chair, wondering where to begin. At the very least, there would be some justice done.

"Mr. O'Hare, as I understand it, your brother was killed in this factory by accident," Freddie said. "And no charity for his wife and children was provided."

"Yes, sir," muttered the dark-haired man.

"In addition, I have been told that your brother was an excellent worker and that his death was caused by the carelessness of another, who is still employed here."

“Yes, sir.”

“That is unconscionable and unacceptable,” Freddie said. He pulled a check from his jacket pocket. “The man at fault has finally been reprimanded and his wages temporarily docked. I also ask you to forgive us for the delay in seeing that your brother’s family is taken care of, and please give them this check to help them in their hour of need.”

“Th-thank you, sir,” said the shocked man. He took the check and gaped. “Thank you.”

“Mr. Watson, I understand that you were unfairly fired,” Freddie said, looking over a piece of paper that had been left on his desk.

“Yes, sir. I was only a few minutes late here and there.”

Freddie’s eyebrow lifted. “They called you a union sympathizer. Well, if you weren’t, I’m sure you are now.” He sighed, then looked at Mr. Watson. “Do you think you can avoid fomenting any strikes while you’re here? Because I would like to give you your job back.”

“I sure can, sir,” Mr. Watson said quickly with a cough. “And I won’t be late no more. The baby’s sleeping through the night now.”

Freddie nodded and turned to Mr. O’Hare. “Unfortunately, your little adventure at my parents’ home has lost you your job. I’ve instructed Mr. Hansen, in personnel, to employ you, as well.”

“We sure are sorry about that night,” Mr. Watson said as fast as he could. “We just wanted to scare your father. We didn’t want to hurt him.”

Freddie smiled inwardly. “So, what did happen?”

“Nuthin’,” said Mr. O’Hare. “Truly, Mr. Little. We got up on that terrace and then this lady comes out from the house. And she’s got this gun.”

“Yeah,” Mr. Watson said. “It was a rifle. Not a big one. Maybe it was a shotgun, but it weren’t no pistol. And she’s aiming at trees and another building.”

“She didn’t shoot nuthin’” Mr. O’Hare said. “At least, she didn’t right away. Me and Eddie, here, we just got off that terrace and down the wall as fast and as quiet as we could.”

“Yeah, but when we got to the sidewalk, we heard the gunshots,” Mr. Watson added. “We knew they weren’t coming at us, so we decided to maybe look like we weren’t trying to hide nuthin’ by sticking around. But the copper caught us a bit later and you know how that worked out.”

“I do, indeed,” said Freddie. “Do you have any idea who she was?”

“No, sir,” Mr. Watson said. “I guess she was at the party. She was all dressed up.”

“Why didn’t you tell the police what you saw?” Freddie asked.

The two men looked at each other, puzzled.

“They never asked us,” Watson said simply.

Freddie sighed, then sent the men to the personnel chief, who was expecting them.

The rest of the afternoon passed peaceably enough, even though Mr. Sims had plenty to say. Freddie mostly reassured the manager that there would be greater oversight and that Freddie was not nearly as lax as his father had been. Mr. Sims seemed somewhat mollified. Freddie made a point of leaving by six so that he could get back home in good time to have dinner with his family.

At dinner, Freddie forbade any conversation about the murders until they were finished eating. He had good reason, he explained. It turned into quite a convivial meal in spite of the tension. Ivy had taken the night off and she and Honoria had arrived together. Gloria was there, as she had promised. Gam was allowed to join the adults and was quite pleased, even if he struggled through eating his soup without slurping. Uncle Dan even stopped in, a little late. The only person not present was Lowell.

Once dinner was over, they moved into the living room. Gam helped Freddie move the extra easy chairs around so they were grouped into a circle more or less.

Ivy pulled out a leather covered diary and a pencil and made ready to make notes. Kathy looked around as she poured the final cup of coffee and gave it to Freddie

"So where is the mangy cur?" Kathy asked Freddie.

"Lowell?" Freddie checked his watch. "He said he'd be late, but he should be here any minute."

Indeed, the phone in the hall rang at just that moment, and two minutes later, Lowell strode into the living room pushing along a much smaller, milder man by the arm.

"This, everyone, is Mr. Everett Lewton," Lowell announced, jostling the man. "He has important evidence for us."

"Excellent," Freddie said. "But first, Gam has told me that he has news, and to accommodate his earlier bedtime—"

"Aw!" Gam groaned.

"He will get to share it first," Freddie finished. "Gam?"

"I found out how the newspapers got the idea that Freddie was taking the company public," Gam said. "Miles Johnson gave the Times the story hoping to force Freddie's hand."

"And how did you find this out, young man?" Kathy asked.

"There's reporters on the corner," Gam said. "I talk to them sometimes when the footmen and I go out for my walk every day. They keep asking me for tips, but I keep telling them I'm just a kid and don't know nothing."

"Anything," corrected Kathy.

"Anything," Gam repeated, rolling his eyes. "Anyway, I did finally get the fellow from the Times to tell me what happened. He said his boss was awful sore about it, too."

"That's a nasty bit of skullduggery," Gloria said, clearly anxious to share her news. "But I don't see how that could make Mr. Johnson guilty of murder."

"It doesn't," said Uncle Dan.

"However, it does show how far Mr. Johnson will go to get what he wants," Kathy said. "Something he says he always does. Wait. I remember your father telling the person in the conservatory that he wouldn't get what he wanted this time. And he was about to say something about a tart. Could he have been talking to Mr. Johnson?"

"It's always possible." Uncle Dan paused, then slurped his coffee. "But that would put him in the clear because he wouldn't have been on the terrace."

"Which is perfectly all right, because it wasn't Mr. Johnson," Gloria said, proudly. "It was either Wilfrid or Aldrich."

She recounted her discussion with Thelma, about the Coates brothers' questionable movements the night of the party, and what Aldrich had done to his mother, and received appropriately shocked looks at how bad Thelma's situation was.

"So, both Aldrich and Wilfrid were seen leaving the house around the time the gunshots were fired," said Ivy, scribbling away. "Along with Constance. They already had their coats and wrap, and the whereabouts of both those men were unknown at the time the shots were fired."

"That does sound bad," Uncle Dan said. "But I don't see the proof."

"I think it's coming." Freddie set his cup down. "Honoria, you spoke with Aunt Miranda today, didn't you?"

Honoria sat up excitedly. "Yes. She knew that Uncle Stephen had been beating Aunt Thelma. And she had a very convincing tale for why she thought the ruby should have come to her. Her mother used to let her try it on when she was a little girl. Said that she, too, would have her turn to wear it."

"She's still spouting that story?" Gloria sighed. "Both she and Thelma have been telling that tale for years. I suspect their mother let both girls try on her jewels, and probably Wilma, as well. Alas, Wilma was too little to remember.”

“But it does mean she has a motive,” Honoria pointed out.

“Quite probably,” Freddie said. He turned. “Ivy, what about Mr. Marston?”

Ivy looked up from her diary and shook her head. “He did confirm that Mr. Little was prone to teasing his businessmen friends, and was doing so with the ruby in January, but said nothing that would lead me to believe that he was behind the killings.”

“Which brings us to you, Mr. Lewton,” Freddie said. “According to what Mr. Winters told me on the phone, you said you’d spent a good part of the party in the game room, which means you were not upstairs.”

Mr. Lewton nodded with a bit more interest.

“And you saw a fair number of people come and go in the game room, including Freddie’s two cousins, correct?” Lowell said.

“Yes,” Mr. Lewton mumbled.

“And what were the two cousins talking about?” Lowell’s glare bore down on him.

“They were angry with Fred,” Mr. Lewton gathered himself together and as he told his tale, he sat up straighter. “He’d been flirting with Wilfrid’s wife, Constance. Aldrich said they could take care of him later. Wilfrid disagreed rather loudly, but he left, then came back and said that Constance was back in the ballroom and they should take her home. That’s when they left.”

“Very well, then.” Freddie took a deep breath and pressed a hidden call button. “Sadly, it’s time for Gam to go to bed.”

Gam groaned very loudly. Roberts appeared from the hallway.

“Roberts, would you be so good as to escort young Master Briscow to his room and ensure that he stays there?” Freddie asked, gently shoving Gam toward the valet.

“Yes, sir.” There was almost a whisper of a smile

on Roberts' face, as if he didn't expect Gam to stay in his bed.

Kathy, however, sent Gam away with a solid glare, and from the look on the boy's face, Freddie felt reasonably confident that Gam would at least stay in his room. Kathy waited only just long enough for the door to shut behind her brother before all but pouncing on Mr. Lewton.

"I had a chance to speak with Mrs. Lewton this afternoon. She confirmed that she and Father Little were..." Kathy glanced at Everett and Gloria. "Eh, intimate, and that Father Little had promised to give her the ruby when he inherited it. She also hinted that Mr. Lewton killed Father Little. She said she didn't hear the shots as she came downstairs, but that he met her outside the game room and insisted they both leave immediately, leaving their things behind." Kathy glared at Mr. Lewton. "And that you were more nervous than normal, Mr. Lewton. How do you answer that?"

Mr. Lewton looked even more miserable and nervous. "I was afraid. Your cousins, you know. Then I'd heard the gunshots and thought it had to be one of them. I didn't want to be anywhere near them."

"What made you think it was one of them?" Freddie asked.

Mr. Lewton swallowed. "I... I don't know. They were angry. And, well, one hears rumors about them."

"I don't doubt that," grumbled Honoria.

Lowell cleared his throat loudly. "And they're very convenient to blame things on, aren't they, Mr. Lewton?"

"I didn't kill Mr. Little!" Mr. Lewton squeaked. "I was downstairs the whole time. I swear it!"

"Actually, I'm reasonably sure you were," Freddie said. "But just because I have reason to believe so does not mean that you actually were. I think that if I were you, I would not go anywhere or do anything to make yourself look suspicious." He pressed the hidden button again and a moment later, Roberts appeared. "Roberts, would you please see Mr. Lewton out?" Freddie smiled at the small, nervous man. "And, Mr. Lewton, thank you for sharing what you know."

As Roberts led Mr. Lewton out, Kathy glared at Freddie.

"Why did you let him go?" she demanded. "He could have killed your father."

"He has no motive to have killed Uncle Stephen," Freddie said. "And I have reason to believe he didn't do it." There was a small uproar in the living room, but Freddie put his hand up. "I want to be sure I am placing blame in the correct place, so I want to give all of our suspects full consideration. I hope I have scared Mr. Lewton into staying in New York. But if he doesn't that will tell us a great deal, even if it might make it harder to apprehend him. It's a risk I'm willing to take."

"I'm not," grumbled Uncle Dan, getting up. "With your kind permission."

"Of course," said Freddie and Uncle Dan hurried into the hall.

"Hmph!" Kathy folded her arms across her chest.

"Very well," said Gloria, cutting in gracefully. "If we are going to give all of our suspects their due, what about Mr. Carter? Now that I think about it, he did get one of your father's guns. I gave it to him after the funeral."

Ivy sat up. "If he is truly that persistent in his attempts to marry, Mrs. Little, it still does not account for Mr. Coates' murder."

"Unless Uncle Stephen saw something," Honoria said, as Uncle Dan slid back into the room.

"Even so, why would Mr. Carter want to shoot at Freddie and me?" Kathy asked. "Nor does it account for Gam's kidnapping, either."

"That's precisely the issue," said Freddie. "He doesn't have any real motive beyond wanting Mother. When I spoke with him this afternoon, he told me he doesn't want the ruby. He said that he has a finer one than ours."

“Since when?” snorted Gloria.

“He seemed to believe so,” said Freddie. “As for his pursuit of Mother, he claims he has been in love with her for years, but when I pressed him on the issue, it seems he is fonder of the woman he perceives her to be rather than the woman she actually is.”

“And that is no surprise to me,” said Gloria with an injured sniff. “I do not understand why so many men seem to believe that they are so desirable that it does not matter what we women think about them.”

Freddie, Uncle Dan, and Lowell exchanged a quick look as if to say that they had never thought of themselves that way.

“In any case,” said Kathy. “It would certainly seem as though we can eliminate Mr. Carter.”

“It would,” Freddie said.

“Which leaves us with Wilfrid or Aldie,” Honoria said.

“Or Constance,” said Freddie. “And I have information that might implicate her even more strongly than the Coates brothers. But let’s consider the evidence.”

Ivy looked up from her diary. “Well, we have been operating under the assumption that Mr. and Mrs. Johnson left well before the shooting. But if Mr. Little was, in fact, addressing Mr. Johnson when he left the conservatory, then we know they left far later than we’d assumed. However, placing them in the conservatory eliminates them from suspicion because they couldn’t have been on the terrace.”

“Mrs. Johnson could have been up there,” Freddie said. “In fact, it’s possible Mr. Johnson set up the meeting in the conservatory with Father just to put him in the right place so that Mrs. Johnson could shoot him.”

“That doesn’t quite fit with the argument I overheard,” Lowell said.

“But that does mean either Aldrich or Wilfrid could have arranged for your father to be under the terrace in the same way," Kathy said. "It will be hard to say who did the arranging and who did the shooting, but Father Little seemed very surprised by who was up there."

"Or it could have been Constance doing the shooting," Freddie said.

Roberts appeared in the doorway. "Mr. Van Schuyler has just arrived from an errand and says that he has information for you."

"Show him in, please," said Freddie, and the group waited until the small man slid into the living room.

"I believe I have what may be called incriminatory evidence," Van Schuyler said. "Only, on account of my past, dere may be a problem wit' me testifying in a court of law."

"What did you find out, Mr. Van Schuyler?" Gloria asked.

"Mr. Little, here, he made a request to see what I could find out about de burglaries dat were perpetrated upon you good people," Van Schuyler said. He looked a little guilty as he glanced at Gloria. "De idea was to visit some of my old associates to see if dey'd heard anyting. I'm not no snitch or nuttin', and I made no promises. But I might have offered the odd hint or two dat I was taking up my former trade again. It took a while, and I talked with several of de guys. I ain't saying who. But today, I was told dat dey could use a good can opener, uh, someone who can open safes, and if I wanted to work for a team dat paid good money, plus offered excellent legal resources should I run afoul of de law, I should apply to First National Bank of New York for work as a security expert."

"That's Miles Johnson's bank," Freddie with a shocked frown.

"It is, indeed," Van Schuyler said with a grin. "In fact, based on what I was told, he has a whole crew of less dan savory individuals in his employ to take on de unpleasant tasks of breaking the occasional kneecap, roughing up people making da boss's life difficult, and burglaries, of course. Dey even said dey did a kidnapping in de recent past.”

“Gam’s kidnapping!” Kathy gasped.

“So I would surmise, Mrs. Kathy.” Van Schuyler sighed. “But to be honest, I don’t tink dey killed your father, Mr. Little. I told dem I don’t want to be associated with no killers, and dey swore dey didn’t do no stuff like dat.”

“It also suggests that Mr. Johnson didn’t kill Mr. Little, either,” growled Uncle Dan. “A man who has a whole crew of thugs to do his bidding isn’t going to get his hands dirty shooting someone himself.”

Van Schuyler looked distinctly nervous upon noticing the detective.

Uncle Dan waved him off. “You’ve done us an excellent service, young man. We’ve been hearing all manner of rumors about Miles Johnson’s crew, but nothing strong enough to substantiate. Maybe you can help us crack that group.”

“I absolutely forbid it!” Gloria snapped. “You are not going to put Mr. Van Schuyler’s neck at risk.”

“I’m not about to, Mrs. Little.” Uncle Dan said calmly. “But he does have information that might help us stop Mr. Johnson’s merry little crew and put them away for a good long time.”

“I ain’t givin’ no names,” Van Schuyler said with a gulp.

“That’s neither here nor there,” Freddie interrupted. “We will find some way to trap Mr. Johnson later. I think the more immediate danger is the woman who killed Father and Uncle Stephen and who is trying to kill Kathy and me.”

“A woman?” Honoria asked. “Are you sure?”

“Yes,” said Freddie. “This afternoon, Mr. Sims, the manager at the Yonkers factory brought to my office Mr. Edgar Watson and Mr. Ronald O’Hare. Having good reason to believe they are innocent, especially since neither would have occasion to even know about the ruby, much less covet it, I sought to rectify the injustices done to them as well as ask them a few questions about what happened that night. They told me they'd climbed onto the terrace and hid as a woman came out of the house. She was holding a gun and began aiming at various things. They left the terrace as quickly and quietly as possible and did not actually see her shoot. But they did hear the shots. They could not identify the woman, which I believe adds credence to their report. If they wanted to cause trouble, they would have been able to name someone."

"Oh, dear," Gloria whispered.

"Why didn't they tell us that?" Uncle Dan asked, sounding very annoyed.

"They, eh, said they were not asked," Freddie said.

Uncle Dan groaned and shook his head. "I keep telling those boys."

"Which means the shooter could have been Constance or Mrs. Johnson or even..." Freddie paused. "Aunt Thelma or Aunt Miranda."

"It was Miranda," Gloria said sadly.

"Mother, how can you be so sure?" Freddie asked.

"Because that's what Miranda does when she's upset," Gloria groaned. "She grabs the first available gun, then goes and aims it at things. If she's far enough in the country, she'll even let off a shot or two. And we know that she was furious that Kathy had the ruby."

"She participates in shooting competitions," Honoria said. "She was complaining this afternoon that the committee didn't think it was fair of her to compete because she's also on the committee."

Ivy tapped her diary with her pencil. "But if she left Father Little's rifle in the bedroom, as Mr. Taylor said someone did, and he returned it to the game room later, then how did she get it again to shoot Mr. Coates?"

Kathy groaned. "I saw her wrapping something rather long in an afghan from the game room on the day of Father Little's funeral."

"It would be the perfect opportunity," Honoria said.

She sighed suddenly. "But to think of Aunt Miranda as a cold-hearted killer."

Gloria sniffed sadly. "I seriously doubt she sees it that way. Both she and Thelma took it very hard when their mother died and felt utterly usurped when Fred was born. I know everyone paid little heed to their complaints about the jewelry and everyone doting on Fred and forgetting them."

"Of course not," said Freddie. "Not if you'd spent your entire life listening to them complain about it."

"That wouldn't have made either of them feel any better," said Honoria.

"No, it didn't," said Gloria. "That's why I always tried to be understanding whenever the subject came up, even if it was rather tedious. There was some justice to their complaints, not that I would dream of saying so to Wilma. Thelma and Miranda's mother was, by all accounts, a very warm woman, whereas Fred's mother was less so. She was kind enough to the girls, but only Wilma got on with her, probably because she has no memory of her own mother."

"Wait a minute," said Kathy with a frown. "When Aunt Thelma told us what Uncle Stephen had said, she said 'he,' as if Uncle Stephen had seen a man."

Gloria thought. "You're right. But, she also said Uncle Stephen had been slurring so much, she could barely understand him. Perhaps he said, 'she,' and Aunt Thelma thought she heard 'he.'"

"Or could Uncle Thomas have picked up Father Little's gun and killed Uncle Stephen?" Kathy asked. "That's the whole problem with Miranda as the killer. While she has motive enough to go after Freddie and me, because we have the ruby, she doesn't have much of a motive for killing Uncle Stephen."

Honoria snorted. "She had plenty of reason to shoot Uncle Stephen. She hated how cruel he was to Uncle Thomas, and there was the fact that he was beating Aunt Thelma. There might even be more." She frowned. "Unfortunately, there is something that

I witnessed that's actually rather chilling, now that I think about it." She looked abashed and swallowed. "I had an opportunity to question Aunt Miranda about the murders. She didn't know it was me and didn't have anything to say, really, so I thought she was being her usual self-absorbed self. But now that I think about it, she simply did not care that her brother and brother-in-law had been murdered. It had nothing to do with her, she said. She was impressed that I knew about the murders, but that was all."

Uncle Dan shifted and got up. "Perhaps I should leave."

"But, Uncle Dan, we're so close," Kathy said.

"Yes. And I can't pretend I haven't heard what I have tonight," he said, then sighed. "But if the killer is a relative of yours..." He shook his head. "I'd have a hard enough time making charges stick against one of you society ladies."

"Charges?" Gloria gasped. "Oh, my goodness! The scandal!"

"Honestly, Mother," Honoria growled. "It is horrible, but the scandal won't kill us. Aunt Miranda can and has already tried."

Gloria gaped for a moment, then flushed deeply. "Well." She shifted uncomfortably. "I dare say the physician has been asked to heal herself. I gave Aunt Thelma that same advice regarding her boys this very afternoon." She sat up straight, her innate dignity forming almost a glow about her. "Sergeant Callaghan, I do appreciate your discretion. However, allowing Miranda to continue with her murderous behavior not only puts the rest of the family at risk but herself, as well. Perhaps there might even be a medical solution to the problem. She clearly can't be sane."

Uncle Dan sat down and nodded. "That may yet be the best way out of it. But we'll need a confession at the very least. Or better still, the gun."

"And I know how to get it," Honoria said, sitting up. "We'll invite her and Uncle Thomas to a séance with the famed Madame Krichevsky.”

Kathy pressed her lips together. Freddie thought she might be laughing.

“Oh, I’ve heard of her,” Gloria said with a sneer. “She’s very popular among our set. Not that I hold with spiritualism. It’s nothing but flummery.”

Freddie became certain that Kathy was trying not to laugh and couldn’t help noticing that his wife was looking at anyone and anything but Honoria and Ivy. He wondered how long before whatever shared secret came out.

“That’s exactly what it is, Mother,” Honoria said. “But flummery we can make use of.”

“Are you certain you can convince this Madame Kriche-what-sky to have Aunt Miranda bring the gun?” Freddie asked skeptically.

“More than certain,” Honoria said, smiling. “Because I am Madame Krichevsky.” She looked at her mother. “I told you I have a bit of a double life.”

“But as a spiritualist?” Gloria tried not to gape and failed. “Why, in Heaven’s name, would you want to get mixed up in all that?” She suddenly glared at her daughter. “You don’t believe in it, do you?”

“No. Not at all,” Honoria said, with a giggle.

“It was a bet,” Ivy said. “And entirely my fault. We’d gone to see a palm reader on a lark and I was very impressed with the accuracy of the woman’s insights. Honoria insisted that almost anyone with any perception at all could come to the same conclusions. So, I bet her ten dollars she couldn’t convince anyone she was a spiritualist. I, obviously, lost the bet.”

“I only kept doing it because I was so bored,” Honoria said. “And it helped people. You know, offering a little common sense.”

“I thought you’d retired,” Kathy said.

“I can’t,” sighed Honoria. “Too many people depend on me and I have a couple clients I don’t dare let go to another spiritualist. Some of them are not very ethical and I shudder to think what harm they’d cause my dear ladies. But I only take it up once every other month or so." Honoria looked at her mother. "Fear not, I have yet to be recognized, even by Aunt Miranda."

"Oh, good Heavens!" Gloria groaned. "She told Aunt Thelma about you. Just this afternoon, Thelma said she was thinking of going to Madame Krichevsky because Miranda thought she was so wonderful."

Freddie sighed. He still wasn't very comfortable with that evening's conclusions, even though he'd begun to fear the same ever since he'd heard O'Hare's and Watson's account.

"Are we absolutely sure it couldn't have been Constance?" Freddie asked.

"It can't have been," said Gloria. "Aunt Thelma saw her in the ballroom just before the shots were heard. Which means she wasn't upstairs, especially since she and the boys left with their wraps. They'd had time to get them before the commotion."

"Besides," said Kathy. "Constance had motive to kill your father and probably Uncle Stephen. But she has no reason to kill us. I've barely spoken five words to her." Kathy reached over and patted Freddie's arm. "I know it's not pleasant thinking of your dear old aunt as being a dangerous lunatic. But isn't better to see her taken care of?"

Freddie nodded. "Very well. Let's try Honoria's plan. But how do we set up a séance? I've never been to one."

"Your job will be to get Aunt Miranda and Uncle Thomas here," Honoria said. "I'll take care of the séance."

"The play's the thing, eh?" asked Lowell.

"Wherein we'll catch the conscience of the queen," said Gloria a little grimly.

CHAPTER TWENTY

"I should have put my foot down about this playacting nonsense," Uncle Dan groused at luncheon four days later. "It's no fun arresting a relative. I've done it. No good comes of it. You should have just left her to me."

"We're not arresting her," Kathy said, yet again. "We're taking her in for medical treatment."

Gam had been banished to his bedroom for a nap so that he could stay up late for the séance that evening. Kathy and Uncle Dan were waiting for Freddie to come home from his office before Dan and Freddie went off on another errand.

No one had been in a very good mood those four days. Freddie, who preferred to get the unpleasantness over sooner rather than later, had found it incredibly frustrating that it had taken four days to get their "little party" arranged and Aunt Miranda and Uncle Thomas there that evening. Gloria had mostly kept to herself, although she did report in, with considerable disdain, that Aunt Thelma had gone back to live with Aldrich. Honoria had complained repeatedly that it was no fun having a relative who was a homicidal lunatic and wondered if they were all screwy. Kathy, Ivy, and Lowell had borne the complaints patiently but had to give all of the Little family some justice.

Uncle Dan, however, had been the worst. He had accepted the séance initially as the best chance they had at a confession. But as the days passed, his skepticism grew.

"Even so, there are too many things that could go wrong," Dan complained, wagging his finger at Kathy over the lunch table.

"We've taken precautions, as you know. And even you admit that it would be hard to make charges stick any other way." Kathy caught a glimpse of Rogers heading through the foyer to the front door. "It looks like Freddie's here. Will you please give him five minutes to eat something before you go make the collar of your life?"

That was the one bright spot. Thanks to the information provided by Van Schuyler, Uncle Dan, and his men had been not only able to identify some of Miles Johnson's thugs, but they'd also been able to quietly arrest the fellows. Freddie was going with Uncle Dan to Johnson's offices to distract Mr. Johnson while the police arrested the remaining "security experts."

Freddie was not looking forward to the interview. But Mr. Johnson admitted him into the spacious office with the oversized teakwood desk, gold filigree in the wainscoting and the crown moldings. Heavy gold silk drapes covered the windows and two richly colored oriental rugs laid across the floor. Mr. Johnson hefted himself into the rather large leather chair behind his desk, gesturing for Freddie to take the smaller one in front. As Freddie settled himself, he noted to his discomfort and also to his amusement that the height of the chair was just slightly shorter than normal and the back raised slightly. In his chair, Mr. Johnson looked somewhat taller than he actually was.

"Well, how can I help you, Mr. Little?" Mr. Johnson said. "Does your visit today finally mean you've seen the light?"

"I'm not sure to which light you are referring, Mr. Johnson," Freddie replied.

"About taking your company public. I can offer some very attractive terms."

"I'm sure you can, Mr. Johnson. But as I told you before, my hands are tied."

"Now, come on, Mr. Little. We're both men of business. Surely a man who is astute as you are can see the advantages. Not just for us, but for your entire family.”

“That’s neither here nor there,” Freddie said. “I gave my word to my grandfather and I know how much you value a man’s word.”

Mr. Johnson’s eyes narrowed. “So, why are you here?”

“I am curious as to your interest in the family ruby.”

The man appeared to be salivating yet played calm. “You mean that, uh, rock your wife was wearing at the big party? My wife wants it, and what my wife wants, she gets. You know how wives are.”

“Indeed,” said Freddie. “However, what if my wife wants it, also? Shouldn’t she have what she wants?”

“Buy her another one. Come on, Little. You know I’m gonna get it sometime.”

Freddie stood. “Over my dead body.”

“I can arrange that, you know.” Mr. Johnson smirked, then glared as the phone on his desk buzzed. Ignoring Freddie, he picked it up, went a little red at what he heard, glanced at Freddie, then yelled into the handset. “Get them out of there... I don’t give a damn about no warrants. Get them out of there!”

“You could have arranged it, Mr. Johnson,” Freddie said. “Not anymore.”

Mr. Johnson slammed the phone onto its cradle. “What the hell are you doing here, anyway?”

Freddie didn’t get a chance to answer as the door to the office burst open and Uncle Dan, flanked by several harness bulls, strode in.

“Mr. Johnson, I’m here to arrest you for conspiracy to commit kidnapping, assault and battery, and burglary,” Uncle Dan announced. “I advise you to come quietly. You’ve got quite a few birdies singing quite loudly downstairs.”

“Those bastards!” Mr. Johnson yelled. “They owe me everything. I pay them. They love me.”

Freddie shook his head. “Surely a man as astute as you are knows that the price of associating with people of unsavory character is that their loyalty is ruled by expedience."

Mr. Johnson sulked as the harness bulls got the handcuffs on him. Freddie hurried out of the office and left the building as fast as he could. Mr. Johnson's arrest was going to be big news, but Freddie had convinced Uncle Dan not to flaunt it to the papers, as the possibility of causing a run on the bank was all too real. Not that Freddie was worried about Mr. Johnson's assets. But there were probably a variety of small depositors who could be severely hurt by the bank's failure. Instead, Freddie quietly alerted several of the bank's executives that it might be wise to show that the bank was still on very solid ground. Freddie hoped fervently that it was.

That evening, all was ready. Uncle Dan was there as Kathy's guest, while Detective Crowley was hidden in the servant's quarters with a couple of harness bulls. Kathy had finally gotten Freddie to tell her where all the call buttons were in the living room. Somehow or other, "Madame Krichevsky" had convinced Aunt Miranda to give Father Little's rifle to Gloria the day before. Gloria had promptly brought the rifle to the apartment, insisting that Uncle Dan arrest Miranda at once, until Uncle Dan explained, at great length, that possession of the rifle was damning enough had Miranda been anyone else. But since Miranda was of New York's Elite, unless Gloria had proof positive that Miranda had been pulling the trigger at the time of the murders, it was not likely that Miranda would be charged, let alone taken in for treatment.

Kathy gulped. She did not believe in ghosts and spirits but had to admit there was something incredibly creepy about a séance.

"This is the easiest séance I've ever put together," Honoria said, giggling as she looked around the living room.

Kathy smiled weakly. Honoria always giggled

when she was nervous. Still, it was not immediately obvious why anyone would doubt that the intent of the séance was real. The living room looked appropriately mysterious, even with the electric lights on. The big double pocket doors that led to the dining room had been covered by a tall silk screen draped with red velvet. At the far end of the room, one of the windows was open, which added an eerie chill. The velvet drapes on the other window were pulled back. Candles had been scattered about the room with one large one on the round table that had been placed in front of the screen. Even the weather was cooperating, with gusts of wind rattling the windows every now and then.

Kathy patted Honoria on the shoulder and smiled. Honoria had her wig and costume on, but the veil was pulled back. Ivy and Gloria were actually in the dining room and the dining room door was open, but that could not be seen from the living room. Lowell and Uncle Dan had already arrived and were lounging in the foyer with Freddie.

The call came from the front desk. Honoria smiled and Kathy left the living room, pulling the sliding doors closed. Kathy checked her watch. Miranda was true to form. She and Uncle Thomas were at least half an hour late. Roberts was ready when Aunt Miranda and Uncle Thomas buzzed the front door. The valet disappeared with the coats and hats. Freddie waved his hand at the table set up in the corner with several decanters and some hors-d'oeuvres.

"Madame is in the living room," he explained. "She's preparing herself for her trance state and asked us to wait out here until she's ready."

"I told you she's the most authentic spiritualist in New York," Miranda said, excitedly, as she took a glass of whiskey and soda from Freddie. "I can't imagine why Gloria and Thelma didn't want to come tonight."

"I can't either," said Freddie blandly while Kathy wondered how he was able to spout such gentle fibs without it showing, as it would all too easily on her face.

Uncle Thomas approached Freddie and clapped him on the back. "I hear you've got the Yonkers factory back under control.

"Yes, we're quite optimistic," Freddie said.

Kathy couldn't help noticing that both Aunt Miranda and Uncle Thomas studiously ignored Lowell, Uncle Dan, and herself. She debated trying to strike up a conversation with Miranda, but then Honoria slid open the living room doors.

"Welcome," she said in low, heavily accented voice from beneath the veils which now covered her face. "I am ready. Please to come in."

She waved everyone inside the room and slid the door shut behind them. With the lights off and only the light of the scattered candles, the living room was transformed.

"I can feel the spirits," Madame said. "But for them to contact us, we must form a strong connection around the table and my crystal ball."

Kathy noticed that the ball had been placed before Madame's seat directly in front of the screen. As planned, she sat next to Madame, with Aunt Miranda on her other side. Freddie sat between Aunt Miranda and Uncle Thomas, while Lowell was seated on Uncle Thomas' other side, and then Uncle Dan between Lowell and Madame. Madame instructed everybody to join hands and breathe slowly and deeply.

Once everyone was settled, Madame began a keening chant, then began to rock back and forth. Kathy tried to focus on her breathing and noticed Uncle Thomas looking a little nervous. A cool gust of wind suddenly chilled the back of Kathy's neck.

"Is that a spirit?" Aunt Miranda chirped excitedly.

"The window's just open," grumbled Uncle Thomas, getting up. "I'll close it."

He went to the window just behind Kathy, then stopped.

"It's closed," he said, reaching for his glasses.

"Do not break the circle again," Madame warned.

Thomas stuffed his pocket color back into his breast pocket and slid his glasses back onto his nose as he settled back in his seat. He glared at the window behind Kathy one more time, then joined hands with Freddie and Lowell.

Madame had returned to her tuneless keening. Then suddenly she stopped and sat up straight.

"They are here! The spirits are here!" she cried softly. "Speak to us, spirits, speak to us!"

"You killed me," rasped a voice from behind her.

Aunt Miranda stared at a spot just between Lowell and Uncle Dan. Kathy couldn't see anything there, but Aunt Miranda's gaze was fixed.

"Fred!" she said, almost happily.

"You killed me!"

"Well, of course, I did," Aunt Miranda said as if what she were saying was perfectly reasonable and to be expected. "I was angry. That's why I was on the terrace with your gun. And then you had to yell at me as if I had no right to be there."

Kathy looked around at the others at the table. The shock was holding them as frozen as she was.

"You killed me!" rasped an even deeper voice.

"Oh, hello, Stephen." Aunt Miranda's gaze shifted to just above Uncle Dan's head, and her voice was a touch disdainful.

"You killed me!" the voice rasped again.

"It's your own fault," Aunt Miranda said. "You shouldn't have teased me about the ruby. You know very well that Mother promised it to me and not Thelma."

Kathy was fairly certain there was no need to continue but had no idea how to stop the séance. A rifle drifted down, as if on air, the candlelight making the golden barrel glow.

"Oh, that's your gun, Fred," Aunt Miranda said, lightly. "I should take that now. It belongs to me."

"You killed me!" rasped the two ghostly voices.

“And we have come for you!”

“No, you haven’t,” Aunt Miranda finally began looking worried.

“We’re coming for you!” the voices rasped again.

“No!” Aunt Miranda cried. “You wanted to be dead. You did. That’s why you made it so easy for me. You wanted to be dead!”

“That’s enough!” Uncle Thomas suddenly roared. Bouncing up, he grabbed Aunt Miranda and pulled her away from the table and close to him. “It’s just nonsense. I told you. I don’t know what Freddie is trying to pull, but it’s just nonsense.” He reached over and ripped the gun off the wire from which it had been suspended. “See? It’s on a wire.”

Aunt Miranda sobbed into his shoulder. “Don’t let them have me.”

“I won’t.” Uncle Thomas glared at the rest of them. “It doesn’t matter what you heard here tonight.”

“She’s obviously not well,” Freddie said, rising slowly.

“Stay down!” Uncle Thomas looked around the room frantically, then gestured with the gun. “Every one of you. Just stay put!”

Aunt Miranda looked up and began screaming hysterically. The table rose as if all by itself. Kathy shuddered, even though she knew who was causing the table to rise. Then a violent gust of wind burst through the room and blew all the candles out.

“Stay put!” Uncle Thomas screamed. “Stay put!”

Kathy did as she was told, even though she heard a sudden thud and oomph. Then the roar of the gun and the flash from the barrel shattered what little calm she had.

“Freddie!” she screamed.

The table had stopped moving and a minute later, the lights came on. Gam was standing at the switch near the door, the table’s cloth trailing in his direction. Freddie and Uncle Dan were rolling on the floor, trying to get Uncle Thomas contained. Aunt Miranda sat nearby, rocking and crooning softly to herself. Madame had her head face down on the table. Kathy gasped and felt Honoria squeeze her hand.

"Are you?" Kathy whispered.

"I'm fine," Honoria hissed back quickly.

Kathy left the table and hurried over to Aunt Miranda. The older woman seemed physically unhurt. Kathy sat down next to her and held her.

It was another minute or two before Freddie and Uncle Dan could get Uncle Thomas handcuffed. They dragged him up and seated him on the sofa. He sobbed and shook his head again and again.

"She was perfectly all right until that party," he gasped. "Then she came downstairs all glassy-eyed. I took her home as fast as I could. Had the doctor give her a sedative. But then she became obsessed with that damned ruby. It was all she talked about, and if anyone dared to suggest that it wasn't hers, she'd go all glassy-eyed again."

"You knew," Freddie gasped.

Behind him, Ivy and Gloria slid cautiously out from behind the screen.

"I didn't know," Uncle Thomas said. "I thought maybe." He looked up and saw Gloria. "I really didn't know for sure."

"Are you done with your wrestling match?" Uncle Dan asked Uncle Thomas with gruff kindness.

Uncle Thomas nodded and Uncle Dan took off the handcuffs. "I'll have to take her tonight. It's my duty, you know. But I will see to it that she's treated well. And then, after I talk to the commissioner and the district attorney, I don't see why we can't find her a nice, comfortable place to stay where they can take good care of her."

"She'd be horrified by the scandal." Uncle Thomas hiccuped.

Gloria sat down next to him. "There are worse scandals, Thomas. It sounds to me as though she was perfectly sane until she did something she never intended and was horrified by what she'd done. And that's when she became not herself and came up with a way to justify it. What she did was terrible, and I suppose I should hate her for it. But I am confident it was by reason of insanity and it's awfully hard to hate someone who is noncompos mentis."

Kathy wasn't sure if Gloria was being genuinely that generous or just trying to get everyone out of possibly the most awkward situation one could imagine. Either way, Kathy was glad and pressed the button for Detective Crowley and the harness bulls.

CHAPTER TWENTY-ONE

The next morning, Uncle Dan called with the news that the district attorney had definitely agreed with him that the public good would be better served by packing Aunt Miranda off to a good sanitarium, and by that afternoon, Uncle Thomas called to let them know that he had found a suitable place. Freddie got the particulars on the home on the pretext of offering to visit. Uncle Thomas wasn't entirely fooled but thanked Freddie for his discretion. Even better was that the newspapers didn't find much interest in an old lady going batty, for which Gloria expressed considerable relief.

The shock of the night's events wore off over a few days, to the point that Lowell had the temerity to ask Honoria if she'd ever been to a séance one evening over dinner in her apartment.

"Not really," Honoria admitted. "But I've read the odd novel or two."

"I thought as much," Lowell growled as Freddie, Kathy and Ivy all rolled their eyes. "Honestly, Honoria, that was the most ridiculous séance I've ever been to."

Freddie quickly told Lowell to shut up and dinner went on without another reference to the evening.

Gloria called for luncheon the day after that to tell Freddie, Kathy, and Gam that not only had she decided that the land the mansion had been on should be sold to a well-known developer (pending Freddie confirming the gentleman's bona fides and approving of the venture, of course), the developer wanted to erect a luxury apartment building and had offered her one of the first apartments. In the meantime, she had found a perfectly lovely place to rent.

Uncle Dan had gotten a commendation from the police commissioner and the mayor's office for the arrest of Miles Johnson, which the rest of his family decided only served to swell his already swollen head, and they remained bent on keeping him in his place.

A week and a half after the séance, Freddie returned home from the office feeling utterly exhausted. He handed his hat and overcoat to Roberts and was about to ask where Kathy was when she came into the foyer from the study.

"Hello, dearest," she said, giving him a solid kiss, then slipping her arm through his. "There are some lovely hors-d'oeuvres in the study, along with a couple of nice glasses of whiskey and soda. And I've some even better news."

"What?" he asked as they moved into the study.

"Gam will be dining with your mother tonight and she's promised not to let Van Schuyler teach him how to crack safes, not to do any experiments that might involve an explosion, and to not bring him home until his bedtime."

"Good Heavens, what will they talk about?" Freddie eased himself into his favorite chair and accepted the whiskey and soda from Kathy.

"Gam is explaining the stock market to her and they are making plans for the half of your father's estate that the judge says she'll get when your father's will finishes probate." Kathy slid down onto the couch next to him and passed him a tray of tiny, cold, asparagus spears.

"He ruled on that already?"

"Yes, and he ruled that she'll get her half of the estate before debts are deducted, assuming they can prove any, so I'm afraid you're getting the short end of the stick."

"I simply do not care." Freddie nibbled on a bit of asparagus.

"I also told her that I'd rather she kept the ruby necklace for the time being," Kathy said, smiling. "She does have the odd gala or two to go to and it would look lovely on her."

"Given how much trouble that blasted necklace caused us, I'm surprised she accepted it."

"She took it philosophically and pointed out that it's probably been causing trouble in the family since your ancestor first bought it. And it's also been giving pleasure, too. It's not the gem that's the problem, it's everybody coveting it."

"To be sure." Freddie chuckled, then shifted and picked up his briefcase. "And I have something else that sparkles for you. Or at least, I hope it does."

He pulled out a thick box of typed paper and handed it to her.

"You finished?" Kathy grinned, holding the box close.

"Isn't it about time? I've been working on it for almost a year now. And I finished it late last night," Freddie yawned. "That's why I'm so blasted sleepy. I had one of the typists at the office type up the last pages for us, so that you can turn your pencil on it as soon as possible. But why don't you look at the first page or two?"

Kathy opened the box. "Let's see. Temporary title, by Frederick Gordon Little. You don't need to put in a dedication now—" She paused and her eyes misted a little. "Freddie, you dedicated it to me."

He reached over and touched her cheek. "Of course, my darling. Who else?"

"Oh, Freddie. Now that is worth a king's ransom, and I don't have to worry about the string breaking."

Sneak Peak

The next Freddie and Kathy mystery is tentatively titled No Crystal Stair, *in which Kathy goes on the hunt for the killer of a young poet from Harlem. However, I can't provide a look at it because it's not written yet. But I have a new series that is scheduled for release in November 2019,* Rage Issues, *a contemporary mystery featuring theatre producer and sometimes PI, Daria Barnes as she has to step up for her friend and find out who killed the drummer in a country band. And don't forget to look for the exciting second installment in the Old Los Angeles series,* Death of the City Marshal, *coming in May 2019.*

RAGE ISSUES

It started the day I snapped. I was working at a domestic abuse shelter in the northern part of L.A. I'd been there almost eighteen months, which was pretty good for that job. I was technically the secretary for the group. But there was a lot of hand holding involved as well, and not just the hands of the women. The case workers needed their fair share of propping up, although, to be fair, they were always available when I needed to whine and weep.

Martina Rivera was in my office, a miserable puddle. For months, the poor woman had been calling, trying to find a way to get away from her husband, an exceptional son of a bitch, even among the bastards we usually dealt with.

Now, I know how incredibly hard it is for an abused woman to break away from her abuser. The stats say seven tries, on average, before she finally gets out, and that's about right. It's even harder for Latinas, who face tremendous cultural and family pressure to stay with the louts. If the woman is an immigrant and her husbands is here legally and she's not, such as was Martina's case, the bastard has even more power over her.

Only now, Juan Rivera had seriously injured one of the kids. The cops got called in, Children's Services had removed the rest of the children, and the D.A.'s office was talking about prosecuting Martina as an accessory because she didn't stop her husband. Great idea, punishing her when she was just as much a victim.

Only that's exactly what I wanted to do. Cripes, the woman had been calling and calling. We'd given her option after option. She still didn't leave.

So, I left, and a week later went to lunch

"I wanted to ask her why the hell didn't she get out?" I told my friend Berto Esparza, who was buying. "And, of course, I didn't. I got her case worker and got out the lawyer list." I shook my head and blinked back tears. "Berto, I just couldn't take it anymore. I was building up a shell just to keep from caving in from all the sadness. Anyway, that's when I quit. Merrilee gave me all the vacation time I've accrued, like they can afford it. She was pretty grateful, actually. I held out longer than most people do there. I just have no idea what I'm going to do now."

Berto had taken me to one of those hot shot places in Pasadena where all the movers and shakers do lunch, which was why he was buying. It's a brass rail and wood sort of place, with an open pizza oven and a fancy schmancy menu featuring things like currant emulsions, for crying out loud. But the meat is damn tender.

Berto is on the fringes of moving and shaking. He's a private investigator with fancy offices next to Beverly Hills and a nice house in the Valley, which means he's doing pretty well for himself. But it's been a long haul for him.

I met him back in the days when he was mostly process serving. In fact, that's how I met him. He served a subpoena on a partner of mine. Berto tipped me off that the son of a bitch was embezzling the entire budget of a play we were producing. What's really ridiculous is that the show was run on a freaking shoestring even for the cheap house we were in.

Since then, Berto and I have been close friends. He's about medium height, with gray flecks shot through his thick, dark hair. His build is pretty stocky and muscular – he's built like a cement block and his face is almost as square. For somebody who's spent as much time as he has dealing with the dregs of humanity, he's pretty cheerful.

Berto was in full dress uniform that afternoon, as in a custom-tailored dark wool suit with a snowy white Egyptian cotton shirt with French cuffs. His tie was more colorful, but still a subdued melange of dark greens and grays.

Berto chuckled. "There's plenty of jobs out there."

"Oh, yeah. Some I might even like." I munched on some lettuce. "It's like here I am, forty years old. I've got a masters degree, however many years experience producing cheap theatre so local actors can show off for casting directors, a website column, lots of clerical experience. Hell, I've even got a bunch of acting credits, and believe me, I don't want to get any closer to the Industry than I've already been." I paused as I poked some more greens onto my fork. "I guess what I want is a career, something where I'm not still on the bottom, starting out. Does that make sense?"

"I think you know what you want, hermanita. You just don't want to face it," Berto said. He wiped his mouth and laid his fork in his now empty plate.

"Face what? I'm tired of drifting, is all. I suppose I could go back to the theatre. Heaven knows, I loved it. But I just got so tired of living on the edge all the time."

"You could find a good man and marry him." Berto's eyes sparkled.

"Don't you give me that shit again. I've been as close as I want to get to that whole game and I want none of it."

He sighed exaggeratedly. The waiter came by, removed our salad plates and slipped the restaurant's version of coq au vin in front of me and beef tenderloin in front of Berto.

"Marisol is going to kill you when she finds out you're eating all that fat," I said, digging in.

Marisol is Berto's wife.

"Marisol is going to kill me when she finds out I had lunch with you," Berto laughed.

I groaned. "Does she still think we're having an affair?"

Although Berto and I have been friends for years, for some reason late the previous summer, Marisol had raised a monster fuss that Berto and I were getting it on behind her back. Patently ridiculous, of course. Berto's been married to her ever since I've known him and I don't sleep with married men.

Berto shrugged. "She doesn't want to listen, it's her problem."

"Have you guys considered counseling?"

Berto shrugged again. "Maybe. Have you considered career counseling?"

I made a face.

He grinned. "How about I save you the hassle? Come work for me as my assistant."

"What happened to Franny?" Franny is Berto's administrative assistant, as in the lucky person who gets to keep Berto up on all his paperwork, see that his billings go out and the money comes in.

"No, no, no. Not that kind of assistant. Someone to help me investigate. I've got business coming in. At this rate, I'm going to need an associate. You practically work for me as it is. What do you say? Work under my license for two years, you'll be eligible for your own, then. Take the test and boom, we're partners."

I winced. "I don't know, Berto. Snooping isn't my style."

Berto laughed loudly. "Bullshit, it's not!"

Connect with Anne Louise Bannon

Thank you for sticking it out this long! Please join my newsletter. It's the best way to stay up-to-date on my upcoming projects, blog posts and even games and giveaways.

Sign up here: http://eepurl.com/zH0Ab

Or connect with me on your favorite social media platforms:

Visit my website: http://annelouisebannon.com

Friend me on Facebook: http://facebook.com/RobinGoodfellowEnt

Follow me on Twitter: http://twitter.com/ALBannon

Favorite my Smashwords author page: https://www.smashwords.com/profile/view/MsBriscow

Connect on LinkedIn: http://www.linkedin.com/in/annelouisebannon

Follow me on Pinterest: http://pinterest.com/msbriscow

Other books by Anne Louise Bannon

I'm so glad you liked this book! Check out my other novels, available in print or ebook at your favorite retailer:

Freddie and Kathy Series:
Fascinating Rhythm
Bring Into Bondage
The Last Witnesses
Blood Red

Old Los Angeles
Death of the Zanjero

Operation Quickline Series
That Old Cloak and Dagger Routine
Stopleak
Deceptive Appearances

Brenda Finnegan
Tyger, Tyger

Romantic Fiction
White House Rhapsody, Book One

Fantasy and Science Fiction
A Ring for a Second Chance
But World Enough and Time

And I would be honored if you left a review for this and any of my books on GoodReads or any other retail site. It really helps.

About Anne Louise Bannon

Anne Louise Bannon is an author and journalist who wrote her first novel at age 15. Her journalistic work has appeared in Ladies' Home Journal, the Los Angeles Times, Wines and Vines, and in newspapers across the country. She was a TV critic for over 10 years, founded the YourFamilyViewer blog, and created the OddBallGrape.com wine education blog with her husband, Michael Holland. She also writes the romantic fiction serial WhiteHouseRhapsody.com, Book One of which is out now. She is the co-author of Howdunit: Book of Poisons, with Serita Stevens, as well as author of the Freddie and Kathy mystery series, set in the 1920s, the Old Los Angeles series,d the Operation Quickline series and Tyger, Tyger. She and her husband live in Southern California with an assortment of critters.